02/13/12

D0394242

REPLICATION

REPLICATION

[A NOVEL]

JILL WILLIAMSON

ZONDERVAN.com/
AUTHORTRACKER
follow your favorite authors

ZONDERVAN

Replication
Copyright © 2011 by Jill Williamson

This title is also available as a Zondervan ebook. Visit www.zondervan.com/ebooks.

Requests for information should be addressed to:
Zondervan, Grand Rapids, Michigan 49530

ISBN: 978-0-310-72758-3

Cover design: Cindy Davis
Cover photography: Getty images
Interior design: Sarah Molegraaf

Printed in the United States of America

11 12 13 14 15 16 17 18 19 /DCI/ 18 17 16 15 14 13 12 11 10 9 8 7 6 5 4 3 2 1

To Amanda Luedeke, for believing in me

MARTYR'S MAP OF JASON FARMS

Level 1

Security	?	?	Dr. Dumas	Dr. Jeng	Dr. Wilkenson

Isolation				Bathroom
Isolation	Monitor Room	Dr. Kane's Office	Reception	
Isolation				
Stairs				Elevator
?				Bathroom

Infirmary	Dr. Sautin	Dr. Goyer	Dr. Max	Dr. Elliot

Level 2

Section 3	Section 4	Section 5	Playground	
Stairs				Elevator
Section 2	Section 1	Kitchen	Cafeteria	

Level 3

Classroom	Classroom	Classroom		
Stairs			Running Track	Elevator
Classroom	Classroom	Classroom		

[CHAPTER ONE]

MARTYR STARED AT THE EQUATION on the white-board and set his pencil down. He didn't feel like practicing math today. What did math matter when his expiration date was so near?

His wrist still throbbed from Fido's teeth. Martyr touched the strip of fabric he'd ripped from his bedsheet and tied around his wrist to stop the bleeding. He hoped the wound would heal before a doctor noticed it. A trip upstairs to mend it would be unpleasant, as the doctor would likely use the opportunity to perform tests. Martyr shuddered.

To distract himself, he glanced at the other boys. Every Jason in the classroom except Speedy and Hummer scribbled down the numbers from the whiteboard. Speedy sketched Dr. Max's profile, staring at the doctor with intense concentration. His hand darted over the paper, shading the dark face with a short, black beard.

Hummer—as always—hummed and rocked back and forth, hugging himself. Martyr never understood why the doctors made Hummer take classes instead of putting him in with the brokens. Perhaps it had to do with Hummer's being so much older than the other brokens, or the fact that he could walk and didn't need special medications.

Movement at the back of the room caught Martyr's attention, and he twisted around to get a better look. Dr. Kane stood outside the locked door, looking in through the square window. A stranger wearing glasses stood beside him, much shorter and a little rounder than Dr. Kane. The man's head was also shaven like Martyr's, but the way he carried himself next to Dr. Kane showed he was nothing like a clone. Martyr's pulse increased. There hadn't been a new doctor on the Farm in a long time.

Dr. Kane opened the door, and both men stepped inside. Martyr gasped. The new doctor wore color! A narrow strip of fabric ran from his neck to his waist. Martyr jumped up from his desk and headed for the stranger.

"J:3:3!" Dr. Max's tone slowed Martyr's steps. "One mark. Take your seat immediately."

Yes, but one mark was not so bad. Martyr quickened his pace. *If I could just touch the strip once ...*

Dr. Kane shooed the new doctor back into the hallway, pulling the door closed behind him. Desperate, and knowing the door would lock once it closed all the way, Martyr stepped into the shrinking exit. The door slammed against his bare foot, and a sharp pain shot through his ankle. He winced and wedged his torso into the crack.

He was met by Dr. Kane's hand pressing against his chest. "J:3:3, return to your seat this instant. Two marks."

But the color on the new doctor was too tempting.

Something indescribable stirred inside Martyr. "He has color,

Dr. Kane." He tried to remember the word—like carrots, like the caps on the doctors' needles, like the slide. "It's orange!"

Martyr pushed the rest of his body through the doorway, and Dr. Kane moved with him, keeping his imposing form between Martyr and the new doctor—the same way Martyr did when a Jason picked on Baby or another broken.

Chair legs scraped against the floor, and the Section Five math class rushed from their seats. With a quick glance that seemed to hint more marks were coming, Dr. Kane reached around Martyr and yanked the door shut before any other Jason could escape, leaving Martyr in the hall with the doctors.

Identical faces filled the square window, but Martyr could barely hear the Jasons inside. The silence in the hallway seemed to heighten the severity of Martyr's actions. He glanced from Dr. Kane's stern expression to the new doctor, to the strip of orange color.

The man stepped back, face pale, eyes wide and slightly magnified through his thick glasses. He clutched the orange fabric with both hands as if trying to hide it. "Wh-What does he want?"

Dr. Kane rubbed the back of his neck and sighed. "It's my fault, Dr. Goyer. It's been so long since I hired someone. Years ago we stopped allowing any adornments below level one. They were a danger to the doctor wearing them. Plus, the boys don't encounter much color down here. It causes problems, as you can see." Dr. Kane turned to Martyr with a tight smile. "J:3:3 is harmless, though."

Dr. Kane's casual tone emboldened Martyr to carry out his plan. He reached out for the orange color, exhaling a shaky breath when the doctor allowed him to touch the fabric. It was smooth, softer than his clothes or his sheets or the towels in the shower room. A napkin, perhaps? Maybe it hung there so the doctor could wipe his mouth after eating. "What's it for?"

The new doctor tugged the orange fabric from Martyr's grip. "It's a tie."

"Enough questions, J:3:3," Dr. Kane said.

Martyr cocked his head to the side. "A napkin tie?"

"Three marks, J:3:3. Back against the wall, or it'll be four," Dr. Kane's deep voice warned.

Martyr inched back and glanced down the hallway. Rolo jogged toward them, clutching his stick at his side, his large body bouncing with every step. Johnson, the other day guard, loped along behind.

Martyr fell to the ground and immediately wrapped himself into a ball, covering his head with his arms. His curiosity had gotten him in trouble again. Three marks meant three hours of lab time. All to touch the orange napkin tie.

It had been worth it.

"What's he doing?" the man named Dr. Goyer asked.

Rolo and Johnson's footsteps on the concrete floor drowned out Dr. Kane's answer.

Rolo jabbed the stick between Martyr's ribs. "What's up, Martyr?" Another jab. Rolo liked when the Jasons fought back. "Getting into mischief again?"

Johnson's familiar crushing grip pried Martyr's arm away from his face, despite Martyr's efforts to keep it there.

Rolo stopped poking long enough to whack Martyr on the head, sending a throbbing ache through his skull. "Get up, boy."

Martyr complied as best he could with the stick still poking his side. He hoped the stinger wouldn't engage.

Rolo grabbed Martyr's other arm, and Martyr bit back a groan as the guards dragged him up and pushed him against the wall.

Rolo slid his stick under Martyr's chin and pressed up, forcing Martyr to look at him. "See, now? We're not so awful, are we?" Rolo's eyes were clear and cold. Martyr knew it was best to nod.

Johnson smirked at Martyr over Rolo's shoulder. Johnson had thick brown hair, a bushy brown beard, and a mustache. The boys were not allowed beards or mustaches or hair. They visited the groomers once a week to be shaved—to keep from looking like Johnson.

"These are our day guards," Dr. Kane said. "Robert Lohan, known as Rolo to the boys, and Dale Johnson. Men, this is Dr. Goyer. He'll be starting next week."

"Was it necessary to strike him?" Dr. Goyer asked Rolo. "He wasn't being violent."

Martyr looked from Dr. Kane to Rolo, then to Rolo's stick. Rolo always used his stick. Most of the time it wasn't necessary.

Rolo snorted, like Dr. Max sometimes did when one of the boys asked an ignorant question. He tightened his grip on Martyr's wrists.

"The guards know how to keep the boys in order," Dr. Kane said. "I don't question their methods."

"But why sticks?" Dr. Goyer asked. "Why not something more effective? A taser?"

"We use tasers if things get too far." Johnson bent down and snagged up Martyr's pant leg, revealing the stinger ring on his ankle. "They're remote controlled, and each has its own code. Lee, up in surveillance can turn each one on manually or in a group. If the boys gang up on us and manage to swipe our weapons, the tasers knock 'em flat in a hurry."

Dr. Kane put his hand on Martyr's shoulder and squeezed. "But J:3:3 doesn't cause those kinds of problems. He sometimes gets a little excited, that's all. Take him up to Dr. Goyer's office, Robert." He turned to Dr. Goyer. "This will give you a chance to try our marks procedure and get to know one of our subjects."

Martyr eyed Dr. Goyer. Would the new doctor be angry that he had touched the orange napkin tie? Would the marks be miserably painful?

"What do I do with him?" Dr. Goyer asked.

The guards pushed Martyr toward the elevator, and he struggled to look over his shoulder at the new doctor.

Dr. Kane's answer made Martyr shiver. "Whatever you want."

Martyr lay strapped to the exam table in Dr. Goyer's office, which he'd discovered was the third door on the right. He twisted his head to the side and squinted. The lab-like office rooms were always so bright. The lights buzzed overhead and the smell of clean made him sick to his stomach, reminding him of the hundreds of times he had lain on a table in such a room while a doctor poked and prodded. All the labs looked the same: a desk for the doctor, an exam table, and a long counter stretching along one wall with cupboards above and below. It had been five years since Martyr had been in this particular lab, though. He would never forget the last time.

The third door on the right had belonged to *her*. To Dr. Woman.

Many years had passed since the incident. Martyr was certain Dr. Kane would never allow another woman to enter the Farm because of what had happened, and the thought made him feel lonely. Dr. Woman had been kinder than any other doctor.

But it had gone bad.

Martyr blamed himself.

The door opened and Dr. Goyer entered. The light glinted off the man's head as he looked down at a chart, and Martyr wondered why this doctor had to see the groomers when the other doctors were allowed to grow hair.

Dr. Goyer jumped back a step when he saw Martyr on the table and put a hand to his chest, but then moved about the lab as if he hadn't seen Martyr at all. Martyr waited and watched Dr. Goyer file some papers, wipe down his counter, and sit at his desk. He was no longer wearing the orange napkin tie, only a white coat over a white shirt and black pants. Martyr frowned. Dr. Goyer would probably never wear the orange napkin tie again.

He hoped Dr. Goyer wouldn't use pain today. Occasionally he got lucky with his marks and only needed to answer questions or try new foods. Dr. Goyer hadn't carried in a steamy sack full of food, though.

Dr. Goyer suddenly spoke. "What am I supposed to do with you?"

Martyr met the doctor's eyes. They were brown, like the eyes of every Jason on the Farm. Martyr knew the color brown well. "What do you *want* to do?"

The doctor rubbed a hand over his head. "I don't know ... I

don't know. They gave me a list of starter questions, but you've probably had all those by now."

Martyr had answered them often. "What's your number? Do you have a nickname? What's your purpose?"

Dr. Goyer smiled. "That's right. Can we just ... talk?"

Martyr relaxed. Talking would likely be painless. "Yes, we can."

"Do you like living here?"

The question confused Martyr. Where else would he live? "What do you mean?"

"Do you enjoy it? Do you find it fun?"

"Some days."

"What makes a good day?"

"No marks. No fights. Food with color. Being with Baby. Especially a day where no one is trying to hurt Baby."

"Is Baby your friend?"

Martyr nodded. "He needs me."

"Why?"

"Baby is a Broken, so a lot of Jasons pick on him."

"Broken."

"Yeah, you know. Something went wrong when he was made. He's small and doesn't speak. The doctors think he's ignorant and can't learn, but they just don't know his language. He talks with his hands, so I'm the only one who understands him."

"Why did the guard call you Martyr?"

"It's my nickname. I got it because I help Baby and the other brokens."

Dr. Goyer paused for a second. "Tell me about a time you helped one of them."

Dealing with bullies wasn't Martyr's favorite thing to talk about, but it was better than being poked with needles. He didn't want the doctor to change his mind, so Martyr answered quickly. "A few days ago, Iron Man and Fido attacked Baby, and I called Johnson to stop them. Fido found me later and was angry."

"What happened?"

Martyr saw no harm in pointing out the wound since he was

already in a lab. He jerked his head to the strip of bedsheet tied around his wrist. "Rolo was close by, so Fido only bit me."

Dr. Goyer stood and walked toward the exam table. "And that's why they call him Fido?"

"Fido is a dog's name." Martyr knew this because Rolo said it almost every time he spoke to Fido. "Rolo says that Fido acts like a dog."

"Have you ever seen a dog?" Dr. Goyer released the strap holding Martyr's wrist to the table, loosened the sheet, and inspected the bite marks. Then he went to his counter and opened a cupboard.

"Only pictures we're shown in class. Have you seen a real one?" Martyr had heard dogs were small and hairy and drooled a lot. Sometimes Hummer drooled, but no one called him a dog. Baby drooled a lot when he cried, but no one called him a dog either. Apparently Fido's dog-ness was due to something else, because he certainly wasn't small or hairy.

Dr. Goyer closed the cupboard. "I've seen lots of dogs."

Martyr's eyes flickered around the lab while he waited. A thick, black coat was draped over the back of Dr. Goyer's chair. "You can go outside?"

"Of course." Dr. Goyer stepped back to Martyr's side and rubbed cool alcohol on his wrist.

It stung and Martyr stiffened. "You take the antidote?"

Dr. Goyer paused and looked away. His throat bobbed. "I, um … yes."

Martyr blew out a long breath. He couldn't even imagine what it must be like in the outside world. "I know I'll never see things like dogs, but someone has to stay underground so people and dogs can exist." Sometimes, the knowledge of his purpose was the only thing that made the Farm bearable. "You took off your napkin tie. Will you wear it again?"

"It's a necktie, not a napkin tie, and I'm not allowed to wear it. I'm sorry I broke the rules today. It was a mistake."

"I'm glad you did. Orange is very rare on the Farm. So is red. Red is my favorite. Where did you get the … necktie?"

Dr. Goyer peeled a bandage and stuck it to Martyr's wrist. "My daughter gave it to me for Christmas."

A tingle traveled down Martyr's arms. Daughter was woman. He lifted his head off the table. "You have a woman?"

Dr. Goyer's eyebrows crinkled over his eyes. "My daughter. She's seventeen."

"What does she look like?"

Dr. Goyer reached into his back pocket. He unfolded black fabric and showed Martyr a colored picture. The doctors sometimes showed them pictures, but never in color. Martyr had never seen so many colors in one place. He stared at the face and exhaled a long breath. The daughter had orange hair! And it was long, past her shoulders, and very curly, like spiral pasta. His eyes were the color of peas.

"He is very colorful." Martyr's eyes did not leave the picture when he asked, "What are the colors of peas?"

"Green."

Martyr stared at the daughter's eyes. "His eyes are green."

"Her eyes."

Martyr glanced at Dr. Goyer. "Her?"

"Women's belongings are *hers* instead of *his*. They're called *she* instead of *he*. Personal pronouns are gender specific."

Goose pimples broke out over Martyr's arms. This was why Dr. Woman had been called *Her*. Martyr wished he could remember more about Dr. Woman, but it had been so long ago, and he had been so young. "I would like to see a woman."

Dr. Goyer's eyebrows crinkled together again. He put the picture back into the black fabric and tucked it into his pocket.

"What's that you keep the picture in?"

"A wallet. It holds my money and credit cards, my driver's license."

Martyr shook his head slightly, confused by the strange terms. None of the other doctors ever showed him things like this. He wished he could see the picture again—wished he had his *own* picture—but Dr. Goyer had seemed upset when he put his wallet back into his pocket. Martyr hoped Dr. Goyer wouldn't stop showing him fascinating things in the future.

As the silence stretched on, Martyr tried to think of something to say so Dr. Goyer wouldn't get bored and decide to use needles. "What is Christmas?"

Dr. Goyer leaned against the wall by the door and folded his arms. "It's a holiday. You don't celebrate Christmas here?"

"What's *celebrate*?"

"Celebrate is … being happy together." Dr. Goyer straightened and looked into Martyr's eyes. "What do the other doctors do when you have marks?"

Martyr swallowed, torn over how to answer. If he didn't tell Dr. Goyer the truth, the other doctors would, and Dr. Goyer would know Martyr had lied. Lying always made things worse. "Mostly they use needles to test the contents of different vials. Medicines for outside, I think. Sometimes the vials cause pain, sometimes they make us sleep. Other times the doctors put sticky wires on our bodies that buzz our insides. And occasionally they just ask questions."

"What kind of questions do they ask?"

"Questions about pain. Questions about math and science. Questions about Iron Man and Fido, or Rolo and Johnson."

"Who is Iron Man?"

"The doctors call him J:3:1. He's the oldest who is still living, which makes him the leader. But many of us choose not to follow him. He's cruel. He's cruel to Baby."

Dr. Goyer walked to his chair and sat down, glancing over the papers on his desk. He picked one up and read from it. "What's the most important rule here?"

It was the standard list of questions. "Obey the doctors."

"What is your purpose?"

Martyr swallowed and closed his eyes. "My purpose is to expire. To be a sacrifice for those who live outside." Martyr opened his eyes and met Dr. Goyer's. "Like you."

Dr. Goyer folded his arms and stared at his lap.

Did the doctor want a longer answer? "I expire in twenty-five days, when I turn eighteen. Then my purpose will be fulfilled."

Dr. Goyer looked up. "Does that scare you?"

No one had ever asked if he were scared. "I don't want to expire."

"Because you want to live?"

"Yes, but not for myself. I'm content to sacrifice my life to save thousands from the toxic air. But if I'm gone, who will take care of Baby? And if Baby doesn't live until he's eighteen, he'll fail to serve his purpose. That wouldn't be fair."

"It's important to you to serve your purpose?"

"It's why I'm alive."

Dr. Goyer rubbed his mouth with his hand. "Can I answer any questions for you, Martyr?"

Martyr thought about the orange necktie and the picture of the daughter. "How do you celebrate Christmas?"

"You give gifts to those you love."

Dr. Max had explained gifts once, when they talked about being nice to others. But the other word was new. "What is love?"

Dr. Goyer ran a hand over his head again. "Uh ... it's when you have kind feelings for someone."

Dr. Goyer had been kind. He had given enjoyable marks and mended Martyr's wrist with no lecture. "Will you give me a gift?"

"Maybe someday."

"An orange necktie?"

Dr. Goyer pursed his lips as if fighting a smile. "Probably not."

[CHAPTER TWO]

CON NUMBER ONE: *coming home to a vacant apartment.*

Weighing the pros and cons always helped Abby Goyer deal with stressful situations. She stood in the open doorway, heart racing, unable to move. Her eyes drifted to the number on the door just to make sure she had the right place.

4B.

Right apartment, but everything else was plain wrong. No furniture. No pictures on the walls. Nothing. She dropped her sleeping bag and pillow, then shrugged off her duffle bag, letting it thud to the floor. After the long ride from Philly, she should be enjoying a deep, peaceful sleep, not dealing with this. She fished her cell phone out of a pocket in her quilted bomber jacket and called her dad.

The phone rang and Abby scanned the bare carpet for her Silver Persian. "Einstein?"

Con number two: no sign of my cat.

Dad picked up on ring four. "Abby, honey. You okay?" His voice had a guilty edge to it.

Abby scowled at the parallel vacuum stripes on the carpet. Dad must have paid a service to clean the place. "What's going on, Dad? Either we were robbed by some pretty thorough burglars or you've done something crazy again."

"Why are you home early? You didn't get my message?"

"Evasion: con number three, Dad." Abby ended the call. She took a deep, bleach-scented breath and checked her messages. Sure enough, one from Dad. She held the phone to her ear.

"Abby, honey? Call me before you get in so I can pick you up. Got big news."

Abby's posture slumped as she surveyed the bare apartment. *Big news?* "Einstein?"

She kicked her things inside and slammed the front door. At least the heat was still on. She hurried to her bedroom and found it had been emptied as well. *Where is my cat?* She picked up a forgotten red ponytail holder off the floor and stretched it over three fingers, plucking it like a guitar string.

Her dad's synthesized ring of Elton John's "I'm Still Standing" echoed in the empty room. He'd changed his ring last time he borrowed her cell, his way of telling Abby he was fine and she could stop worrying about him. That he'd gotten over Mom's death.

The vacant apartment proved one thing: he was a liar. Abby let the phone ring until the loathsome song stopped. A moment later her cell trilled, signaling a new text message. She opened her phone to see what Dad had to say for himself. They did this when they were angry; speaking by way of text messages kept the screaming to all caps.

ABBY HNY. STY PUT. ON MY WAY.

"Great," she said to the empty room. "I'll just hang here and do nothing."

She settled on the lilac carpet and mourned the loss of her private bath, balcony, and view of the Washington Monument. They'd only lived in this apartment three months. Clearly Dad had found a new job—pro number one—but did the man have enough courtesy to mention an interview? At least drop a hint he'd accepted an offer before packing up everything without a word to his only daughter?

Abby sighed. Mom's death had messed him up. He *so* needed to see a shrink.

Fighting tears, she gathered her red curls over one shoulder, braided them into a single plait, and fastened the end with the forgotten ponytail holder. Mom had died nine months ago, and ever since Abby kept busy at school and youth group, taking care of Dad in her spare time. She grieved in silence, refusing to fall into despair. She needed to keep a level head—for Dad's sake. Despite her anger over what he'd done at his old job and his emotional checking out since Mom died, she was all he had. It was up to her to hold things together, which was why his sudden meddling was so unfair. He had put her in charge of their family by his own evasion. How dare he move them without consulting her first?

Abby sniffed away her tears and pulled the latest issue of *CRS Quarterly* out of her duffel bag. Midway through reading *La Brea Tar Pits: Evidence of a Catastrophic Flood,* the front door whooshed open.

"Abby, honey?"

She slammed her magazine shut and murmured, "I'll 'Abby, honey' you …"

Dad's footsteps creaked through the apartment until he stood in her doorway. He wrung his hands together, his usual frown of concentration replaced with a fake smile. Snow dusted the top of his bald head. He wasn't even wearing a coat over his dress shirt and tie.

Abby clunked her head against the wall. "Good grief, Dad. Where's your coat?"

He turned to look down the hall then ran a hand over his head, turning the flakes of snow to water. "I don't ... recall."

Abby held in a sigh. "Evidently we're moving somewhere. Please say it's not far."

Dad kneeled on the floor in front of her and took her hands in his. "Just hear me out."

She shivered at his icy touch. "You've got to dress for the weather. Your hands are freezing!"

"I will, I promise." He grinned like she'd just given him a lifetime subscription to *Biochemical Journal*. "Especially since ... we're moving to Alaska."

Abby sucked in a ragged breath but couldn't exhale. It was one thing to move across town without checking with her. It was another thing to drop her in the middle of Alaska, where the temperatures favored below zero. As if the DC winters weren't cold enough. She opened her mouth to argue, but Dad spoke first.

"We leave tonight. The stuff is already on its way."

His behavior over the past few weeks suddenly hit her. She hadn't said anything because she thought it had to do with Mom. That simply moving from the house to this apartment hadn't worked. That Dad was still trying to avoid dealing with his grief by stuffing memories into boxes.

And then there was the trip he consented to, and paid for, only two days before she'd left. "This is why you let me go to Philly. To soften the blow." Dad had barely let Abby leave the house since Mom died; he never would have let her go to Philly otherwise, especially because it had been a church trip. Dad had major God issues. *What other signs did I miss?*

"I needed to fly up to sign some confidentiality agreements, see the facility, buy a house. It seemed like the perfect time—"

"To get rid of me."

He tried to work his brown puppy dog eyes. "You wanted to go to Philadelphia."

"Not so you could pull a fast one on me while I was gone. Dad, it's halfway through the semester."

"You're way ahead. I'm sure you'll be fine." Dad forced a smile. "It's a good job."

"I'm sure it's fabulous, but why do *you* need to take it? Couldn't you have found something a little more ... south?"

"Alaska has very nice summers. And wait 'til you see the house."

"You're too good for Alaska, Dad. I've seen your resume. They can't possibly have anything going on up there that requires someone of your caliber."

"I know what I'm doing."

For himself. For his career. He wasn't doing this for her. Abby seethed. Just like that, she was supposed to give up what little she had left of her life. Her youth group. Her studies. Her friend Claire. Visits with Uncle Pete. All because Dad wanted to run away.

"Where's Einstein?"

"He's in the car."

"Dad!"

"He's fine. He's in his cat carrier. I gave him food and water."

Abby jumped to her feet and held up her phone, forcing her hand not to shake. "I'm not fighting with you, Dad. Text me the pros and cons, then we'll talk." She grabbed her magazine, pushed past him, and headed for the exit to rescue Einstein.

Dad's muffled voice drifted behind her. "Okay, but our flight leaves in three hours."

Fishhook, Alaska, slept in the heart of the Matanuska Susitna Valley. The population of 2,640 consisted of farmers, schoolteachers, retail workers, and their families. Fishhook had one mall, but most of the stores were empty. As far as Abby could tell, the new Super Walmart got most of the business.

No Nordstrom. Major con.

The next thing she'd noted was how white everything was. She'd expected snow in early March, just not so much. Snow banks edged every road like retaining walls, and it just kept coming down. Dad had shipped up her shiny red BMW from DC, and it sat in the driveway under a mound of snow. She'd need to put her first Alaskan purchase, an ice scraper, into action and clean off the car before driving to school on Monday.

Which gave her two days to get settled. The new two-story log house was spacious, the surrounding snow-covered forest was beautiful, but classes and making new friends consumed her thoughts. She spent most her time deciding what to wear to school, knowing how first impressions could forever label her—like it or not.

When Monday morning finally came, she settled on a cashmere cream-and-brown-striped sweater, a brown matte-jersey skirt, and her cream suede knee-high boots. Very chic, very warm, very cute.

Unfortunately, she didn't give herself enough time to use the new ice scraper. By the time she'd cleaned the mound of snow off the car and scraped a patch of ice big enough to see through, school had started.

She also wasn't used to driving on snowy roads in the dark. With a speed limit of thirty-five through Fishhook, Abby crawled along at twenty until the front and back windshields defrosted. *This car is going into the garage the second I get those stored boxes unpacked. And when does the sun rise around here, anyway?*

Lost in her thoughts, she sailed past the high school and had to turn around in a random driveway. Her tires spun in the snowdrift until her car jerked back onto the icy road.

No wonder she'd missed it—the high school looked like a warehouse, a big, rectangular, windowless, two-story building with a lit-up sign that read simply: *Fishhook*. Hopefully, looks were deceiving.

Abby parked her car in the first spot she saw, eager to walk on solid ground. She soon regretted that wish—and her decision to wear the suede boots—as she slipped and fell on the icy pavement. She sat still a moment in the dark, wincing at her throbbing tailbone, thankful she was late and no one had seen. The cons against life in Alaska were climbing rapidly.

Abby checked in at the school office. Back in Washington, DC, she'd been a junior at George Washington High School, with a 4.2 grade point average, taking four AP classes, and auditing Gross

Anatomy at the university three nights a week. Now, four days later, she was one of seventy-six juniors at Fishhook High School, where only two AP classes were offered—English and calculus—both of which Abby had taken her sophomore year. She opted to take them again, hoping the teachers would let her serve as a teacher's assistant. She handed her choices to the frog-eyed administrative secretary.

"Ooh!" The woman's bulging eyes grew wider. "Calculus is tough stuff."

Abby faked a smile. "That's me. I like a challenge."

"Well, our Future Farmers of America program is stellar. You can talk to Mr. Lester about it. He's your biology II teacher. Now, here's your locker combination and your schedule. Your first class is AP English with Mr. Chung. He's such a nice young man."

Abby's cheek cramped slightly from the cemented-on smile. Sure, all of these Alaskans were nice people, but this wasn't home, and she couldn't keep up the relentless cheer much longer. She accepted the papers and stalked away.

Her locker stood at the end of a long hallway and took three tries to open. When she succeeded, she hung her bomber jacket and backpack inside, taped a picture of Einstein to the inside of the door, then checked her schedule for the room number of AP English.

"New student?" a deep voice asked.

Abby peeked around her locker door to see Mr. Smallville himself walking toward her. She sighed with relief. Despite his Clark Kent looks, he didn't dress like a farmer.

"I'm Abby, from Washington, DC. I'm a junior." She winced, hoping that her TMI response hadn't come off too hyper.

The guy sent her a wide smile that undoubtedly cost plenty in orthodontia. "JD Kane, from Fishhook, Alaska. I'm a senior."

Ooh. Handsome *and* older. Two marks in the pro column. "You aren't in the Future Farmers of America are you?" Not that there was anything wrong with that.

His eyebrows wrinkled in a smirk. "Not me. I play football."

Hmm. Jock. She twisted her lips, contemplating whether being a jock was a pro or a con. JD stepped beside her, and a plume of cologne attacked like exhaust from a city bus. She coughed in search of clean air and mentally marked a check in the con column for *reeks*.

His chocolate-brown eyes searched hers. "You don't like football?"

She pulled a notebook and pen out of her backpack. "I'm not really into sports."

He leaned one arm against the locker beside hers, pinning her between him and her open locker door. "Are you into fame? 'Cause you're looking at it. I'm the star quarterback."

Abby gagged inside. *Ego. Major con.* Why did all the hot guys lack personality? She dodged out of his predatory lean and slammed her locker.

"See you around, JD." She lowered her voice. "Good luck with all that fame."

Abby floated through her first day like it was a bizarre dream. The place had the feel of a normal high school, but so far students had only stared, gaping like Abby bore the face of a third-degree-burn victim. The teachers had been friendly, and she participated in the discussions, but sensed that was a bad way to get started. Becoming the overachieving teacher's pet was not on her list of high school goals.

Abby hadn't been popular at George Washington High, not that she'd cared. With eight hundred plus in the junior class, she had plenty of room to find friends with similar interests. Unfortunately, girls interested in DNA and fingerprinting were likely scarce at Fishhook High, and although Abby didn't really care about popularity, the fear of being the only science-minded girl in the school made for lonely thoughts. She prayed God would lead her to more of her type.

At least one of her type.

When the bell rang after second period Government, she gathered her things and inched out the door with the crowd. Every eye tracked her as she made her way down the hall, as if she were some creature to be gawked at. She clutched her books to her chest and raised her chin. Why did this bother her? She wasn't the type to be intimidated.

"Hey, new girl. Smile."

Someone whistled. "Nice boots."

Abby tensed and marked the cluster of blue and white letter jackets ahead on her right.

Jock cluster.

"Your locker or mine, angel?"

The guys burst into laughter.

There were five of them. She scanned the faces and her eyes locked onto JD's.

He wasn't laughing, but when their eyes met, his lips twisted in a lopsided smile. "Hi, Abby."

She couldn't help but smile back despite the company he kept.

"Ooh, I got one," a short, wiry guy said. "Abby, if I said you had a great body, would you hold it against me?"

JD elbowed him. "Shut up, fool."

"Mine's better," a beefy blond guy said. "Girl, if you were a burger at McDonalds—"

JD tackled him and tried to clamp a hand over his mouth.

"You'd be McGorgeous!"

Abby pursed her lips together as she passed. They might be obnoxious, but at least they verbally acknowledged her presence, which was more than she could say for the girls. She stopped at her locker, twirled the combination, and opened the door. Someone tall stopped at the locker beside hers, sending a dark shadow over her things. A familiar scent soon followed.

"Sorry about the guys. They were just messing around," JD said. "How's your first day?"

Abby glanced up at his towering form. "Okay. People aren't very friendly though."

"Give them a day or two. They're just intimidated. I mean"— JD raised his dark eyebrows—"you look like an actress or some-thing with that hair and those boots."

Abby glanced down. "What's wrong with my boots?"

"Nothing. I love them." He leaned closer. "It's just—the girls around here might not be ready for the competition."

She put her government book into her backpack. She shut the door, twisted the lock, then glanced past JD's toned arm at a group of girls. They wore non-designer jeans, pleather shoes, and layered knit tops. Plain, comfortable, and not likely from anything close to a department store. Maybe JD wasn't that far off. Tomorrow she'd choose more casual clothing.

She checked her schedule. Calculus. Room 204.

"I've got Volkman next too," JD said, peering over her shoulder. "It's upstairs. I'll walk with you."

Abby didn't want to encourage him but saw no reason to be rude. "You're in AP calculus?"

"Yeah. That surprise you?"

Absolutely, but Abby switched gears. "What's the teacher like?"

JD started up the main staircase. "She's cool. A stickler about homework. I have a feeling you'll like her."

Abby did like Mrs. Volkman. And, to her mild annoyance, JD was growing on her. He was the only student who'd gone out of his way to make conversation. Abby had never realized how lucky she'd been to have friends in DC.

Somehow she made it through the day, though she'd chewed her poor thumbnail down to the quick. She walked outside and the bitter cold blasted her face, forcing her to snuggle into her bomber jacket and step carefully over the icy pavement. As she crossed the lot, not only did she feel the stares of every person within eyesight, she realized her car was the only BMW in a lot filled with two-tone pickup trucks and run-down cars. There were a few exceptions. JD waved at her from a new cobalt-blue Ford F–150 with gun rack and snowboarding accessories.

Rich misfits? She squirmed at having so much in common with the likely-to-be-elected prom king. His type had never paid much attention to her before, and she had yet to figure out his intentions. In a town this small, it was probably just the thrill of the new girl.

Abby slid into the sanctuary of beige leather seats and tinted windows. Once she was inside, she started the car and turned up the heat. While the car warmed up, she pulled out her cell and texted Dad.

FEEL LKE SNOB N A HALF. NO 1 DRIVES BMW.

The trip home went much faster in daylight. As she pulled up the narrow driveway and parked the car outside the log cabin house, she found herself peering around the perimeter. So used to living in an apartment in the city, it creeped her out to be home alone surrounded by trees and the occasional bark-eating moose. Not that she'd admit it to Dad, of course. Still, she could barely see the lights of the neighbor's house through the trees. Only 4:35 and the sky was growing dusky.

Abby locked the front door and turned on all the lights as she made her way into the living room. Einstein padded up to greet her, and she snuggled into his soft, white fur. "You love me, don't you, Einstein?"

She checked the cat's food and water, then tucked herself onto the living room couch with her homework. She read her government chapter first, then did her calculus problems, and finally curled up with Einstein to start reading *The Great Gatsby*.

Six chimes of the grandfather clock jolted her away from 1920s New York. She sat up. Six o'clock and pitch black outside. She walked to the huge wall of windows that stretched to the vaulted ceiling. All she could see was her reflection staring back. The image reminded her of the array of horror films she shouldn't have watched over the years. Forest-dwelling weirdos could be spying on her right now, planning her murder, and she'd never know. How might the forensic scientists enter the scene? They'd take photos first, then analyze how the intruder might have broken in, estimate the time of death—

Abby shook her head. Not the best line of thoughts when one was home alone. This room needed drapes. She walked to the front door, flipped on the porch light, and peered out the narrow, full-length window that edged the front door. Empty driveway. She shouldn't be surprised. Dad had never gotten home early before; why would Alaska be any different?

She contemplated making dinner, but why bother? Dad would likely wander in after she was asleep. She microwaved herself a potpie, gathered *The Great Gatsby* and Einstein, and climbed the stairs to her room, wondering where might be the best place to order drapes online.

She ate and read more of *The Great Gatsby* until she nodded off. After brushing her teeth, she twisted the mini-blinds closed on her bedroom window so she wouldn't have to see the inky blackness, then crawled under her purple comforter and clicked off the lamp. The hallway light filtered through her cracked-open doorway, casting shadows across the bare, lavender walls and carpeting. See? Her dad wasn't completely self-centered. He'd gone out of his way to make sure her room was purple. Tomorrow she'd put up some posters.

Einstein jumped up beside her and kneaded the comforter with his paws, purring like a distant lawnmower. She pulled the cat close and stroked his fur, missing her mom more than ever.

[CHAPTER THREE]

ROLO OPENED THE DOOR TO Dr. Elliot's office and shoved Martyr forward. "In you go, boy."

Martyr fought to keep his balance as he entered the chilled lab.

Dr. Elliot, the only doctor on the Farm who conducted health examinations, looked up from his desk, a wide smile stretching across his narrow face. His small, dark eyes glittered over a long, oily nose. He stood and glided to the counter.

Martyr couldn't help but stare every time Dr. Elliot walked, amazed he was able to move at all. The man looked like the stick figures Baby drew in art class: tall and very thin.

"You know the drill. Clothes off. Then up on the table." Dr.

Elliot always sounded like he was pinching his nose when he spoke. He opened an upper cupboard, clinking glass vials together as he searched for something. "Fasten him tight today, Rolo."

As he did each time he visited Dr. Elliot for a check-up, Martyr removed his shirt and pants, draped them over a chair sitting beside the door, then lay back on the paper-covered exam table. Within seconds Rolo strapped his wrist into the restraint, pulling the buckles until they pinched. Martyr barely noticed the pain as he watched Dr. Elliot. Bad vials were kept in that cupboard. Things that made Jasons sick. What was the doctor looking for? This was to be an exam, not marks.

Rolo hooked the last restraint on Martyr's leg and left. Once the door clicked shut, an eerie silence blanketed the lab. Dr. Elliot still busied himself at the cupboard.

Martyr swallowed. He shifted slightly and the hairs on his right calf pulled. He looked down and adjusted his leg as much as was possible within Rolo's handiwork. When he straightened, Dr. Elliot stood over him. Martyr jolted, heart thudding in his chest.

Dr. Elliot's wide smile returned. "And how are we feeling today?"

"Fine."

"Eighteen days now."

Two-and-a-half weeks until expiration. Martyr stared at his feet, which hung off the end of the table. He, like most boys in Section Five, had long ago grown too tall to fit on it comfortably.

"I've been thinking." Dr. Elliot held Martyr's left eye open with his thumb and shined a light into it, then did the same to his right eye. "What will happen to Baby when you're not here to protect him?"

Martyr squeezed his hands into fists.

Dr. Elliot patted Martyr's head, his rubber glove scratching against the prickly stubs of hair that would be shaved off tomorrow during the J:3s weekly grooming. "Don't you worry about Baby," Dr. Elliot said. "I promise to take good care of him."

A wave of heat flashed over Martyr, and he clenched every

muscle to remain calm. Dr. Elliot liked to taunt; he would not get the satisfaction of a reaction today.

As if nothing had occurred, Dr. Elliot commenced with his tests, scribbling information onto his chart after each step. Martyr had been through it hundreds of times over the years: Blood pressure, temperature, then a look in Martyr's eyes, ears, and throat. Blood drawn from his arm. Poking and prodding all over his body. Listening to his heart and lungs.

At the end of the exam, Dr. Elliot would call Rolo to escort Martyr to the bathroom, where Martyr would have to urinate in a cup. Dr. Elliot claimed it was all to make sure he stayed healthy, but Martyr wondered if there was another reason.

Someone spoke in a raised voice just outside the closed door. "You know I'm worth more than that." Dr. Max's voice. Muffled, but angry. "Why not give me top clearance?"

"I see no reason to change things." Dr. Kane, cool and calm.

"I've sacrificed more than the others. I deserve to be involved at Camp Ragnar."

Martyr looked at Dr. Elliot, who stood motionless, staring at the closed door. What had Dr. Max sacrificed? And why was he so upset?

"You're welcome to work at Gunnolf full time, Dr. Jordan," Dr. Kane said. "I don't know why you refuse. Your bedside manner with the surrogates is matchless."

Martyr held his breath, straining to hear Dr. Max's response, hoping his favorite doctor would not leave Jason Farms to work at any other facility.

"We've been over this," Dr. Max said. "Deborah and I deserve more—"

"Then we have nothing further to discuss." The door handle lowered, and the door opened a crack, increasing the volume of Dr. Kane's voice. "Now if you'll excuse me, Dr. Elliot is waiting."

Dr. Max's voice lowered. "At least let me see the shared consciousness data. Some of the specimens are mine. I've got a right to—"

"Good day, Dr. Jordan."

The door to Dr. Elliot's office opened completely, and Dr. Kane swept in, quickly shutting the door behind him. He studied Martyr. "How is he?"

"Perfect, as usual," Dr. Elliot said. He glanced at the lab's entrance. "Is there a problem I should know about?"

Dr. Kane followed Dr. Elliot's gaze. "Dr. Jordan wants top clearance."

"Why not give it? His expertise would be an asset to the project."

"He never offers expertise, only asks questions. Demands to see the data and the formulas. He's too ambitious." Dr. Kane turned his eyes back on Martyr. "We're on schedule?"

"Of course." Dr. Elliot lowered his gangly body into the chair behind his desk and read from Martyr's chart. "Friday the twenty-eighth. We'll put him under, transport him to Gunnolf that night, and you can meet us there in the morning."

Put him under. Transport him. They spoke of Martyr's death as if it was a mundane routine, like sweeping the floor or making a bed. Martyr supposed it was that way for them. For people who had approval to go outside. But why couldn't they wait until he left to talk about it?

"And how are you feeling?" Dr. Elliot asked Dr. Kane.

"Nauseous. I haven't eaten yet today."

Martyr scrutinized Dr. Kane's appearance. His tall and muscular body seemed as forbidding as ever, but his pale face and red eyes ringed with creases hinted all was not well.

"You need to eat," Dr. Elliot said, "whether you're hungry or not."

"I will." Dr. Kane slumped onto the chair by the door, sitting on Martyr's clothes. "I need to hire a personal assistant, but the idea of screening someone ..."

"Two-and-a-half weeks and you'll be good as new. You won't need an assistant."

Dr. Kane rubbed his face, sighed, then stood and walked to Martyr's side, his commanding presence returning with each step. "Well, J:3:3, are you ready to serve your purpose?"

Martyr looked away from Dr. Kane's bloodshot eyes. "Yes." But his voice cracked, betraying his cowardice.

Dr. Kane patted Martyr's shoulder. "It will be painless, I assure you." He walked to the door and pulled it open. "Dr. Elliot, let me know if there are any complications."

"Of course."

When the door closed behind Dr. Kane, Dr. Elliot stood and walked to the opposite side of his desk. He perched on the front edge, crossed his ankles and arms, and fixed his beady eyes on Martyr. "You remind me of my older brother."

Martyr glanced away and swallowed. Now things would get weird, like they often did in Dr. Elliot's lab once the testing was complete. Martyr usually distracted his thoughts from Dr. Elliot's ranting, but all he could think of today were the conversations he'd just overheard.

"Eighteen days now."

"You're welcome to work at Gunnolf full time, Dr. Jordan."

"Friday the twenty-eighth. We'll put him under, transport him to Gunnolf that night—"

"Richard did everything right." Dr. Elliot puffed out a short breath. "I don't think he ever got in trouble once, not even a lecture. It wasn't normal."

"I get into trouble," Martyr said.

Dr. Elliot tipped back his head and chuckled, an almost silent, wheezing sound. "Only because you play the hero. If you simply minded your own business, you'd never get marks at all."

But Martyr didn't mind marks if it meant keeping Baby and Hummer from getting hurt. He glanced away from Dr. Elliot's penetrating gaze and noticed a small vial sitting on the counter. A chill washed over him—the vial hadn't been there when Martyr first entered. Dr. Elliot must have removed it from the cupboard while Rolo hooked Martyr's restraints.

A smile swelled under Dr. Elliot's greasy nose. "Always so sharp, you are." He strode to the counter and held up the vial, which was filled with yellow fluid. "This is for an LD:50 test. Do you know what that means?"

Martyr's mouth went dry.

"A lethal dose-fifty test determines the amount of substance required to kill fifty percent of the test subjects used in a study. I've been documenting the side effects of EEZ for the provider."

Martyr worked to keep his panic at bay. The doctors often tested different vials on the Jasons as a consequence of misbehavior and a way to conduct the research necessary to save the lives of those who lived outside. But exams were not meant for marks. Surely Dr. Elliot wouldn't do testing on him now, especially when Dr. Kane was concerned about Martyr's health.

Yet Dr. Elliot often did things that Martyr did not understand.

The doctor poked a needle into the vial and filled the syringe. As he stepped toward Martyr, he tapped the barrel of the syringe with his index finger. "One cc of EEZ has been enough to make some of the boys ill for a week. I'm sure you've seen them in the bathroom, puking violently into the toilets after marks with me. I've been saving a larger dose for someone special: Baby."

Martyr pulled against the restraints.

"I want you to have a small taste of what your little friend will experience once you're dead. My farewell gift to you."

Dr. Elliot clamped a hand down on Martyr's forearm. The needle stung as it pierced his skin, and Martyr looked away while the yellow liquid emptied into his veins. He waited for the pain, but nothing seemed to be happening.

Dr. Elliot tossed the syringe onto the counter and pulled off his rubber gloves, then threw them into the trash can and pressed the intercom button on his phone. "Send Rolo up. I'm all done in here."

It wasn't until Rolo steered Martyr out into the hall that Martyr felt his chest itch, then his arms. He scratched, but the sensation did not abate. Martyr slowed to scratch harder, leaving long red marks on his arms.

Rolo prodded him in the back with his stick. "Keep moving. Into Dr. Goyer's office."

Martyr's head snapped around. "Dr. Goyer?"

"You still have two marks to serve with him." Rolo smacked his stick against his palm.

Martyr moved on, not wanting to be struck. As he walked, his heart suddenly thudded irregularly. His chest burned. He tensed and willed himself to reach Dr. Goyer's office.

This day continued to get stranger. Marks were usually done daily until completed, so when a week had passed from the necktie incident and he'd not been escorted to Dr. Goyer's lab, Martyr had assumed the doctor had decided not to work at the Farm, and that his marks had been forgotten.

But Dr. Goyer was sitting behind his desk when Rolo steered Martyr inside and strapped him to the exam table.

As soon as Rolo left, another burning throb singed Martyr's insides. He gasped and clenched his muscles against the pain. His clammy back stuck to the thin paper sheet that lined the exam table and he shivered, wishing he could itch or fold his arms to hold himself together.

Dr. Goyer's chubby face rested in one hand, elbow propped on his desk. "Hello, Martyr. How are you today?"

"I …" Martyr winced, gritting his teeth at the burn that now radiated through him like pronged fire.

Dr. Goyer straightened. "Are you all right?"

Fluid rose in Martyr's throat and he gagged, trying to hold it back. His body shook, rustling the paper sheet beneath him.

Dr. Goyer leapt to his feet and scurried to the exam table. He laid his hand on Martyr's head and frowned.

Martyr vomited. He twisted his head to the side to get the stuff out of his mouth. Dr. Goyer jumped back, then lunged forward and fumbled with the restraint buckle on Martyr's left wrist. Once he freed both arms and helped Martyr to a sitting position, Dr. Goyer ran to open the cupboard under the sink. He returned with a plastic tub and sat it on Martyr's lap.

"I'm calling Dr. Elliot."

Martyr shook his head and began to speak, but Dr. Goyer had already turned away.

The doctor spoke into the intercom. "I need Dr. Elliot in here right away. Martyr is sick."

But Martyr felt somewhat better now. All but the burning

itch and the taste in his mouth had vanished. He swiped his wrist across his mouth and scraped his tongue with his teeth. "Could I have some water?"

"Of course." Dr. Goyer scurried to the sink and returned with a tiny paper cup.

Martyr sucked the liquid into his mouth, swished it around, then spit into the tub Dr. Goyer had brought. He held out the cup. "More?"

As the word left his lips, the door burst open. Dr. Kane rushed in, followed by Dr. Elliot.

"What's happened to him? Why is he loose?" Dr. Kane demanded.

Dr. Goyer removed the tub from Martyr's lap. "He threw up and was practically convulsing. I didn't want him to drown in his own vomit."

Dr. Elliot pushed Dr. Goyer aside. "There's a bug going around." He grabbed Martyr's head and tipped it back, shining his little light into Martyr's eyes again.

Martyr wrenched away then grabbed Dr. Elliot's throat. "If you give that to Baby, I'll …" But there was nothing Martyr could do once he was dead, so he squeezed harder, pouring his hate and frustration into his hands.

"J:3:3, no!" Dr. Kane pulled at Martyr's fingers. "Help me get him off!"

Dr. Goyer shoved the tub on the counter and pried at Martyr's other hand until they managed to free Dr. Elliot.

Martyr breathed through his nose, fast and deep. "He gave me something called EEZ. He says he's going to give a lot of it to Baby after I'm gone. Please, Dr. Goyer, you have to help Baby. Don't let them kill him early. Baby wants to serve his purpose too. He has every right."

Dr. Kane's chest swelled. "You gave him *what*?"

"He doesn't know what he's saying," Dr. Elliot said. "I took a routine blood sample, that's all."

"No! He said he wanted me to know what Baby would feel when he gave it to him. He said—" Another wave of nausea seized Martyr's stomach and he retched into the tub.

When he looked up, Dr. Kane had rounded on Dr. Elliot. "Are you a fool? Why him? Why now?"

"I didn't do anything to your precious candidate."

"J:3:3 does not lie."

Dr. Elliot pressed his thin lips together then shrugged. "I didn't give him enough to do any damage."

Dr. Kane's face reddened. "This is insubordination. How could you be so rash? Do you see me? I'm barely standing, the pain is so fierce. I can't afford the risk of your torturous hobbies."

"Oh, be reasonable. Do you honestly think I would jeopardize the plan? I've already tested this sample on eleven subjects. I know my limits. The adverse drug reactions are strictly flu-like. No one's suffered any permanent damage."

"Don't touch J:3:3 again without me there."

Dr. Elliot held up both hands. "You're the boss." His long legs carried him from the lab in three smooth strides.

Dr. Kane ran a hand through his hair and blew out a long sigh.

Martyr trembled. He didn't understand what had been said. Why should Dr. Kane's health depend on Martyr's heath? Perhaps Dr. Kane's condition was what happened to the people who didn't get the antidote. Dr. Kane must be in the next group to receive it.

Dr. Goyer's forehead wrinkled, as if he, too, were suffering some ill side effect. "Dr. Elliot purposely gave Martyr an unapproved pharmaceutical? As a … hobby?"

"His identification is J:3:3, Dr. Goyer. Their numbers are on their sleeves and wrists if you can't remember. Calling them by their numbers makes it easier not to become attached."

Martyr had never heard it put quite like that.

"Right. Sorry."

"I've explained our reasons for pharmaceutical testing. We all do it, and you will too. But Dr. Elliot, he … enjoys it."

"I understand the need for testing. But he already knew the side effects and administered it maliciously, not as a scientist seeking a cure or test results."

"I know what he did. That said, it doesn't matter. What matters is that J:3:3 lives a healthy life for eighteen more days. That's all I care about right now. Keep an eye on him until you leave today, then tell Erik to watch him tonight. If his condition worsens, call me immediately."

With a final nod to Dr. Goyer, Dr. Kane left.

As Martyr watched Dr. Goyer cross the room, he was shocked that the doctors—especially Dr. Kane—had not remembered to re-hook his wrists to the exam table.

Dr. Goyer sat behind his desk and once again pressed the intercom button on his phone. "This is Dr. Goyer. Can I get one of the assistants in here? I need a mess cleaned up."

"Right away, doctor."

"Thanks."

"What made you come back to the Farm?" Martyr asked.

"I always intended to come back, Mar—J:3:3. I simply lived far away and had to move, and that took a few days."

"I'm glad you're here."

"You are? Why?"

"I like talking to you." *You're one of the few doctors who see me as more than an experiment.*

Dr. Goyer leaned back in his chair. "Well, we have the rest of the day to talk. Would you like that?"

Martyr winced as the burning itch surged. He nodded, unable to speak over the pain.

"You don't like Dr. Elliot, I imagine."

Martyr gritted out his words. "He's a bad man. The things in his cupboard ... Please"—he took a sharp breath—"keep him from hurting Baby when I'm gone."

Dr. Goyer shifted in his chair. "When I met Dr. Kane last week, he seemed a different man. Now that I'm here, he's not only deathly ill, but absentminded and moody. I'm afraid he hasn't given me very efficient training, so I really can't say what I'll be permitted after your ... your ... expiration. I will do what I can for Baby, though."

Martyr relaxed his posture. "Thank you. Hummer will also need someone. He and Baby are the two Section Fives who don't speak."

"I'll make a note of that."

"When Iron Man and I are gone, Fido will take over. He will be a horrible leader, worse than Iron Man because he's ignorant and barely talks. Plus, Fido hates Baby. Maybe Baby could move into Section One? Do you think Dr. Kane would allow it?"

"I can ask him."

An awkward silence stretched between them as Martyr struggled to find questions appropriate for a doctor—even someone like Dr. Goyer—to answer. Each thing that came into his head seemed somehow forbidden.

Finally, Dr. Goyer said, "Would you like some more water?"

"Thank you."

Dr. Goyer got up and retrieved another tiny paper cup. He filled it and handed it to Martyr. "Do you have anything you'd like to do, you know, before you … expire? Any desires?"

Could the doctor sense his thoughts? "We aren't allowed things we cannot normally have."

"I know, but that doesn't mean you can't wish, right?"

Martyr hid a smile. His wishes never came true. But it was still fun to think about them.

"Well, then? I'd like to know what you want, besides keeping Baby and Hummer safe."

"I want to see the sky."

Dr. Max had taught them about sky in science class seven years ago, and Martyr had never forgotten. It was blue, but he was not sure what blue looked like. It was rumored Rolo's eyes were blue, but if anyone asked, Rolo smacked them with his stick.

"We're not allowed outside because of the toxic air, but since I'm going to expire anyway, I'd like to see the sky before I fulfill my purpose. Do you think I'd be infected if I went outside just long enough to see it?"

"I don't really know."

"If I knew Baby and Hummer would be safe and I could glimpse the sky for only a moment, I would die happy. It isn't too much to dream for, is it?"

Dr. Goyer rubbed his face with both hands. "No. Not at all."

[CHAPTER FOUR]

ABBY DRESSED CASUALLY FOR DAY two at Fish-hook High. In her *concern* for her Dad's welfare, she followed him that morning. He'd traded in his Lexus for a Chevy Silverado. The only similar thing about the vehicles was the gunmetal color.

Abby squeezed her steering wheel as she tried to keep up with his speed on the dark, icy road. Dad pulled into a narrow drive, where two wheel ruts snaked through the snow into a thick forest. The sign at the end of the drive read *Jason Farms*. Abby drove slowly, not wanting to be seen or get stuck. She rounded a sharp corner that spilled into a small parking lot in front of a run-down red barn.

What on earth?

Two dozen cars and a delivery truck from the local grocery store confirmed the farm was still active, but the barn's peeling paint and small size made Abby wonder what all the owners to these vehicles could be doing and where their activities took place. Whatever they were up to, she prayed it was legit.

Fishhook High operated on a rotating schedule, so today Abby had Spanish II, Biology II, PE (which, to her surprise, was co-ed due to the school's small size), and computers. Naturally, JD was also in her Biology II and PE classes. Abby couldn't help being impressed by his challenging schedule, even though he was a year older. The cliché jock in her mind would be coasting by on electives his senior year. Of course, JD excelled at volleyball, which was the PE sport of choice that day. Abby had never been very athletic, but she had used her former gym membership three days a week to keep in shape. She had yet to find a suitable alternative in Fishhook but heard some girls in the hall saying that Sarah Palin took kickboxing someplace nearby.

She skipped showering after PE, having done little more than sit on the sidelines and watch. She had lunch before computers and so made her way to the cafeteria, wondering if she'd be sitting alone again. When she got her tray and scanned the tables, each girl she made eye contact with averted her eyes. Ug. Why was this so hard?

JD waved her over to sit at the popular table. She froze, realizing she had a choice. She could blend in and accept her place as the solitary brainiac/rich girl of Fishhook High, or she could go with the flow and see what life in the spotlight felt like for once.

JD flashed his perfect smile, seeming eager to help her make a decision.

Though momentarily blinded by the brightness of his pearly whites, he really only tempted her for a millisecond. Abby wasn't a spotlight kind of girl, unless ranting on controversial issues of science, of course. She bypassed JD's table and plopped down beside a pretty, African American girl she recognized from calculus class, who had amazing, dark chocolate skin, perfect lips, and silky black hair that flipped out like a bell above her shoulders. Average-looking kids filled the table. *Pro number one.*

"Hi," Abby said.

The African American girl smiled, chomped on her gum a few times, then turned to a shaggy-headed boy across the table. "Dylan, you totally lost me again. I just don't get what you subtract from what for the fundamental theorem."

Warmth filled Abby from inside. They were talking math. Pro number two!

Dylan sighed as if the girl had said she couldn't figure out how to get her straw into her milk carton. "Okay, Kylee. Listen closely this time. I'll make it as simple as possible." He shook his hair out of his eyes. "The theorem uses a definite integral instead of an indefinite one. So, if the function f of x is nonnegative and continuous between the interval of a and b, you find the integral of that function by doing the antiderivative and plugging in the numbers of b and a respectively to get an exact number, as opposed to a general solution like you'd get from an indefinite integral."

Kylee blew a tiny bubble and sucked it back in, the gum crackling and popping in the silence around the table. Her unresponsiveness told Abby she still hadn't understood a word Dylan had said.

Abby seized the silent moment. "Once you have the antiderivative, you do the top number minus the bottom. b minus a."

Kylee sucked in a sharp breath and slapped her palm on the table. "Thank you! You don't know how long I've been trying to get that." She turned to Dylan. "Simple is best with me."

Dylan frowned at Kylee. "But that's exactly what I said."

Abby smiled and bit into her slice of pizza. She'd found her people. *Thanks, God.*

After lunch, Abby weaved through the students crowding the lobby on her way to computer class.

JD cornered her by the trophy case with his cool-man—stalker?—lean. "Second day better than the first?"

She backed against the glass to get some personal space. "Yes, actually." *Ooh.* Her stomach flip-flopped. Six feet tall with thick, tousled brown hair and eyebrows that could flirt all on their own. She fought back the girly sigh trying to abduct her rational side and reminded herself this boy had trouble written all over him.

And he still reeked.

"You didn't sit with me at lunch."

"I had to help a girl with her calculus."

"Ah. So you think you're going to waltz in here and steal my valedictorian spot?"

Valedictorian? Abby made the mistake of looking into his chocolaty eyes. She slid down the glass as if she actually melted a little. "I don't—aren't you a senior? I'm only a junior. I thought I told you that."

He chuckled softly, his smile lighting up his face. "I'm just teasing."

"Are you really valedictorian?" Abby asked.

"So far." He raised a finger just over her shoulder and tapped the glass. "That one there is all me. I ran a thirty-yard touchdown against Colony with no time left on the clock. Took MVP of the tournament."

Ug. How easily JD bounced between interesting, smart hunk and cliché über-full-of-himself quarterback. And now he was way too into her personal space. His body was so close that, even if she wanted to, she couldn't turn to admire his football award. Abby peered under his arm, mapping a getaway route. Resorting to violence on her second day might make a bad impression, but she wasn't completely opposed to the idea.

Second option: If she could duck and turn, she might be able to snake her way free. Too bad she wasn't the most graceful of athletes. This plan could backfire into an embarrassing sprawl across the crowded lobby floor. She glanced back to JD. His eyes closed and he leaned down.

Uh oh.

She turned her head and his lips met her ear.

Abby gasped. "*What* are you *doing*?"

He recovered with a raised eyebrow. "I like you."

"Like me? We just met yesterday."

JD's lips stretched into a grin, and the brainless fool came in for another try. Abby ducked and he lip-locked the trophy case. How apropos.

Two of his letter-jacket-wearing friends who were standing by the school's front doors burst into laughter. Abby darted away, cheeks blazing. Before she could make it to the main hall, however, someone grabbed her hand.

She turned back to see JD staring at her like she was the last donut in the box. "Hey, I'm sorry. I thought you liked me. I misread your signals."

She jerked away. "I wasn't giving you any signals." Was she? She had smiled a lot, but she was only reciprocating. Well, she *had* swooned for a second ... But a smile didn't translate to "please make out with me." Not in any language. She strode toward computer class, heart racing.

Her high school goals did *not* include dating. But even if she were interested, she would never move *that* fast. She had standards, and his behavior wasn't even *near* measuring up. She knew she was pretty and guys liked her hair, but she tried not to give off mixed signals. As a result she wore very little makeup, almost always kept her hair tamed in a braid or ponytail, purposely trying to make herself plain. Plus, she didn't want to risk using cosmetics tested on animals—but that was beside the point.

JD darted in front of her and held out his hands. "Come on, Abby. Give me another chance. I'll be good, I promise. Come hang out with me and the guys at Reggie's. It's a pizza and ice cream place a few blocks from here. I'll buy. It'll be fun. As friends, okay?"

Not okay. JD Kane had one too many cons against him, even for pizza and ice cream. Abby stuck out her bottom lip in a pout. "I'm sorry, JD, but I'm busy until you go to college."

Abby stared at her reflection in the massive windows in the living room and ran her fingers through Einstein's fur. She'd completed all her homework, even finished reading The Great Gatsby. She glanced at the grandfather clock and sighed. 8:47. No sign of Dad, no messages, no texts. She dragged her feet into the kitchen, set Einstein on the counter, and pulled out the bread and a block of cheddar to make herself a grilled cheese sandwich.

Plate in hand, she settled in front of the TV. She prayed over her meal and went looking for old episodes of CSI. Grilled cheese and CSI. Two pros. See, it was all about looking for the positives.

But it bothered her that Dad was so secretive about his new job—and that his workplace itself seemed intent on keeping secrets of its own. Old memories surfaced, fights between him and Mom over research ethics, and the newspaper article that brought the truth to Abby, Mom, and the rest of the world.

Oh, Dad. What are you doing now?

She finished her sandwich, then snuggled under a blanket and into the Las Vegas world of crime.

The sound of keys in the front door jolted her awake.

Her dad's enlarged shadow floated along the hallway. "Abby, honey. You still up?"

CSI had ended while she'd slept, and now the TV blared a cable talk show. How long was I out? Abby sat, knocking the blanket and Einstein to the floor. The cat stretched and pranced to his food dish in the kitchen, his tail raised behind him like a flag. Abby picked up the remote, yawned, and clicked off the television. She looked over the back of the couch to see her dad standing in the foyer. "Just waiting for you. You could text, you know, if you're going to be this late."

Dad shrugged off his trench coat and hung it in the closet. "I'm sorry. I'll try to remember to check in tomorrow."

"Why you so late?"

He lifted his scarf over his head and put it with his coat. "We're working on some important research."

"What's so important? ... at an old barn in the middle of the woods?"

Dad ambled toward the kitchen and, as usual, evaded questions requiring specific answers. Though she was surprised he didn't jump on the fact she knew where he worked. Was he even listening?

"Did you make dinner?"

It was always all about his needs. Did she do her homework? Pick up the mail? Make dinner? Do the laundry?

Why wouldn't he be open with her? She didn't understand his secrecy. What could be so hush-hush about a barn? At George Washington U, before *the incident*, he'd taken her to the lab and showed her his work. She'd met his colleagues and ate barbecue at their homes on Saturdays. She wished he'd let her in now. The fact that he wouldn't didn't bode well.

She stood up and walked to the island that separated the kitchen from the living room. "What do you do there, Dad?"

"Abby..." His voice held a warning tone. He set his briefcase on the counter between them and met her eyes long enough to say, "It's a *private* lab. They have the right to confidentiality. I signed several agreements stating I wouldn't discuss my work with anyone."

"Not even your own daughter?"

"Not even you." He looked away. End of conversation.

"You're not doing something bad again, are you?"

He opened the fridge. "Any leftovers?"

She set her jaw to keep from saying something she'd regret. She was too tired for a text war, but stomped toward the stairs just to show him his answers were not acceptable. "Good-night, then."

He didn't seem to catch on. "Night, Abby, honey."

In her bedroom, she burrowed under her purple comforter and closed her eyes. Seeing the barn that morning, and Dad's secretive behavior, dug up all kinds of memories she'd been trying to suppress. Her mom's death had devastated them both, but Abby's parents hadn't exactly been happily-ever-after. They'd never argued about normal things, like whose turn it was to take out the trash, or how to raise Abby, or money—well, that one wasn't entirely true. Dad hated that Mom tithed at church, claiming she was throwing away his hard-earned salary. He never understood

Mom's relationship with God. That foundational difference led to the other, more passionate debate: Dad's work.

Dad had started out with a craving to save the world. That was what Mom had said she first loved about him. He wanted to find a cure for diabetes, cancer, AIDS, you name it. But Mom's breast cancer diagnosis turned ambition into obsession. As the years went on—genius that he was—he found his way onto a Nobel Prize-nominated team that used embryonic stem cells of mice to modify genes. It wasn't until some undercover reporter's story made the front page of the *Washington Times* that Abby learned the truth.

Dad's team had also been experimenting with embryos and fetal tissue, trying to clone human cells and organs in the name of science, in the search for a cure for cancer. The lab had used anonymous human donors, but since federal funding for human cloning was illegal, and Dad was at a federally funded lab, the government shut them down. Dad was out of a job.

All this went on while Mom was dying from cancer.

So Mom and Dad had fought. Big time. Yelling and screaming on the way to a doctor's appointment. Harsh whispers and evasion when Mom got back from a round of chemo. Mom called Dad a murderer. Dad called Mom a brainwashed fool.

And Abby had spent a lot of time in her room reading *Forensic Magazine*.

[CHAPTER FIVE]

NINE DOCTORS WERE NOW ON the Farm. Before Dr. Goyer had come—and not counting Dr. Woman—Dr. Max had been Martyr's favorite. Dr. Max taught math, as well as other subjects when the Jasons were younger. He was strict, as all the doctors were, but he made Martyr laugh. Plus, his skin fascinated Martyr. It was brown, like the dark gravy that sometimes came over mashed potatoes. Martyr had never seen anyone like him.

Martyr sat in the math classroom waiting for the clock to switch from 2:59 to 3:00, when he could attempt to talk privately with Dr. Max. He'd never made a personal request from a doctor until yesterday, when he asked Dr. Goyer to watch over Baby and Hummer. Today he would ask Dr. Max for an even bigger favor.

The clock buzzed. Three o' clock. The door clicked, unlocked for the next five minutes by an automatic timer. The Jasons trailed up the aisle to place their math papers in the basket on Dr. Max's desk, but Martyr stalled, slowly closing his book and writing his identification number at the top of his sheet. When he did stand, his vision spun and his stomach cramped. He gripped the back of his chair and waited for it to pass; the burn from Dr. Elliot's EEZ had gone, but he was still nauseous and dizzy.

Martyr again took his time, staying at the very back of the group. When he reached the desk, he placed his math problems in the basket and lingered. A glance over his shoulder revealed Hummer still holding open the door, a job he assigned himself daily.

Martyr waved. "You go ahead, Hummer. I'll see you at dinner."

Hummer left and the door fell closed. Martyr turned back to Dr. Max's desk.

Dr. Max looked up from his paperwork. "Can I do something for you?"

"I want to ask you a favor."

"Shoot."

Dr. Max's dialogue sometimes confused Martyr. He often spoke in slang, as Dr. Sautin, the language arts teacher, said. Dr. Max folded his hands and leaned forward, apparently waiting for Martyr to speak.

"I expire in sixteen days." Martyr hated the sound of those words. "I wonder, if you wouldn't mind, maybe … do you think you could help to … I—"

"Just spit it out, boy."

Martyr stared at the basket overflowing in all directions with math assignments. "I want to see the sky. Just a glimpse." He glanced up, gauging the doctor's reaction.

Dr. Max's forehead wrinkled. "Oh, Martyr, my man, I can't do that. I'm sorry. I can sneak you in some fast food and all, maybe even a book with some colored pictures of the sky, but I can't take you above ground." Dr. Max's black eyebrows scrunched together. "I—It's not … well, it's not safe."

"But I'll be dead soon. Does it matter if I get infected?"

"It might. Are you willing to risk your purpose? What if you get infected and it makes you unable to provide the antidote? Or you infect everyone down here?"

"But the doctors go outside and you don't infect us."

"But we take the antidote."

"Then give me the antidote, just enough for five minutes. One minute." Martyr's throat grew tight. He sucked in a sharp breath. "Please?"

"Naw. There's no way. You liked that chocolate ice cream I brought last year, didn't you? I can bring you a half gallon tomorrow. You can eat the whole thing yourself."

Martyr's eyes moistened, and Dr. Max's face went out of focus. "Thank you." He turned and jogged toward the door. His head tingled. Black spots swept across his eyes. He stumbled, crashed into a desk, and fell.

Dr. Max was at his side in seconds. "Martyr, buddy, you okay?" He clutched Martyr's arm and helped him stand.

Marty jerked away, swallowed, and walked toward the door, careful not to move too fast.

"Martyr," Dr. Max called.

Martyr pulled the door open and stepped into the hall.

"Tomorrow, man," Dr. Max yelled. "I'll bring you some."

"It's not that I don't appreciate his offer. Ice cream is *very* good," Martyr told Dr. Goyer, swinging his foot against the side of the exam table. After Rolo dropped Martyr off, Dr. Goyer had removed the restraints, allowing Martyr to sit on the table like a real person. It was a very kind thing, to break the rules in such a way. "I shouldn't have allowed myself to dream."

"Well, I apologize, Martyr, for putting the idea in your head."

"It's not your fault, Dr. Goyer. I never expected to behave so foolishly at the end. I wanted to be brave."

"You're being very brave, son."

Martyr cocked his head to the side. "Sun? The big star in the sky?"

"Oh, no. S-U-N, *sun*, is the big star in the sky. S-O-N, *son*, is kind of a nickname. It's what people sometimes call their male children or other boys."

Some adults who lived outside had children who were not created the way Martyr had been. The doctors talked very little about this subject. Maybe Dr. Goyer would tell Martyr something he did not know if he asked the right questions. He may not be able to see the sky, but learning new things still thrilled him.

"Tell me about your daughter. How did you come to own her?"

Dr. Goyer chuckled. "I don't think of it as owning her. I raise her, much in the way the doctors raise you. I teach her things, take care of her, love her."

"But she was not made?"

"Well, of course she was made."

"How?"

Dr. Goyer reddened. "Does it matter how?"

"I want to know the difference." All Martyr knew about how the Jasons were made was that they arrived as infants from the Gunnolf facility.

"Let's talk about something else as this is probably our last day together. It's doubtful you'll be assigned marks with me again since I'm not a teacher."

"You might not lead a class, but you are the best teacher, in my opinion, because you answer truthfully. Tell me what it's like to live outside."

Dr. Goyer rubbed his face. "I'll tell you as much as I can, but if I think it is going to break the rules, I'll stop, okay?"

Martyr nodded.

Dr. Goyer began to tell Martyr of the sky and the birds and something called *airplanes* that flew through it, and the *rainbows* and clouds that sometimes appeared in it. He spoke of the land covered in green grass and trees and how a strange blowing, *wind*, made them dance, of the rivers that gurgled and lakes that sat still, the mountains that climbed to the sky and jagged *canyons* that cut into the earth. He spoke of seasons, where the same land looked different, how water drops from the sky called *rain* made the sky dark and flakes of ice called *snow* covered everything in a white blanket. Martyr soaked in every word, asking questions whenever Dr. Goyer paused for breath.

The clock on Dr. Goyer's desk buzzed at five o' clock.

Martyr asked another question, before Dr. Goyer could call Rolo to escort him downstairs. "Do you believe I will get infected if I went outside for one minute?"

Dr. Goyer rubbed the back of his neck. "Oh, I … I doubt it. But don't go telling Dr. Kane I said that, or I'll end up having marks with Dr. Elliot."

Martyr laughed. "You wouldn't like that, trust me."

"Do you feel better today?"

"Somewhat. I haven't vomited, but I'm very dizzy, especially if I move too fast. I've fallen down twice so far."

"I'm sorry Dr. Elliot caused that."

"Yes." Martyr pursed his lips, then figured he had nothing to lose by asking. "Dr. Goyer, would you take me outside?"

Dr. Goyer sucked in a deep breath. "Martyr. I— No. I can't."

It was no use. Martyr would not see sky before he expired. He should be thankful for Dr. Goyer's talks and the ice cream Dr. Max would bring. It was more than some received.

Martyr could not bear to look Dr. Goyer in the eyes, so his gaze fell to the doctor's desk. Piles of papers cluttered the surface. Martyr had never seen such disorganization. His eyes stopped on a keycard sitting on the front corner. He chanced a glance at Dr. Goyer and noticed a tear dripping down the man's cheek. Dr. Goyer removed his glasses and rubbed his eyes.

While he felt compassion for Dr. Goyer and wanted to comfort him in some way—and find out what was causing the doctor to cry—Martyr's eyes shot back to the keycard. His mind whirred with possible scenarios to get the card without being caught. *Even marks with Dr. Elliot would be worth it.*

Dr. Goyer pressed his intercom and spoke with a somewhat strained voice. "This is Dr. Goyer. Could you send Robert up?"

"Sure thing, doctor."

"Let's get you strapped back down before he gets here." Dr. Goyer rose and walked to the exam table, stopping at Martyr's side. "I enjoyed our time together, Martyr. I'm glad I got to know you."

Martyr did not like good-byes. Good-byes were forever. Dr. Woman. The J:1s and J:2s.

Now it was his turn.

Though he hated any kind of deceit, he could see no other option to get what he wanted. Closing his eyes, he remembered yesterday's pain and willed it back. He groaned, gagged, and shook, trying to look convincing. He clamped a hand over his mouth and moaned.

Dr. Goyer raced for the cupboard under the sink, crouched, and opened the door.

Martyr slid off the table and snatched the keycard, tucking it into the waistband of his pants before jumping back on the exam table. He lay back and took deep breaths, heart pounding.

The cupboard slammed and Dr. Goyer appeared at his side with the plastic tub. "You okay?"

"Yes," Martyr said. "Lying down helped." His whole body trembled and burned—not from Dr. Elliott's poison. From the lie.

"You scared me half to death." Dr. Goyer set the tub on his desk, then fastened the restraints.

A wave of remorse seeped into Martyr's heart. He hoped Dr. Goyer wouldn't get into trouble because Martyr had taken his keycard. "Thank you, Dr. Goyer. You've been very kind."

"You're welcome, son."

Martyr felt another stab of guilt race through him.

The lab door flew open and Rolo entered. He removed the restraints and led Martyr out of Dr. Goyer's lab.

"Good-bye, Martyr," Dr. Goyer called, voice raspy.

"Good-bye."

Rolo led Martyr down the stairwell to level two and out into the hallway. He shoved Martyr's shoulder, and the force knocked the keycard a little lower. "Get yourself to dinner."

Martyr walked carefully so that the keycard would not fall out of his waistband. He went to the cafeteria, plotting when he would make his move.

Martyr looked down at the bumpy gray cardboard tray in his hands, searching for color. Tonight's meal consisted of creamy pasta over chicken, along with cauliflower, a roll, and a small box of milk. He carried his tray across the cafeteria. Five white-and-black tables stretched across the open eating area, each seating a different section. Almost everything was white, black, or gray on the Farm.

Tonight, Martyr hoped to see blue.

The fifteen boys in Section Five were aged fourteen to seventeen. Their table was farthest away, near the wall of mirrors, where Baby was already seated.

Martyr slid onto the bench beside Baby, trying to act as if nothing were different, despite the stolen keycard tucked into his waistband. The deception made him hot all over.

He forced a big smile to Baby. "Hungry?"

Baby stuffed a handful of cauliflower into his mouth. His blotchy cheeks puffed out, and he bobbed his unusually large head from side to side as he chewed.

The bright lights hanging from the ceiling glared off Baby's head. The sixteen-year-old J:4s had been groomed that morning, and Baby's head and chin were clean-shaven, his nails clipped short, and he should smell fresh. Martyr wasn't going to risk taking a whiff in case the groomers had cheated him of soap. Everyone knew Baby couldn't complain.

Martyr winced at the fresh bruise shading his friend's neck. Iron Man could have killed Baby this morning if Martyr hadn't found Johnson. And it would have been Martyr's fault, just like last time.

He had tried so hard to protect the ones who couldn't protect themselves—but he'd be gone soon. Maybe tonight. He hoped Dr. Goyer would be able to keep Baby and the others safe.

Fido darted forward and snatched the milk off Baby's tray.

Baby clutched his ears and wailed, rocking back and forth on the bench.

Martyr jumped to his feet. "Put it back."

Fido's tongue lolled out of his mouth. He panted while staring at Martyr with wild eyes, and reached for Baby's bread.

Martyr slid over the tabletop and grabbed Fido's arm. "No." He yanked the milk free and set it back on the tray.

Fido growled and swiped for the milk again, but Martyr caught him by the wrist and squeezed, digging in with his fingernails, thankful J:3s weren't groomed until Thursdays.

"Fido!" Rolo lumbered between the tables and slapped his stick against his palm. His bulging body jiggled beneath his tight, gray uniform. "You causing trouble, boy?"

Martyr quickly let go and sat down. He reached across the table and pulled his tray in front of him.

Rolo smacked Fido's knee with his stick. Fido wailed. "That's right. Howl, you mongrel!" Rolo prodded Fido in the back. "Now, get back to your seat before I chain you to it."

Fido slunk away, glowering at Martyr as he settled at the end of the table. Martyr turned back to Baby, who had stifled his cry by sticking his thumb in his mouth, though he still rocked on the bench.

Martyr patted his shoulder. "Hey, it's okay. He's gone now. Eat up."

Baby's big brown eyes flickered to Martyr's. He grinned around the thumb in his mouth.

Baby would only be saved if he managed to get placed in Section One. But for tonight, Martyr would do all he could to please his friend. Who knew if he would even survive the toxic air to see Baby again?

He shoveled the cauliflower off his tray and onto Baby's.

Baby grunted with glee.

[CHAPTER SIX]

ABBY AND KYLEE SAT AT the end of an empty table in the cafeteria. Kylee's friends had yet to arrive. Abby eyed the pile of noodles on her tray, feeling like she should bag it for evidence. She looked up from the tomato and bean nightmare. "What's this supposed to be?"

"Sign said *cowboy mac*." Kylee spit her wad of gum into a napkin and opened her milk carton. "So where do you live?"

"On Alpine, right off Dawson Road, in the woods behind that Salmon Laundromat."

Kylee's eyes lit up. "I don't live that far from you. Think I could come over sometime to study? I could use help in calculus."

"Sure." Abby fought the urge to squeal at the prospect of a friend. "My dad's never home."

"Neither is my mom. She's working on her PhD."

Abby tore back the foil lid on her juice cup. "In what?"

"Something about science. Biology, I think."

Abby slumped in awe. "That is *so* cool. I can't wait to meet her." Abby's mom never had an interest in science, except to debate Dad's ethics.

Kylee lowered her gaze, and her silky black hair, which usually sat in a bell-like curve above her shoulders, slumped with her. "Like I said, she's never home."

Abby could relate. "You can come over anytime."

Kylee sipped her milk and flashed a dimpled smile. "This is such an answer to prayer. I'm so glad you moved here."

Abby grinned. Pro number three for Kylee Wallace. "You go to church?"

"Fishhook Community Church. My brother is the youth pastor there."

"You have brothers and sisters?"

"Just Scott. He's twenty-six. He and his wife are expecting their first baby in May, which means I'm going to be an aunt."

"How fun! I never liked being an only child."

"It's been hard since Scott moved out, but at least he didn't go far. Dad left when I was seven. He never came back."

Abby ate a bite of pasta. Were there no unbroken families left in the world? Maybe Kylee's brother, his wife, and their child-to-be would fare better. "I'd like to visit your church sometime. I really miss my youth group. We went on a trip to Philly right before—"

"Hey, friend." JD slid onto the bench beside Abby and draped a heavy arm around her neck. His overpowering cologne tickled her nose, making her wonder how he was able to keep sneaking up on her.

She shrugged off his arm. "JD, you know Kylee?"

He barely glanced across the table. "Sure. Listen, Abby. There's a basketball game tonight. I don't play or anything, but it's fun to watch. You game, *friend*?"

If I don't look at him, his brown eyes and dazzling smile can't tempt me. She focused on Kylee, who had gone stiff, eyes bulging. "Can't. Kylee and I are going to hit the books, right, Kylee?"

Kylee hadn't managed to avoid JD's charms. The girl sat straight across from him, staring, lips still pursed around the straw sticking out of her milk container.

Abby kicked her under the table. "Kylee?"

Kylee jolted. The straw flicked free from her lips and a few drops of milk dribbled down her chin. "Huh?"

"We're going to study at my place tonight, *right*?"

Kylee squeaked out, "Calculus."

JD's hand found Abby's shoulder again, and he massaged it as he stood. "Maybe next time, then. Later, Abby."

He strode to the lunch line and cut in where some jocks were standing. Abby blinked away from him to focus on Kylee. The girl still hadn't cleaned off her chin.

"Kylee." Abby offered her napkin and tapped her own chin. "You've got some milk …"

Kylee snatched the napkin and wiped her chin. "Did JD just ask you out?"

"I guess. I turned him down once. I don't know why he won't give up."

Kylee snorted then clapped a hand over her mouth. "I am such a dork. Did I actually drool in his presence?"

"I think you just had a faulty straw."

A smile spread across Kylee's face. "You know, I don't usually go for white boys—Mom would kill me—but I think I'd face the wrath for JD Kane."

Abby wrinkled her nose. "Really? But he's so cocky. Plus, he tried to kiss me yesterday. Yesterday, Kylee. He'd only known me for twenty-four hours, less if you only count the time we've actually talked." Abby shook her head. "Not that I'm looking, but I want a guy who is my friend first and—"

Kylee grabbed Abby's wrist. "Back up, girl. He tried to kiss you?"

Abby related JD's near-assault at the trophy case.

"Wow," Kylee said. "I'd always imagined he'd be more … romantic than that."

"Sorry to kill the dream."

"You're still lucky, even if you don't like him," Kylee said. "At least you got asked out by someone—a cute someone. There's such a shortage of cute guys around here, Danny Chung is starting to look good."

AP English Mr. Chung? Abby grimaced, but Kylee was on a roll.

"And don't even get me started on the lack of ethnicity. How many other black kids do you see at this school?"

Abby's lips parted. Was that a rhetorical question? There wasn't another person with anything close to the dark chocolate complexion of her friend, but she glanced around the cafeteria and caught sight of Mr. Chung in line at the vending machine. He had kind of a cute, John Cho-Hikaru Sulu thing going on, but it was hard to guess his age.

"I rest my case," Kylee said, stabbing her Tater Tots with her fork.

"Two more years and you and Mr. Chung will be legal. He looks really young."

"He's twenty-six. Graduated with Scott."

Abby had been joking, but Kylee's information took her by surprise. "Really? It must be weird to teach at your own high school."

"Danny even played football here. Got a scholarship to Oregon State but wasn't good enough for pro. When Coach Reimers retired, Fishhook High hired Danny to teach and coach."

"So the old coach taught English?"

"No. Mr. Lester taught English then."

"Bio II, Mr. Lester?" Abby could not imagine Mr. Lester talking about the lyrical prose of F. Scott Fitzgerald without tying it to formaldehyde.

Kylee's black lashes flicked from side to side, and she lowered her voice. "You really want to hear the soap opera that is Fishhook High?"

Intrigued, Abby said, "Please."

Kylee took a deep breath. "Corrine Markley taught biology quite a few years ago. Mr. Lester wanted the job, but they needed him in the English department. Anyway, Mrs. Markley didn't show up one day. No one knew where she was, and her husband reported her missing. The cops even questioned him but had to let him go for lack of evidence. Scott and Danny thought Mr. Lester knocked her off for the biology position. And sure enough, next year Mr. Lester was head of the science department."

A missing biology teacher. A chill tingled up Abby's spine. "Did they ever find her?"

"Nope. She vanished. No body, no crime. Scott had a few of her classes when he was in school, and he was really depressed when the cops gave up on the search. He said it was because she was a great teacher, but I think he had a thing for her. This was way before he married Aliza, of course."

"How long ago?"

"I was in sixth grade when she disappeared, and Scott was just out of college. And I remember Danny was subbing in the valley, looking for a fulltime job. The school hired him that fall to coach and fill Mr. Lester's English spot."

Welcome to *CSI: Fishhook*. If Abby could find the public library, she could look up the old newspapers, read the official story. The cops probably had done all they could, and the case *was* pretty old, but still. In a town like this, they probably couldn't afford the best forensics specialists. Not that Abby had enough training to do any good, but her mind was suffering from lack of academic stimuli. It might be fun to look up the case and build some theories. And possibly find out what really happened to Corrine Markley.

"In your role as genetic counselors, you'll investigate an inherited disease and prepare a PowerPoint presentation for a client who has just been diagnosed."

Now this was the kind of assignment she got back at George Washington High School, and Mr. Lester was the kind of teacher she was used to. He was wearing a white lab coat. Big pro for Mr. Lester. Abby liked that he took science seriously.

She really hoped he wasn't a murderer.

He draped an arm over the tall cane-like faucet of the sink on his marble desk. "Your presentation should provide medical information to help your client live a long and healthy life. Things like"—he walked to the whiteboard and began to write— "symptoms, causes, diagnosis, treatment, prognosis, and pedigree." He put down the marker. "I also want to see the impact of the disease on the victim, their family, and society. Make sure you create a Punnett square to predict possible genetic outcomes for the patient's offspring."

Abby's mind spun through the genetic disease possibilities. Cystic Fibrosis? She'd always been fascinated with little Emmy, who had lived in their apartment building back in DC. A freshman guy in her PE class here had hemophilia. He'd gotten a bloody nose playing volleyball yesterday and an ambulance had taken him to the hospital.

She snapped out of her thoughts as chairs scraped the floor and students began moving around the room. Mr. Lester must have dismissed them to find a partner. She stood and scanned the classroom for a lone student but saw only pairs.

"I guess that leaves you and me," a deep voice said.

Abby swung around to see JD sitting in the once-vacant seat beside her. *Of course.* "I'm not working with you."

He raised an eyebrow. "Why not?"

She stammered, "I … There's no … Just because."

He grinned and opened his notebook to a clean sheet of paper. She fell back into her chair and propped her cheek on her fist. He'd better not mess this up.

She hadn't bothered to take note of JD's outfit today, but now she couldn't help but notice. He wore a blue sweater over a white turtleneck. The colors popped over the black marble tabletop. He pushed the sleeves up over his sculpted forearms and leaned back in his chair, looking like something out of *GQ*.

Abby twisted her lips. Too bad he had no IQ.

She snickered at her private joke then caught a whiff of his cologne. Her snicker morphed into a cough that morphed into, "What do you want to do the project on?"

JD leaned forward and propped his elbows on his knees. "How about, how long it will take you to forgive me?"

"It's not a statistics project, JD. It's biology. Biogenetics, technically." Instead of looking chastised, JD seemed amused. "Look, my grade is important to me. I'm a straight-A student. So if you're not going to help, you can find yourself another lab partner."

His eyebrows rose in innocent protest. "I'm a straight-A student too, remember? Valedictorian?"

"Right. Well, are you interested in any disease in particular? Because if you're not, I—"

"Lupus."

"Really?" Abby blinked, surprised how quickly he'd spat out the word. "Do you know someone with lupus?"

JD frowned. "You think that'll get us extra credit?"

"I doubt it, but if we could interview someone—"

He shook his head. "I don't know anyone." He straightened in his chair, scratched his neck, cleared his throat, and fidgeted until he crossed his arms back over his chest.

O-kay. Talk about your tells. Wonder boy was exhibiting some serious lying symptoms.

And under her penetrating gaze, JD's ears pinked. "I don't really care what we do."

"Lupus is fine with me. I don't know all that much about it." Which was a major pro. She'd finally have something to focus her energy on.

He loosened up again and delivered a smile that could thaw the deepest freeze. "Why don't you come to my house later and we could—"

She shot him a scowl.

"—study." His smile drooped. "Or not." Then he laughed, the dopiest laugh Abby had ever heard. Much worse than Kylee's snort.

Good grief. Jock boy's geek was showing.

Abby hung out at the school library for a few hours after school, looking for books on lupus. There weren't many. They also didn't keep any newspapers past four years old. She checked out the couple books they did have then took the scenic route home, driving past Jason Farms.

She pulled her BMW into the parking lot and eased into an empty space between a Lexus and a Land Rover. Nice cars; Jason Farms must pay well. She bit her lip and tapped her gloved fingers on the steering wheel, staring at the dark opening in the barn where one of the big doors was propped open with a mound of snow.

Maybe they were working on something to do with cloning fruit or vegetables. Something to help the FDA? She turned off the engine and the cab chilled almost instantly without the fan blowing heat in her face. Not exactly ideal weather for growing vegetation. She pulled her hood strings tight around her chin, wrenched open the door, and walked toward the barn.

Just a quick peek.

Her breath puffed out in front like exhaust. Her nylon bomber jacket rustled with every swing of her arms or turn of her head. She stepped through the large entry onto a concrete floor and pushed off her hood to get a better look around. The floor was entirely concrete, the barn itself vast and empty except for stacks of mildewed hay bales. A wide, steel vault door stood to her left, a keycard slot perched on the wall beside it.

High security. Not your everyday barn.

Further down the wall that held the mysterious vault door were several aluminum storage cabinets. Abby opened one. Oddly enough, they weren't locked.

The first revealed nothing but canned cauliflower. Weird. The second cabinet was filled with cartons of dried goods: instant mashed potatoes, boxes of pasta, napkins, and plastic spoons.

The next held nothing but diapers in all sizes. Lots and lots of diapers.

Perhaps they had chimps behind that Fort Knox door. Her toes clenched in the bottom of her boots. Had Dad gone from one unethical lab to another? Jason Farms sure looked like it had something to hide.

The last door was steel, about two-feet wide by three feet high, and opened at waist level. A track ran along the wall on the opposite side, descending underground. She leaned in and peeked down a dark hole, where only a tiny crack of light shone somewhere below. She spotted a switch on the outer wall beside the door and was tempted to flip it. She laughed to herself. Surely there was nothing to be afraid of. It was a dumbwaiter, a shortcut designed to take the food and supplies down below.

But why did they need so much food and supplies down there? And diapers?

Did chimps eat cauliflower?

She exited the barn and circled the perimeter. There couldn't be more than a ten-foot square room behind that vault door. Not big enough for a lab upstairs.

Abby huffed, sending a cloud of foggy breath in front of her face. Her nose and cheeks were growing numb. She really wanted to see this underground lab, but Dad would freak if she tried the door and somehow caused a scene. And it was already starting to get dark. The land of the midnight sun wasn't so sunny in early March.

Reluctantly, she climbed back into her car and started the engine. Her cheeks tingled as the heat thawed her extremities. She drove home and pulled into her driveway only to find a familiar Ford F–150 sitting in front of her house, the twilight and a plume of exhaust misting its signature cobalt blue.

JD Kane.

She slammed her car into park, switched off the headlights, and wrenched up the handbrake. What part of no did JD not understand? They'd made plans to meet in the library tomorrow during lunch to work on their project. But clearly stalker man thought he could do whatever he wanted.

JD opened his door as she opened hers. Man, he was cute. She shook the wretched thought away as she stepped carefully across the icy driveway.

"Hi, *friend*."

His deep, smooth voice and movie star looks would not sway her. Abby narrowed her eyes. "What are you doing here? How do you even know where I live?"

He grinned that all-American smile. "Steph Abrams works in the office fifth period. She gave me your address—she's got a little crush on me."

Little? According to Kylee, 98 percent of the girls at Fishhook High would pawn their iPods to exchange three words with JD Kane. "And the first question?"

His eyebrows rose up under his shaggy brown hair.

"What. Are. You. Doing. Here?"

The grin again. "I thought you were having a study session." He opened his truck door and reached inside, pulling out a tousled pile of papers. "I found some pamphlets on lupus I wanted to show you. Plus I have this ..." He held out a book titled *Genetic Disease*.

Abby feigned disinterest, but the book was like a magnet. She stepped closer, slipped a bit on the ice, but steadied herself, lest he try to "help" her. "Where'd you find that?"

"Uh ... I think it's from Amazon."

She rolled her eyes. "That's *not* what I meant."

He shrugged one shoulder, the leather sleeve of his varsity jacket crackling in the cold. "My dad's library. He's into diseases and stuff."

Abby studied his expression. He seemed earnest, but she didn't buy the fact his dad just so happened to collect books on genetic disease. Either JD had improved his lying skills since biology class, or she wasn't the only one with an eccentric and scientific father.

Abby met his eyes and her pulse tripped in the awkward silence. What to do? "I'm not letting you into my house without backup."

He shot her a confused—and incredibly cute—expression. Wrinkled brow, partial frown ... "Backup?"

I can't believe I said that out loud. She turned away, pulled her phone out of her pocket, and dialed Kylee.

"Abby?"

"Hey ... when are you coming over?"

"Today?"

"Uh ... you know. Calculus?"

"That was just an excuse to avoid going to the game with JD, right?"

Abby turned to find JD's eyes roaming where they shouldn't

and tugged the waistband of her parka lower. She whispered, "JD is at my house, and I don't feel safe … without … you know, a buffer friend."

A squeak came through the phone, followed by heavy breathing. Kylee hyperventilating.

"Kylee? I need you coherent. Please, stay calm."

"I'll be right over." She sounded like a nervous prank caller.

Abby shut the phone and crammed it into her pocket. "Kylee will be joining us shortly."

JD crossed his arms and leaned back against his truck. "You don't trust me."

"Nope."

His mouth twitched up in a grin. "Smart girl."

The voracious capacity of his eyes shot a nervous thrill through Abby's limbs. She walked it off by going to her passenger door to unload her schoolbooks. Every sense was aware of his presence as she pulled the books into her arm, shut the door, and walked up the porch steps. They creaked behind her.

She whirled around. He stood inches from her; the toes of his shoes bumped against hers. Before she could react he put one hand against the doorframe in his characteristic lean. Abby felt herself swimming until his aggressive cologne snapped her back to her senses.

She slammed her books against his blue-and-white letter jacket. "Hold these, will you?"

He leaned back to balance all the books in his arms, and she took advantage of his vulnerable state to lay down some offense. "Kylee will be here any minute. Try anything and I have a ten-pound flashlight that masquerades as a nightstick."

A smile flitted across his face, and she was suddenly aware that her lack of interest probably fed his persistence. Nothing like a challenge to interest a guy who could have anything—anyone— he wanted. She frowned, shoved her house key into the lock, and turned it.

She might have to change strategies.

JD shadowed her through the house. She upped the thermostat

and settled into the armchair in the living room, leaving him to choose between the couch, the loveseat, or the barstools at the kitchen counter. JD dropped his stack of papers and Abby's books on the counter then sat down on the couch and stared at her with hungry eyes.

Einstein padded into the room and leapt onto her lap, and she ran her fingers through the cat's fur to calm her nerves. Maybe she should have waited for Kylee outside, thirty below or not. How many episodes of *CSI* would it take to remind her that inviting a guy into your home when you were alone was S-T-U-P-I-D? Where was her brain?

She tried to give off an air of nonchalance, as if the hunky predator in her home was no big deal. "Let's see that brochure."

He didn't move at first, then clambered to his feet and wandered to the kitchen counter. He brought the pile of papers to Abby's chair, kneeled in front of her, and pulled out a brochure.

When she reached for it, he pulled it back out of her grasp. She reached again, and he lifted his arm into the air.

The doorbell rang.

Abby pushed Einstein off her lap and jumped up. She snatched the pamphlet out of JD's hand on her way to the door, thankful her reinforcement lived so close.

Abby opened the door.

"Study buddy to the rescue!" Kylee squeaked out. She held her calculus book in front of her face, but Abby could still hear her chomping her gum.

"You. Are. My. Hero." Abby shooed Kylee inside and secured the door. She led her friend into the living room. JD was no longer in sight.

"Where is he?" Kylee's voice was still not quite normal. And her eager expression made Abby smirk. Her new friend should make a more-than-willing distraction for JD Kane.

"JD?" Abby tipped her head back to peer up the stairs. She didn't see him. *Where did—*

Suddenly Abby was airborne and floating in JD's arms. He'd scooped her up and was spinning her around and around.

She screamed, "Put me down!" and clutched the front of his jacket. The room blurred around her, making her stomach lurch.

JD laughed deep and long, and finally stopped spinning. He didn't release her, though. The room still whirled as she tried to focus on Kylee's face. JD's right hand shifted too close to inappropriate, and Abby slapped him. He cursed and dropped her. Her tailbone bashed against the wooden floor and sent smarting pain up her spine.

Kylee rushed to her side. "Are you okay?" She glared at JD. "I can't believe you!"

JD's lips parted. "Me?" Shock and surprise were foreign expressions to his usual smugness, as was his whining tone. He rubbed his cheek. "That really hurt!"

Kylee smacked her lips. "Oh, poor baby." She helped Abby to her feet and whispered, "His stock just dropped a few points, girl. That was so out of line."

Kylee's chagrin was the perfect bandage for Abby's sore tush. She inched back to the armchair and nestled her aching rear into the soft leather. Einstein instantly jumped back into the chair, settling protectively on her lap.

"You have a cat?" Kylee sat on the couch, leaving JD standing in the middle of the room.

"Einstein," Abby said.

"He's so cute!"

"He's a Silver Persian."

"Is that expensive?"

Abby had never considered it. "He's a purebred."

"I have two cats. I've had one forever. Shadow's totally black. The other is some kind of calico mix we got from a box at the mall. I'm a sucker. Named him Bitsy."

"I've had Einstein for two years. Dad got him for me—"

JD cleared his throat.

Abby glared at him, ignoring his pouty frown. "Are you ready to work?"

"Yes, ma'am." He walked to her chair and stood beside it. "You want to read me that pamphlet?"

She exchanged a quick eyebrow raise with Kylee. "Do you mind, Kylee?"

"Not at all." Kylee opened her calculus book and picked up a pencil.

Abby shook open the pamphlet, and read aloud.

"Systemic lupus can be mild or severe and sometimes fatal. For mild cases of lupus, when there is little disease activity and no major organ involved, treatment may be managed by a primary care doctor ..." She stopped reading aloud and continued in silence.

> ... such as a pediatrician for children and teens, a family practitioner, or an internal medicine physician for adults. However, when lupus is active and the person needs to be watched for complications, he or she should be under the care of a specialist, usually a rheumatologist.
>
> If lupus has caused damage to a particular organ, other specialists will be consulted: a dermatologist for skin disease, a cardiologist for heart disease, a nephrologist for kidney disease, a neurologist for nervous system involvement, and others as the symptoms require.

JD perched on the arm of Abby's chair. "Anything good in there?"

"Yeah. This will totally help with our project."

"You think they'll ever find a cure?"

"For lupus?" Abby shrugged. "If my dad has anything to say about it, there will be a cure for everything."

"Your dad interested in medicine?"

Abby huffed a laugh. "You could say that."

[CHAPTER SEVEN]

MARTYR FINGERED THE KEYCARD UNDER his pillow. He felt bad about stealing from Dr. Goyer. He would likely get many marks—maybe ten—if he were caught, but it didn't matter because tonight he would see sky.

A rattling rose from below his bunk. Brain, snoring. Martyr listened to the steady drone, and wondered if everyone was sleeping now. He leaned over the side and saw that his skinny bunkmate lay above his covers, eyes closed. Brain hated covers or close spaces or being confined. Marks were very hard on Brain.

Martyr scanned the other bunks; everyone appeared to be asleep. He withdrew the keycard from under his pillow and climbed down. As he crept to the exit, he placed a quick kiss on Baby's forehead, the way Dr. Woman had once done for him. He waited to the side of the narrow window in the door until the night guards, Erik and Wilson, passed, heading toward the cafeteria. Martyr counted to thirty, knowing it was thirty steps to the cafeteria from his room. He'd checked twice today.

Martyr swiped Dr. Goyer's keycard in the slot at the door, the way he'd seen Johnson and Rolo do so many times. The light turned green, like peas. Without a sound, Martyr twisted the handle and pulled the door open a crack. He peered down the hallway and caught sight of the guards rounding the corner. Martyr slipped out the door, closing it gently behind him, and padded on bare feet to the exit at the end of the hall. He didn't need to use the keycard at the door to the stairwell—it didn't have a lock since the Jasons moved between levels two and three daily. He darted inside the stairwell and ran up the stairs two at a time, stopping at the door to level one. He had never come this far without an escort. No Jason had.

The door to level one was locked. He swiped the keycard and pushed the door in, hoping no one would still be working at this hour. His heart pounded as he stepped across the cool, white tile. What would he do if he got caught? What would they do to him? Isolation? More EEZ?

They would use the stinger on his ankle, that much was certain.

Martyr shuddered, heart racing as he crept slowly down the white hallway. Everything seemed so bright. He counted three doors and paused in front of Dr. Goyer's lab, hoping to borrow his white lab coat. But as he glanced in the window on the door, he saw Dr. Goyer still sitting behind his desk.

Martyr shrank back against the wall, heat flashing over him. He crouched and scurried to the next door. A quick peek in the dark window confirmed Dr. Max had gone. Martyr slipped inside and rummaged through a closet until he discovered a white lab coat and a pair of eye goggles. He put both on, hoping to look like a doctor, or as much as was possible. Unfortunately, his bald head was a giveaway, he was too tall and thin to be mistaken as Dr. Goyer. And he didn't have shoes.

It was okay. He only needed to see the sky for a moment.

He stole back into the hallway and edged along the wall, listening for voices. The last door on his right—Dr. Elliott's door—creaked open. Martyr darted left through an open doorway. Chairs lined up along one wall. On the other wall, a vacant desk sat in front of an open door.

"Dr. Elliot? Are you coming?" Dr. Kane's voice called from beyond the doorway.

"Yes." Dr. Elliot's steps drew near the place where Martyr had entered.

Martyr dove onto the cool floor underneath the desk and pulled the chair in.

Dr. Elliott's brown leather shoes with the tassels passed by the desk and stopped in the open doorway. "How are you feeling?"

"As well as can be expected. Have you confirmed everything?"

"Martyr is still the best choice."

Martyr tensed at his name.

"J:3:3, Dr. Elliot. Calling them pet names will only make us all feel like jerks."

Dr. Elliot shifted from one foot to the other. "J:3:3 is by far the healthiest specimen in batch three, almost in all of Section Five. Iron Ma—er, J:3:2 is physically stronger than J:3:3, but only because he does weightlifting in the athletic program. Also, J:3:2's urine has high protein counts, so he's out."

Martyr's mind filtered this dialogue. Healthiest for what? Every Jason had the same purpose. Health didn't matter, did it?

"Which program is J:3:3 in?" Dr. Kane asked. "Is it art?"

"Knowledge. He's top of Section Five under Brain. Excuse me, under J:4:1."

Dr. Kane chuckled. "Well, I don't need anyone's brain, just a pair of kidneys."

Martyr sucked in a sharp breath, making a soft noise in his throat. He clamped his hand over his mouth.

"The surgery is still scheduled for the twenty-eighth. Falls right on the J:3s' expiration date. We'll take the other two first, that way we won't have to rush with Mart—with J:3:3. Of course you know there are no guarantees. Martyr is the best—"

"You mean J:3:3."

Dr. Elliot cleared his throat. "Yes. J:3:3 *is* the best candidate, but he's a clone. His kidneys likely carry the disease as well. Only time will tell."

"Time is all I'm looking for, Dr. Elliot. Time. Dr. Parlor is making excellent progress tweaking the hybrid chromosomes at Gunnolf. We've only lost three this year, so far. The others appear to be perfectly healthy."

"Should you need my assistance at Gunnolf, the offer is still open."

"I *have* a surgeon at Gunnolf. And she's not nearly as reckless with her experiments as you."

"It was a safe dosage."

Dr. Kane came out of the open doorway, wearing a long brown coat, a black hat, and black gloves. The light in his room went out. "Good night, Dr. Elliott."

Dr. Elliot followed Dr. Kane into the hall. "I wouldn't have done anything to jeopardize his health."

Martyr released his mouth and a silent breath. None of this made sense. Dr. Elliot thought Martyr might already carry a disease? How could he be used for a cure? And what did Dr. Kane want with Martyr's kidneys? He'd implied transplant. A cold tremor ran up Martyr's arms. They had talked about transplants in biology class, as a procedure doctors used to help sick patients, but the organs came from dead people who had volunteered their bodies for the cause in the event of a premature death.

Martyr relaxed slightly. The Jasons were special. They were created to die, to save the earth's population from the toxic air. It made sense that their organs would also be used after their blood was taken.

I must have misunderstood the conversation. Everything was on schedule for his expiration. That was all that mattered. He gripped the keycard to his chest. Once he saw the sky, he would feel much better about—

The elevator dinged. Martyr peeked out from under the desk to see the elevator doors slide open. Dr. Kane stepped inside. When the doors closed, Martyr crawled out from his hiding place and into Dr. Kane's cell. As far as he knew, no Jason had ever been inside.

He was afraid to turn on the lights, so he pulled off the goggles and waited for his eyes to adjust to the dark. The light streaming in from the doorway was just enough to see by.

Many things in Dr. Kane's cell looked strange. There was some kind of thick fabric on the floor and a lot of color. Even in the dim light shining through the doorway, Martyr could see the flowers in the corner, the pictures on Dr. Kane's desk, the balls in a dish— many of them red and orange.

What were all these other colors called?

Martyr picked up a small red ball and smelled it. He put his tongue to it and discovered it had a slight sugary taste. Cautiously, he placed it in his mouth and sucked on it. Sweetness melted across his tongue, and when he bit down, it crumbled and continued to melt. He set down the goggles, grabbed a handful of the colorful balls, and dumped them into his mouth.

He sat on the floor, took the glass dish in his lap, and continued to eat the little colors until they were gone.

His belly felt very full, but he got to his feet and continued to peruse the office. A large picture hung in the center of one wall. It was different from Dr. Goyer's picture of his daughter. This one had a large frame around it and the colors were textured. Martyr ran his finger along the rubbery surface then studied the faces.

Dr. Kane sat in the center of the picture on a fancy chair. A woman stood beside him, but although she was fascinating Martyr spent little time looking at her, because of the familiar young man to her left. He had thick brown hair, dark brown eyes, and his face was identical to Martyr's.

He was a Jason.

A sound outside the door made Martyr fall to the floor and curl into a ball. He listened carefully and forced his breath to stay even. *It was only the muffled whir of the elevator.* Martyr crawled to the doorway and peeked out. Dr. Elliot, dressed in a thick black coat, stood in front of the elevator. When it opened, he went inside and the doors closed.

As a precaution, Martyr stayed on the floor a bit longer before running to the elevator himself. He pushed the up arrow and it glowed. As the elevator whirred again, his heart pounded. His shirt felt damp under his arms, under the doctor's white coat. Would this elevator take him to the sky? He stood with his nose almost touching the crack where the doors would open.

When they did, he jumped back in surprise, then grinned at his nervous behavior. He stepped inside and felt the floor move slightly under him. The doors closed, but the elevator didn't move. He examined the buttons: G, L1, L2, and L3. He pressed G.

The elevator buzzed but still did not move.

Martyr swallowed. A new wave of heat swelled inside him. There was a slot above the buttons—maybe he needed the keycard here too. He pulled it out of his waistband and stuck it in the slot. The small light on the box lit up red.

Red was Martyr's favorite color, but red on the keycard box was not good. Whenever the keycard box lit up red, Rolo struck it with his stick.

He pushed the card in again. Red. He whacked the box with the end of his fist.

Nothing.

Martyr looked around. Another keycard box hung on the other side of the doors, where a card dangled from the box by a chain. Martyr stuck it in the slot, then slid his card in the first slot. The light turned green. He pushed G again.

The elevator started to move.

Martyr looked around the elevator and grinned as it rose, until he noticed a camera hung in the corner, watching him. He winced. He'd forgotten the goggles in Dr. Kane's office. *Maybe the guards who watch through the cameras leave to sleep each night.* He turned so his sleeve pointed away from the camera, then remembered he wore the lab coat and relaxed slightly. At least the camera could not see his number.

The elevator chimed. Martyr jumped. The doors whooshed open. He peeked out into a cold room; what if a guard, or Dr. Elliot, were nearby? To his relief, the room looked deserted. Another metal door stood in front of him with an empty desk beside it. Two keycard boxes hung on the wall, one on each side of the door. Martyr frowned. No extra keycard hung from either box.

He grabbed the keycard dangling from the chain in the elevator and pulled it off, then hurried across the cold floor to the door and stuck the card into one slot. When he inserted his card in the other slot, the light glowed green, and he pushed open the door. He reached back and snatched the elevator keycard in case he needed two cards to get back inside.

A shock of chilly air gripped him, causing him to gasp. Everything was freezing and dark. A dim light shone overhead but spots danced in front of his eyes. He stepped over the shockingly cold floor and shivered, taking in his surroundings. He stood inside a vast building. Large, yellow rectangles stacked up to the ceiling along the wall on his right. Martyr reached out to touch one. The rectangles were prickly like the bristles of a broom.

He stepped toward the dark opening where two bright red lights stared at him, humming loud and moving away. He ran after them then stopped as his feet left the cold floor and touched the freezing white ground.

Ice. Very, very cold icy ground.

Was he outside? Why was it dark? He looked up to see the sky, but everything was black. He sucked in a hesitant, icy breath, heartbeat thudding in his head. Did the cold and darkness have something to do with the toxicity?

His feet burned, so he ran back inside and found the floor warm compared to the icy whiteness. He turned back to face it, body quaking from cold and the thrill. *Snow.* Dr. Goyer had told him about the white substance that covered the ground in winter. A slow smile spread across Martyr's face.

The door he'd come out of opened slowly. Martyr dove behind

a stack of the yellow rectangles and sat down, rubbing his cold, stinging feet, hoping no one had noticed the keycard missing from the elevator.

"Even I need to use the can sometimes," a voice said, "although Dr. Kane probably wouldn't approve. But I don't ever get a break up here and it's a long night."

"I'll bet," Dr. Goyer's voice said.

"Again, sorry to keep you waiting, doc. You have a nice evening."

"You too, Stan. And be sure to tell Dr. Kane about the missing keycards. I likely misplaced mine, but the one gone from the elevator is strange. If Dr. Jeng hadn't still been here, I might have been stuck in the office till morning."

"Will do, doc."

Martyr heard the door click shut, the clacking of shoes across the floor, and then crunching as Dr. Goyer walked over the snow.

Martyr looked out from behind the stack of prickly bristles and watched Dr. Goyer approach a place where many cars sat. Martyr had never seen a car, only a drawing Dr. Max did a few years ago to explain how he came to the Farm each day.

Dr. Goyer climbed inside a big car with a long, flat back. Martyr breathed hard and fast, trying to decide what to do. A roar split the silence, and Dr. Goyer's car lit up and rolled backward. *This could be my only chance.*

Martyr sprinted over the icy snow in a crouch. The car stopped. Martyr peeked inside the flat back of the car; it was a pocket. The car lurched forward, so Martyr grabbed the cold metal and climbed inside, lying flat on the cold, hard, vibrating surface of the pocket. He curled into a ball to warm himself, but it did little to help. The snow had melted on his feet, leaving them wet and numb.

With each lurch Martyr slid forward, and his head struck the metal wall of the pocket. The repeated bouncing banged his limbs against the rigid surface. Just as he felt he could take no more, the car suddenly went very fast and smooth. Above him, black tree branches reached toward a lighter black background full of tiny lights like those on the keycard box, but very far away, and not green or red, just white. Martyr reached up a hand. Yes. They were very, very far away.

Why wasn't the sky blue? Could it be because of the toxic air? Martyr stopped breathing a moment, then sucked in a short, icy breath. The cold air entered his nostrils and burned slightly. Something was wrong. If the air was toxic, shouldn't he be having some difficulties breathing? If Martyr's blood carried the cure, perhaps he would be immune. But Dr. Elliot had implied Martyr might already carry a disease. If so, could he infect others?

He shivered and hoped Dr. Goyer would not be angry once the car stopped.

[CHAPTER EIGHT]

WHO KNEW JD KANE COULD COOK?

Abby promised herself this interesting fact would not alter her feelings toward him, but the fact that he volunteered to cut the onions—and diced them like a sous chef—carried more weight than she liked to admit. She loved cooked onions, but raw ones were lethal on her eyes.

JD diced on the cutting board. *Chop, chop, chop.* The conversation had been pleasantly surprising, centering on genetic disease before drifting to treatments and how everything could relate to their assignment. Now they were talking about research and cures. JD actually knew more than most about science. Against her will, her respect for Mr. Full-of-Himself had taken a major upturn.

Poor Kylee added little to the conversation, her furrowed eyebrows proof the subject matter was not one of her interests.

JD dumped the onions, peas, and carrots into a frying pan of heated olive oil. A hiss of steam rose up around his face. "Yeah. But clinical trials are essential to developing drugs. If the laws weren't so strict against human testing, we'd have cures by now."

Human testing? Abby should have known more cons were lurking below the surface. This was worth two strikes on JD's already con-heavy list. "Um, those are good laws, JD."

JD stirred the sautéing veggies. "Whatever."

An eerie déjà vu moment flashed over Abby. This was her mom and dad's late-night arguments all over again. What was that saying about girls choosing guys like their dads?

Not in a million years.

Abby took a deep breath. JD would not win this debate; she knew her stuff. "Pharmaceutical companies sometimes go too far. Most have no code of ethics when it comes to dollar signs. Do you know what happened with testing on prisoners?"

JD popped a slice of carrot into his mouth. "Doesn't matter. They were volunteers."

"It was abuse. Inmates earned ten times more as human guinea pigs than they ever earned from whatever prison jobs were available. Those who did agree may have been mentally ill or addicted to drugs, and some were probably too illiterate to read what they were agreeing to. Plus, they were offered the worst types of testing. Sensory deprivation, chemical treatments, psycho surgeries—"

"You don't know that's fact. Besides, it's their bodies." JD dumped in the rice and stirred. "If they wanted to donate their bodies for science, I say, good for them. It's a noble cause."

The food smelled fabulous, but Abby was too annoyed to savor the aroma. "It's *insane*. People were warped for life after some of that stuff. I agree that certain amounts of human testing are necessary, but only after the results on animals prove it's safe. The laws the FDA set up are to protect people."

"You think they should test on animals?" Kylee's voice took on a high-pitched squeakiness.

JD cracked an egg into a glass bowl. "That's what they're here for."

"You know what …" Abby should never have let JD into her house. She'd already marked him as trouble. What had she been thinking letting him worm his way inside for a second chance? Being an animal lover herself, she smiled at Kylee and tried to word things more sweetly. "Testing on animals saves human lives. Virtually every medical achievement of the twentieth century relied on the use of animals in some way."

Kylee smacked her gum. "That is *so* mean."

"Uh," JD said in a nasty tone, "cancer is mean."

Kylee asked, "Why can't they find cures without testing on animals?"

"They can," JD said. "If the FDA would ease up. They've got such strict rules on testing these days. It needs to change, or we'll never cure anything."

Abby fumed. "You think it's right to harm one person to cure another? If a healthy person gets sick trying to help, then you're only making more people sick."

JD rolled his eyes. "Yeah, yeah. Which is why embryonic stem cell research is so perfect. But there are lots of people against that too. Mostly religious types."

Abby set her jaw. An inner heat cascaded over her. "Embryonic stem cell research is testing on humans, JD. It's the same thing. That's why people are against it. Human beings are not guinea pigs."

"Um … it's cells in a petri dish, Abby. Last time I checked, embryos don't need to eat, sleep, or use the john."

"An embryo is alive from the moment the sperm fertilizes the ovum. It's called conception."

His mouth twitched. "So you say, religious type."

"Are you trying to insult me by calling me religious?"

He lifted his hands, then had the audacity to wink.

Abby jerked the spatula from his hand and pushed him away from her fried rice. "You think this is funny? I suppose you think we should destroy life to prolong life? That concern for the people on earth inflicted with diseases demands we sacrifice the lives of those waiting to be born?"

"Abby," Kylee said. "These are really cool stools. I like the cushions."

JD mumbled, "Girls."

Abby raised her voice. "*Excuse* me?"

"You think you're so smart. You're just emotional. Oh, poor little micey wicey. Poor little cells."

Abby's jaw lowered in slow motion, like a drawbridge.

JD smirked and motioned to the frying pan. "You need to add the egg now, or are you afraid it's alive too?"

Abby dumped the egg into the pan and vented her frustration by stirring the mixture. What a surprise to discover that JD was more than a self-centered wonder jock—he was also a chauvinist and a liberal extremist.

What a waste of a stunning male specimen.

Kylee's small voice rose over the stirring and sizzling. "So, Abby. Would you mind going over this logarithm with me? I'm having a really hard time understanding the whole base of a positive number thing."

Thank goodness for Kylee. Eternally grateful for the change of subject, Abby switched off the burner and opened the cupboard. "You bet. Get your book while I dish this up."

"You need to put the soy sauce in it first," JD said.

Abby thrust the spatula against his chest and went to the cabinet to get plates. As much as she enjoyed this lupus assignment, she couldn't wait until it was over and she would have no more reason to mix company with JD Kane.

Dinner long gone, Abby and Kylee sat on the loveseat in the living room, working through an equation. JD slouched in Abby's armchair, reading the genetic diseases book.

The front door whooshed open. "Abby, honey? What's going

on here? I can't pull into the driveway." Dad slowed to a stop, his eyes fixed on JD.

Chilled air drifted over to Abby. Dad had left the door open. She watched as he dropped his briefcase on the floor, Adam's apple bobbing as he swallowed, eyes boring into JD like lasers.

Uh oh.

Last March, Abby had gone on a group date to the movies. Afterward, everyone came back to Abby's house to hang out. This had sparked the first and only fight between her parents on the subject of Abby and the opposite sex. She'd been careful not to let it come up again—her parents had enough problems without her adding to them.

Now Dad wore the same expression he had the night he found them all sitting in the backyard talking. His wild eyes flickered from face to face, his lips were drawn into a tight line, and his forehead was as wrinkled as a pug's.

JD seemed to speak the silent language of territorial father. He jumped up and started across the room. "I should get home. I'll see you tomorrow, Abby."

"Yeah, bye."

Abby's eyes never left her dad's smoldering ones. He looked like he might blow a gasket. She hoped he waited until everyone was gone.

He didn't.

He shadowed JD to the door. It was a humorous sight; JD's muscular body towered a foot above her dad's plump one, but the odds didn't deter her father. "What's your name, son?"

"JD Kane."

"Ah. Hmm." Dad's "Hmm" morphed into a moan, an odd sound somewhere between looking to answer a question and pain.

Abby jumped up and ran halfway to the door. "Dad? You okay?"

"I don't allow boys in this house when I'm not home." Dad's voice came in a hoarse whisper. "Is that clear?"

JD gripped the knob and yanked the door open. "Yes, sir. Sorry."

"Dad," Abby said in her most soothing, round tone. "We were *just* studying."

Dad waved a hand at Kylee. "You should go home too."

Abby's jaw dropped. "Dad!"

Eyes wide enough to show all the white, Kylee shut her calculus book, grabbed her purse, and stood.

"Kylee," Abby said. "Thanks for coming over. Really. My hero."

Kylee winked. "No problemo, girl. See you tomorrow."

Abby chewed her thumbnail as she walked Kylee out. When both vehicles had left the driveway, Abby shut the front door and rounded on her dad. "I can't believe you kicked out my friends!"

Dad hung up his coat and scarf. "I can't believe you invited friends over without asking, especially JD Ka—a boy."

"Asking? Who would I ask, Dad? It's not like you're ever home!"

Dad picked up his briefcase and started toward the kitchen. "You could have texted. I would have texted you back."

Abby trailed behind him. "To say 'no'? News flash, I have a life too, Dad. It's not all about you. Maybe I *need* friends. Maybe I need to study with them outside of school. If you're never home to *chaperone*, what should I do? Hire someone? A nanny, Dad, for a seventeen-year-old girl? Maybe I should homeschool myself. Then I could give myself assignments I already know. Easy As."

"Don't be ridiculous." He set his briefcase on the counter and inspected the pan of half-eaten stirfry on the stove.

"You're right. I'll just sit in my room each night like a good daughter and come when you call me to dinner— Wait, I'm the one who makes dinner. In fact, I'm the one who does all the house-work. Maybe you should go to your room!"

Dad spun around. "That's enough."

"Whatever!"

Abby stomped upstairs to her room and slammed the door. She flopped onto her bed, and when she saw JD Kane crouched in the corner, she screamed.

[CHAPTER NINE]

"**WHAT ARE YOU DOING,** you idiot?" the daughter whispered. She jumped off the bed and propped her hands on her hips. "You can't be in my room. My dad will call the cops. Do you have a death wish?"

Martyr fell to the soft floor and curled into a ball. His heart thudded in his chest. Certainly he had done something very bad and would be punished. Did daughters give marks?

"What are you …? Get up." The daughter nudged him in the back.

He would not get up so she could strike him. Martyr knew that trick—it was one of Rolo's favorites. Besides, he liked this floor with the soft, warm fibers that cushioned his body. It was safer to stay in a ball and see what she decided to do next.

A moment of silence passed, and he slowly peeked out between his elbows to see her puzzled expression. Her hair practically glowed; the reddish orange color was so vibrant. He had never seen anything so beautiful.

"What are you wearing?" she asked. "And what did you do to your hair? *JD!* Your hair is your best feature."

Something sang on the daughter, a noisy, metallic rhythm. Martyr scrambled to a sitting position and backed against the wall, afraid of the strange sound. Was it some kind of alarm?

The daughter stood up and removed a small, red device from her pocket. She held it to her ear. "Hello?"

Martyr frowned as he watched her, puzzled by the strange device and her reaction to it.

"Don't be stupid. Who is this?" Her thin eyebrows sank low over her pea-green eyes. "It is *not* ... Because I'm looking at you right now ... You *shaved* your head. Is it a wig?" She leaned closer, peering at Martyr's head. "How are you doing this?"

The daughter reached a hand towards Martyr, but a loud honk outside caused her to jerk her hand back. She went to the wall, peeked through the strips of metal that hung there, and looked out a window. "What in the world?"

She tossed the device onto the bed. "Stay here." She pointed a finger at Martyr, who pressed back into the corner again. The daughter opened the door and went out, slamming the door behind her.

Maybe I should leave. This might be his only chance to get away. But it was so warm and colorful inside the daughter's cell. He was thankful Dr. Goyer had left the door open when he had yelled at his daughter. Martyr rubbed his cold feet, which had finally started to thaw. It was so much warmer inside the facility than out in the icy darkness.

Martyr did not want to go back to Jason Farms. He did not want to expire. He did not want Dr. Kane to take his kidneys. It was selfish to run away—and he hadn't intended to. If he never went back to the Farm, how many people who lived outside would not get an antidote? Would he still expire when he became eighteen? What would happen to Baby?

Martyr crawled to the bed and tapped the red device with one finger. It was hard and smooth and did not make noise for him. He looked around the daughter's cell. He couldn't name the color, but almost everything was the same shade, similar to gray but more pleasant. A huge picture hung on the door of a man with frizzy white hair and a thick mustache. Martyr stepped closer to read the words.

$E=MC^2$

The door burst open, and the daughter closed it quickly behind her. Martyr scurried back to the corner and crouched low. The daughter leaned against the picture of the man for a long moment before turning to look at Martyr. She stepped toward him and squatted down to his level. She was holding something in her arms. A white and hairy animal. A dog?

"Who *are* you?" Her intense eyes trained on his.

Martyr suddenly grew very hot, saliva filling his mouth. The dog squirmed. Its round eyes met his and he noticed they were the same color as the daughter's: green. Martyr swallowed and said in a near whisper, "I am Martyr. J:3:3."

Her sculpted eyebrows sank over her eyes. Martyr focused on the sprinkle of tiny dots on the top of her cheeks and nose, dots the same color as her hair.

"What kind of name is that?" she asked.

Her question knotted his thoughts. His identification was not acceptable? "It's what I'm called."

"Where do you live?"

"The Farm."

"What farm?"

"Jason Farms."

The daughter sucked in a sharp breath. "No. That's not possible. How did you get in this house?"

"I rode in the pocket of Dr. Goyer's car."

"Doctor? In the back of the Silverado?"

What was a Silverado? "I-I do not know."

"Just how do you know my dad?"

"Dr. Goyer works at the Farm. I met him the day he wore his orange necktie. I touched it."

The daughter wrinkled her lips. Martyr must have said something incorrect. Perhaps neckties were forbidden in this facility too.

She took a deep breath and exhaled. "How did you get to the Farm?"

Martyr cocked his head to the side. He did not understand the question.

She asked another. "When did you first go there?"

"I have always lived on the Farm."

"No!" The daughter jumped up and strode across the room. The dog leapt from her arms, arched its back in the air, then hopped onto the bed. When the daughter reached the door, she turned and strode back to face him.

Martyr shrank back into the corner. He had somehow upset her again. He did not want her to be upset. "I'm sorry."

"Why are *you* sorry?"

"I angered you. I shouldn't have ridden in the pocket of Dr. Goyer's car and come into his facility, but the snow was freezing my feet. The door was open, and I wanted to get warm."

Tears flooded the daughter's eyes. She walked back to the door, leaned against it, and slid down against the picture of the frizzy-haired man until she sat on the floor, staring at Martyr, her eyes out of focus like Hummer's.

"JD forgot his books and he had some homework due tomorrow, so he called …"

Martyr could not look away from the daughter's face. It made his heart race. Round cheeks, creamy skin peppered with dots, glossy lips, and her hair—bright and wild, it swung soft and long and curly around her face when she moved. He wanted very badly to touch it.

Something pounded softly outside the door. The daughter scrambled to her knees and poked a button on the doorknob. She stood and whispered, "Get over here. It's my dad." She lunged forward, grabbed his hand, and pulled. "Come on."

Her touch inflicted a pleasant nausea. He was much taller than she was. The top of her head reached his chin. How was it she had such power over his senses?

"Abby, honey? Can I come in?" Dr. Goyer's voice came from the other side of the door.

The daughter herded Martyr into a tiny closet filled with clothing. He stood in awe of so many colors and textures. She pushed the door shut, closing him in darkness, but the door swung slowly back open, letting in a stripe of light. Martyr could see the daughter scramble to her bed and find the noisy red device. She opened it and began to push on it with her thumbs.

Something pounded on the door again, the doorknob rattled, and Dr. Goyer said, "Honey, open the door. We need to talk."

The daughter opened her mouth like she was about to respond, but instead started pushing buttons on her red device again.

Dr. Goyer's voice carried from outside the room. "Because I said so."

She pushed more buttons.

"That wasn't a fortune cookie answer! Listen, I know I'm gone a lot, but that doesn't mean you can do whatever you like."

The daughter rolled her eyes, and began hitting buttons again.

"True," Dr. Goyer said, even though the daughter hadn't spoken, "but you're not old enough to have a boyfriend over without supervision either."

The daughter gasped. "He's *not* my boyfriend!" she yelled. "We're doing a project together. And he invited himself over!"

Dr. Goyer's voice softened. "What's the project?"

She heaved a sigh and began pushing buttons on the device again.

"I *do* care," Dr. Goyer said. "Tell me more about it."

The daughter ignored him and kept on hitting buttons. Martyr was amazed. Clearly she was communicating to Dr. Goyer through that thing in her hands. He wanted to see how it worked.

"Sounds interesting," Dr. Goyer said slowly, "but why lupus?

And is there any way for you to get a different partner? Perhaps a female? I would feel better about it."

The daughter looked like she had just received an injection of EEZ. "I chose lupus, Dad!" She threw the device on the bed and flopped down. "If you care that much about keeping me away from boys, maybe you should go down to the school and talk to the principal." She snorted. "But guess what, Dad? The principal is JD's mom. So that should go over really well."

It was quiet for a moment, and Martyr wondered if Dr. Goyer had left. But then he heard Dr. Goyer clear his throat and say, "Abby, honey, I'm sure JD is not a bad kid. I just—his being in the house surprised me."

The daughter sighed and grabbed the device off the bed, causing the dog to dart out of the way and settle near the wall. She communicated one more time, and Dr. Goyer said, "Okay, honey. Come downstairs when you're ready."

The daughter sank onto the edge of her bed and dropped the device beside her. She sat quiet and still, pet her dog, then turned her head slowly toward where Martyr stood in the closet. The angry expression on her face sent Martyr stepping back until colorful fabrics fell over his head. He crouched onto the floor to escape them, and when he looked back out the door, the daughter stood right above him.

She held out her hand. He leaned forward to look, but there was nothing in it. Her fingernails were long and glossy red except for one jagged thumbnail. He reached a finger out to touch one and found it smooth. Her lips twisted a bit. She took his hand in her small, warm one, and drew him back into her cell.

Again her touch wiped away all reasonable thought. Martyr's hand began to shake. He dragged in a long, deep breath and stumbled after her.

"Sit there." She pointed to the edge of her bed, climbed onto the other end, took the pillow in her lap, and sat against the white wooden bars by the wall.

The dog got up and moved to her side—settling into a ball of white fluff beside her. It closed its eyes and a gentle noise came from it, like the hum of a furnace.

For a while the daughter did nothing but watch Martyr, so he stared back. A strange tension bound them somehow, like an invisible string from her eyes to his. Like when she had touched him, her attention mesmerized him, spinning his stomach like a ceiling fan.

"My name is Abby."

"Abby." He felt taller just knowing her name.

"How old are you?" she asked, so calm and confident, like she spoke to Jasons every day.

She probably did.

"I am seventeen years, eleven months, and twelve days old."

One of her eyebrows arched up, wrinkling part of her forehead. He grinned and tried to mimic her expression.

"That's pretty accurate." She scowled. "Stop that."

He relaxed his face immediately and waited for her next words.

"You lived all those years on the Farm? Even as a baby?"

"Yes."

"Why do you look like JD Kane?"

Dr. Kane? The question was so ridiculous, Martyr laughed. "Dr. Kane is in charge of the Farm. I don't look like him."

They sat silently again, looking into each other's eyes. Martyr did not mind. He could look at Daughter Abby all day long.

She broke the silence. "What about your parents?"

"What are parents?"

She breathed out a laugh. "Are you for real?"

Martyr did not know what this question meant either.

"You know, a mom and a dad? Did they die? Are you an orphan?"

Ah. Mom and dad were slang for mother and father. Children who lived outside had these special adults to care for them. "Only children who live outside have mothers and fathers."

"Everyone has a mother and a father—at some point, anyway."

"We don't."

"We? How many, um … are there?"

"There are fifty-five of us."

She sucked in a short breath. "Are you all boys?"

"Yes. There are no woman at the Farm."

"Women."

"*Women.*" Of course. Like *man* and *men.* Singular and plural. How obvious. Martyr's face warmed at the simplicity of his mistake. She must think him ignorant.

But Daughter Abby only looked pale. Her next question came so softly, Martyr almost couldn't hear it. "Then how were you born?"

He did not understand. "Born?"

"Produced. Made. Created." Her voice rose with each word.

Martyr hoped she was not frightened. Did she think he would hurt her? He hoped his answers would bring her comfort. "We were created at the Gunnolf Lab and brought to Jason Farms as infants."

She scowled again.

Martyr couldn't help but copy her expression. This scowling look was by far his favorite Daughter Abby face, and mimicking her only made her scowl more.

"Why are you called Martyr?"

"Because I protect Baby and the other Brokens. My official identification is J:3:3." He pushed up the right sleeve of the lab coat and turned his wrist over to show her the numbers inked into his skin.

Her eyes swelled. "What does that mean?"

"Product Jason: batch three: number three."

Her eyebrows scrunched together like she was thinking very hard. "But you're ... normal. How could they have kept you hidden all this time? Why?"

"We're created to save the world. That's our purpose. The world is toxic and we are the cure." According to Dr. Kane, the program at the Farm was famous, and the Jasons were worldwide heroes for their sacrifice. Why did Daughter Abby not know this already? "You haven't heard of our sacrifice?"

"No, JD—Martyr. Is that what you want me to call you?"

"Martyr is my name, but you may call me whatever you like."

She smirked and Martyr fought the urge to try this expression on his face as well. "Then I'll call you Marty. It's more of a normal name. Why do you think the world is toxic, Marty?"

Her words chilled him. "Your question implies the world is *not* toxic."

"It's not. A little polluted, maybe, but no one needs to be cured from simply breathing the air."

"But ..." Martyr's chest burned, like the EEZ side effects had come upon him again. "If the world is not toxic ..." He squeezed his knees. Dr. Kane's words flashed over him like a bucket of water on grooming day. His deep, smooth chuckle followed by, *Well, I don't need anyone's brain, just a pair of kidneys.*

"Aaaaah ..." Martyr clutched his temples and doubled forward, propping his elbows on his knees. There had to be a logical explanation.

He felt a pressure on his back—a hand—then Daughter Abby's worried voice. "Are you okay?"

Martyr closed his eyes. "When I came outside to see the sky and didn't die from breathing the air, I knew something was wrong." Still hunched over, he turned his head toward Daughter Abby. "They lied to us. But if our purpose is not to save the world, why do we expire? For kidneys?"

Her forehead wrinkled. "I don't understand. Expire? Who expires?"

"Me. In sixteen days. On April twenty-eight."

"You said you were seventeen years and eleven ..." She scoffed. "People don't just die on their eighteenth birthday."

Martyr's throat was dry. He licked his lips and glanced at the soft fibers on the floor. "We do."

Daughter Abby slid off the bed and stood in front of him. Her feet were bare and he saw her toenails were also red. The oddness of it flushed the confusion from his mind. He smirked and looked up to find her hands on her hips. The confident, in-control Daughter Abby had returned.

"Are you hungry?"

"We never eat at night. Only during meal times."

"That's not what I asked, Marty. Are. You. Hungry?"

"Yes." Martyr was always hungry.

"I'll get you something." She walked to the door. "Lock this behind me—push the button." She touched a tiny circle on the doorknob. "I'll knock three times, like this." She softly tapped her knuckles against the door, taking a long pause between each knock. "I don't want my dad to know you're here … yet."

She slipped past the door and closed it behind her.

Martyr jumped up and pressed the little button with a click. He hoped she would not be gone long.

[CHAPTER TEN]

ABBY TOOK HER TIME GOING DOWNSTAIRS, a hand pressed over her pounding heart. There had to be another explanation for the gorgeous guy in her room. No one could have successfully cloned humans almost eighteen years ago and kept it secret. Someone would have talked by now ... right? In her experience, scientists tended to have pretty big egos when it came to breakthrough discoveries. How was it no one knew?

And why did Marty look like JD's identical twin? Marty said Dr. Kane was in charge at Jason Farms. Since Helen Kane was the high school principal, Dr. Kane must be JD's dad, which explained a lot about JD's extremist views and his claim of having an eccentric scientific father. It did not explain why a man would clone his own son. How weird was that?

And intelligent! From what little interaction they'd had, Marty was healthy and perfectly cognizant. A little odd from living in an underground lab all his life, but other than that … it was beyond amazing. At some point, she would have to ask her dad why they educated them.

Abby reached the bottom of the stairs, thankful her dad had gone to bed, and crept across the wooden floor into the kitchen. She took a large plate from the cupboard and set it on the counter. What would a guy want to eat at quarter to ten at night? She pulled the peanut butter out from the pantry then put it back. *What if he's allergic to something?*

She rummaged through the fridge and pantry looking for a decent hypoallergenic selection. Settling on a turkey sandwich, she added cheese, lettuce, and tomatoes, but spread the mayo and mustard thin, in case he didn't like it. She grabbed the plate, a package of Oreos, and a bag of Doritos, and headed for the stairs. She paused and went back, set everything on the counter, shoved a bottle of blue Gatorade under her arm, and picked up everything again. She'd gathered all the food she could hold, but how in the world was she going to knock?

She managed to kick the door three times with the side of her foot. Marty opened it, staring at her with those deep brown eyes. Gah, he was even cute bald, although technically, his head was covered in fine stubble. She edged past him, and he shadowed her as she set the food on her bed. She whispered, "Shut the door!" and he jumped to it.

Obedient. A mark in the pro column. Add another pro for: *looks like JD but doesn't behave like JD.*

She nodded at the food. "Go ahead."

He sank onto his knees beside the bed and stared at the food like it had just spoken or something.

"What's wrong?"

He drew a slice of tomato out of the sandwich. "What is this?"

He didn't know what a tomato was? O-kay. "It's a tomato."

"Tomato. I've never had one before. They don't let us eat tomatoes."

"Why not?"

"Color causes fights. We all want to have it, but there's never enough for everyone."

What was this, some sort of sterile *Lord of the Flies*?

Marty brought the tomato slice to his tongue and tasted it. His eyebrows rose and he tucked the tomato back inside the sandwich. Well, he was certainly a tidy clone.

She winced at the word *clone*, still not quite convinced he was for real. Maybe Dr. and Mrs. Kane had twins and gave one up for research? She shuddered. No matter how hard she tried to find a logical explanation, nothing seemed to make sense.

Especially since Marty had said there were more than fifty like him.

Marty ate slowly, savoring every morsel like a death-row inmate eating his last meal. Abby opened the Gatorade and set it beside his plate on the floor. He eyed the liquid as he chewed his sandwich and didn't speak until he swallowed.

"Is it water?"

"It's like juice. It's sweet."

"What color is this?"

"Blue."

His lips stretched into a slow smile. "Blue like the sky."

He set his sandwich down and scooted the plate closer to him, like he was afraid she might take it away before he finished. Then he lifted the Gatorade to his lips and drank.

His eyes went wide again. What on earth did they feed them at the Farm? Then she remembered seeing the cans of cauliflower and the instant mashed potatoes. Bland colored—and tasting—food.

Martyr set the Gatorade down. "When I came outside, the sky was black. Why was it not blue with white clouds and a massive star?"

"Um, because it's nighttime. And also because it's Alaska. Trust me, I'm still getting used to the hours-of-daylight issue here." But he probably didn't know what that meant either. She reached for her bedside table, opened the small drawer, and pulled out a stack of postcards. Uncle Pete didn't own a cell phone and hated email, but always kept in touch with Abby with short-and-sweet post-cards. She had dozens from Philly, and dozens more from various places around the globe.

She shuffled the stack until she found a card with a picture of Myrtle Beach. "This is what you were hoping to see, I bet." She passed him the postcard. "Depending on the weather, the sky here could be blue in the morning. Well, by eight a.m. or so anyway."

His JD Kane eyes danced over the picture. It was so weird to be with him and not feel like she had to have a can of pepper spray ready.

"It's beautiful," Marty said. "So much is beautiful in the out-side." He looked at her then, his expression so intense she had to look away. Too much of JD in that look.

"Yeah … nature rocks." She passed him a postcard of the Phila-delphia skyline during the day. "But check this out."

His eyes shifted as he studied the postcard. "What's this place?"

"It's a city. Alaska has a few cities, but they're far from here and are nothing like that one. Not too many skyscrapers in Alaska." She paused, then answered before he asked. "A skyscraper is a really, really tall building."

His eyes flickered back and forth between the postcards. She grabbed the Oreos and slid the tray out of the wrapper. "Have you ever had cookies?"

"No." He set the postcards on the floor in front of his plate and took another sip of Gatorade.

She grabbed an Oreo and popped it whole into her mouth, then remembered how black they made her teeth. She was such an idiot. She dumped a few cookies on Marty's plate then pushed the bag across the room where she couldn't reach it.

Marty picked up a cookie and bit into it. His face scrunched up, like eating new foods was a serious job requiring deep thought and concentration and he might have to give a detailed report on it. Suddenly he grinned, his teeth caked in chocolate. "I like cookies."

Abby laughed. She watched him eat until all the food was gone.

He leaned back against her bed and pulled his knees up, wrapping his arms around them. It was eerie how much he looked like JD, with the exception of the lack of hair. His demeanor was completely different, though. Hesitant. Nervous. His eyes were always observing, collecting information. And the sound of his own voice didn't seem to thrill him like it did JD.

She took in his clothes for the first time. He wore gray sweatpants and a white lab coat over a white T-shirt. His feet were bare and pink.

Abby brushed the back of her knuckles over the top of one foot. "Your feet are freezing!"

He jolted at her touch and scrambled to the side.

"I'm sorry." She crawled over to her dresser and opened her sock drawer. She had a pair of men's socks in there somewhere. Dad had loaned them to her once when he took her skiing at Liberty Mountain Resort.

That had been a joke. She hoped Alaska's jagged peaks would not inspire Dad to try again.

She spotted the cream-colored socks with the wide red band and pulled them out. "Here." She tossed them to Marty, who eyed them curiously. Was he kidding? "Don't tell me you don't know what socks are?"

"I've never …"

She scooted up to him and took the socks back. She scrunched her fingers up inside one and held it out. "Give me your foot."

He extended one leg. "The doctors wear socks, inside their shoes. We're not allowed shoes."

Wild, dark hairs stood out on his pale ankle. Apparently he could grow hair just fine. Abby stretched the sock over his toes and past his heel, leaving the long sock bunched around his ankle. "Does someone shave your head?"

He nodded, but kept his eyes glued to his foot. "J:3s have grooming every Thursday morning. They shave our heads and faces and clip our fingernails and toenails. That's when we also get bandages if we're hurt."

Abby readied the second sock, and he offered his foot without her having to ask. "Once a week? For Band-Aids?"

"They don't always discover our injuries right away, and we don't like to say."

"Why not?" You'd think the scientists wouldn't want the clones bleeding to death.

"Because we get marks for fighting."

Marks? As Abby pulled the other sock on, she noticed a silver ring poking out from the cuff on his pant leg. She pushed up his pant leg and drew the ring out. "What's this?"

"A stinger."

Abby's felt her breath snag. She leaned closer to study the crude device. "How does it work?"

"The people watching through the cameras make it sting."

A remote-controlled taser? "When?"

"When we get out of control."

"Does that happen often?"

He shook his head. "No one likes to be stung."

Abby swallowed back a sarcastic remark and patted his shin. "All done."

"Thank you." He pulled his knees back up to his chest and wiggled his toes. "They are soft and warm ... and red." He stroked the red band on his right leg.

Her mind raced with questions. "What's a mark?"

"A consequence for misbehavior. One mark is one hour with a doctor in their lab room."

"What happens in the lab?"

"Different things. It depends on the doctor. Some—like your father—are kind and just want to talk. But most test how our bodies react to different vials."

Abby trembled at his words. "They do pharmaceutical testing on you?"

"That's right." Marty had apparently heard the word *pharmaceutical* from the doctors before.

It ticked Abby off to hear her dad was involved in this Farm business. That he knew human clones existed and was party to using them as guinea pigs … She exhaled through her nose to calm herself and chewed her thumbnail. She should be thankful Dad was one of the kind, talking doctors at least. "You had a mark with my dad? What did he ask you?"

"Much of what you are asking."

"I still don't understand why they told you the world is toxic. Maybe to keep you from trying to escape. Why *did* you escape?"

"I wanted to see the sky before I expired."

Abby's heart broke at the desperation in his voice. Right. He'd said something about that. His one dream in the world was to see the sky and the outlaw scientists wouldn't let him? Insanity.

"Do you think they also lied about expiring?" Marty's gaze was filled with so many things: hope, desperation, confusion, fear. "That maybe I won't expire on April twenty-eight?"

She grimaced. Expiring. Beyond disturbing. But why would they kill their own clones? "I don't know, Marty. We should ask my dad."

Marty hung his head. "Will he make me go back?"

She threw up her hands. "I don't know. I won't tell him yet. I need to think about this a little more." If Marty weren't a carbon copy of JD, her skepticism would be greater. But she knew JD's gene pool. The guy couldn't act. Marty's behavior, the things he said, the way he said them … no one could pretend that. Not even for a very sick and twisted joke.

Marty was real.

Abby went into her closet and pulled out her purple sleeping bag with the fuchsia lining. She had used it for her trip to Philly, then for the first night in the house until she could unpack her bedding. She rolled it out along the wall across from her bed and checked to make sure the door was locked. "Sorry. This is all I have, but it's warm."

Marty didn't seem to know or care that purple and fuchsia were girly colors that no guy his age would be caught dead sleeping in. She gave him one of the pillows off her bed, explained how to wiggle inside the sleeping bag, then zipped him up. Once he was settled she rolled up the bag of Doritos and set them on the floor next to the Oreos.

She needed to go brush her teeth, but she didn't dare leave his side. Not yet.

"What are the names of these colors?" Marty asked, looking at the sleeping bag.

"Purple and pink—hot pink."

"The floor is also purple and pink hot pink?"

She snickered. "No. The outside of the sleeping bag is purple, like my comforter. The floor and walls are lavender, which is a lighter shade of purple. Purple is my favorite color."

"Red is my favorite color."

She smiled at their pre-school-level conversation. "The inside of the sleeping bag is hot pink, which is a very bright shade of pink."

"Sleeping bag."

Abby crawled under her comforter and watched Marty. He stared at the ceiling for a moment before turning to face her. His eyes were unnerving. They were as dark and insatiable as JD's, yet Marty's presence didn't threaten. He was everything good about JD—and unique. Sweet and innocent and nice to talk to. A clone.

A thought popped into her head that both amused and shamed her.

Can I keep him?

She clicked off the light next to her bed. "Good-night, Marty."

"Yes, it is, Daughter Abby. A very good night. Thank you."

[CHAPTER ELEVEN]

WHEN MARTYR WOKE THE NEXT MORNING, Daughter Abby was gone and the door to her cell hung open. He sat up, and the sleeping bag sat up with him. He wiggled free from the stifling fabric and stood, wondering what to do. The sky was still dark, and Daughter Abby had not told him what to do when he woke up. The only thing he knew was he did not want to go back to the Farm. *Will Baby worry when I don't show up for breakfast?*

Martyr inched out the door. The facility was dark, but light glowed from the lower level. He stopped at the wooden railing and peeked over the ledge. Noises clunked and water sloshed somewhere below, but he saw no one. He wanted to call out to Daughter

Abby and see if she was the one making the noise. He simply wasn't ready to meet Dr. Goyer yet.

A sudden odor met his nose. Someone was cooking food on level one.

Then he saw her. Daughter Abby passed under the ledge into the room with long, soft chairs and the high ceiling. She touched a long, flat monitor with her finger and walked back under the ledge, out of view. The monitor suddenly glowed bright and a voice spoke from it. Martyr crouched to the floor and peered between the bars.

"… mushers may push on this afternoon, preferring to take their twenty-four in Cripple. Live from Ophir, I'm Lisa Haberton."

"Thank you, Lisa," a man said. "And speaking of Cripple, nobody was more surprised than Kenai musher Roxi McAlpine to have won the Dorothy Page Halfway Award, which comes with three thousand dollars in gold nuggets. McAlpine, who was first into Cripple this morning, was excited about the accomplishment."

"I had no idea I was even in the lead," a high-pitched voice said. "That snowstorm threw me off a bit. I thought I'd overshot the trail. I was thinking about backtracking when I caught sight of it. Sure feels good to know I'm still in this thing. I'm real proud of my team."

Martyr crept along the bars until he reached the stairs. The floor was covered in the same thick fibers as Daughter Abby's floor, but instead of the purple shade, this was the color of pancakes. He liked the feel of it under his feet.

He sat on the top step and scooted over the ledge to the next one, holding on to the bars while keeping his eyes focused toward the talking monitor. It appeared to be speaking of huge dogs pulling people over the snow on pieces of wood. Martyr had only seen a few pictures of dogs years ago, and now the white, fluffy one Daughter Abby kept in her room. He hadn't known dogs could be so big. He also hadn't known people who lived outside used dogs for transportation. Martyr supposed it would keep them from having to walk on the cold snow, but wouldn't a car be faster?

Martyr slid down the stairs one at a time until he reached the bottom. Then, keeping his back to the wall, he edged slowly toward the kitchen. Daughter Abby darted around behind a tall counter covered in shiny, white tile. A billowing cloud of steam rose above her head. It smelled delicious. She had fastened her wild hair on top of her head and it poked up in a strange bubble. It was her dark red sweater, however, that made Martyr's heart race.

He stopped at the end of the wall and hovered, trying to decide what to do. He swallowed and took three long steps to stand in front of the counter. It was taller than the ones in the labs and came up to his stomach.

He faced Daughter Abby's back. She cracked an egg in a pan over a blue flame and tossed the shell into a trash can. Then she stirred something Martyr couldn't see that was cooking in another pan. He sniffed in a long breath and immediately wanted to eat what she had created.

She turned slowly and jumped when she saw him. "Oh! You scared me!" She clapped her hand against her chest. Then she motioned him to a tall, round chair beside the counter. "Sit down. Are you hungry?"

"Yes, please."

She grinned. "You're so polite. You'd put all the boys at school to shame." She turned back to the pan, filled a plate, and set it before him. Everything looked different. Instead of yellow eggs in a pile, these were smooth and white except for a round circle of yellow in the center. Some kind of brown meat shaped like large pills were also on the plate. The toast was rectangular instead of square, and Daughter Abby had cut it diagonally to form two triangles. There were also wedges of bright, wet fruit.

She set another plate next to his before coming around the counter to sit beside him. His heart pounded as he smelled her fragrance over the food. He couldn't describe her smell. He blinked, trying to focus, but found it was impossible next to her.

"I usually pray before I eat. Would you like to pray with me?"

He craned his neck to look into her green eyes. They were so many more colors of green than plain peas. Dr. Goyer's picture had not been a good representation.

She stared at him, waiting.

His cheeks warmed. She'd asked him something that he didn't understand again. "Yes," he said, hoping his answer would be the right one, that she wouldn't think him ignorant.

She bowed her head and closed her eyes. "Dear God, I thank you for this beautiful morning and this meal you've provided. Thank you for bringing Marty here and for creating him and letting me meet him. Show me how to help him, no matter what that might mean. Please keep him safe. In Jesus's name, amen."

Martyr cocked his head to the side, more confused than ever by her words. He glanced around the facility, but saw no one else. Who was she talking to?

She picked up a shiny metal fork and cut open her egg. The yellow circle bled over the tender white of the eggs. Martyr gasped and turned to his own plate. Would his eggs bleed too?

He picked up his fork and stabbed the circle, causing the dark liquid to ooze out of the small puncture holes. He glanced at Daughter Abby. She dipped her toast into the liquid. Martyr picked up his toast but did not eat.

"Who is God?"

Daughter Abby hummed and chewed. She held up a finger until she swallowed. "Uh, well, God is … um … He's the creator … of everything."

"Does he work at the Farm?"

She giggled. "Yes, but not how you mean. God isn't a person like you or me or my dad, he's a deity … wh-which is a … um … I'm not so good at explaining him, I guess. Basically, he made life, the earth, and everything in it. He made people and animals and trees and—"

"And you speak to him here, where he is not"—Martyr looked around the facility again to be certain they were alone—"and he hears you?"

"God hears every prayer. He knows everything that happens, even your thoughts."

"How can he know my thoughts?"

"Because he's omniscient."

"What is—?"

"It means he has unlimited knowledge and understanding."

"But how can he—?"

"Because he's God."

"You're certain he made *me*?"

Daughter Abby frowned and took a bite of her toast. Martyr watched her chew and swallow before she spoke again. "I don't know, Marty. I've always believed it was wrong to clo—" She cleared her throat. "Not that I'm positive you're a clone."

"I am a clone. The doctors say it sometimes. I'm not sure what it means."

She set her fork down and dropped her face into her hands. "Of course they didn't *explain* anything." Her voice was muffled. "Clones are … well, they're copies of people who already exist. And it's wrong to clone people. It's like playing God, but humans can't create things as well as he can. We mess stuff up, even with the best intentions." She lifted her face to look at him. "Didn't you say there were … *Brokens*?"

"Yes."

"How many Brokens, Marty?"

"Uh … officially four, but probably half of us have serious conditions. And the doctors call them Brokens too."

"Half?" Her eyes glistened and her eyelashes fluttered. "What kind of broken?"

"Well, Baby is small, though he has a large head. He doesn't speak with words, and he sucks his thumb. But he's smart, unlike Hummer, who only hums and rocks and drools all the time. Also, Hummer's face is a little crooked and his eyes are extra large. Several have misshapen appendages, like arms, a foot, or fingers or toes. Fido likes to pick on the Brokens, especially since many of them can't run or fight back." Martyr paused and remembered the little boy in the box. "One J:9 or 10 didn't grow legs. They keep him in a glass box in Section One. He moans all the time, like Hummer, but I think he's in pain where Hummer is not. He is one of the four."

A tear ran down Daughter Abby's cheek. Martyr reached up and brushed it away with the backs of his fingers. He did not mean to make her sad.

"Marty, doctors in a lab can't give you a purpose—only God can do that. I know he has a plan for you, for your life. Maybe escaping was part of his plan. Maybe you and I can rescue the others."

Rescue. As if their life at the Farm had been wrong in some way. As if they had been prisoners. The sudden realization turned his stomach. He was a copy. They all were. Copies of a real person. And the doctors had lied to them. Used them. Could they get away? Could they each have a new purpose? Could all the Jasons have a life like Daughter Abby's? "I would like the purpose of freeing the others. How can I find out if this is God's purpose for me?"

"Oh." This time she scowled like she was thinking very hard. Suddenly she gasped and grabbed his wrist. "I know! I'll take you to meet Kylee's brother. He's a youth pastor, so he'll know what to do … I think. But first, Marty, I've got to go to school, which means you'll have to stay here alone while I'm gone. You must stay inside the house. Don't answer the door or the phone. If you hear someone coming, go back up to my room and hide in the closet. I made you another sandwich for lunch. It's in the fridge." She pointed at a large rectangular box with two white doors. "Eat anything you want. Just make sure the doors to the fridge close when you're done or all the cold air will get out. The TV is on—I'll show you how to change the channels." She took his hand, led him to the picture monitor, and explained how to use a tiny device with buttons that made this *TV* change to different scenes.

"I'll be back at about three twenty-five." She pointed to a wooden clock taller than he was. "Can you tell time?"

He nodded.

She walked over by the door, opened a closet, and put on a puffy black coat. She removed the binding from her hair and pulled a black hat over her head, making her curly hair poof out around the edges of the hat. She stepped into a pair of black boots filled with white fur, then came to him, wrapped her arms around his waist, and squeezed.

He tensed and flushed at her touch, but she quickly let go and said, "Be careful."

Then she pulled on a pair of black gloves, heaved a black bag over her shoulder, and left.

Abby couldn't concentrate on the drive to school. She shouldn't have left Marty alone. What if he went outside? What if someone came and took him away and she couldn't prove he existed? She could just see herself trying to convince the cops that Jason Farms had an underground cloning lab.

Jason Farms.

She shuddered, figuring JD stood for Jason something. See? Crazy scientists did have egos.

But did JD know what his father did for a living? JD held some liberal views about scientific research, but that didn't mean he knew about his father's work. Another question nagged at her. Clearly Dr. Kane thought it would be a good idea to clone his son, but why? Wouldn't seeing a mutilated version of your own son be heartbreaking? How could a parent do that?

And how could Abby's dad be a part of it?

She wanted to text Dad and let him have it, but that would tip him off about where Marty was, and she didn't want Marty to have to go back. The lab sounded horrible. No color? No socks? No hair? She could only imagine the extent of psychological abuse the clones had suffered at the hands of Dr. Kane. Toxic world … death at age eighteen? Purpose to expire? Not to mention physical abuse involving tasers and pharmaceutical testing. Unbelievable!

And completely twisted.

A thought sparked in her mind. She shivered, not liking where it led. A facility that cloned humans would have some level of security. They were bound to have surveillance cameras. Abby didn't remember seeing any, but she hadn't been looking. Maybe they didn't have someone monitoring the feed 24/7, but when they discovered Marty was missing, they'd go back and look. They'd see her snooping around outside. They'd see Marty climb in the back of her dad's truck.

And they'd come looking.

Abby had to find answers before then, and JD was the place to start.

She parked her car and entered the school, eyes peeled for that familiar to-die-for hair. She didn't see JD until third period calculus.

He was sitting at his desk, his book open in front of him, studiously working on the problems Mrs. Volkman had left on the board.

He was so cute when he acted normal.

She needed to snoop around his house, see if his dad had a home office. If she could find something concrete, she could go to the cops. The trick was getting to JD's house without encouraging any romantic notions. An idea formed as she made her way across the room; she'd play the assignment card. JD knew she was all about academia. In light of their major project, her request shouldn't seem suspicious. She sank into the empty desk beside his and, having entered his proximity, held her breath.

JD looked up, a smile defeating his studious expression. "Hey, gorgeous."

It was disturbing how identical JD's and Marty's faces were. Only Marty was well-mannered and shy, and didn't reek like the cosmetics department at Walmart.

Oh, she hoped he stayed safe today.

Abby opened her notebook. "Could I come to your house this afternoon? I want to see what other books your dad has in his library that might help our project."

"Anything for you." She could hear the smile in his voice, the eagerness, the triumph. "I'll meet you in the parking lot after sixth."

"Perfect."

She copied the first problem into her notebook, only she didn't actually do the logarithm. Her mind dwelled on Marty. She glanced at the clock. 9:57. What was he doing right now? She hoped he was okay and wouldn't freak out when she didn't come home right at 3:25.

Maybe going to JD's house today was a bad idea—*duh, Abby!* She didn't have the training or the gear for infiltration. But she needed hard evidence since the cops wouldn't buy her story without probable cause. She needed reason enough for a judge to approve a search warrant for Jason Farms.

The Kane residence had to have something.

[CHAPTER TWELVE]

MARTYR WATCHED THE TV FOR HOURS. It was fascinating, filled with endless knowledge. On some numbers the people talked to him, but he quickly realized they didn't hear the questions he asked back. Other numbers showed people living their lives as if Martyr wasn't watching. It felt wrong to spy on these people, especially when some of them did things that made his cheeks flush. But again, the people didn't seem to know he was there.

He pushed through all the numbers looking for a view of the Farm, hoping he could see what Baby was doing. He found none.

On level two, he located a small bathroom next to Daughter Abby's cell. Her smell hung in the air. Something moved to his left, startling him until he realized it was his own reflection. This reflecting glass was much clearer than the mirror wall at the end of the cafeteria and track on the Farm. Martyr studied himself in the shiny surface and noticed he seemed pale compared to people aboveground. He touched his prickly head. When Daughter Abby had called him JD, she had said his hair was his best feature.

The groomers never said why they shaved the Jasons' hair. They just always had. *Why did I never question these things?* Martyr's eyebrows were thick and dark, as was the hair on the rest of his body. That was the color his hair would be if it ever grew out. He wished he had hair, since Daughter Abby liked it so much.

He also wished he could wear something colorful. He walked into Daughter Abby's cell. As soon as he entered the dog jumped off the bed and strutted over to him, arching its back and growling its strange, non-threatening growl. Martyr reached out to touch it. His fingers sank in the soft, white hair that was unlike anything he'd ever felt before. The dog raised its head, pressing against Martyr's hand, increasing its continuous hum. Martyr smiled and studied its scrunched-up face and bulging, gray eyes. The animal seemed to like him. It followed him to the drawers then stood rubbing its body against Martyr's leg.

Martyr opened the drawer where Daughter Abby had found the socks. Many colorful socks were in the drawer, but they were all too small for Martyr's feet. He opened the next drawer and pulled out something that was not socks.

Underwear. The pair he held were red and soft like nothing he had ever felt. Amazing! He held them up and frowned. They were also too small.

The other drawer held more colors and shiny fabrics, but Martyr couldn't understand the purpose for such stringy garments. While he puzzled, the dog walked away as if bored and leapt back up on the bed, curling into a ball, watching with its huge eyes.

Martyr walked into the closet where the clothing hung down. He pulled out items in the colors he liked best, carried an armful of things into the bathroom, and tried them on in front of the reflecting glass. They were all too small. Daughter Abby was a tiny person.

An idea came to him. Dr. Goyer lived in this facility. Perhaps he had a cell of his own. And bigger clothing. He walked down the hall to the only other door and slowly pushed it open.

Dr. Goyer's cell was dark. Martyr found the switch on the wall that made the lights come on and entered. The walls were green—much darker green than peas. A large bed sat in the middle of the cell, covered in a thick, green blanket. Martyr climbed onto it and lay down. It was very comfortable, wide, and so long his feet didn't touch the end. He stretched his arms and legs out like an X, and still he didn't hang off any edges.

He got up and looked in Dr. Goyer's drawers. He found more socks and underwear, but Dr. Goyer's were white or gray or black—nothing colorful like Daughter Abby had. This was disappointing. In the very back of the bottom drawer, he found a pair of long, red socks with bright green triangles on them. Martyr grinned. He sat down on the floor, removed the socks Daughter Abby had given him last night, and pulled the red socks on. They were thinner than the other socks, but the bright red and green colors made him smile.

Dr. Goyer also had a closet filled with hanging clothes. Dr. Goyer and Daughter Abby must be special people to have so many personal things. Martyr had never been allowed such things. Even his clothes were shared, the dirty ones traded in for a clean set each week at grooming. What freedom to get to choose what colors you wore each day.

By Martyr's count, this was Thursday. Grooming day. For once he could choose what fresh clothes to wear. Martyr tried on several things that made him look like a doctor. He imagined he worked at the Farm and had to give marks to Fido and Iron Man for picking on Baby.

He settled on a dark red shirt that buttoned up the front and a pair of stiff blue pants that snapped around the waist. It took him a long time to thread the buttons through the holes on the shirt. The pants wanted to fall down, but Martyr found a belt that helped them stay up. He also found the orange necktie, but he couldn't figure out how to knot it around his neck, so he did the best he could. He approved his appearance in the bathroom mirror before going back down to level one.

At 12:10—when he knew Baby and the others were eating lunch at Jason Farms—Martyr went to the white box where Daughter Abby claimed to have put his sandwich. He pulled the door open and immediately a light blinked on and cold air drifted over him. His eyes widened at all the color. He spotted the plate with the sandwich and removed it. He also saw more bottles of the blue drink Daughter Abby had given him last night and took one. He looked from item to item inside the white box, marveling at the choices of things to eat, then slammed the door shut, remembering how Daughter Abby had been concerned about leaving the door open too long. He took his food and drink and sat at the tall counter where they had eaten breakfast.

He wondered if he should speak to God, like Daughter Abby had that morning. He very much wanted the Creator of Everything to like him.

"Hello?" Martyr swallowed. His nervousness made it hard to concentrate. "I-I thank you for this sandwich Daughter Abby made for me to eat. She is a very kind daughter. I, um, also thank you I got to meet her, a real women—woman. I hope I can stay here forever and Baby can come too, and Dr. Goyer and Daughter Abby will want to take care of us. I hope I won't expire in fifteen days."

Daughter Abby had also said something to end her communication—Martyr couldn't remember what. "Thank you for listening, sir."

After Martyr finished his sandwich, he wandered back to the room with the TV. Light now streamed in the windows from outside. Martyr spent a long time staring out the large window. Snow covered everything like cotton balls. The TV had said more was expected to come by Sunday and Martyr wondered how it would arrive.

He stared at the sky, bits of blue peeking out from the tops of the trees. He pressed his palms to the window and craned his neck to see above him, but the trees were too close to the house and the windows had no way to open. Martyr went to the front door and opened it. A gust of icy air swept inside, chilling his cheeks. But he could not see the sky at all with the way the ceiling hung out over the platform and stairs that led to the ground.

He closed the door and explored the house, looking for a better view of the sky. On level one, he found an exit that led to the backside of the house. It had a small platform with no ceiling and wooden steps leading to a large, snow-covered clearing that was surrounded by a wall of dark trees. Martyr knelt in the doorway at the top of the steps, careful to keep his body inside the house as Daughter Abby had asked of him.

The sky stretched overhead like a very high, blue ceiling—a lighter color of blue than the picture of *Myrtle Beach* but darker than Rolo's eyes. The sun hung up in the sky, as well, somehow staying there without falling to the ground. It did not have a smiling face or long beams stretching out on all sides like the pictures Dr. Max had drawn. It was a pale, round ball of brightness. It hurt his eyes to stare at the sun, so he studied the clouds instead. They were fluffy and white like the snow.

Air gusted around him suddenly, shaking the leaves on the trees so that they sounded like running water. Martyr shivered, and listened for other sounds. There were noises like the beeps of the doctor's machines, but lighter, longer, and erratic—almost musical. A black knife cut across the yard and landed at the side of the facility, where a tiny structure had been mounted on a pole. The knife was a creature… a bird? It bit at the snow around the pole, made a string of beeping music, then went back to … eating, perhaps? Two more birds joined the first, then one flew away, then three others came. Two left. They were very busy and quick.

Engines hummed in the distance, but Martyr could not see anything that could be making such noise. Something moved in the trees to his left, beyond the birds.

It was alive—an animal of some kind, but nothing Martyr had ever imagined. It was much bigger than Daughter Abby's dog, even bigger than the dogs Martyr had seen on the TV that morning. Maybe it was a horse; Dr. Max had once said people could ride on horses' backs.

The animal bit a tree branch and snapped it off. Martyr stared as it chewed and chewed. The horse looked bored standing in the snow. Maybe it wanted someone to ride on it? Martyr tried to imagine climbing onto the animal's back. He did not want to try that at all.

Soon the horse moved away, and Martyr got so cold that he closed the door and returned to the soft, long chair in front of the TV. This was called a *sofa* or *loveseat* or *discount item*. A man on TV had told him several times he should come on down and purchase one today. He didn't know how to make the TV stop talking, so he found the device that Daughter Abby had given him and examined it. He pushed the POWER button and the picture box clicked off.

He smiled and put the device down.

A stack of books and papers lay on the floor by Martyr's feet. He leaned over to examine them. One word in particular stuck out.

Lupus.

A word he had heard before.

"What's the deal?" Kylee asked Abby when Mr. Bunker instructed the debate class to split up and practice for the last five minutes of class. "He's walking you to class now?"

Abby sighed. She was beyond weary of her six-foot shadow. Unfortunately, inviting herself over to JD's place had only encouraged him, despite her business-only study proposition.

"There's no deal, Kylee. Trust me."

"Then why is he trailing you like a puppy?" A dreamy grin stretched across Kylee's face. "Must be nice."

Abby rolled her eyes and changed the subject. "So can I meet your brother sometime?"

Kylee shrugged. "Church on Sunday."

"Before then. I have something I really need to ask a pastor. Would it bug him if we just showed up?"

"At his apartment? Probably not. Kids do it all the time. What do you want to ask him?"

Abby didn't want to give Kylee any information on the whole Jason Farms problem. The less people who knew about it, the safer Marty would be. "Well … my dad's a scientist. He's also not a believer. So I wondered about how I can, uh, you know, talk to my dad about God and my beliefs about science without us always fighting." It wasn't a lie. She could use all the help she could get in that department.

"We can go after school, I guess."

Abby wasn't ready to explain her non-date sleuthing expedition to JD's house. Kylee would probably go into permanent swoon. "Can I call you? I need to make sure it's okay with my dad first."

"Sounds good."

The bell rang. Kylee leaned over and slapped a package of gum on Abby's desk. "My gift to you, just in case you need minty breath." She leaped from her desk, and as she passed JD, who was waiting for Abby outside the classroom door, she broke into a fit of the giggles.

Ha ha. Abby pocketed the gum and sulked toward the door.

JD walked with her from Mr. Bunker's classroom, to her locker, and out to the parking lot. He tried convincing her she should ride in his truck, but Abby insisted on following in her car. She didn't want to be stranded at his place without means of escape, nor did she want to waste time having him bring her back to the school to get her car, which would leave Marty home alone even longer.

She had to drive faster than she liked on the icy roads to keep up with JD's F–150. He passed the public access road to Lake Praydor and wound down a long driveway surrounded by dense forest.

JD's truck slid to a stop in front of a massive, multi-gable brick home overlooking the lake. Abby held in a deep breath. The vast whiteness of the frozen water peeked through the trees behind the house, and on the lake a small airplane with skis perched on the frozen expanse like a weightless bird.

She climbed out of her car and met JD on the neatly shoveled walk. "Is that your plane?"

"Not mine personally. It's my dad's. I've flown it, though. I'm getting my pilot's license."

My, my. The things the mega-rich got to do—*like I can talk, Miss BMW Sports Car*. If she wanted a pilot's license bad enough, her dad would find a way to make it happen. The reality of that made her feel dirty somehow. Must have something to do with the company she was in.

At least she didn't wear a whole bottle of perfume every day. That was just wasteful.

JD led the way into an immense living room. As a buffer, Abby stopped beside the polished wooden banister of a large staircase while she took in the sight. Black leather furniture stood in contrast to a sandy-white hardwood floor. At the opposite end of the room, a large bearskin rug laid in front of a stone fireplace that stretched up the wall and out the ceiling. Wide picture windows reached two stories high along the wall between fireplace and staircase, overlooking the lake. The view drew a small, involuntary gasp from Abby's lips.

Hello, Lifestyles of the Rich and Not-So-Famous.

"Like it?" JD walked up behind her and grabbed one of the bars halfway up the stairs. She could feel his arm behind her head, which meant he was leaning again. Could the guy not stand up straight?

Talk about walking into the lions' den. On purpose.

She'd be lucky to leave alive or at least unmauled. She glanced back to the bearskin rug on the floor and wondered what a JD rug would look like on her living room floor.

Hopefully it wouldn't come to that.

Abby stepped toward the windows and out of JD's rapacious reach. "Rich people who live on a lake. It's like something out of a movie."

JD laughed. "Are there a lot of movies about that?"

"Tons." Abby needed something to calm her nerves. She reached into her coat pocket, pulled out a stick of Kylee's gum, and folded it into her mouth. She held out the pack to JD. "Want some?"

He took a piece. "Does my breath smell bad?" He put the stick in his mouth and chewed. "Oh, I get it. You want us both to have good breath."

One-track mind on this one. She shrugged off her coat and dropped her backpack onto the floor. "So where's this library?"

"Upstairs. Next to *my* room."

Good grief.

She glanced at the clock—3:20. If she was quick, she wouldn't be that late getting back to Marty. She started up the stairs that climbed along the far wall of the living room and JD came close behind. She felt self-conscious with him behind her and hoped she didn't lose her balance and trip. How embarrassing would that be?

Upstairs, a hallway stretched in two directions. She paused on the stairs to let JD lead, but he stopped behind her and moved her hair over her shoulder. His breath tickled the back of her neck. A tingle shot down her spine, and she whipped around.

"No funny business, JD."

He stepped up onto her step, grabbed her shoulders. His chocolate eyes melted into hers. He was so tall. *Had Marty been this tall?*

"There's nothing funny about how you make me feel."

Abby poked a finger against his chest. "I'm serious, JD. Knock it off!" She ducked under his arm and climbed the last three steps. She turned to face him, put her arms out at her sides, and turned in a circle. "This is my personal space. You stay out of it. I'd hate to throw you down the stairs. Don't think I won't."

A smile twitched at the corner of his full, perfect lips—*Stop it, Abby! Focus!*

She walked to the right. "Where is the library?"

His voice floated over the top of her head. "Third door on your right."

She pushed open the door and walked into an office. A massive cherry desk took up most of the floor space, but the walls were solid bookshelves. JD walked past her and sat on the edge of what must be his father's desk. She needed to lose him for a few. Time for some creative thinking.

"You got anything to eat? I'm kinda hungry."

JD waggled his eyebrows. "Are you sure you're hungry for food, because I can—"

"I'm sure, JD. Something munchy. Anything really." As long

as it got him out of there so she could snoop for probable cause. "Ooh, do you have any hot chocolate? I'd love some hot chocolate." Which would take him a lot longer than grabbing a bag of chips.

"Yeah, I think so." JD jumped off the desk and left the room. "Be right back," he called from the hallway.

"Thanks for the warning." She sat down in his dad's leather chair. *Ergonomic. Nice.*

She pulled open a drawer full of office supplies: paper clips, rubber bands, envelopes, pens, a letter opener— Ooh! She drew the letter opener out and set it on the desk. It would be a good weapon if JD got too frisky. She shut the drawer and opened the next one. Looked like bills waiting to be paid. Electric, doctor, phone—she took a closer look at the phone bill. Calls to Washington D.C., New York, somewhere in Europe, Japan, Boston. She put the bill back.

Just what was she hoping to find? Dr. Kane must keep everything work-related in his lab office. He would be a fool to keep anything at home. And anyone who managed to successfully clone humans eighteenish years ago was not a fool.

Drat.

How could she get into his lab office?

She stood and perused the books on the shelf closest to her. Her heart flooded with longing. What she wouldn't give for a personal scientific library like this. She ran her finger over the titles and stopped at *Lupus and You.*

Hello.

She pulled the book out. The spine was creased, the pages heavily dog-eared, but the top was dusty. Someone had once made good use of this book, but not in a really long time. The copyright date was 1989. She frowned, her mind circling around something familiar. She hurried back to the desk, pulled open the drawer with the bills, and shuffled through them until she came to the doctor bill. After a moment's hesitation, she opened it.

It was a co-payment receipt for immune suppressants. A lot of them. For a Jason Dean Kane.

Did JD have lupus?

Footsteps echoed in the hallway. Abby shut the drawer, stuck the doctor bill inside the lupus book, and tucked it under her arm. She stepped back to the books, pretending to look at more.

"Can I help you?" a woman asked in a cold and formal tone.

Abby spun to face the door to the office, heat flushing over her. "Mrs. Kane! Wow. How are you?" Scary. With the school principal for a mom, no wonder JD was so popular.

"I repeat my question. Can. I. Help. You?"

Abby swallowed. "Um, I'm just waiting for JD. We're doing a science project together on lupus for Bio II, and he said his dad had a lot of science books. I'll say. I've never seen such an extensive home library, Mrs. Kane. It's totally impressive that—"

"You have an interest in my son?"

Abby's cheeks warmed. "Oh. No, ma'am. Strictly academic. Bio II. Big project. Lupus."

"There is no reason for you to be in our home."

"Excuse me?"

"I suggest you schedule your little study sessions at the school library from now on. And if you do have a romantic interest in my son, I strongly urge you to set your sights on someone else, immediately. Jason is not allowed to date."

Abby laughed out loud—she couldn't help it. JD not allowed to date? "You're kidding, right?"

Mrs. Kane raised her penciled eyebrows. "Have you ever known him to have a girlfriend?"

Abby sobered. "Well, I … um. I'm new. I've only lived in Fishhook a few days."

Not that JD hasn't tried, lady.

"Well, let me enlighten you. My son is not allowed to date. He is not allowed to invite girls over to our home. He is not allowed a *girlfriend*."

Awkward. The one time Abby would like JD to show up … She shifted her weight to her other foot.

Mrs. Kane faked an icy smile. "Off you go, then."

Abby stepped toward the door, but Mrs. Kane still blocked the way out. The woman held out her hand. "The book can stay here."

"Right." Abby reluctantly set the lupus book on Mrs. Kane's hand, and the woman stepped aside. Abby scrambled out the door and down the stairs. She slipped into her coat, heaved her backpack over one shoulder, and headed for the front door.

"You're leaving?" JD stepped out of the kitchen with a tray in his hands. It had a plate of chocolate chip cookies and two mugs of hot chocolate. *Awww. How cute.*

Abby grabbed a cookie off the plate and whispered, "Yeah. Your mom kicked me to the curb."

JD seemed to deflate a little. "I didn't hear her. She must have come in through the garage. Look, Abby, my mom's a little bit … strict."

"Yeah. I caught that. Makes for an efficient high school principal, though. Hey, she took this book that looked perfect for our project. It was called *Lupus and You*. Think you could bring it to school tomorrow?"

"I'll try. Unless she locks it in her vault." He grinned. "Kidding."

Abby started for the door. "See you tomorrow, JD. Thanks for the cookie."

"Bye, Abby." JD's voice had never sounded so sad, but Abby remembered his plans to have *her* for a snack and was secretly relieved Mrs. Kane had sent her packing. Too much weird in this house anyway. She needed a plan B.

She stuck the cookie in her mouth and let herself out.

[CHAPTER THIRTEEN]

MARTYR SAT ON THE LONG CHAIR, bouncing his leg. He looked at the clock: 3:44. Only one minute later than the last time he had checked. He turned his attention back to the TV, watching the *dolphins* swim in very deep water. They were fascinating creatures, but his thoughts were fixed on Daughter Abby. Where was she? He hoped nothing had happened to her.

Something touched his leg, causing him to lean forward. It was the dog, rubbing its body against him. Martyr lifted the creature onto his lap and stroked its thick fur. It closed its eyes and hummed, low and content. Martyr smiled. The dog made him feel like—

The front door rattled. Finally! Martyr pushed the dog off his lap and stood up.

"Abby, honey? I'm home!"

Martyr scrambled up the stairs. He had just reached the top when the front door slammed shut. Martyr paused at the railing and looked down on the room, where the strange sounds of the dolphins still came from the TV. He'd forgotten to turn it off.

"Abby? Where are you going?"

Martyr ran to Daughter Abby's cell and darted into the closet, pulling the door closed behind him. He plowed past the hanging clothes, burrowing his way to the back wall. His heart thudded. It was dark in the clothing, and Martyr hoped Dr. Goyer would not see him even if he opened the door.

"Abby?"

The doctor was in his daughter's cell now. Martyr curled into a ball and held his breath. Something slipped underneath his leg and clunked onto the floor. He winced.

The closet door swung open. Martyr hugged his head and begged the Creator of Everything for Dr. Goyer to go away.

The light turned on.

Martyr could hear the doctor's breathing, the creaking floor. Martyr waited, hoping, pleading.

"Come on out, son, or I'll have to call the police."

Martyr did not know what the police were, but it sounded like a threat. Someone grabbed Martyr's arm. He screamed.

"I'm not going to hurt you." Dr. Goyer pushed the clothing aside. "I just want you to come out of there."

Martyr relaxed some. Dr. Goyer had been nice during marks; if he said he wouldn't hurt him, then Martyr believed he wouldn't.

Martyr crawled backward out of the closet until he was in the main room, then sat back on his heels and looked up at the doctor. Guilt pressed down like a heavy blanket.

Dr. Goyer's eyes widened, looking huge behind his thick glasses. "*Martyr*?"

Martyr shrank back until he bumped into the leg of Daughter Abby's desk.

Dr. Goyer hissed a string of words that Martyr had only ever heard the guards use when they were very angry. Martyr scooted under the desk, watching Dr. Goyer carefully to see what he might do next. He didn't appear to have a stick. Would the taser work in Dr. Goyer's facility? He braced himself for the pain just in case.

"Dad?" The muted sound of Daughter Abby's voice drifted up from level one.

Dr. Goyer spun in a circle. Then he motioned to Martyr and said, "Stay right there."

Martyr was more than happy to comply. The floor under the desk was small enough that no one else could fit there.

Dr. Goyer bounded out of the room and closed the door behind him.

Abby almost cried when she saw Dad's truck in the driveway. What on earth was he doing home so early? She should have driven straight home from school or skipped it all together. What if she were too late?

What if Dad had found Marty?

The house was fairly messy. Marty had eaten the sandwich at the counter but left his plate. A documentary on dolphins blared from the television. A box containing Dad's office décor sat on the kitchen counter. Hope swelled in her chest. Had Dad been fired? Did he quit?

"Dad?" she called again.

"Abby, honey?" Her dad's slightly strained voice came from upstairs.

He knows.

She raced to the stairs and met her dad halfway up. "Hi, Dad. How was work?"

His eyes darted away from hers. "Good. Good. Did you know …? How was school?"

"Great. I made some real progress on my big science project." Sort of. Not really. Dad stood sentry on the stairs, not moving. Guarding what, exactly? "Uh, Dad? You okay? I'd like to change out of this sweater. It's fine for school, but it's always too hot to wear at home."

Dad didn't speak. He just looked over the railing into the empty space above the living room.

"Dad?"

He jumped and looked back to Abby. "Huh?"

"Can I get by?"

"No!"

"No?" He definitely knew. "Why not?"

"Your homework. You should finish it first. Downstairs."

"Before I can change my sweater?"

"Yes."

"Have you gone insane?" Not a real nice thing to ask under the circumstances, but on the plus side, Marty must still be here. In Abby's room, to be precise. No sense in beating around the bush. "You found Marty?"

Dad's eyes bulged out in a Halloween freak-show kind of way, then he turned a pale, pale yellow. She hoped he wouldn't puke.

"Dad, it's okay. He's safe here, right? You didn't tell Dr. Kane anything, did you? Do they have surveillance footage of him getting into your truck?"

Dad's eyes bulged further. Abby was afraid they might pop over the top of his glasses and roll down the stairs. When his mouth dropped open, she shrank back a hair and put a firm grip on the banister, just in case he lost it completely.

"How do you know …? Where I work is my … How do you, you, you …?"

"Dad? Chill, okay and I'll explain. Deep breaths. I found Marty last night. He rode here in the back of your truck and got into the house somehow. I let him sleep in my room."

The color came back to Dad's face real quick.

"In my sleeping bag, Dad. You watch too much TV. I told him to stay here today because I need to come up with a way to help him. I was thinking about—"

"*Help him?* He's not a stray dog, Abigail. He belongs to Dr. Kane. He must go back!"

This time Abby's face flushed. "No, Dad. He doesn't *belong* to Dr. Kane. People don't belong to anyone, not like that. He's not a car or a boat that has a title of ownership."

She tried to push past her dad, but he wouldn't let her. "Hold on, honey—"

"You hold on, Dad. I can't believe you'd take another job like this. Didn't you learn anything from the last time?" She didn't wait for an answer, but she did quit trying to shove him out of her way. "Did Dr. Kane really clone his own son over and over and keep them imprisoned in an underground lab? Who does stuff like that?" When her dad still didn't answer she dropped her gaze. "Marty says he's going to die in two weeks. He thinks the air is poison and his purpose in life is to die to save humanity."

Sighing deeply, her father sat down on the steps, putting their faces at the same level. "They need to tell the boys something so they won't run away. If you thought about—"

"I should have known you'd take the scientists' side!" She wanted to rush past, to go to Martyr, but this might be her only chance to reason with her dad. She sat down on the step his feet rested on and leaned against the wall. "Please, Dad. This isn't your pet project. They did all this long before you went on the payroll. You have to admit it's abuse. Psychological abuse. Physical abuse. Please don't condone that!"

Her dad put his hand on her knee. "I don't condone abuse, Abby, honey, ever, but you have to accept that these clones are not people. They are *copies* of people."

Abby jerked her leg away from him. "Have you talked to him? He's as real as you or me, and he's scared!"

Her dad stood up. "Not everything in this world fits your black and white beliefs, Abby. I will not allow you to meddle in things that—"

Abby stood up too. "Me, meddle? You're the one playing God! You're just no good at it." She paused just long enough to see the question in his eyes. "What about the brokens? The boy without legs?"

Something must have snapped in her dad's brain, because he

suddenly buried his face in his hands. Abby seized his moment of sagging posture and barged past. He turned and grabbed for her waist, but she wriggled free and burst into her room. She went to the closet and peeked behind armfuls of clothing but couldn't find Marty. Her foot snagged on something and she looked down. Clothes were strewn about the closet floor. She turned back to her room and saw her bras, underwear, and socks poking out of open drawers.

Awkward.

Dad stepped into the doorway, rubbing a hand over his forehead. "He's under the desk."

Abby sank to her knees and pulled back the desk chair. Marty lay curled in a ball, arms cradling his head. He was wearing her dad's clothes.

She smiled. "Looks like Marty likes those Christmas socks I bought you, even if you don't."

"He likes red."

Abby glanced at her dad and saw he was smiling a bit. "Look at him," she said, hoping her dad was no longer on the dark side. "Why would a guy his size cower like this? What do they do to them at that place?"

Dad sank onto the foot of her bed. "He's just not confrontational. Some of the other clones are very aggressive."

"But not Marty?"

"He'll fight to protect someone, which is how he got his nickname, I guess. If I attacked you, I bet he'd come out in a hurry."

"What if I attacked you?" Abby grinned.

"I'm not sure he likes me. I'm a doctor. The enemy."

Abby set a hand on Marty's thigh. "Come on out, Marty. Dad's not going to hurt you."

Marty didn't come out, but he relaxed a bit and let go of his head. He peeked out at Abby, his dark eyebrows wrinkled. "Will he take me back?"

"No," Abby said firmly over her father's whispered, "Yes."

Marty crawled out from under the desk. Dad's orange silk tie hung around his neck like a scarf. Abby pursed her lips to keep from laughing. He looked good in Dad's shirt. It was buttoned off kilter, but the maroon color brought life to his pale skin. The jeans were a little baggy around the waist, short in the legs. He sat against the wall and hugged his knees to his chest.

"Nice socks," Abby said.

Marty grinned that wide, unguarded smile and Abby melted.

Marty looked at her dad, eyebrows scrunched together. "I'm sorry I took your keycard, Dr. Goyer. I wanted to see the sky and no one would help me."

"I know, son. I know."

Heat flared up inside Abby again. "He says he's going to expire. Why would that be?"

Dad shrugged one shoulder. "I'm not sure yet. They don't tell me everything. But I don't think they die on their own."

"So they kill them when they turn eighteen?"

Dad gripped the edge of Abby's bed and leaned forward. "I'm the newest scientist at the Farm, honey. Privileges and knowledge come with time."

"But you know JD stands for Jason something, right?"

Dad motioned to Martyr. "Why do you think I flipped out when I saw JD Junior in our living room?"

"Because you don't want me dating any—wait. Junior? JD is named after his ... dad?"

"Yes."

Abby fell back on her rear. "Dad, I think Dr. Kane is sick."

"I know you don't agree with cloning, but he's actually quite brilliant. They're doing some fascinating research—"

"No, I mean sick as in *has a disease*. At first I thought it was JD, because I saw the name Jason Kane on a co-payment receipt for immune suppressants in Dr. Kane's house. I assumed it was JD, because it was his idea to do our project on lupus and he brought me the pamphlet—"

"Whoa." Dad's face flushed. "When were you at his ... *why* were you at his house?"

"—on genetic disease. So after I left his house—where I went strictly for research—I figured JD must have lupus but … Dad? I think it's Dr. Kane."

Dad pushed his glasses up his nose and groaned. "Abby, I cannot reveal confidential information about my work."

"Oh, Dad. We're way past that now."

"Dr. Kane *is* sick," Marty said. "I think he wants my kidneys. I heard him talking to Dr. Elliot. He said I was the healthiest of the J:3s." He looked at Dad. "But transplants come from donors, right? So why wouldn't Dr. Kane find a donor?"

Abby froze. Kidneys could fail in some extreme cases of lupus. She'd read it in the pamphlet JD gave her.

"Because not all donors are a match," Dad said.

Abby gasped, the truth clicking in her mind like the combination on a lock. "Dad?" Her eyes were wide, and she wondered if they were bulging as much as Dad's had back on the stairs. "Dad, they're all Dr. Kane's—" She took a long, deep breath. "Dr. Kane cloned himself?"

Dad hung his head.

Marty looked slightly bewildered. Abby reached out and took his hand. It was bigger than hers and warmer too. She wrapped her fingers with his and squeezed. He squeezed back.

She turned her anger back to her dad. "How could he do that? Clone himself when he's sick?"

"He's trying to find a cure."

"That's a strange way to go about it. No wonder so many are broken. If they already have lupus, what chance do they have?" Abby brought her thumbnail to her lips and said, "We can't let him go back there."

"He might not be safe on his own," Dad said. "He doesn't know our world."

"He can learn. He's super smart. In fact, I'd been meaning to ask why they educate the clones."

"It keeps them occupied and healthy."

Abby paused, prayed for patience, and put on her most pleading only-child face. "Even if you and I don't agree that cloning humans is wrong, you've got to admit that keeping over four dozen boys in an underground lab their whole life is false imprisonment. Kidnapping, even. And then killing them for their kidneys, Dad? Murder. Surely these are laws you can't argue with."

"But if clones aren't human, they don't have the same rights as …" Dad took off his glasses and rubbed his face.

Abby sucked in a sharp breath, ready to spout out that no judge in America could look at Martyr's sweet face and say he wasn't human.

Be still.

Abby blinked. Everything in her wanted to fight, but the soft voice prodded again.

Be still.

When Dad looked up, his eyes were moist. "One of the last things your mother ever said to me was, 'Please don't kill to avenge my death.'" Dad put his glasses back on. "I told myself she was very sick, that she didn't really know what she was saying. That the disease had …" Dad squeezed his eyes shut and swallowed. "I don't understand a lot at Jason Farms, but I've run enough tests this week to know that most of the boys are perfectly healthy. I can see no reason for them to … expire."

A chill ran over Abby. Dad would help. Jason Farms had gone too far, even for him. It was a start, one she would accept for now.

Thank you, Lord, for helping him see that much.

Dad stood. "They'll come looking for him. We need to get the tracker out of his ear, or it will lead them straight here."

"Tracker?" Abby swatted her dad's leg. "When were you going to mention this?"

Marty looked from Abby to Dad and back to Abby. "What's a tracker?"

Dad walked to the door. "Come on into the bathroom, son."

Abby stood, took Marty's hand, and helped him up. Marty didn't let go of her hand, so they trailed after Dad together.

"Wait here," Dad said. "I need a razor blade."

Once Dad left, Abby stared at the reflection in the mirror above the sink. Was it bad that she liked how they looked holding hands?

She bumped her shoulder against his arm. "Red looks good on you."

Marty's face tinged pink and his throat bobbed as he swallowed. His presence made her heart start up like a generator. He turned his head to look down on her. She made eye contact. Big mistake. His hot chocolate eyes heated her to the core. Like JD, he was so intense, but about different things. Marty was just plain curious about life.

Dad returned with a little pile of first aid supplies and a pair of wire clippers. He set his goods on the counter and shut the toilet lid.

"Put your right foot up here."

Marty complied but wobbled. Abby let go of his hand and slid against his side, wrapping her arm around his waist. To keep him steady, of course.

He turned his intense eyes on her again, then settled his arm around her shoulders.

Dad took the wire clippers to the ring on Marty's ankle. "I don't think the taser will work this far from the lab, but better to be safe." He squeezed the clippers and emitted a tiny grunt before a crack rang out. Dad set the clippers on the floor, wrenched the ring off Marty's ankle, and tossed it on the counter.

Marty put his foot down, so Abby left his side and picked up the taser. A plastic shell coated the outside of the ring, but inside, pairs of electrodes were evenly spaced.

Barbaric.

"Go ahead and sit down," Dad told Marty.

Marty obeyed. Dad placed his hand on the back of Marty's head and tipped it forward. "Hold very still. I'm no surgeon."

Dad folded Marty's left ear forward and ran a finger over the top edge. Abby could see a black line through the skin. *Eww.*

"It's going to hurt for a second," Dad said, putting the razor into position. "One … two … three."

Abby winced as Dad carved along the black line. Marty twitched. Then Dad tossed the razor into the sink and pushed at the black line with his thumbnail.

Marty's breath hitched.

"Got it!" Dad held a bloody black chip in the palm of his hand. He snapped it in half with his fingers and set it on the counter. "I'll take that into town and drop it somewhere just in case."

Dad moved to the sink to wash his hands, and Abby took over. She swabbed Marty's cut with an alcohol wipe and covered it with a bandage.

"All done," she said.

"Thank you, Daughter Abby."

"She's not daughter to you," Dad said. "She's just Abby. Abby Goyer."

Marty looked from Dad into Abby's eyes. "Thank you, Abby Goyer."

How sweet was that? Abby beamed. She liked the way he said her name, without the baiting intonation JD used.

Dad turned the water off. "They hadn't known he'd left the building until just before I went home. All day they thought he was hiding somewhere. Martyr has a lot of little hiding spots, don't you?"

"I help Baby hide, and sometimes Hummer."

Dad patted Marty on the shoulder. "Dr. Kane was out of the office all morning and by the time he arrived, the guards had started to suspect you'd gotten outside somehow—mostly because of the missing keycards."

Marty's face flushed.

Dad went on. "When Dr. Kane demanded to see the surveillance tapes from last night, the lab went into an uproar. I guess he hadn't asked for surveillance tapes in so long no one remembered how to do it. Then he wanted them to pull Martyr's code up on the tracker system, which is something they've *never* had to use. They didn't even have the computer software set up. Got spoiled with the video surveillance, I guess. Dr. Kane put a guy on it, but he'd barely started when I left. The lower levels were on lockdown. Dr. Kane sent everyone home who wasn't necessary.

"Long story short, we've got to get him out of our house. If the parking lot has a surveillance tape, and I'm sure it does, we need to find someplace else for him before they see it, otherwise—"

"I can take him to see Kylee's brother. He'll be able to help us, I think." Didn't all pastors take vows to help the orphans and widows or something?

"We can't drag more people into this," Dad said.

"But we need someplace to keep him outside of our house, in case anyone from the lab comes looking. Kylee's brother is a pastor. He'll keep everything confidential."

Dad groaned softly, so Abby kept going. "And I think you should call the police—after Marty is safe, of course. Tell them Marty came here in the back of your truck, but you didn't know."

"I *didn't* know."

"Exactly. But then we say I freaked out when he snuck inside my room, and you came running, then called the police. We make it seem like this just happened."

Dad tipped back his head. "That way we won't look involved."

Marty's eyebrows sank. "What are the police?"

"Police are people who enforce order and safety and laws," Abby said.

"Like Rolo and Johnson?"

"Kind of," Dad said. "But police aren't … They don't … They're nicer. They're on our side."

Abby squeezed Marty's hand. "It'll be okay. Then Dad can call Jason Farms and report it, saying he didn't realize it was you until after he called the police." She turned to Dad. "You should ask them what you should do next. Make them think you're still on their side."

Dad shot Abby a withering glare. "I never said I wasn't on their side."

Marty looked terribly confused. "You want them to find me?"

"No." Abby took Martyr's hand. "But we don't want to look suspicious. They won't find you at Pastor Scott's place. Trust me."

"I trust you, Abby Goyer."

She smiled. Cloned boys were way nicer than the regular ones. Cloned JDs, anyway.

[CHAPTER FOURTEEN]

MARTYR HAD NEVER RIDDEN inside a car. He liked the red color of this one very much, but the *seatbelt* reminded him of the restraints on the exam tables at the Farm. He shifted in his seat, pulling at the confining strap across his chest and staring at the surroundings flashing by. The only thing that made it bearable was the fact Abby's car smelled sweet like her. He gripped the handle above the door as she steered around the curves in the road. The car moved very fast over the hard snow, and twice, when Abby slowed at a red sign that said STOP, the car skidded over the white line.

Martyr wasn't convinced this was normal.

Abby steered the car into an open area with many other cars

of different sizes, colors, and styles. She stopped and climbed out. Martyr followed her toward a tall facility with many windows. The sky was starting to grow dim, and the lights shone brightly from the glass panes.

Martyr slipped on the icy ground, not used to the boots Dr. Goyer had loaned him. He was glad to have them, as they—and the red *Christmas* socks—kept his feet from touching the freezing ground, but they were tight, pinched his toes, and felt awkward to walk in.

Abby grabbed his arm. "Careful. It's really slick here."

Martyr wanted to answer, but her statement seemed so obvious, he wasn't certain she sought a response. As she drew him closer, her sweet smell reached his nose. It was harder to detect in the cold air, but still pleasant. He liked how she worried over him. No one had ever worried over Martyr like this. Not since Dr. Woman, anyway.

"Kylee said he's in apartment 5C," Abby said. "Try to remember that in case you leave for some reason. But don't leave unless I come for you or tell you otherwise."

"5C," Martyr repeated as Abby pressed a button on a silver box attached to a black gate.

"And keep my cell phone in case you need it." She held out the red device.

Martyr took the device from her, running his fingers over the smooth, red top. *Cell phone?*

"Hello?" The voice came from the box.

"Pastor Scott? This is Abby Goyer. Kylee's friend? She said she called you. Is this a bad time? We really need your help."

"Not at all, come on up."

The box emitted a metallic buzz, one Martyr wasn't sure he liked. Abby pushed open the gate, took Martyr by the hand, and went inside, towing him along. Her touch—even wrapped in the black glove—sent a wave of heat through his body. Her hand was small and always seemed to know what to do. Her hands would never hurt anyone, either; Martyr just knew it.

A tall man with dark brown skin answered door 5C. His hair

was very short and black, and a short beard shaded his chin. He opened the door wide enough for Abby and Martyr to enter. Martyr tried not to stare, but the man's skin was even darker than Dr. Max's.

"Have a seat, guys." The man motioned to a long, brown, L-shaped *sectional*, similar to the one shown on TV. This room also had a TV, much smaller than the one at Abby's facility.

Abby sat in the center of the sectional. Martyr sat beside her. A woman with short, curly black hair stepped out of a doorway at the back of the room. Her skin was lighter brown, like Dr. Max's. And there was something wrong with this woman: her stomach protruded out in front abnormally, making the fabric of her shirt stretch tight over her belly like she was hiding something. She took her time lowering herself onto the end of the sectional, as if her body were injured.

The woman's smile took up most her face. "Hi, I'm Aliza, Scott's wife." She leaned over and held out her hand.

Martyr stared at her hand. Was he supposed to do something? He turned to Abby and whispered, "What's *wife*?"

"I'll explain later." Abby reached across Martyr's lap and grasped Aliza's hand briefly. "I'm Abby."

Martyr whispered again, "Is she a broken?"

Abby gave him a curious smile. "Why do you ask?"

Martyr touched his stomach. "She has an abnormal growth."

Abby giggled, her green eyes sparkling. "Aliza's pregnant. I'm sure she's perfectly healthy."

Martyr wanted to ask what *pragment* was but figured now was the wrong time.

Pastor Scott sat on the arm of a recliner across the room. There had been many recliners "on sale now" on the TV as well.

"You're JD Kane, right?" Pastor Scott asked. "I saw you play against Colony at regionals."

Again Martyr looked to Abby, not knowing what to say.

Abby scooted to the edge of the sectional. "Pastor Scott, something amazing has been going on in this community for a long time. Completely unethical, but amazing. Did Kylee tell you anything about my dad?"

"Only that the two of you have some major differences of opinions."

"My dad's a molecular biologist. For years he's been seeking cures for diseases via embryonic stem cell technology. It's a pretty controversial line of work, but my mom had cancer, and even though Mom disagreed with Dad's line of work, he was desperate. Anyway, this is the first job Dad has taken since we lost Mom last year. I had hoped he was working someplace … normal."

Martyr had no parents, but he could imagine that losing a mother must be horrible. Losing Dr. Woman and the J:1s and J:2s had been hard enough.

"JD Kane is my lab partner at Fishhook High," Abby said. "He was at my house last night studying. Kylee was there too. When they left, I went up to my room and found Marty." She placed her hand on Martyr's thigh, causing his stomach to lighten. "I thought it was JD, playing some weirdo prank, until JD called my cell phone from his truck. He'd forgotten some of his books and wanted me to run them out to him since my dad didn't seem to like him much."

"JD was on the phone, but this guy"—Pastor Scott pointed at Martyr—"was in your room?"

"Exactly," Abby said. "I ran out to give JD his books—he really was out in his truck, *with* hair—and when I came back inside, Marty was still in my room. He said he stole my dad's keycard, got out of the lab, and rode to my house in the back of Dad's truck. I guess I should explain my dad works at an underground lab called Jason Farms, which is run by Dr. *Jason* Kane. According to Marty, there are fifty-five Jasons on this *Farm*. I think they're all clones of Dr. Kane."

Pastor Scott's lips twisted in a small smile. "Real cute, guys. Did Danny Chang put you up to this? 'Cause I'm gonna get that guy good."

"You have to believe me," Abby said. "Marty is in danger—the scientists want him back. Please, can he stay here for now? Just until things calm down? Dad is worried they'll come to the house any minute."

Pastor Scott glanced at Aliza. "Abby, we've just met JD—I mean, your friend. I don't think—"

"Marty's the nicest guy in the world, I promise. You don't have anything to worry about. May he sleep on your couch, at least for tonight? He has a lot of questions about God that I don't know how to answer. The Bible doesn't really talk about cloning, so—"

"Okay," Aliza said. "He can stay while we sort this out, but if his dad comes looking, we have to let him go. We want to help, but we can't harbor a runaway."

"O-kay. Good. Thank you." Abby closed her eyes for a moment. "But he's *not* JD Kane. Look, if you stop by the school tomorrow at lunch, I'll sit with JD, so I can prove it to you. Trust me, I wouldn't offer to sit with him unless it was important." Her voice rose. "If we don't help Marty, they'll kill him. If he dies, the other fifty-four boys will likely die too."

Martyr tensed. Could that be true? Only the J:3s were scheduled to expire soon.

Pastor Scott raised his hands. "Okay, okay. Calm down. We'll keep an open mind."

"Can we talk to your dad about this?" Aliza asked.

"Yeah," Abby said. "I'll have him call you after we deal with the police."

Aliza raised an eyebrow, and her voice squeaked out, "Excuse me?"

"Don't worry. It's only to throw off Dr. Kane's guards." Abby stood, and Martyr stood with her. She turned and looked into his eyes. "I'd better go before they change their minds. You'll be safe here. I'll call when I know what to do next." She bit her thumbnail, then leaned up on her toes and pressed her lips against his cheek. Martyr's body tingled with electricity, like when the ankle taser was activated but without the pain.

Abby pulled away too soon, and the pleasantness of her touch faded into a sensation of fear. She was really going to leave him with these people? She said she would call, but how? He followed her to the door, still clutching the cell phone in his hand. Perhaps she meant for him to talk into the device like she had. Would Pastor Scott or the pragment Aliza show him how to use it? "Will I see you again?"

Abby grinned, but her eyes did not sparkle. "Of course, silly. I'll come back as soon as I can."

Then she threw her arms around him, like she did before leaving that morning for school. Martyr felt another small burst of electricity. He buried his nose in her hair and inhaled, hoping to commit her scent to memory.

"Don't worry, okay?" Abby said. "I'm really smart about these things. Once I get a project, I never fail. You'll be okay, I promise."

Then she was gone.

When Abby walked into the house, the first thing she saw was the box on the counter. She peeked inside, wondering why Dad had brought his things home.

"Abby, honey? That you?" Dad walked down the first two steps from upstairs and paused when he met her eyes.

Abby motioned to the box. "I meant to ask you earlier. What's all this?"

"Dr. Kane asked us to take home any personal belongings, just in case."

"In case the cops came snooping around?"

Dad sighed and walked down the stairs. "Looks that way." He sat on a stool at the counter. "I know you've always disagreed with my work, but—"

"Dad, can we not do this right—"

"You're right. About a lot of things. I'm not saying you're right about everything, but a lot, okay? What Dr. Kane is doing with those boys is wrong."

"Thanks, Dad."

She put her arm around his shoulder, and he pulled her close. "Thank you, for not letting me lie to myself about it, honey. You ready for me to call the police?"

Abby took a deep breath. "I think so."

Dad placed the call, explaining how his daughter had found an intruder in her room and scared him away and that Abby wasn't hurt. They promised to send a car as soon as possible.

Abby went up to her room to pray. She went over the situation with God, hoping to feel some validation about their plans, but instead her prayers drifted from Marty to her dad's involvement in a cloning lab, then settled on her mother.

Mom would have known exactly what to do.

Tears streaked down Abby's cheeks. People always said you never know when it might be the last time you do certain things in your life. Most of Abby's final memories with her mom hadn't been that way. They'd known Mom was dying and had plenty of time to fit in a last trip to various places, but the memories weren't completely joyful because they all knew it had been the last: The last trip to Niagara Falls. The last trip to New York City. The last time standing together on the Empire State Building. The last time making cookies. The last time sitting in church. The list went on and on. Abby relived them all, forgetting that she had been praying. Dwelling on the loss that now felt so fresh. So raw.

Why had it happened? In her heart, Abby knew she didn't need to know; she trusted God. Still, her heart ached for what could have been. She longed for the moment when she would see the good in this loss, how God had made beauty from ashes.

For just a moment, Abby indulged herself in trying to make an answer fit, trying to understand God's plan. If her mother hadn't died, Dad might not have quit his job at GWU, because he wouldn't have been as desperate to try and save Mom. They all would still be living in Washington DC, and they wouldn't know Marty existed. Marty might not have even managed to escape, for surely the scientists who worked there for years knew better than to leave their keycards lying around.

The bittersweet reasoning eased some pain in Abby's heart. A new sorrow overtook her mind: the idea of Marty living underground, never seeing the sun or sky, never breathing fresh air, fifty-five of him, all different ages, some strong, some broken, all prisoners in the name of science. Baby and Hummer and the one without legs …

Abby spiraled into another wave of emotion, pleading to God that he would expose the wrongness and protect the boys. If it wasn't done just right, the government might take the boys away to a new prison to be studied by different scientists. The doorbell jolted her back to reality. She snapped out of prayer mode, said a quick amen, and peeked out the window. The cops were here.

She smoothed her hair and went into the bathroom to rinse off her face, which didn't bring down the swelling as much as she'd like. She ran cold water over a washcloth and held it against her eyes. It seemed like she stood there forever. She turned the wash-cloth over and put the cooler side on her eyelids. What was going on downstairs? Would Dad even involve—?

"Abby, honey?" Dad's voice called from downstairs.

Finally. She draped the washcloth over the towel rack and took a deep breath. "Coming."

Abby descended the stairs and found two officers sitting on the couch in the living room—a man with a thick brown moustache and a woman with a long blonde ponytail. The woman's crystal-blue eyes made Abby think of a human lie detector. She hoped her perceptions were wrong.

Dad was sitting in the armchair across from them. "Here she is."

Abby walked over to her dad and perched on the arm of his chair.

He put his arm around her waist. "Abby, these officers have come to ask some questions about the intruder."

Abby forced a small smile and glanced from one cop to the other. "I'm not sure how helpful I'll be."

"I'm Officer Jackson," the female cop said. "This is Officer McNear." She gestured to the guy with the mustache. "Were you hurt at all?"

"No," Abby said.

"Your father already told us his version of what happened, but we'd like to get an official statement from you. You feel up to that?"

"Sure. I went up my room, mad because Dad made my friends

leave. We were just studying, but Dad kicked everyone out. I was"—Abby glanced at her father—"really embarrassed."

Jackson's gaze drilled into Abby. "What happened next?"

Abby looked to where Einstein was eating out of his dish. "When I turned around, a boy was in my room, crouched in the corner."

"Did he speak to you?" McNear asked, his voice a rumbling bass.

The sound pulled Abby's gaze away from Einstein. "No. He just sat there. I yelled at him to get out and he ran."

McNear turned to Dad. "Did you see him leave, Mr. Goyer?"

"I didn't. I'd stepped into my office in the den. I heard Abby yell, then the door slam. That's it."

McNear smoothed his moustache and looked to Abby. "Why did you wait until today to call this in?"

Abby jerked her head to look at her dad. He was supposed to have said that this had just happened. Talk about raising a red flag in an investigator's mind. "Uh ..."

"It's my fault," Dad said. "I didn't want to blow things out of proportion for a high school prank. But Abby was so insistent about what she saw, well ... after I slept on it, I thought it wouldn't hurt to report it."

Abby sighed inside. Then a sudden overwhelming feeling of shame overtook her. She had talked her dad into lying to the cops and now they were getting caught in their deceit.

Jackson wrote something down in her notebook, then glanced at Abby. "Could you describe him?"

"Uh ... he was bald ... and tall and ... thin." Abby scrambled to think if her answer might hurt Marty. She didn't see how it could. "He was wearing gray sweats and a white lab coat. Like the kind a doctor wears."

Jackson turned to Abby's dad. "So he changed his clothes after your daughter saw him?"

Abby frowned at her father.

"I guess he must have." Dad shrugged. "All I know is that I found those clothes on my bedroom floor."

Abby followed Dad's nod to the kitchen. Marty's sweats, T-shirt, and lab coat were folded in a neat pile on one of the kitchen counters. Ug. They really should have rehearsed what they were going to say, which only confirmed the inkling in the back of her mind that this was wrong. They were making up a story, wasting the officers' time. She hated people who did stuff like this.

"How old did he look, Miss Goyer?" Jackson asked.

"Seventeen or eighteen."

"Did you recognize him?"

Abby paused. She wasn't supposed to know any clones existed, so in her mind, the boy in her room would have been JD Kane. She didn't want to lie anymore, nor did she want to get JD in trouble. If she said the intruder looked like JD, would that help the case against Jason Farms? If JD had an alibi, would that give the police reason to search the barn? Perhaps.

"He looked kind of like JD Kane, a boy at my school. But the thing is, JD has hair. Even more strange, he had just called me on my cell because he'd forgotten some books when our study group ended. JD was waiting outside when I brought him the books, and when I went back upstairs, the guy was still in my room."

"So you saw JD outside when he was supposedly in your bedroom?" Jackson asked.

Now Abby was having second thoughts about the tell-the-cops plan. What if the police started looking for a JD lookalike? How was that going to help Marty?

"You and JD Kane are friends?" Officer Jackson's gaze bored into Abby's.

"He's my lab partner."

"Have you ever dated?"

"He asked me out, but I turned him down. He's not really my type."

"How did he take that?"

"Take what?"

"Your rejection?"

Great job—you just handed them a motive. Officer Jackson thought JD had come into Abby's room because he was stalking her or something. "Oh, JD's fine. Actually, he seemed more determined than ever to get me to go out with him once I—"

Dad coughed.

"—said no." She glanced at her dad. Oh. Her answers weren't helping, and now it really looked like JD was stalking her. She should have left it at "strange bald guy I didn't recognize" and been done with it. She would never lie again. It was one of the Ten Commandments for a reason. Doing it only made things worse.

The cops asked a bunch more questions, mostly about JD. Abby did her best to paint JD in a favorable light, but she got the impression the cops had their own preconceived opinion of JD Kane.

When the cops finished asking questions, Dad walked them to the door. "Thanks for looking into this."

"We'll head over to the Kane residence next," Officer Jackson said. "We'll call if we find out anything. Let us know if there are any more … strange visits."

"Will do."

Abby winced inside. JD was getting pulled into this mess, but it was his *dad's* fault for cloning himself.

Dad called the lab next. He told them he called the police because of an intruder and that later his daughter had described him as JD Kane. Dad assumed it had been Martyr.

While Dad talked to the lab, Abby escaped to her room, conscience nagging. She was glad Marty was at Pastor Scott's place and that they'd thrown the Jason Farm scientists off the trail, but could she have accomplished the same thing without bending the truth? Calling the police had seemed like the perfect idea at the time, but now that it was over, it wasn't sitting so well. What if JD got in trouble for something he didn't do?

She crawled under the covers on her bed and snuggled against Einstein. Her obsession with forensics and detective work had gone too far. She, Abigail Goyer, a girl whose goal in life was to enforce the law, had broken it today. Mom would have been disappointed. Mom had always told her it was up to the two of them to show Dad what loving God was all about.

Abby had failed today in a big way.

It had been her idea to lie to the police, and Dad had gone along with it. She'd led her father astray. This thought sent Abby into a long bawl-fest. It had been ages since she cried, and this made twice in one day. She cried so long it hurt. She couldn't breathe. Snot dripped everywhere. Her eyes stung. Her sobbing scared Einstein so much he squirmed out of her grip and darted out the door.

The exit of her dearest friend made her cry harder. She prayed long and hard. She knew God had forgiven her for the lies, but that didn't mean there wouldn't be consequences for her actions. She dreaded those consequences.

Good thing Abby wasn't in charge of running the universe. Things would sure get messy in a hurry. Deep down, she trusted that God would take care of Marty and the other clones, but it wasn't in her nature to sit back and not get involved. She really needed to work on giving up control. She only hoped her meddling hadn't made a bigger mess for God to clean up.

[CHAPTER FIFTEEN]

MARTYR SHIFTED UNCOMFORTABLY on the brown sectional.

Dinner had been filled with new and interesting foods he was still struggling to describe, but it also had been awkward because Pastor Scott asked many strange questions. Martyr sensed Pastor Scott becoming frustrated. The man seemed to suspect that Martyr had done something wrong.

Now they sat in the *living room*, which was what Aliza called the room with the sectional, recliner, and TV. Martyr didn't understand this title since there were no beds here. Clearly it was only one of several rooms in the facility that was being lived in.

Again, Aliza sat on the end of the sectional and Pastor Scott sat in the recliner. Martyr sat in the corner of the sectional. The pillows squished around him and gave the sense of protection against Pastor Scott and Aliza's unnerving gazes.

"Abby said you had questions about God," Pastor Scott said, fixing his brown eyes on Martyr. "Why don't we focus on those for a while?"

"Where does he live? Can you take me to his facility?"

Pastor Scott glanced at Aliza, his lips nearly frowning. "God doesn't live in any building—on earth, at least—not even a church."

"I don't understand." How could someone live nowhere? Did God roam the land like the birds and horses? "Abby said God hears my words and thoughts. But how can I hear him if I cannot find him?"

"Through prayer and reading the Bible," Pastor Scott said.

Prayer, like Abby had done before eating her food. "Is this Bible a book?"

"Here." Pastor Scott got up and pulled a book off a shelf. He flipped through it and handed it, opened, to Martyr. "This is a pretty easy-to-understand Bible. Go ahead and read some. Let me know if you have any questions. I recommend starting here, in John."

"You don't start at the beginning?"

"You can if you want, but John is probably going to give you some of the answers you're looking for. The red letters, those are God's words."

Red letters intrigued Martyr, but if Abby was wrong, and this God was not Martyr's creator, then he was wasting his time looking for answers here. "Abby told me that God made me. How do I know if that's true?"

"The only way to know for sure is to believe it. Listen, the Bible says in Jeremiah 1:5, 'Before I formed you in the womb, I knew you.' God made every human on the planet. He loves each one dearly. He created you for a purpose. And if you believe that, it can change your life."

Martyr perked up at the word *purpose*. "I want to believe so I can discover my true purpose before it is too late."

"Marty," Pastor Scott began, "why are you in such a hurry?"

"Because I will expire in fifteen days."

The house phone rang. The second ring cut off midway.

Dad yelled from downstairs, "Abby! Phone!"

She took a deep breath and picked up the receiver. "Hello?"

"Hey, it's Scott. Abby, I need you to come back over here. I'm a little worried about JD. I mean, uh … Marty. How much do you know about him?"

Abby winced. "Is he trying on your clothes?"

"He seems mentally ill, maybe even suicidal."

"Oh, he's not suicidal, he just thinks he is going to die on his eighteenth birthday. Personally, I don't think it will happen. Dad doesn't either. But you never can tell with scientists and their experiments."

"Abby, please. You're not making a lot of sense."

"I know. I'm sorry. Would it help to talk to my dad? I'll get him. Dad!" Abby carried the phone down to the kitchen. "Dad, will you explain to Pastor Scott about Marty? I don't think he believes me about the clones. He thinks Marty is mentally ill."

Dad stepped back from Abby, staring at the phone like it was infected with some kind of incurable disease. She wondered if his hesitation was more due to talking to a real live pastor than betraying any confidentiality agreement with his soon-to-be former employer.

Abby dragged him to the armchair in the living room, pushed him down, and put the phone in his hand. "Just tell him, Dad."

Dad answered Pastor Scott's questions as best as a paranoid molecular biologist who was involved in illegal activities could. Not that Abby had much experience in determining that. At first he tried to evade the truth, saying things like, "Well, that's a teenager for you," and "Well, I'm sure I don't know," and "That sounds more like your department than mine." But he seemed to give in when he said, "Well, how would you act if you were a cloned teenager who was raised in an underground lab and had never seen the light of day?"

Things were progressing now. Abby sat on the couch across from him, watching her dad's expressions as he spoke to Pastor Scott. Maybe she should have taken him over there. This was really more of an in-person type of conversation, and the situation might even cause Dad to open up to the pastor. Abby—and God—knew that Dad had plenty of questions in the faith department. He was just too proud to ask.

Dad clicked off the phone.

"What's Marty doing?" Abby asked.

"Reading a Bible. And apparently asking questions after every other sentence. Seriously, Abby, I don't think taking him there was the best plan. Are you trying to convert him or something?"

"Dad!" Abby glared at her father, whose normal response to religion was, *No, I don't believe there is a God, but I'm really angry with the way he's running things.* Real logical. "I just wanted to take him to someone trustworthy who likes to help people. Do you have a better idea?"

"No. It's just typical that the first thing that happens over there is to hand the poor kid a Bible. Talk about shoving God down your throat."

"It's my fault he's asking them about God."

"And why is that?"

"Because I prayed for our breakfast this morning."

Dad frowned.

"You know I pray over my food, Dad."

"I didn't know you did it all the time. I figured it was just to annoy me."

Abby exhaled a groan. "I pray because I want to talk to God. It has nothing to do with you ... or Marty. I thanked God for our breakfast this morning and asked him to help me and Marty. Then Marty had a lot of questions, so I answered them as best as I could."

Dad let his head fall back against the armchair.

"Dad, don't you know why Mom was so mad about your experiments? Because she trusted God to take care of her life. If God wanted her to be with him, she was okay with that."

For a moment Dad didn't say anything. He stared up at the ceiling, and Abby wondered if he had even heard her. Then he slowly, almost painfully moved his head from the back of the chair and looked straight at Abby. "That's the stupidest thing I've ever heard."

Abby stared back for a long moment, then nodded. She didn't blame him for thinking it was crazy. If you didn't know God, how could you trust him? "The thing is, I believe that too," Abby said softly. "I trust God with my life, so I try to share as much of it with him as I can. I thank him for every breath, every bite of food, every blessing. I want to spend my time on earth fulfilling the purpose God designed me for."

Dad slid to the edge of his armchair. "Wouldn't you think it was unfair if your God allows you to live only until the end of the week?"

Abby took a deep breath. "Life isn't about how many days I live, but how I live the days I have." She kicked herself when her dad leaned back in his chair; he wasn't going to accept her fortune cookie answers. "Listen, Dad, you spent your marriage trying to find a cure for Mom and you missed out on what little life she had. You took her joy, Dad, and yours, trying to save her." He looked a bit startled at what she was saying, but he appeared to be listening. And it had to be said. "Now you work for more people with that same philosophy. They want to take the lives of others because of their fear. They don't understand, so they try to find a way to control things. But God will always get his way. No scientist can change that. The only way to really live is to give up your fear and trust God." Abby's eyes got misty. "Mom taught me that."

Dad's face had a red tinge. Abby had pushed her luck way past her original bet. Another word would undoubtedly push Dad too far, and she wasn't in the mood for a text fight. Not that she had her cell phone anyway. She stared at the reflection of the living room in the picture windows.

Dad pushed himself out of the chair. "Go to bed, Abby, honey. I'll see you tomorrow."

Martyr lay on the couch with the Bible. He found this book-filled-with-smaller-books fascinating. And confusing. He read John, then Luke, and then went to the beginning and read the first few chapters of Genesis. He asked Pastor Scott dozens of questions until he and Aliza went to bed.

Martyr continued to read. He couldn't believe the doctors had kept this information from him. Everything in his heart told him it was truth. But Pastor Scott had said many people didn't believe in this book. How could that be? If the Creator of Everything made the people, how could they deny that? How could they not want to know everything about their maker?

Something clinked in the kitchen and Martyr sat up.

"Sorry," Pastor Scott whispered. "Just getting a drink."

"Pastor Scott, what is *wife*?" The Genesis chapter had told about Adam and his wife, Eve. Aliza had introduced herself to Abby and Martyr as Pastor Scott's "wife."

Pastor Scott walked into the living room and took a seat in the recliner. "Wife is a woman who's married." He held up a finger. "Before you ask, let me explain."

Martyr smiled. After a long day of questioning, Pastor Scott had figured him out.

"When a man finds a woman he loves, he asks her to marry him. If she agrees, they have a ceremony where their friends and family come to witness their vows before God. Then the woman will move in to her husband's house—which is a facility where people live. Eventually the husband and wife may decide to start a family. Aliza and I are going to have a baby. I know you noticed her belly."

"She is pragment."

"*Pregnant*. It means our baby is growing inside her. She's going to be a mother."

Martyr straightened. "How can a person be inside her?"

Pastor Scott chuckled. "That's a lesson for another day. But I told you so you'd understand where life comes from."

"Abby said the Creator of Everything makes life."

"And this is how he does it."

"It is the only way?"

"Yes."

Martyr wanted to think this over. "Thank you for answering my questions."

"You're welcome. I'm going to go back to bed now. I'll see you tomorrow morning, okay?"

Martyr lay back down. "Yes, that is okay."

Pastor Scott disappeared down the dark hallway. Martyr heard a door close.

So many new words confused his mind. *Wife, married, pregnant, mother, family, love.* Martyr suddenly wanted to ask Pastor Scott about love. He sat up again and reached for the thick black book. Maybe the Bible would say something about it.

He searched the *index* in the back for the word *love.* He was thankful Abby had brought him to such a knowledgeable man. Pastor Scott had showed Martyr how to use the index, and it had been a very valuable lesson. Martyr read several of the suggested verses with great interest, but 1 Corinthians 13:4–8 held his attention more than any other.

> *Love is patient, love is kind. It does not*
> *envy, it does not boast, it is not proud.*
> *It does not dishonor others, it is not self-*
> *seeking, it is not easily angered, it keeps no*
> *record of wrongs. Love does not delight in*
> *evil but rejoices with the truth. It always*
> *protects, always trusts, always hopes,*
> *always perseveres.*
> *Love never fails.*

Martyr read this again. Then he read it several more times.

Abby had loved him. She had been kind when she could have beaten him with a stick. She'd given him socks to warm his feet. She'd shared her sleeping bag and her cell. She'd made him breakfast with bleeding eggs. She'd taught him about the Creator of Everything. She'd hid him from Dr. Goyer so he wouldn't have to go back to the Farm, then fought for him so that Dr. Goyer removed the stinger and the tracker in his ear. She'd brought him to Pastor Scott's house to keep him safe and to learn about the Creator of Everything.

Plus, Abby said she never failed, which was exactly what the Corinthians chapter said about love.

"Once I get a project, I never fail. You'll be okay, I promise."

Abby was love, and Martyr had found her.

He never wanted to go back to the Farm. He wanted to find his own house with large windows where he could see the sky and horses that ate trees. He wanted Abby to live with him and take care of him. And he wanted to take care of her. If he had socks, he would share them with her. If he knew how to cook eggs, he would cook them for Abby.

"When a man finds a woman he loves, he asks her to marry him." That was what Pastor Scott had said. But what would Abby say? Pastor Scott hadn't been clear about what happened if the woman said no.

Friday. Abby hadn't wanted to come to school, but if the scientists were watching, they might be suspicious if she didn't. She pulled *Fahrenheit 451* out of her locker for AP English class and grabbed her government book as well, since the classrooms were close. She closed her locker and jumped when she saw JD leaning against the locker beside hers.

"You scared me!"

He grinned, but the joy didn't reach his eyes. "You know what's really scary? Prison."

Abby shifted the books in her hands until the right corners

were flush. Her heart beat wildly in her chest. She inched backward and turned toward class, deciding to play dumb. "I imagine that would be scary."

"Do you?" He strode beside her and handed her a book. *Lupus and You.* "I said I'd get it for you, didn't I? Friends keep promises. And we're friends, *right*?" His tone was odd. Taunting.

"Thanks, JD. This will totally help our project." And if the bill was still inside, it would be evidence for the police.

"I hope you were able to work on it some last night. I was a little busy at the *police station*. They questioned me for hours after some girl accused me of breaking into her house and attacking her. They wouldn't say who it was."

Abby turned down the west hallway and wove her way toward American Lit. A tinge of hope flooded her. If JD didn't know she'd been the girl who'd spoken to the cops, maybe it would all go away.

JD caught up and slipped his arm over her shoulder, walking alongside her like a boyfriend. "I had no clue what they were talking about." He suddenly stepped into an alcove where the doors to the shop class cut into the wall, pulling Abby with him. "I tried to tell them that, but they didn't believe me." He spun around and pushed her up against the cool, cinderblock wall, his eyes inches from hers. "Why would you tell them that, Abby? Do you hate me that much? Am I so awful to be around? The other girls like me— *all of them.* Why don't you?"

Abby's heart pounded in her ears. So much for hope. She shook her head, tears welling in her eyes at the pain of JD's thumbs boring into the tender muscles of her rotator cuffs. If he murdered her, the mortician would find bruises there. *Only I would think about gross anatomy at a time like this.* She shook the tangent away. "He looked just like you, I swear."

"Just like me, huh?"

Abby swallowed and looked over his shoulder to where Kylee stood watching.

Are you okay? Kylee mouthed.

"No," Abby said answering both questions. Kylee vanished.

Abby looked up into JD's dark eyes. "I told them it wasn't you. Because he was bald."

"They thought I was wearing a disguise." His gaze boiled into hers, and heat seeped all the way to her toes. "Why do you have to be such a self-righteous little snob, huh? Why does everything have to be your way?" Then he kissed her. Hard. She dropped her books, reached up, and pushed at his face. He jerked back and flashed an angry grin. "Does he kiss just like me too, Abby?"

"Stop it!" She stomped on his suede sneaker and tried to slap him.

He dodged her assault easily, but his face flushed red and he kept her pinned.

"Let go of me!"

"Jason Dean!"

JD stepped back instantly at the sound of his mother's voice and swiped the back of his hand across his lips.

Mrs. Kane stood behind him to the left, arms crossed, expression smoldering. "To class, Miss Goyer!"

Abby didn't have to be told twice. She crouched to gather her books and ran to Mr. Chung's classroom without looking back. She slid into a desk in the back row—a place she never sat—buried her head into her arms, and burst into tears.

When she arrived in calculus class, JD was already sitting in his assigned seat to the left of hers. Abby slid into her desk and scooted it a few inches to the right.

"Abby—"

"This *self-righteous little snob* doesn't want to talk to you."

He slumped back in his chair and ran a hand through his hair. "You deserved it. I was there for *three hours* with that man-hater detective, Jackson, ripping me a new—"

"I *said* I don't want to talk to you."

He growled to himself. "Mom said I'm not allowed to talk to you anyway. She said your dad is trying to cause trouble for my dad, and you only came over to snoop in Dad's office."

Abby stared straight ahead, trying not to show that JD's words had any meaning. Did Dr. Kane suspect her of something? Did that mean he didn't believe the story she told the cops? Had he seen the footage of her snooping around the barn? Did he think she knew where Marty was?

JD leaned across the aisle. "Abby, if you know something about my dad, please tell me. I know he and my mom are keeping something from me."

Abby looked at him then, not knowing what to say. Clearly he'd been raised by two maniacs. Was he telling the truth? Or had his parents put him up to this to see what she knew? She couldn't trust him. "I don't know what you're talking about. Why don't you just take no for an answer and leave me alone?"

He combed his fingers through his hair again. "Come on. Don't think about it like that. I didn't mean to scare you."

"It's way too late for *that* apology, JD. No one deserves to be attacked."

"I didn't attack you."

She turned her head toward him in slow motion and folded her arms.

"Fine." He sat back again and started scribbling the math problems on the board into his notebook. "Try to leave the cops out of it this time, will you?"

Abby sighed. "Just—" She prayed she was doing the right thing. "Just go to work with your dad sometime and see what goes on at Jason Farms."

"They kill cows."

Abby let out a fake laugh. "They kill more than that."

[CHAPTER SIXTEEN]

MARTYR SAT IN THE FRONT SEAT of Pastor Scott's car, which he called a *van*. Pastor Scott had driven to Abby's *high* school. The building was not a skyscraper, though. It was only two levels, very long, and the color of pancakes.

"School is out, so they should be coming any minute," Pastor Scott said.

He'd parked his white van that said "Fishhook Community Church" on the side, next to a blue truck. Pastor Scott had explained the different types of vehicles to Martyr on the ride over, and Martyr was still amazed at how many kinds and colors there were. He especially liked the shiny, blue truck sitting beside the van. Pastor Scott said it belonged to JD Kane. For some reason, Pastor Scott had hoped Martyr might recognize it.

He did not.

Two students left the high school facility together—two women. Martyr's posture straightened. They looked so different from Abby. One had hair the color of corn, long and straight. The other's hair was cut short like Aliza's but was hot pink—like the inside of Abby's sleeping bag—and stuck up all over in a way that fascinated him. He wanted to get out of the van to look closer, but he'd promised Pastor Scott he would stay inside.

Suddenly people were everywhere. Boys and women of all shapes and sizes, wearing many colors. Several boys wore matching coats that were blue with white sleeves, but other than that, everyone looked different. And they all had hair.

How could everyone be so unique?

A tall boy approached the van. Martyr cocked his head to the side and examined him. He had a familiar gait, a familiar posture, a familiar shape. It came to him suddenly. It was the boy in the painting in Dr. Kane's office. The Jason who had hair and did not live on the Farm.

The Jason stopped at the blue truck. As he went to open the door, his eyes flashed toward Martyr's. The Jason froze, his mouth hanging open like Baby's did sometimes when he was having a frozen fit.

"Unbelievable." Pastor Scott's voice shook slightly, making Martyr jump. "Marty, lock the door."

Martyr studied the door, unsure of where the locking device was.

"The button thingy. Push it down!" Pastor Scott leaned over Martyr and swatted at the button, but the door swung open.

"What the …?" The Jason leaned his face close to Martyr's. "Are you the creep who's been harassing Abby?"

Martyr's chest swelled. "What happened to Abby?"

The Jason grabbed the front of the thick shirt that Pastor Scott had loaned Martyr and dragged him from the van. The cold air gripped Martyr as tightly as the Jason did.

"Hey, now!" Pastor Scott yelled. "Let's not do anything stupid."

The Jason squeezed Martyr's shirt in his fist. "Why'd you go in her house?"

Pastor Scott appeared at the Jason's side. "JD, let him go. Let's talk this out."

Martyr straightened. JD? Yes. This was the boy Abby knew. She liked his hair. Martyr looked at JD's hair and wondered if his would look the same if it ever grew out.

"Answer me, you freak. Why'd you attack her?"

"I would never hurt Abby. I have love for her. I want her to be my wife."

JD drew back a fist and punched Martyr's face.

Martyr's nose burned. His legs collapsed out from under him, and he fell onto the cold, gray ground. JD crouched over him, still clutching the front of his shirt. He struck Martyr again, this time hitting Martyr's left eye. Martyr rolled onto his side and curled into a ball. *Perhaps this Jason is similar to Iron Man.*

JD grabbed the back of his shirt and tried to pull him up. "Not so tough now, are you? You only pick on girls? Huh?" JD kicked Martyr's back.

Pastor Scott's voice floated somewhere above. "Come on, that's enough. Break it up."

"Listen up, freak." JD's voice was so near Martyr could feel warm breath on his ear. "You stay away from Abby, you hear me? If you lay a hand on her, I'll kill you."

"JD?"

Martyr's heart leaped at the sound of Abby's voice. He scrambled to a sitting position and forced open his throbbing eye. Abby stood at the front of the van, face pale, lips parted. Martyr hoped she wasn't angry with him.

"Don't you worry about this loser anymore, Abby," JD said, strutting toward her. "He's nothing I can't handle." JD reached out and pulled Abby into an embrace.

She shoved him away. "Don't touch me!" Her eyes, wild with fright, jumped from JD to Martyr.

Martyr didn't want to move for fear of what she might say. The power of her words amazed him. She held all that mattered in her hands.

From the look on JD's face, it was the same for him.

"Marty?" Her voice was soft and unsure. "Pastor Scott, is that Marty?"

"I'm sorry, Abby," Pastor Scott said. "I just wanted to get a look at JD. I shouldn't have parked so close to his truck."

"Get a look at *me*? Who are you people? Abby, what is going on? Who is this freak?"

Abby pushed past JD and crouched beside Martyr. She turned to look at JD. "What did you do?"

"I was helping you," he said. "You said some bald JD look-alike attacked you. Well, here's a bald JD look-alike, so I attacked him first."

"You didn't!"

"The dude stole my face. He attacked you. Be mad at him, not me."

But Abby turned back to Martyr and touched his cheek, brushing her warm thumb under his throbbing eye. He closed his eyes and relaxed at her contact.

She whispered, "I'm sorry. This is all my fault." She stood up and faced JD. "I didn't mean for you to get in trouble when I talked to the police. I hoped you had an alibi."

"What are you talking about?" JD said.

Pastor Scott helped Martyr stand.

"I only talked to the police because I was trying to help Marty," Abby said.

JD sniffed in a long breath, his chest swelling. "My mom grounded me for a month! She thinks I did it. She thinks I'm obsessed with you."

Martyr had to agree with JD's mother. JD looked quite obsessed.

Pastor Scott opened the van door and helped Martyr inside.

JD's angry eyes flickered from Martyr. "Why does *he* need your help?"

Abby turned to look JD straight in the eye. "He escaped from your dad's lab. Your dad's been cloning people, and here's the weird thing: I think you might be a clone too."

JD stared at Abby, eyebrows crinkled, then laughed. "You can't clone people."

Abby's serious expression didn't change. "Your dad has lupus. It's getting bad, and I think he needs a kidney transplant. Problem is, all his clones have lupus too."

JD's face relaxed into a frown.

Pastor Scott pushed down the locking device on the door and slammed it shut, muting Abby and JD's conversation. Martyr strained to hear what they were saying. He could no longer hear Abby, but he could hear JD loud and clear.

"That's not true!"

Abby yelled something and poked JD in the chest.

"You think he's better than me? He's a weakling!"

Abby responded by shaking her head and gesturing to the van. Martyr felt useless. He wanted to protect Abby, but what could he do?

"I was right the first time!" JD yelled. "You are a self-righteous snob!"

Abby slid open the back door to the van and climbed in.

JD stepped closer. "He said he wants to marry you, just so you know. You think I'm obsessed? Must be my *DNA*."

In one swift yank, Abby slid the door shut. Pastor Scott started the van.

JD stood by the blue truck, staring after them as the van drove away. Martyr felt sorry for him.

"Move back here by me, Marty. I want to look at your eye."

Martyr unclasped his seatbelt, stepped awkwardly to the long seat, and buckled himself beside Abby. Her black coat was unzipped, and he could see that she was wearing a purple shirt today.

She touched his cheek again, staring at his face with furrowed brows. Martyr copied her, not meaning to at first, but it was easy to keep his face in that position when he realized what had just happened.

"Will JD speak about this to Dr. Kane?" he asked.

She released his face and slouched down in her seat. "Probably."

"What must I do?"

"I don't know."

"Send me back to the Farm. I don't want to bring danger to you or Dr. Goyer. Besides, Baby needs me. I should never have abandoned him."

She trained her green eyes on his. "Did you tell JD you wanted to marry me?"

He saw Pastor Scott's eyes in the tiny reflecting glass, looking at him. Martyr was suddenly very warm. "Yes."

"Why?"

"Because you are love. I read it in One Corinthians. And Pastor Scott said when a man finds love he asks the woman to marry him. Did I understand correctly, Pastor Scott?"

Pastor Scott chuckled. "Well, sort of. But Marty, you've only known Abby for what, two days?"

Martyr felt like he was falling inside himself. "That's not long enough to know love?"

"Not really," Pastor Scott said.

Shame washed over Martyr. He was a fool to think that someone like Abby would love him. What if he expired before he knew love?

"It's just that usually the girl and guy date for a while before getting married." Abby took his hand in hers. "Let's slow things down just a bit, okay?"

Martyr squeezed Abby's hand and breathed until his heart settled back into its normal cadence. Her smell filled every breath, and Martyr ignored his disappointment at having misunderstood love and enjoyed simply sitting beside her.

But Abby had more to say. "Still, even a second is long enough to experience what's described in 1 Corinthians. I'm thrilled that you see me as a personification of that kind of love, Marty. Many would disagree with you there." She huffed a wry laugh. "JD being first in line."

Martyr could not imagine how anyone could see Abby as anything but love.

They sat in silence as Pastor Scott drove away from the school, but instead of looking out the window, Martyr focused on Abby's hand, which still was wrapped around his. He found it very hard not to think about what she had said.

"It's just that usually the girl and the guy ate for a while before getting married. Let's slow things down just a bit, okay?"

Slow down and eat?

"I think we should go to the cops," Abby said suddenly, pulling Martyr back to reality. "With the whole truth this time. We need to get Baby and the others out. I don't know what will happen, but we have to try."

"Okay." Martyr would do whatever Abby thought best.

"Are you sure?" Pastor Scott asked. "They won't believe you at first. I sure didn't. Unless they see JD and Marty together, they'll think you're making it up."

"What else can we do? JD saw Marty, and as soon as he can he'll tell Dr. Kane that we're with you. So Marty shouldn't go back to your house. He isn't safe anywhere. The police have to help."

"The police might just call Dr. Kane to come down and pick up his son, thinking he's drugged out. Marty looks like JD. It's what I'd do."

"Will you drop us at my house, then? We'll see what my dad thinks."

"You got it." Pastor Scott said. "And Abby, I'm sorry I didn't believe you. It's still so odd. Let me know when you decide to go to the police and I'll come with. The more people you have to corroborate your story, the better."

When Pastor Scott dropped them off, Dad wasn't home, which raised a lot of concerns Abby didn't want to deal with. She was tempted to call Pastor Scott and ask him to take her back for her car at the school—the scientists could just as easily come to her house as to Pastor Scott's apartment. But with no cars in her driveway, maybe they'd assume no one was here. Plus, she needed time to think. She hung up her coat in the front closet. Marty took off the green and brown plaid quilted flannel shirt he was wearing and hung it next to Abby's coat.

"Where did you get that?" she asked.

"Pastor Scott loaned it to me."

How very Fishhook, Alaska.

Marty's eye was swollen; she needed to get some ice on it. But first, she had to know where dad was. "Do you have my phone?"

Marty dug it out of his front pocket and handed it to her. She left a message on Dad's cell, then ordered a pizza.

"Why don't you go lie down on the couch? I'll get something for your bruise." Abby went into the kitchen, took a package of frozen corn from the freezer, and wrapped it in a dishtowel. She walked back to the sofa and kneeled down. "Hold this on your eye. It's cold, but will help the swelling."

Marty placed the wrapped corn on his face, and Abby sank to her rear on the floor and leaned her head back on the edge of the couch. What a day. Her mind spun with the bizarre events. She felt sorry for JD. Not for how he'd treated her—the creepazoid—but for the trouble her accusation had caused.

She wasn't really a self-righteous snob, was she?

Something tickled her scalp. Marty was touching her hair.

What to do with him?

He was so sweet and naïve and innocent—like no other boy on the planet. He might have the same DNA as JD, but he was not the same person. And he wanted to marry her—because she was the first person ever to show him kindness without an agenda. Marty knew how to love instinctively, but she doubted anyone had ever truly loved him. No mother had kissed him good-night, no father had played catch. No wonder he wanted to stay with her.

He was feeling her hair by the handful now. It actually felt kind of nice. What must he feel to have been raised in captivity all his life? To have never seen a girl? It must be confusing, especially since he was a boy. Teenage boys had more hormones raging than anyone. That was a biological fact.

And JD's mom wouldn't let him date. Probably because she

was afraid someone would find out he was a clone. As a result, the poor guy didn't know what to do with himself. Attacking girls in the hallway was the best plan he could come up with.

Poor, dumb boy.

Marty had stopped touching her hair. Abby rose onto her knees and turned to check on him. He lay with one hand holding the corn to his ear, the other dangling off the couch.

Sleeping.

He looked so peaceful. His long, dark eyelashes fell softly against the rosy skin of his swollen face. His cheeks, chin, and upper neck were scruffy with brown hair. Did Marty know how to shave or had the groomers taken that bit of his independence?

Abby gently pried the corn from his hand and set the package on the floor by her knees. Marty inhaled a long breath and opened his good eye. His eyelashes fluttered as he blinked the swollen eye back into use. She stroked the side of his face, feeling the chill left by the corn. His prickly cheeks darkened at her caress.

So cute.

"Is something wrong?" Marty pushed up onto one elbow and swung his legs to the floor.

Their faces were inches apart now. She sat back on her heels to give herself room to breathe. "No. I-I'm sorry I woke you."

He gazed at her. His eyes had a way of ensnaring hers so that she couldn't look away. He gripped her shoulder in one hand, leaned toward her, and, even though she knew she shouldn't allow him to kiss her, she couldn't move or form the words to stop him.

But his aim was *way* off for a kiss, and his lips pressed firmly against her forehead. She closed her eyes, startled by his sweet gesture. When she opened them again, he had sat back and was watching her with a small smile on his lips. Lips that were full and perfect, unharmed by JD's fist. Twice now JD had forced kisses without asking. Would Marty's kiss feel different from JD's?

Abby stood on her knees and pressed her lips against his. They were soft and warm and nothing like JD's. Marty tensed and uttered a little whimper.

For a fleeting moment she wanted to stay connected to him

forever. Everything about him felt right. His eyes, his lips, his smell, his sweet kindness, the way he looked at her … then she snapped to her senses and pulled back. What had she done? What had happened to her standards? She hadn't known Marty much longer than she'd known JD.

The horror! She had just pulled a JD Kane!

Marty sucked in a powerful breath of air and slowly opened his eyes, staring at her with wonder. "More?"

She laughed and shook her head. "No more today."

For the briefest moment, a hungry look flashed across his face. The same look JD wore daily. A flutter of fear danced through her stomach; maybe it was wrong to have introduced Marty to his physical side, especially right after he'd wanted to marry her and she told him to slow down.

But then he fell back against the couch, closed his eyes again, and drifted back to sleep, a faint smile on his lips.

Abby sat watching him, wondering what to do with her feelings, wondering how to keep Marty safe, wondering if his life would last beyond his eighteenth birthday.

Abby and Marty sat side by side on the sofa.

"May I thank God for the meal?" Marty asked.

Abby turned to him, startled. "Oh. Of course."

Marty bowed his head over the steaming pepperoni and green pepper pizza. "Hello to you, Creator of Everything. Thank you for this *pizza*, and for keeping us safe at the high school facility, and for Abby's *kiss*. Please tell me your purpose for my life so I can follow it. Thank you for listening."

Abby smiled. She considered telling him about saying amen after a prayer, but she didn't want to make him feel like he'd done it wrong. And she supposed he hadn't—the intent was the same. She bit into the warm pizza and Marty's eyes watched, probably to see how to eat it. She doubted they ate pizza on the Farm, since it had so much color.

"Should I have said 'In Jesus's name' at the end of my prayer?" Marty asked. "You spoke it that way, as did Pastor Scott."

"That's okay. I'm sure God understood."

"Why do you say it?"

"Because Jesus said to. I'm not so good at Bible references, but he said something like, 'whatever you ask for in my name ...' So I guess that's why we say it."

"Why did they keep this information from us at the lab?"

"Probably because not everyone believes the Bible."

"How could they not? It is written."

"Well, yeah. But just because something is written doesn't make it truth. Anybody can write a book. Do you believe everything you read?"

"Of course."

"You've never questioned anything?"

Marty looked confused. "I have many questions."

"About the Bible or something else?"

"Is Jesus a clone of God? Who wrote the Bible? Where does the Bible explain what my purpose is? How will believing in God change my life? What does—"

"Whoa! Slow down." Marty's stay with Pastor Scott was supposed to have answered his tough questions, not raise more complicated ones. "Those are all great questions, but let's just focus on the most important one for now. Believing in God changes your life because he lets you start over. Believers call this being born again."

"How can anyone be created again? Humans do not grow smaller."

"Not literally born again. But spiritually reborn. We're all born with sin—with a badness in our hearts. And we do bad things in our life. But rather than have God punish us for that when we die, he sent Jesus to take that punishment for us. That's the example he set for us in 1 Corinthians. God is love. Jesus died so we could live. But we have to believe it. We have to tell him we accept his sacrifice."

"How do I accept this sacrifice?"

Abby shoved a huge bite of pizza in her mouth. She'd always hoped the first time she had this conversation, it would be with her dad. But who was she to argue with God?

She swallowed her bite. Marty had still not touched his food. His pizza was going to get cold.

"Okay, I'll tell you, but after that you have to eat." She didn't know why she was bossing him around like she did her dad. As if eating pizza compared to his eternal salvation. Man, she was a control freak sometimes.

She thought back to what her youth pastor had taught them. Giving your life to Christ was as easy as ABC. "It's a simple prayer. First, admit that you're a sinner—that you've done bad things. Then believe that Jesus died for you, so you could be part of God's family. Then confess the bad things you've done and promise to live your life for him." Abby twisted her lips and hoped she hadn't forgotten anything important. "That's pretty much it. Did you … uh … want to do that?"

Marty nodded, his eyes big and childlike. Gosh, he was sweet. She wanted to kiss him again, but this obviously wasn't the best time.

Marty closed his eyes and began talking to God the way he talked to her. She couldn't believe the things he considered sin, and some confessions were so bizarre she didn't have a clue what he meant. Stealing food to give to Jasons with PDR marks. Not reporting when someone had hurt him. Faking ADR results. Lying to the guards. Eating before BMPs. Trying to choke Dr. Elliot. Taking Dad's keycard. Trying on her dad's clothes and her clothes—Abby would have liked to witness that one.

She should have told him he didn't have to individually name each one: a summary would have sufficed. When he spoke of his sin of abandoning Baby and running away from the Farm, Abby wanted to interrupt and tell him that wasn't a sin, that he was being held prisoner there, but his voice cracked like he was going to cry, which instantly brought tears to her eyes.

She decided to let him keep going.

"Most of all, please forgive me for Dr. Woman. I know it wasn't all my fault; the J:1s tricked me. But even when I realized they were hurting her, I couldn't stop them. I tried to but they wouldn't let me. I'm sorry they broke her until she died. I'm sorry I couldn't save her."

Hold up. Who was Dr. Woman?

"And that's all I can think of that I did wrong. If I forgot something, please forgive me for forgetting—"

Good grief.

"—and please help me to know the purpose for my life. Not the plan the doctors at the Farm designed me for, but the plan you have for me. I promise to do all I can to fulfill that plan. Thank you in Jesus's name."

Marty gave one long sniff, and it was as if he never shed a tear. What was up with that? Abby had only been sympathy crying and she probably looked like pounded steak. She wanted to ask about this random Dr. Woman but thought she'd give him a moment.

She smiled. "How do you feel?"

His eyes searched hers, then he examined his hands. "The same. Although I do feel safe. If I must go back to the Farm, if I must expire, this is not the end. I will be with the Creator of Everything." Marty finally picked up his slice of pizza and bit into it. His eyes grew wide, and he devoured the slice in four bites.

"Who was Dr. Woman?" She'd meant to give him a little more time, but she was really curious. If too much time passed, and he wasn't so open, he might not share. And if someone had died on the Farm … someone who was not a clone …

"She was a doctor who worked at the Farm for as long as I could remember. She was the only woman there. She was special. And she made us feel special. She was kind, and when she smiled …" He sighed and picked a green pepper off his plate. "It was almost like the kiss."

Abby brought her hand to her chest. "My kiss?"

Marty grinned. "Almost." Then he broke out into deep laughter. His sparkling eyes locked onto hers, and the laughter became contagious. Abby laughed until her sides hurt, unsure why he found this funny, but unable to stop because Marty was just too cute. Somehow his random laughter was charming, where JD's had been geeky.

Finally his face sobered. "I'm sorry. What happened to Dr. Woman was not something to laugh about. When we got older, the J:1s began to act strangely around her, like it really mattered she was so different. They talked about her hair and her body and they wanted to touch her. A few had tried before and received many marks and stings and beatings with the stick."

"The stick?"

"The guards strike us if we disobey."

Charming place, this Farm. "Go on."

"The J:1s made a plan. Bones—he was J:1:3—asked me to help." Marty picked up a lost green pepper that was on his plate and put it back on his slice of pizza. He kept his gaze on his food and lowered his voice. "I wanted to touch her too, so I went along with them."

Abby and Marty had both become very still.

Marty glanced at her, his forehead creased as if pleading. "Dr. Woman liked me. When I was given marks with her, she never did experiments. I was younger then—we all were—but I still took care of Baby. Dr. Woman often asked what I was thinking when I helped the Brokens. She told me I was brave to face the *bullies*, as she called them.

"She requested me to visit her lab room often. The J:1s teased me about being her favorite. Maybe I was. She told me things she didn't tell the others. When they made the plan, they told me I was an important part. They wanted me to play sick, so I went to the toilet in Section Five and waited. The J:1s were hiding behind a bunk bed. Bones lured her in to help me. When I saw her, I confessed right away. But she didn't understand. She put her hand on my forehead and ..."

Marty drew in a ragged breath. Abby was glad he'd stopped, because his story suddenly horrified her. She'd seen enough episodes of *CSI* to guess what happened next.

"Rock grabbed her first because he was the strongest. She fought well, but Gumby took her radio away and she couldn't call for help."

Again he stopped and took a deep breath. His eyes filled with moisture. Abby recalled the words from his prayer. *I couldn't stop them. I tried to but they wouldn't let me. I'm sorry they broke her until she died. I'm sorry I couldn't save her.*

"Rock held her down and—"

"Marty." Abby put her hand on his. "You can stop now. Thank you for sharing the story."

Marty reached for another slice of pizza out of the box on the floor.

But Abby had one more question nagging at the back of her brain. "Why did they call her Dr. Woman?"

Marty's lips curved in a wistful smile. "Because she told me she was a woman, and I told the others."

"Will you tell me her real name, Marty? Did you know it?"

Martyr turned, his eyes locking with Abby's. "Doctor Corrine Markley."

[CHAPTER SEVENTEEN]

ABBY JUMPED UP. "Did you say Corrine Markley? That's
… wow."

Martyr found it strange that Dr. Woman's name gave Abby joy.
She opened her cell phone, pushed buttons, and held it to her ear.

"Kylee? What are you doing right now?" Abby brushed a
crumb of pizza bread off Martyr's shirt. "Can you come and get
me? I left my car at school, and I need a ride to get it … Thanks!
… Okay, bye."

Abby closed the cell phone. "I don't know what's going to happen, but we can't stay here much longer. Dad hasn't answered his
cell or texted, which is really weird." She bit her thumbnail. "But

your story might be what we needed. If we can get the cops to believe us, knowing what we do about Corrine Markley should be enough to close down Jason Farms. We simply need hard evidence." She walked to the front door and rummaged through her bag.

"Why would they not believe us?" Martyr asked.

Abby came and sat beside him on the sofa, carrying a large green book. "Because in the real world people don't trust each other. You always need proof, which is called *evidence*. Surveillance footage would be a start. I'm sure there were no cameras in the bathroom, and even if there were, that footage has probably been destroyed. But I doubt they destroyed everything with her on it. That would be too much valuable scientific research to just throw out. Any footage of her working there would be enough to at least interest the detectives. And that's all we need, reason enough for the cops to search Jason Farms."

Abby twisted her lips. She opened the book and pulled out a sheet of paper. "This is a statement from Dr. Kane's insurance provider. It's not hard evidence in itself, but it shows he is taking prescription immune suppressants, which proves he's sick." She shut the paper back inside the book. "Could you draw the layout of Jason Farms—as best you can? The way the rooms are?"

"Yes." Martyr could do that easily.

Abby grabbed his arm and dragged him to a small room on the other side of the kitchen that held a large table with six chairs around it. She pushed him onto one of the chairs. "I'll get you some paper."

Abby returned with paper, a pencil, and a ruler, and Martyr started drawing. Abby drifted away. He could hear her rummaging in the kitchen. He finished level two first, then started on level three.

A loud, musical sound caused Martyr to jump out of his chair and seek out Abby. She stood before the entrance of the house, peeking out a window that ran alongside the front door. Martyr stayed out of view, just behind the wall separating the entrance from the living room.

"What is it?" he asked.

Abby turned, a finger over her lips. She shrank back and squatted beside a mismatched pile of shoes. She forced her foot into a boot while her hands scrambled in the pile for the other. The doorknob rattled and someone pounded on the door.

"Abigail Goyer? Hello?"

Abby tossed her bag over her shoulder, grabbed the boots Dr. Goyer had loaned to Martyr, her coat and Pastor Scott's flannel, and scurried toward him in a crouch. She pushed the boots into his arms and whispered, "Put them on!"

Martyr obeyed, not sure what else to do. While he put on the boots, Abby raced into the living room, grabbed her book, and ran through the kitchen. The pounding on the door continued. Martyr found Abby in the room with the table, where she was stuffing his drawing materials into her bag. She shoved the thick shirt at Martyr, put on her own coat, then swung her bag onto her back.

Martyr had barely put his arms into the shirtsleeves when Abby grabbed his hand and towed him through a dark hallway to the exit in the back of the house.

She whispered, "I think JD talked to his dad."

Martyr listened to the voice behind the door and thought so too. At the sound of breaking glass, he pulled Abby into his arms.

"We have to move quickly, Marty." She broke away from him and opened the door. They stood at the top of the steps facing the vast clearing surrounded by forest.

"Where are we going?" He followed her carefully down the icy steps to the ground.

"Out."

Martyr wanted a better answer, but Abby ran across the clearing and into the trees. He traipsed after her, his legs sinking up to his knees in the deep snow, causing the freezing crystals to fall over the top of his boots. He gasped at the cold running down his legs, but kept moving. He hoped they wouldn't come face-to-face with the horse.

"There they go!" a voice shouted.

"Martyr!"

Martyr spun around. A tall man wearing a pancake-colored jacket and red hat emerged from the back of the house.

"Johnson," Marty said.

"What?" Abby called.

"That man is Johnson. A guard from the Farm."

"Then let's move!" Abby threaded her way between the prickly trees. "The main road is just through here. If we get a good lead and they decide to drive, we should beat them there."

Martyr looked back to see Johnson run down the steps, slip, and crash into the deep snow.

Rolo appeared in the doorway, wearing a blue coat that doubled his size. Martyr turned and ran, ignoring the pain from a tree limb that snapped against his cheek. He plunged after Abby with his hands out in front, pushing the other limbs aside.

"We're heading toward Dawson Road." Abby held the cell phone to her ear. "Can you swing that way?"

Another limb managed to get by Martyr's hands and scraped his forehead. Abby didn't seem to be having as many problems with the trees. Maybe it was because she was so short. Martyr crouched lower.

"We're coming out right behind Salmon Laundromat ... Yeah ... Hurry!"

Abby pocketed her cell phone, and her pace increased. The snow in Martyr's boots caked around his numb ankles. The trees began to thin out, though. He was thankful there were no more sharp limbs.

They approached a large, gray facility, with steam pouring out of silver pipes in the back wall. Martyr followed Abby to the front and slipped in dirty snow that had turned gray and mushy. He barely managed to stay on his feet.

Two loud sounds burst from a small, black, two-door car on the edge of the road, and Abby ran toward it. A girl sat behind the driving wheel. Her skin was the same dark brown color of Pastor Scott's.

Abby opened the passenger door and climbed in the back seat. Martyr tried to follow, but she pulled the front seat back into place.

"You can ride shotgun," she said. "Hurry."

Shotgun?

"Girl, what's going on? What are you all running from?"

Martyr squeezed himself into the tiny front seat and pulled the door closed. The dark-skinned girl stared at him, eyes narrowed. "What'd you do to your hair?"

Martyr ran his hand over his scratchy head, uncertain how to answer.

"This is my friend Kylee," Abby said.

"Hello, Kylee," Martyr said.

"What happened to his face?"

"I got scratched," Martyr said at the same time as Abby said, "JD hit him."

Kylee frowned at Marty. "You hit yourself?"

Abby leaned between the two front seats. "Oh, Marty." She pressed her fingers to his scratched cheek. "Does it hurt?"

"It stings."

"Why'd you call him Marty?"

"Because he's not JD, he's Marty. Kylee, I need you to get us out of here. I have an amazing story—you're going to freak out—but if we don't move, we'll be in serious trouble."

Kylee still stared at Martyr. "But he sounds just like him."

"I know! Just drive."

Kylee steered the car out onto the road, and Abby told the story of how she found Martyr in her room, what was going on at Jason Farms, and how JD had attacked him.

Kylee's long black hair fascinated Martyr, but the way she stared made him nervous, so he tried not to examine her too much. She drove them down a winding road until they came to a big clearing with four large, wooden facilities painted brown. Even with so much looking his way, Kylee was a much safer driver than Abby.

"Abby lives in a house, Marty," Kylee spoke slowly, "but I live in an a-part-ment." Kylee stopped the car between two trucks and pulled a clicking lever between the seats. She turned to Martyr and said, "Ah part ment."

"Apartment," Martyr said.

Abby groaned. "He speaks English, Kylee."

Kylee led Abby and Martyr to a set of glass doors, up an elevator, and through a door marked 3D. The apartment house was similar to Pastor Scott and Aliza's home, only smaller and cluttered with stacks of papers, clothing, and books. The kitchen and living room shared the same small space, and something smelled spicy and sweet. All the windows were covered with thin strips of white metal making everything dark.

"Look at his posture. He's so straight."

Abby didn't seem to hear her. "Marty needs a table to work at."

"Yeah, okay. He can work right here." Kylee grabbed a stack of books off a small round table next to the one-wall kitchen. In a few quick movements she set the books on the floor and brushed the table's surface off with her sleeve. "There you go, JD—I, uh …" Kylee's voice hushed to a whisper. "Um … Marty."

Martyr pulled out a small wooden chair, on which sat a messy stack of papers.

"Let me get those for you," Kylee said. "My mom is working on her PhD. She's gone to Anchorage three days a week, and then it's study, study, study." Kylee piled the papers onto the cluttered kitchen counter. "I don't know how Mom finds anything in this mess."

Martyr sat down. The small chair creaked under his weight, but held together. Abby placed his drawing on the table, leaving him to work while she and Kylee went and sat on a sofa in front of the TV, whispering. Every once in a while they burst into laughter. Martyr hoped he was not the topic of conversation. Eventually Kylee turned on the TV and the talking stopped.

He heard Abby make two attempts to reach Dr. Goyer on her cell phone, but it did not sound like Dr. Goyer ever spoke back.

When Martyr finished his sketch, he carried it to where Abby sat. "I hope this helps."

"Let's see it." Abby grabbed his hand and pulled him down between them.

Martyr sank deep into the sofa, and Abby and Kylee fell against him. He straightened himself up the best he could and explained his drawing. "Level three is the lowest level. It's where we exercise and have classes. There's a running track and exercise equipment and classrooms. Up one level is level two, where we sleep. There are four sections divided into cells by age and one other section for the Brokens. The cafeteria is on this level, as well as a play structure with an orange slide for the children. Level one, the top floor, is mostly lab rooms. Dr. Kane's office is here, and Dr. Goyer's office is here. Dr. Goyer's office was once Dr. Woman's office."

Abby's eyes met Martyr's, dipped to his lips and back. His heart thudded at the idea of her kiss. Was she going to kiss him again?

But instead Abby said, "Kylee, do you think Marty could take a shower? I don't think he's been able to for a few days. Right, Marty?"

"Yes," Martyr said. Today was Friday, a day past grooming. A shower would feel nice. Plus, he felt sweaty and smelled bad. Maybe Abby had noticed and this was why she had not kissed him again. The thought caused his cheeks to burn.

Kylee sang out a sigh. "I can't believe JD Kane's clone is naked in my shower."

Abby rolled her eyes and nestled further into the sofa. "I hate to break it to you, but JD is a clone too. His crazy *dad* cloned himself."

"I thought cloning humans was impossible. Mr. Lester said so."

"A successful case has never been publicly documented. And since Dr. Kane is using them for his own gain, he didn't tell anyone. As long as no one realizes what he's accomplished, no one can stop him. I know he's testing pharmaceuticals on them, probably raking in the bucks from it too."

"Human guinea pigs?" Kylee asked.

Abby shrugged. "Who knows? The worst thing is that Marty says he's going to expire on his eighteenth birthday. Dad says there is no reason he would—he's perfectly healthy. That leads me to believe Dr. Kane is killing his clones."

"And using their organs?" Kylee asked. When Abby nodded, Kylee added, "I've heard about human traffickers getting good money for body parts."

"Marty can't live without kidneys; he'd need to keep at least one. But it sounds like Dr. Kane planned to take both of them."

"That's so creepy."

"It wouldn't surprise me if Dr. Kane had cloned someone else; but according to Marty and my dad, there are only Jasons at Jason Farms."

Kylee wrinkled her nose. "Jason Dean Kane?"

"Jason Dean Kane *Senior*." Abby stuck out her tongue. "Pretty gross, huh?"

"All this time I thought it was some farmer named Jason."

Abby shook Marty's drawing. "To shut the Farm down, we need to find proof that Corrine Markley worked there."

"How?"

Abby didn't want to admit it, but she could think of no other way. "We have to go in."

"Take him back there? But what if they won't let you leave?"

"We have to try. I was thinking nighttime should be our best chance of sneaking into the lab."

"Abby, that's crazy."

"Then I hope you have some crazy in you, because you're going to help."

"How?"

"If we don't come back by a certain time, you tell the cops what happened."

"And what if the cops don't believe me?"

"I don't know. I haven't been able to get hold of my dad all day. I'm afraid he went back to the lab and they won't let him leave." Abby took a deep breath. "What else do you know about Corrine Markley's disappearance?"

"Her husband, Jim, caused a lot of trouble, picketing down at the police station, holding interviews. Most people believed he killed her, but Scott didn't think a guilty man would draw so much attention to himself. People thought he was nuts. He was talking about mad"—Kylee paused as if just discovering something—"scientists."

"That would be Dr. Kane and company. Do you think we could find her husband?"

"I don't know. I remember my brother saying he went crazy after all this happened. We could go online and see if he's listed. If not, we could check the *Anchorage Daily News* archives."

Kylee popped up and logged on to her computer. Even after several searches, they couldn't find a listing for a James or Jim Markley. The old newspapers would provide answers, but full articles couldn't be accessed online without paying a fee, and neither of them had a credit card.

Kylee offered another idea. "I could drive us to the Mat-Su library. I bet we could look up old newspapers there."

When Marty came out of the shower, Kylee drove them to the library. It took very little time to locate old newspapers reporting the disappearance and arrest.

> FISHHOOK—Police questioned James Markley, a pipeline engineer, in connection with the disappearance of his wife, Corrine. Markley was taken into custody Tuesday night for questioning. He claimed his wife had been working for scientists who cloned humans, and that the scientists are responsible for his wife's disappearance. Markley is not considered a suspect.
>
> Dr. Corrine Markley, 29, holds a doctorate in biochemistry and molecular biophysics from the University of Arizona. She is white, 5'7" and 120 pounds. She had dark brown to black hair and brown eyes when she disappeared. Anyone with information is asked to contact the Fishhook Police or Mat-Su CrimeStoppers.

"It doesn't say where he lives," Kylee said.

"But look at this one." Abby showed Kylee the article she'd found.

> CHUGIAK – Former senior drilling engineer James Markley has opened Markley's Taxidermy and Souvenirs in his Chugiak-area residence. The shop specializes in big game and small mammal hunting or fishing trophies, head mounts, and rugs.

"This was just a few years ago. If he really had a breakdown like your brother said, maybe he lost his engineering job." Abby clicked open an Internet search window and quickly found a website for Markley's Taxidermy and Souvenirs in Chugiak. "Looks like we're going for a little ride."

[CHAPTER EIGHTEEN]

DR. GOYER HAD EXPLAINED mountains to Martyr, but nothing prepared him for the massive, gray, snow-capped peaks. The drive to Chugiak took about twenty minutes on the *highway*, and Martyr stared at the mountains until Kylee stopped the car in front of a sign that read *Markley's Taxidermy and Souvenirs*.

As they went inside, and a bell over the door chimed. Marty froze just inside the door and stared at the stuffed horse's head staring down from the wall. Large sticks grew out from behind its ears. A dozen other animals hung on the wall around it. Some were whole and some were only heads. One was only a furry paw with long, black claws. Abby took Marty's arm and pulled him toward the counter.

He went reluctantly. "What happened to that horse?"

Abby looked over Martyr's shoulder and grinned. "That's a moose."

Moose? "Why is its head on the wall?"

"I'll explain later."

A short man with a round belly and a protruding lower lip stood on the other side of the counter. Martyr stared at the man's belly. "Is that man growing a baby?"

"Shh." Abby glared at Martyr. "Later."

But Abby had still not explained about the baby in Aliza's belly.

"You here to pick something up?" the man asked.

Abby draped one arm on the counter and smiled. "Are you Jim Markley?"

"What's it to you?"

"We're in desperate need of your help," Abby said, trying to think of a way to broach this topic tactfully. "It involves a place called Jason Farms."

"Out!" The man pointed over Abby's head. "I'm not talking to any reporters."

Abby winced. She had sure botched the tact. "We're not reporters. And we know about the scientists Dr. Markley worked with." Abby shot a quick glance at Martyr. "We know how she was killed."

The man folded his arms. "Who says she was killed?"

"Marty witnessed it," Abby said.

The man fixed his watery eyes on Martyr in a way that made Martyr feel anxious, then he turned away and spit into a red and white can that read *Campbell's Condensed Chicken Noodle Soup.* "Wait here."

Martyr glanced at Abby, whose nose was wrinkled as if something smelled bad. Perhaps spitting into a can was strange, even to her.

The man walked around the counter and locked the front door, then flipped the sign in the window to CLOSED. On his way back, he waved them to follow him back behind the counter. As they passed a long table, Martyr examined various chunks of wood, animal hair, and cans. There were even a few more soup cans. This facility made Martyr wish he could reach out and touch Abby, but she stayed ahead of him as she followed the man toward a blue sheet that hung over a doorway at the back. The man held the fabric aside, and Martyr ducked under and stepped into a small, one-room cell with a tiny kitchen at one end and a dirty mattress at the other.

Martyr moved very close to Abby.

The man gestured to the mattress. "Pull up a seat."

Martyr sat down next to Abby and Kylee on the very edge.

The man picked up a red can off a shelf and spit into it. This can said *Sam's Choice Cola*. The man crossed his arms and leaned against the wall just inside the doorway. "Let's hear it, then."

"It's sort of complicated, Mr. Markley," Abby said. "First I need to explain—"

"No." He pointed to Martyr. "You say he saw it. I want him to tell it."

Abby glanced at Martyr. "Well, he's not really … he doesn't understand how to … uh …"

Martyr squeezed Abby's hand. "Do not worry, Abby Goyer. I can tell him." And he could. Dr. Woman had been a wife to this man; he needed to know what happened.

Martyr told Mr. Markley the same story he told Abby, making sure he knew Dr. Woman was a nice doctor to the clones, that everyone had liked her. He thought the man would like that part. Abby squeezed Martyr's hand long and hard when he got to the part of the story she had not wanted to hear before. Kylee started to cry. Mr. Markley's face remained pale, like one of the masks Dr. Max had shown them once.

When Martyr finished, Mr. Markley said, "I knew it! I knew something had happened with those twisted scientists." His voice cracked a little. "There's still no proof. Only a story, which isn't much better than mine. If I go to the cops with that, they'll still think I'm nuts. 'No body, no crime,' they'd say."

"But that's exactly why we came," Abby said. "We need evidence. Proof Dr. Markley worked at Jason Farms. Do you have anything that might help? Old pay stubs? Any personal research, computer files, pictures, anything?"

"She was real secretive about her work there. I was gone a lot, up on the pipeline. And she paid the bills, so I never saw her pay-checks. I gave her computer to the cops along with her cell phone and organizer. They didn't find anything."

"Maybe they didn't know what to look for," Abby said.

Mr. Markley spit into the Sam can again. "They gave all her stuff back to me. It's in a storage unit back in Fishhook. After Corrie disappeared, and the cops were finally convinced I was innocent, I went through a rough patch. Lost my job with BP. Had to move. And I couldn't deal with all the staring and gossip. Threw almost everything we owned into storage and sold the house. Bought this little shack, learned a new trade."

"Could we look at the storage unit?" Abby asked.

"I can meet you over there tomorrow, say eleven thirty? I'm not much of a morning person anymore."

"Thank you, Mr. Markley." Abby squeezed Martyr's hand and smiled. "That will be perfect."

It was dark by the time Kylee's car entered Fishhook city limits, but for the first time in the past few days, Abby felt hope. They'd found out a lot about the Farm and had a plan that could possibly bring down the cloning operation. She prayed the boys could go into foster homes, maybe be adopted. It would be wrong for them to move from one prison to another.

"Uh oh," Kylee said.

Red and blue lights illuminated the dark night as Kylee slowed the car to a stop on the side of the road.

Abby looked out the back window. A patrol car pulled up behind them almost like it had been waiting for them to drive past. "Kylee, were you speeding?"

"No way. What should we do?"

"I don't know." Abby's heart pounded as a man wearing a tan

Fishhook Police Department uniform stopped outside the driver's window. Abby's gaze focused on his holstered gun, which was perfectly eye level as the officer knocked on the glass with the back of his knuckles. As sweat beaded on her forehead, she forced herself to look up. The cop—Allam, according to his name badge—had blond hair and looked to be twenty-something. He could have been a surfer if this were a beach town.

Kylee rolled the window down. "Was I going too fast?"

Officer Allam clicked on a flashlight and shone the blinding beam on each face. Then he pointed the light at a paper in his gloved hand. "Step out of the car, please."

"But what did I do?" Kylee asked.

"Step out of the car, all of you."

Kylee slipped and almost fell to the pavement as she climbed out. Another officer appeared on Marty's side of the car, and Abby could feel the man's bad intentions coming through the passenger's side. Marty cracked open his door, but Abby grabbed his shoulder and leaned over the seat.

She slipped her phone to Marty and whispered, "Take my phone. If they try to take you, run, okay? Hide somewhere, then use the contacts to call Pete Goyer. He's my uncle. Tell him everything."

Marty nodded and climbed out. As soon as he was standing outside, Abby lifted the lever and pushed the seat forward while the other officer waved for her to hurry up. Marty backed up a few steps, his entire body alert like a deer preparing to flee. A strip mall glowed off to their right. If Marty could get a head start, he might find a place to hide. She slowly stretched one leg out of the car.

"Let's go! Let's go!" the officer said. "Move it along."

Abby squeezed the rest of the way out and examined the cop on her side of the car. This officer—Runstrom—was fortyish, well built, with dirty blond hair, a scruffy face, and the pinked cheeks of a man with rosacea—or an alcoholic, but that was unlikely. Either way, he wouldn't have much difficulty taking down Marty in a fight.

"What's the problem, sir?" Abby asked. Marty was still backing away one small step at a time. With the red and blue lights flickering on his face, he looked like a scared child in the dark shadows.

"Watch the kid!" Allam said.

Runstrom wheeled around. "Hey! Get back here."

"Go, Marty!"

Marty spun around on the shoulder of the highway and started to run, but his feet slipped under him and he went nowhere, as if running on a treadmill. Runstrom ran after him. Marty managed to get going, but the officer's speed was already faster. He tackled Marty, and the bodies slid two yards on the icy blacktop before coming to a stop.

Runstrom rolled Marty facedown on the road and slapped a pair of handcuffs on him. "Your daddy's been looking for you, boy."

Abby jogged toward them and willed herself to stay composed. "You're making a huge mistake. This isn't JD Kane. This is Marty. He's a witness in a murder case. He can tell you exactly what happened to Corrine Markley four years ago."

Runstrom jerked Marty to his feet. "Bet he can tell me where the Easter Bunny lives too."

"We can get you proof," Abby said. "A woman was murdered, and if anyone is to blame, it's Dr. Jason Kane. Please don't let him have Marty."

Runstrom led Marty to the squad car and shoved him into the backseat. Marty's elbow cracked against the side of the door as he went inside.

"Hey!" Abby said. "A little rough, aren't you?"

Runstrom glared down on Abby. "You'll want to watch that mouth. Now, you can climb in after your boyfriend here or I could put some cuffs on you too. What's it going to be?"

"We're only looking for your friends, miss," Allam told Kylee. "You're free to go."

Abby craned her neck over the car. "Kylee, meet Jim tomorrow! Don't forget."

"I won't." Kylee stood next to her open car door, tears glistening on her face in the flashing lights.

Abby climbed into the backseat beside Marty and hugged

herself. Her surroundings froze her train of worry. She'd never been in a patrol car before. The backseat was hard, black plastic, contoured to sit two. No cushions. She reasoned the hard seats would be easy to clean and collect evidence from, then berated herself for having such a thought. A steel barrier wall with an open, thick plexiglass window separated the front of the car from the back.

Runstrom fell into the passenger's seat and began settling into the upholstery while Allam walked back to the squad car and climbed into the driver's seat. Slowly, Kylee's car pulled back onto the road and drove away.

Abby leaned up to the plexiglass window. "Have you heard of Dolly, the cloned sheep?"

"Cold out tonight," Runstrom said. "Might see some northern lights if I get off on time."

Allam glanced at Abby in the rearview mirror. "Doesn't look likely with this load."

"You're making a mistake." Abby couldn't believe how they were treating her. "Dr. Kane is the real criminal. He has an underground lab at the Jason Farms barn. This boy is not JD Kane, he's one of Dr. Kane's clones. Find an old picture of Dr. Kane and you'll see. JD Kane is a clone too. A woman died at the Jason Farms facility. Dr. Corrine Markley. The clones killed her, and Dr. Kane covered it up. You have to go investigate. Dr. Kane and his staff are doing experiments on the boys. He wants to take Marty's kidneys."

Abby paused to breathe, knowing she sounded like a babbling lunatic. Hysteria wasn't making her wild story any more believable, either.

"What say we grab a bite after we drop these perps?" Allam asked.

Runstrom turned to face his partner. "Chepo's or Peking?"

"Chepo's. I hate that Chinese bird food."

Abby kicked the back of the seat. "It's true! Listen to me!"

Runstrom slid the plexiglass window shut.

"Abby, do not be upset." Marty's soft voice calmed her.

"But don't you know what this means? Dr. Kane reported his

son missing. Who knows what story he gave the cops, but they think you're him. It was Dr. Kane's way of finding you and it worked. You'll be back at the Farm in time for bed." Abby leaned back against the hard seat and started to cry. What would Dr. Kane do when he got Marty back? Would he kill him right away? Abby couldn't handle thinking about it.

"Abby Goyer?" Marty whispered in her ear. "I could give you kiss? It made me feel better before."

Abby smiled and turned her tear-streaked face to Marty's.

[CHAPTER NINETEEN]

MARTYR AND ABBY SAT in front of Officer Runstrom's desk at what Abby called the *police station*. The man called Allam had told them to sit there and walked away without removing the restraints on Martyr's wrists. That had been over forty minutes ago. Only two of the seven desks in the large room were occupied, but neither of those men had spoken, despite Abby's attempts at communicating.

Martyr watched the entrance for Dr. Kane. Abby seemed convinced he would arrive soon. She had tried three times to reach Dr. Goyer on her cell phone but had not succeeded.

"This is ridiculous," Abby said. "I mean, they can't keep us here without a reason. Fishhook doesn't have a curfew, and Kylee was driving the speed limit."

Allam walked into the room and sat three desks away from Runstrom's.

"Hey," Abby said. "You don't have a right to hold us. Plus, we deserve to get our phone calls."

"You're not under arrest," Allam said.

"Even more reason why we deserve a phone call."

Allam leaned back in his chair. "You're a minor. The laws aren't the same."

"Besides," a man at one of the desks in the back of the room said, "you've got a cell phone on you. We aren't stopping you from using it. Call someone who'll answer."

Abby's eyebrows sank. "I'm not some idiot teenager, you know. I've got a summer internship scheduled with the Philadelphia PD, and I'm going to Penn State to study forensic science. So you can just cut the fluff and tell me the truth, okay? Why are you holding us?"

Allam stared at her, his lips fighting a smile. "We picked up a runaway. What's *fluff* about that? We've called your dad at both numbers you gave us. No answer. Your boyfriend's dad is on the way."

Martyr stiffened. The men in uniform had used the term *boyfriend* in reference to him, which seemed to indicate he belonged to Abby. He didn't mind that, but he did not have a father, unless the uniformed man meant the Creator of Everything. And Martyr was pretty certain the Creator did not have a cell phone.

"Dr. Kane is *not* Marty's dad. You're making a huge mistake."

Martyr agreed. He did not want anyone to think Dr. Kane was his father.

"It's really not my call, miss," Allam said.

Abby growled, and Martyr wished he could hold her hand. The metal restraints were very uncomfortable.

Voices drifted down the hallway from the front of the police station. Runstrom entered the room with Dr. Kane beside him. Dr. Elliot trailed along a few paces behind. Martyr swallowed the lump that had formed and looked down at his feet. It was over now, and there was no way to fight it. Nothing mattered anymore. At least he would be able to see Baby. He hoped Baby was okay.

"No!" Abby jumped to her feet and sprinted toward the men. What was she doing?

Before she got more than a few feet, Allam grabbed her by the shoulders and pushed her back out of the way. "None of that now."

Abby reached over Allam's shoulder and clawed at Dr. Kane, a violent sneer on her face that shocked Martyr. She managed to grab a handful of Dr. Kane's brown-and-gray hair, which jerked his head sideways, but Dr. Kane did not cry out. He did not get angry or fight back. He simply followed Runstrom to the place where Martyr sat.

Martyr glanced at the familiar faces he'd hoped never to see again. Dr. Elliot looked blank, his face void of any emotion. Dr. Kane, however, beamed, a tear glistening in his eye.

"I'm so relieved. I'd thought I lost you, son." Dr. Kane bent down and wrapped his long arms around Martyr. The embrace felt strange and cold, although to the others it had probably looked kind.

"You … aren't angry?" Martyr asked, certain that leaving the facility would merit at least a dozen marks.

"Beyond so," Dr. Kane said. "But you are my son."

Martyr frowned. "I'm not your—"

"I'm just glad you're safe."

Martyr couldn't stand the deception. "Because you want my kidneys."

"Ah." Dr. Kane placed his hand on Martyr's head and rubbed it. "You've missed too many doses of your medication, I'm afraid."

What is he talking about?

"Marty isn't on any medication!" Abby struggled against Allam's hold, her orange curls shaking wildly with each move. "Dr. Kane's a liar. He wants Marty's kidneys. He'll say anything to get his investment."

Dr. Kane turned to Abby. "I understand your father has dropped the charges against my son. When he heard about JD's mental illness, he was very understanding. No one knows about

JD's condition, Officer Runstrom. We didn't want people to treat him differently because of it. Normally it's very manageable, as long as he takes his medication."

"He's lying!" Abby said. "There were never any charges against JD, because it was Marty who broke into our house. If you get in touch with my dad, he'll back that up."

"Actually, miss," Runstrom said, "your father called earlier today to say there was never an intruder. Just a high school romance gone bad. We haven't been able to reach him this evening, though."

Abby's face paled. She stopped struggling against Allam, but still glared at Dr. Kane. "What did you do to my dad?"

Dr. Kane backed away and Dr. Elliot took his place in front of Martyr; his cold expression froze Martyr's every muscle.

Dr. Elliot set a small case on Runstrom's desk and opened it, removing a syringe. Marty jumped up and turned in a circle, the urge to run, to hide, crowding out every thought. He dove past Dr. Elliot and rolled under Runstrom's desk.

"Leave him alone," Abby screamed.

The desk wasn't safe. Martyr popped up on the other side and ran to the far wall of the room, forced to crouch in the corner.

Runstrom followed him, watching with a puzzled expression. "It'll be for your own good, kid."

"Dr. Elliot's injections are never good." What if the needle was the first step toward expiration? "He cannot take my kidneys. Abby says you need two kidneys to live, and I don't want to die for that purpose."

Dr. Kane looked over Runstrom's shoulder, peering down on Martyr. "Like I said, he's been off his meds for several days. He always gets delusional without them. *Kidneys.*" Dr. Kane shook his head.

Dr. Elliot crouched down beside Martyr.

Having nowhere to go, Martyr rolled onto his side and curled into a ball. He couldn't cover his head with his arms, so he turned his face into the hard floor and tensed, waiting for the pain. He could not escape.

"Make them stop! You're supposed to protect the innocent!"

Abby's screaming only made Martyr's heart beat faster.

Dr. Kane's voice came soft and soothing from above. "I know you like Miss Goyer, son, but there's a reason we don't allow you to date." His tone changed as he spoke to someone else. "In the past he's told stories to his friends, trying to get them to help him run away. If they don't help, he gets violent. It's quite sad."

"He's lying." Abby's voice sounded weak, like she had a cold. "He's a liar."

Footsteps shuffled, and Martyr could hear Abby's continued protests. *But they won't matter. Even the outside world is filled with wrong things.* A sharp pinch preceded the needle plunging into his shoulder. Martyr gritted his teeth as a familiar grogginess flooded his vision.

Abby's sobbing voice sounded far away. "Pray, Marty. God will help you."

Pray.

Yes, Marty could pray. He could call on the Creator of Everything to help.

Hello, Creator? Please help me to …

"You're making a huge mistake." Abby's voice had gone hoarse. "Dr. Kane is a murderer." Allam held Abby back as Runstrom and the "doctor" carried Marty's limp form out of the station. Abby protested, screamed, and cried, but it changed nothing.

Marty was gone.

Dr. Kane stopped in front of her on his way out. For an old guy he was still oddly handsome. Even at three times Marty and JD's age he looked so much like them. Talk about creepy. But handsome or not, he didn't look healthy. His eyes were bloodshot, his skin pale and moist. "You look like you could use a transplant, Dr. Kane."

He smiled coldly, as if she too were suffering the mythical delusions he claimed of his son. "Can we offer you a ride home, Miss Goyer?"

She spit in his face.

Dr. Kane removed a handkerchief from his pocket and wiped the saliva from his eye.

"You're an evil, horrible man," Abby said. "I know about the lupus and the transplants. I know you're dying, and I am sorry for that, but I won't let you hurt Marty and the others anymore."

Dr. Kane's expression twitched, but he walked out of the room without another word. Once he was gone, Allam let go of Abby. She took this opportunity to beat on his chest.

"How could you let that monster take him? You're supposed to protect people. What good are you if you can't even do that? What good are you?"

Allam played the punching bag until Abby exhausted herself. He met her eyes, looking tired, and gave a half smile, as if not at all wounded by her tirade.

Her cheeks warmed. She scowled and stepped away, folding her arms, wanting to hide herself somehow. Her fit certainly hadn't helped matters. She'd acted like a lovesick adolescent. They probably believed every word Dr. Kane had spoon-fed them.

She approached Runstrom, since he appeared to be the man in charge. In her calmest tone, she asked, "Will you at least look and see if there is an underground lab at the Jason Farms barn? I know that's where Dr. Kane will go next." *Let them listen this time, or at least do it to keep me quiet.*

"I've seen JD Kane play football more times than I can count," Runstrom said. "I'm not going to harass that man because his son fed you some wild story."

"Would you like a ride home?" Allam asked. "We don't have to keep you here until we reach your father. You've done nothing wrong, so—"

"Marty didn't do anything wrong either."

Allam blew out a long breath. "Would you like a ride or are you going to attack me again? If I charged you with assault of a police officer, you could stay a while."

Clearly these men would not help without evidence. She would go home—no, she'd go to Kylee's place. Dr. Kane would probably come looking for her at home, especially if he already had done something to her dad. The mere thought made her queasy. She'd research as much as she could at Kylee's, meet Jim tomorrow morning, and hope they found something at the storage unit. She prayed Dr. Kane wouldn't be ready to operate yet, another thought that made her stomach roil.

"A ride to the high school, please," Abby said, pulling her gloves out of her bomber jacket pocket. "I left my car there this afternoon."

Allam drove Abby to the high school and parked the squad car beside her BMW. He gave a low whistle. "Nice wheels."

"My dad is a molecular biologist. He makes serious cash, but he works for a crazy, psychotic man who cloned himself fifty-five times. Maybe you heard me mention him? Marty is one of those clones and you gave him up for dead." Abby knew how bizarre and desperate she sounded. "Look, Officer Allam, could you at least do me a favor and check on us over the next few days? I know you don't believe me, but the thing is, I know too much and so does my dad. I'm afraid Dr. Kane already got my dad and that's why you can't reach him. If you can't find us, please check for a basement lab under the barn at Jason Farms. They have an elevator on the west end behind a vault door. You'll probably need a specialist to break into it."

Allam did look sympathetic. "Look, miss. Guys are good at sweet-talking girls to get what they want, take my word for it. I was guilty of it at your age. I'm sure that boy just wanted your help to get away from his dad. Don't you worry about the stories he told you."

Abby's temperature simmered. "Will you or will you not check on me?"

"I'll check on you, sure. You take care, now."

Abby faked a smile. "Thanks."

Her car was freezing inside. She started the engine and cranked up the heat, her moist breath billowing out in front. She waited, shivering in the cold, while the heater warmed the car's interior. She called her dad, but there was still no answer. When the temperature was bearable, she gripped the frigid steering wheel, wiped away a tear, and pulled out of the parking lot.

To his credit, Allam didn't drive away until Abby did. She turned onto the main road, grateful few cars were out around ten thirty at night. She passed Dawson Road and the Salmon Laundromat, headed toward Kylee's apartment.

God, please don't let Marty die. Please let Dad be okay.

A pair of headlights gleamed in her rearview mirror.

"Yikes. Turn off the brights, buddy." But the headlights drew closer. Abby hunched forward so the glare wouldn't reach her eyes.

Her car jolted. What on earth? *Did that vehicle just hit me?* She sped up a bit, but the roads were icy and she didn't want to push her luck. The other vehicle surged forward and rammed her again. This time her car skidded a bit. Heat flooded Abby's body as she fought to control the BMW. She should have asked Officer Allam to escort her to Kylee's place.

A sharp corner loomed ahead, and Abby was going way too fast. She lifted her foot off the gas, but the speedometer still hovered over the fifty. She turned the wheel a bit and tapped the breaks just as the vehicle rammed her bumper again.

The BMW skidded sideways on the icy highway. Abby slammed on the breaks and wrenched the wheel to stay on the road, but only managed to spin herself in a half-circle. She screamed, facing the blinding headlights a second before her car burst backward through a mound of snow that edged the road. The car scraped into the forest, crunching past several trees and colliding to a sharp stop. Abby's head smacked against the side airbag and she lost consciousness.

[CHAPTER TWENTY]

ABBY FELT HERSELF FALL into an icy blanket that cushioned her body. She wanted to get up, but everything hurt, her shoulder especially. Even more alarming, she heard voices.

"Is she dead?"

"Naw, she's still breathin'."

"Let's get her in the van before someone calls 911."

Abby needed to open her eyes, but they weren't cooperating. Why was she on the ground? How had she gotten out of the car? Who was talking?

That vehicle ... Was I really run off the road?

She felt pressure under her arms. Though the searing cold of the ground vanished as she was lifted up, pain tore at her shoulder. *Where am I?* Her feet dragged over crunchy snow, then suddenly slid faster over a smooth, hard surface.

"Hold her while I open the van."

She suddenly crashed against icy pavement. The fresh pain coursing through her shoulder brought a wave of nausea. She gasped and wheezed on the blacktop, her eyes blinking wildly, trying to focus.

"Oh, come on, Johnson! Why'd you drop her?"

"Thought you said to open the van."

"I said hold her while *I* open the van, you numbskull."

Abby squinted, trying to see her surroundings. As thoughts cleared her foggy mind—or maybe it was simply the cold—she realized she lay on pavement. As there were no flashing lights of an ambulance or a cop car, these men must be her pursuers, not rescuers. She had to get away.

As the two men fought, she rolled onto her front, steering clear of her left shoulder, and struggled to her knees. She stilled and groaned as the dizzy fog swept over her again and willed it to subside, but her traitorous body slumped back to the ground.

"Hurry up with the door. She's comin' to."

A vehicle door creaked open. A pair of boots stepped into Abby's vision. She focused in on the lettering on the heel. *Timberland.* Whoever it was had huge feet. His boots scraped over the icy pavement, her own labored breathing the only competing sound.

Just like before, someone grabbed under her arms from behind and sent her shoulder screaming. She moaned a protest and kicked in a feeble attempt at escape. Her feet barely left the ground.

God, help me, please.

The men were quick. Another one grabbed her floundering legs, and together they tossed her into the back of a van and slammed the door. She blinked in the pitch blackness, struggling to sit, and softly squeezed her shoulder with her right hand, feeling for damage. Probably dislocated. The men had likely pulled her out of the wreckage by her arm. Abby groaned. Her car. She hadn't seen the condition of the BMW. Was it totaled?

A bitter laugh escaped her lips, echoing softly in the metal darkness. Here she was worrying about her car when she'd been kidnapped.

Two doors slammed shut. The engine rumbled to life, vibrating the darkness around her. She prayed as the van moved, probably taking her to her death. Perhaps they'd throw her into Lake Praydor. It was frozen over, but if they cut a hole and shoved her through … She stopped herself, angry that her irrational fear—and too many episodes of crime dramas—had distracted her prayer. She focused on God again and prayed for safety, and that his ultimate plan would prevail. Because she definitely had no idea what to do.

A short drive later, the van stopped. Abby tensed as the cab doors opened and closed. She listened closely as two sets of boots crunched their way to the back of the van. With effort, she got to her feet in a squat position, ready for a fight. *Why didn't I make more of an effort to find Sarah Palin's kickboxing class? That skill would be handy right now.*

The back doors opened but all Abby could see was a single beam of light piercing the darkness. Abby shrank back and shielded her eyes, blinking until she could see two dark silhouettes. One of them hoisted himself into the back, rocking the van with his movement. Abby could just make out his bearded face and the now familiar boots.

"Don't give us no trouble now, pretty lady," the man said as he closed in.

Drawing on her fear, Abby sprang past him and leaped out of the van, tumbling headfirst into the snow. An unbidden cry accompanied the impact to her left side, and the pain only intensified as she scrambled to her feet. Regardless, she ran, taking in her surroundings as she went. She was in the middle of a forest.

"Get her!"

Abby veered around the van, intending to find the road and follow it out. Instead, she plowed right into a man's open arms. His body odor overwhelmed her as he wrapped his arms tightly around her torso, squeezing the tender area around her rotator cuff. Abby fought back a gag but not the sharp moan.

"I got her, Johnson."

The back doors slammed shut and the crunch of snow drew closer. Abby stomped down on her captor's foot. He didn't budge.

Johnson appeared beside them, flashlight clenched between his teeth. He bent down and grabbed Abby's ankles, pulling them together and tucking them under his arm so she was carried between the two men. Abby jerked her legs, hoping to free one and get in a good kick. As she twisted, she caught a glimpse of the foul-smelling man and noticed he was heavyset and bald. *If I ever escape, these men will rot in jail.*

A car sped past on the distant highway, and she risked a piercing scream in a sliver of hope the driver might hear. Who knows? Someone could be driving the winter highway in the middle of the night with his windows rolled down. This was Alaska, after all.

The men carried Abby through a forest so dark she couldn't see where they were headed. After an interminable amount of minutes, Johnson suddenly dropped her feet and crouched. Abby stood on her own legs and stopped struggling in an attempt to see what he was doing. A hinge squeaked as Johnson opened a door in the ground. A storm cellar or something.

She scanned the dark forest around her, unable to see anything to pinpoint her location. Johnson swept up her legs again, and the heavyset man stepped into the dark hole.

"No!" Abby's head sank below the ground. "Why are you doing this?"

The men didn't answer, only led her down a staircase into darkness.

At the bottom of the stairs, Johnson dropped her ankles and climbed back up to shut the door. Abby gave one last piercing scream, eliciting laughter from her beefy captor.

"Scream away, girlie. No one can hear you."

Abby waited, watching the tiny beam of light from Johnson's flashlight descend the stairs and pass her. The beam illuminated a silver surface, then a lockbox. A vault door. A second entrance into the Farm? She hoped the cops had taken her advice and were watching the place.

"Got your card, Rolo?"

Rolo grinned as he dragged Abby toward the lockbox. He released her long enough to shift his grip to Abby's sore arm and pull a keycard from his pocket. His hand stayed poised near a slot in the box.

Johnson stepped away, taking the light with him. A second lockbox entered the beam.

"Hurry up," Rolo said. "I'm sick of this kid. Glad we don't do girls here."

"One. Two. Three," Johnson said, and the men swiped their cards.

The door clicked and Johnson pulled it open. Abby stood tall and walked through the door, despite the violent push from her captor.

Hopefully they were taking her to Marty or her dad.

A stone corridor stretched before her, lit with dim bulbs every twenty steps or so. Abby walked maybe two hundred yards before the tunnel veered right to another vault door. Johnson and Rolo swiped their keycards again.

This door opened to a white hallway floored with gray, industrial carpet. Halfway up the wall on her left, a dark window stretched the length of the hallway, looking in on an empty cafeteria. As the men led Abby into the building, she realized she was looking in on the Farm itself.

They stopped at an elevator and Abby looked over her shoulder. Straight across from the elevator, a set of double doors split the tinted windows, but the two-way mirrors continued on the other side of the doors, overlooking a black barred children's playground with a bright orange slide that was just as Marty had described it.

At least they gave the boys that much.

The elevator dinged and Rolo maneuvered her inside while Johnson swiped his keycard and hit the button that said L1. The elevator rose, and the doors opened to a stark, white waiting room.

Abby shut her eyes against the brightness, then blinked, not wanting to miss where they were taking her.

Straight through a reception area. She thought back to Marty's drawings of the Farm. This level had a hallway that ran in a U shape from one side of reception area to the other, with Dr. Kane's office and the computer lab in the center. The guards were headed for the office.

The men led Abby through a doorway into a vast and richly decorated office. For a place that had little color, this room was an exception. A wide mahogany conference table stretched across the front end of the office, the edge and legs intricately carved. Matching chairs upholstered in black leather surrounded it. An Oriental carpet probably worth fifty grand covered the floor. At the other end of the room, Dr. Kane sat behind a massive antique desk and motioned to one of two high-back chairs that sat before it.

The guards dragged her to the chairs.

"Please, sit down," he said. "Can I take your coat and gloves?"

"No, thanks," Abby said, grossed out by the way his voice sounded like JD's. "I'm not staying."

The guards pulled back one of the chairs and negated her choice. She resituated herself on the soft, low seat, perching on the edge and sitting as tall as her spine would stretch. Apparently the doctor liked sitting above everyone else.

Abby glanced around the room. Fresh flowers brought a sweet smell to the underground office. Candy dishes filled with M&M's sat on every wooden surface. A huge painting hung on the wall: a family portrait of Dr. Kane, his wife, and JD.

How bizarre to have a life-sized painting of you and your clone.

"A handsome family, don't you think?" Dr. Kane asked. He watched her from behind his oversized desk with familiar, hungry brown eyes.

Abby shivered. "There *is* quite a resemblance. Do you have paintings with the other fifty-five?"

"The Jasons are not people, Miss Goyer, like you and me. These are duplications of me, photocopies if you will."

"Then your *son* isn't a person?"

"JD is different. An exception. A gift. My wife wanted a child more than anything, which is what started this all. I know you think it was my illness, but that came later. Creating life is a deep human need. When you can't succeed, it creates a certain … frustration, almost a madness. I had to find a way for Helen to conceive. As a result, she became JD's surrogate, which is what makes him so different from the others. He is the only one who got to stay with his birthmother."

"So she knows her only son is not real?"

"Oh, JD is real. A real copy of the original. But, yes, she knows he's my clone. Why do you think she won't allow him to date?" Dr. Kane chuckled. "Of course children always want what they can't have. I guess our rules and your rejection were too much challenge for JD to ignore."

"Free will is also a deep human need, Dr. Kane."

"Not in my clones. They know their purpose and that's what they live for. JD is no exception, although his purpose is different from the others. To be a child to us."

"JD knows he's a clone?"

"Of course not. I define purpose for my clones, Miss Goyer. I do not want them confused. JD's purpose is to live as my son. J:3:3's purpose is to give his life as a sacrifice for a good cause. In fact all the boys at this facility share that purpose, for now. Come, see what I mean."

Rolo grabbed Abby's left arm and tugged her to her feet. She gritted her teeth, not wanting to call attention to her injury again. Together, they followed Dr. Kane out of the office, sliced across the reception area, through an archway, and into a white corridor. The only sound was everyone's shoes squeaking against the white tile.

They passed one door, and Abby noticed how the doors were identical, about ten steps apart from each other, and stretched down the outer wall of the corridor. Johnson opened the third door, and Dr. Kane led them inside. The interior reminded Abby of an examination room, similar to any that one might see at a physician's office. The only difference was the microscope on the counter. But the man dressed in a white lab coat definitely wasn't a standard physician.

"Dad!" Abby wrenched away from Rolo and threw her good arm around her father.

"Abby, *darling*. I'm so glad to see you. Talk about working overtime." Dad chuckled and stepped out of her embrace.

Something was weird. Dad never called her *darling*. That was his name for Mom—when they hadn't been fighting, anyway. Abby let the questions queue in her mind, waiting for the right time to ask.

She glanced around the room and choked back a scream. Marty was strapped to an examination table, morosely staring at his feet. His head and face were freshly shaven, and he was dressed again in the gray sweatpants and a white T-shirt that had *J:3:3* printed in black on the sleeve. The doctor who came to the police station with Dr. Kane stood on the other side of Marty's exam table, clipboard in hand.

Abby lunged to Marty's side and took his limp hand, wanting to rip off the cruel restraint at his wrist. The bruising on his eye was gone. It was him, wasn't it? Yes, she could see the faint scratch on his cheek from the tree branch. "What did you do to him?" She unhooked the strap and glared at the doctor who stood on the other side. The tall, scarecrow-like man barely reacted. "Let him out of these bindings."

"Very well, Miss Goyer," said Dr. Kane. "Dr. Elliot, if you will?"

The tall man removed the strap on Marty's other wrist. His arm slid lifelessly off the table.

Abby squeezed Marty's hand and shook it. "You've … drugged him or something."

"No drugs, Miss Goyer," Dr. Kane said. "Only instruction. J:3:3 experienced a glitch when he escaped. We've corrected that glitch."

"With drugs?"

"With persuasion. J:3:3 knows better than to disobey. He has been told to forget what he saw outside of the Farm, including you."

"That's ridiculous. You can't force people to forget."

Dr. Kane chuckled, a darker version of JD's cocky laugh. "I can be very persuasive. J:3:3 is due to expire on the twenty-eighth. He would like to spend much of that time with his close acquaintances, isn't that right, Dr. Goyer?"

"Yes."

Abby turned to glare at her dad and caught a tiny wink. Hope burned in her chest like a sip of scalding cocoa. She pulled off her gloves and tucked them in her jacket pocket, then turned back to Marty and squeezed his limp hand again.

"Marty, it's Abby," she whispered. "Look at me, Marty. You don't have to expire. We can still get free. Have faith—God will help us."

Marty continued to stare at his feet, but his fingers trembled and a tear welled in the corner of his eye. He *was* still in there, pretending not to be, for some reason. Was this Dr. Kane's *persuasion* in effect? Had he threatened Marty in some way to be submissive?

Abby rounded on Dr. Kane. "Where is Baby? I want to see him."

"I'm not sure who you mean."

"You know exactly who I mean. Marty's friend, Baby. Show him to me. Now."

"Your daughter is tenacious, Dr. Goyer."

"What harm could come from Abby seeing J:4:4 at this point?" Dad asked. "My daughter is extremely intelligent, and J:4:4 is a fascinating subject. I say what I said before. Abby would be an asset to your work here."

Abby spun back to her dad and caught his stiff grin. He wanted her to play along.

Dr. Kane heaved a sigh. "Dr. Goyer, I'm sure you haven't forgotten what I've told you. If I allow the Jasons to see a female, I cannot guarantee her safety."

Abby tensed at his vague reference to Dr. Markley's death.

"J:4:4 is in Dr. Elliot's lab," Dad said. "No one will see her but him, and he's restrained."

Marty, still feigning a comatose form, squeezed Abby's hand.

She fought back tears and squeezed back. "Take me there. I want to see him."

Reluctantly, she released Marty's hand and stepped toward the door.

"Fine, fine. But first, Dr. Elliot?" Dr. Kane snapped his fingers.

Within seconds Rolo forced Abby into a chair by the door while Johnson unzipped Abby's bomber jacket and yanked it off, jerking her sore shoulder in the process. Abby gritted her teeth. As soon as he tossed her coat on the floor, Johnson grabbed her forearm and pushed her left sleeve up over her elbow.

Dr. Elliot tied a rubber strap around Abby's left upper arm, pinching her skin in his haste. She fought but could hardly budge against the strength of the two men now holding her down. She glanced at her dad. "Daddy?"

Dad's wrinkled forehead gave away his worry. "Is this really necessary?"

"Only insurance." Dr. Kane's smile had an eerie resemblance to JD's when he decided to get his way. "You're the best of the best, Dr. Goyer, without a doubt. And while I do believe your daughter is as brilliant as you claim, word at the high school already pegs her as a crusader. I'm sure you can't blame me for taking a small safeguard. I would hate to come into work tomorrow and find I no longer have a lab."

"I'm not a *terrorist*." Abby winced and shut her eyes as Dr. Elliot plunged a needle into her arm. She cracked one eye to get a peek. He wasn't injecting her, but drawing blood. "What are you doing?"

"I've no intention of cloning females, Miss Goyer. They're weak—physically and emotionally. They can be taken advantage of, and I want order on my farm. Women arouse disorder. But ..." He reached his index finger toward her hair and hooked a curl, drawing it back so that it coiled around his finger, then bounced free. "If you attempt to thwart me in any way, I will not hesitate to experiment with your DNA. Many scientists would be interested in testing female subjects. I'm sure they'd pay top dollar for your clones."

[CHAPTER TWENTY-ONE]

ABBY SHUDDERED AND GLANCED AT MARTY.
Please, God. Help us. Make this right.

Dr. Elliot withdrew the needle and taped a cotton swab over the bead of blood forming on Abby's inner elbow. He left the room, carrying her blood. The potential for a host of Abbys.

Panic temporarily hit Abby, but she didn't want Dr. Kane to see that. She wanted to say something that might scare him as much as his actions were scaring her. "You may not like women, Dr. Kane," she said, as calmly as she could, "but you clearly haven't thought things through. Right now, neither gender is dominant. Men and women need each other. God designed it that way." She paused, doubting God would ever allow her next words to happen, yet said, "But you're changing all that. Since it's possible for babies to be cloned from women without the need of a male, men become insignificant to reproduction and expendable. In a hundred years, thanks to *your* research, women might just take over the world."

Dr. Kane stared at Abby with a cold expression. "Another reason why women will never work in this lab." He set a hand on her shoulder and squeezed. "Your father ensures me you are brilliant, Miss Goyer, but have no delusions. You will never see enough of my research to do any harm—no woman will. Your involvement will be extremely limited. Your father has bargained for your life; if you can be of use, so much the better. But should you become a liability"—his dark eyebrows rose—"you *could* be a surrogate."

Dad gasped. "Now, hold on a minute. That was never part of our agreement."

Dr. Kane released Abby and pulled open the door. "Now ..." He paused to look back at her. "You had asked to see J:4:4, is that right?"

Abby nodded, assuming J:4:4 was Baby. The guards hovered near her as she got up and followed after Dr. Kane. He entered the lab next door to her dad's and flipped on the lights. The lab was set up identically, including the presence of a boy strapped to the table. He flinched when the halogen bulbs flickered to life. His eyes squeezed shut and his head thrashed from one side to the other while he whimpered and squirmed. Martyr had said Baby was small, but she hadn't been prepared for the reality before her. He was a dwarfed teenager. His white T-shirt bunched around his waif-like torso and skeletal arms. His head seemed abnormally large, although it was probably the only thing about him that was the right size for his age. Purple and green bruises covered his face, neck, and arms.

Abby broke free from the guards and stepped closer. "What happened to him?"

"Some of the older boys," Dr. Kane said. "Without J:3:3's protection, J:4:4 was an easy target. They attacked him the first day J:3:3 was gone." He walked over to the table and stroked Baby's forehead. "J:4:4 has a form of hypochondroplasia. His body has not grown in comparison to his head. He's somewhat intelligent—likely mute of his own volition. Only J:3:3 seems to understand him. Those two have developed their own communication, a form of sign language. Fascinating, really."

Baby opened his eyes and Abby's heart broke. They were the same eyes as JD and Dr. Kane's, but with a warmth like Marty's. "Based on his name and the way Marty talked, I was expecting a child."

"The guards give out pet names as it's easier for them to keep track that way. J:4:4 sucks his thumb and doesn't talk, earning the nickname Baby. J:3:3 rescues him from the other's assaults, rescues anyone unfortunate enough to be targeted by the bigger boys, earning himself the nickname Martyr."

"Why strap them to these tables if they're here of their own free will?"

"The bindings are for the subjects' own safety. J:4:4 is here as leverage."

Abby sucked an angry breath through her nose. "To get Marty to behave."

"You see how well it works. J:3:3 obeys because I control his environment."

Abby scoffed. "It's not obedience to you that causes him to submit. You're not bending his will to yours if he makes his choice to protect Baby. He sacrifices himself for a friend, proving he loves another more than himself. Proving he's no photocopy of you. Proving you're not in control. You, Dr. Kane, are not God."

With Dr. Kane gone, Martyr snapped out of his lethargy and looked to Dr. Goyer.

"We have very little time," Dr. Goyer said as he helped Martyr sit. "Don't forget to tape off the sprinkler heads before starting the fire. And the servers are—"

"Under the table," Martyr said. "I remember."

"We've got to make this work. You'll have to really hit me hard."

Martyr did not want to strike Dr. Goyer, but he understood how it would look if he did not. Dr. Goyer stepped back and Martyr jumped down from the table. The tile floor felt cool under his bare feet. He missed wearing socks.

Dr. Goyer withdrew two keycards from his pocket, held them up, and set them on his desk. "The briefcase might be your best bet." Dr. Goyer pointed to the narrow black box on the floor by his desk. "A good swing to my temple should do the trick."

Martyr picked up the *briefcase* and paused.

"It's now or never, Martyr. Give it to me good. Pretend I'm Dr. Kane. Or Rolo or Johnson. Pretend I'm Dr. Elliot."

Martyr sucked in a sharp breath, winced, and swung the briefcase at Dr. Goyer's head with all his strength, thinking of Baby in Dr. Elliot's office and how Dr. Elliot had promised to hurt Baby when Martyr was gone. Dr. Goyer fell back against his shelf, knocking test tubes and flasks over. Some crashed to the floor.

Martyr dropped the briefcase and stared at the drop of blood growing on Dr. Goyer's temple. He needed to go before help came. He hoped Dr. Goyer was all right. He snatched the keycards, wedged them under the waistband of his sweatpants, and stepped out into the hall.

The distant sound of breaking glass made Abby jump. Dr. Kane, in contrast, sped past her into the hall, followed by the guards. Abby stared after them a moment, then unhooked Baby's restraints. She helped him sit, but his lethargic body wasn't cooperating.

"Baby, you've got to get up. Martyr has come back for you," she said, "and if we don't move now, he may have come back for nothing."

Baby's eyes locked with hers. He banged his chest with his fist then pointed to his cheek.

"Find him!" Dr. Kane's voice boomed from the hallway.

Abby peeked out the door and saw the guards running down

the hall away from Abby, Dr. Kane and Dr. Elliot at their heels. Had her dad freed Marty? Were they escaping without her?

She took Baby's hand and darted across the hall, through the reception area, and to the elevator. She pushed the up arrow, but when the doors opened she realized she couldn't operate the elevator from the inside without a keycard. Footsteps neared, so Abby dragged Baby out of the elevator and down the opposite hallway. Halfway down the corridor, a bald Jason poked his head out from a door, looking away from them.

Like an excited chimpanzee, Baby grunted in a language of his own. The Jason turned to face them. *Marty!* His face lit up in a smile, his previous comatose behavior completely gone as he waved them forward. Baby broke into a sprint, almost dragging Abby along. The little guy was surprisingly strong.

Marty crowded them into a dark lab room, then locked the door and pressed his ear to the white surface.

Baby continued to grunt and whimper. After a glance at the door, Marty walked to the middle of the room and put his arms around Baby, shushing and rubbing the smaller boy's back. Baby put his thumb into his mouth and went silent, tucking his head into the crook of Marty's neck. *How cute is that?*

Marty looked over Baby's head at Abby. "Thank you for freeing him, Abby Goyer."

Abby smiled.

"We must hurry to the elevator." Martyr pulled two keycards from his waistband. "I would give you one in case we're separated, but you need two to operate the elevators."

"What about my dad?"

Martyr's eyes shifted away. "He should be safe as long as he's not seen helping us."

"*Should* be?"

"He must look frustrated with our escape, like he's on Dr. Kane's side. Don't believe anything he says when Dr. Kane is in the room. He's playing a part, like the people on *TV*."

Abby pressed her lips together to avoid laughing.

Marty put his ear to the door again and then twisted the

doorknob. Abby followed Marty and Baby back toward the elevator end of the building. They'd only walked a few yards when Marty froze, forcing Abby to bump into his back. Johnson had rounded the corner and was blocking the way.

"Found 'em," the guard yelled, stepping closer. "Always tryin' to save the day, ain't you, Martyr? Can't just toe the line. Always got to make trouble."

Abby grabbed Baby's hand and ran the other way. When she didn't hear footsteps behind her, she stopped and glanced over her shoulder. Marty hadn't moved.

He stepped sideways, skipping slightly as Johnson neared. The guard slapped his stick against his empty palm in time with each step. Heart racing, Abby turned the corner and reached a door. Peeking through the rectangular window revealed a stairway that led down. She yanked the door open.

"No, Abby Goyer!" Marty's bare feet slapped against the tile floor as he sprinted to her side. He grabbed her sleeve to keep her from going through. She bit her lip against the pain shooting down her left arm as Marty pulled her around the next corner, back to the elevators. Dr. Kane, Dr. Elliot, and Rolo ran toward them.

Marty stepped in front of her, inching backward.

Abby darted back to the stairwell. "Marty, what are you doing? There's nowhere else to go."

"But if we go down, we will be trapped," Marty said.

"If we don't, we'll be caught."

Marty's forehead wrinkled. He yelled in frustration and pushed through the double doors. Abby grabbed Baby's hand and followed.

Martyr's hope sank with each step that took them lower. Dr. Goyer would be disappointed. He simply asked Martyr to get Abby out, and already Martyr had failed. How would escape be possible from the lower levels? And what would the Jasons do if they saw him? More importantly, what would they do if they saw Abby? Martyr swallowed the queasy thought, pushing aside the haunting image of Dr. Woman's broken body. He stopped on the landing between levels two and three and ran his hands over his face.

Abby took his hands in hers. "Don't worry," she said. "God will protect us."

She looked frightened despite her brave words.

"We'll go all the way down to level three," Martyr said. "We need to be very quiet. The Jasons are sleeping on level two, and we don't want to wake them." He squeezed Abby's hand. "I have a few hiding spots the doctors don't know about."

Martyr padded down the steps to level three, wincing as the door squeaked open into the dark hallway. They crept past the classrooms and stopped before the vast darkness of the recreational area. Four dim overhead lamps lit the large space.

Please, let everyone be asleep.

Abby clutched his arm. "Marty. Where is the cafeteria and playground?"

"Upstairs. On level two."

"There is a tunnel that leads outside. That's how they brought me in."

Martyr turned to face Abby. "What is a tunnel?"

"A way out. A long hallway that leads outside."

"There is no *tunnel* at Jason Farms."

Abby dragged Martyr toward the double doors in the center of the wall of reflecting glass. "It's on the other side of the doors like these, on the level with the cafeteria. Let's try."

Martyr hesitated, certain Abby was mistaken. Surely he would have heard of a tunnel if one existed on level two. He handed her a keycard anyway. Abby poised it over the keycard box on one side of the doors. He held his over the other and counted to three, like the guards always did, before he and Abby swiped.

The door clicked.

Abby pulled it open. "We'll go up one level and I'll show you the door."

"But what if someone comes down this way?"

Abby glanced up at the ceiling, where a camera's lens glinted. "They're watching us anyway. We may as well try."

They punched the button on the elevator and waited. The elevator's gears seemed to shift in slow motion. He prayed the Creator of Everything might allow the elevator to be—

Ding!

Martyr jumped and pushed Abby and Baby behind him. The elevator opened. Empty.

Thank you, Creator.

They rode up one level. When the doors opened, Abby ran out to the left. Martyr jogged after her, pulling Baby alongside, but stopped when he saw the windows. Dark glass stretched the length of the hallway. Not reflecting glass. Windows. Baby pressed his palm to the window and grunted.

Martyr nodded. He and Baby were both thinking the same thing. *Why?* So the doctors could watch them eat, play, exercise, and study in the classrooms?

"Marty!" Abby said.

He turned to see Abby at the end of the hallway, standing at a door, keycard poised at the top of a keycard box. He furrowed his eyebrows. Where might such a door lead? Perhaps it was another staircase?

Could it really be a way out?

Filled with hope, Martyr immediately held his keycard to the free slot. Abby counted to three and they swiped their cards. A red light flashed on Martyr's keycard box.

"Again," said Abby.

They swiped their cards, but again the light blinked red. Over and over they tried, but the door would not respond.

"Different keycards must open different doors," Abby said. "Whose cards are these?"

"Your father's," Martyr said.

"He probably doesn't have clearance for the secret exit."

Martyr turned, scanning the tinted windows for movement. "We must go back down. We need to hide."

Martyr jogged across the spongy track, grabbing two towels off the pile by the weight bench before ushering Abby and Baby through a door in the middle of the far wall. The moment the door clicked shut, he tucked the towels against the crack at the foot of the door until he couldn't see a speck of light. Then he felt along the wall until he found the switch and flipped it on, illuminating a dull bulb that buzzed softly. They would be found eventually—the guards knew about this hiding place—but at least here they would have some time to think.

Abby looked around at the shelves of sports equipment and sat down on a basketball. "They let you play sports?"

"It's important we remain in good physical health." Martyr sat cross-legged on the concrete floor. He draped an arm around Baby, who had settled beside him and leaned his head against Martyr's shoulder. "I missed you, Baby. I'm sorry I left without saying good-bye. I never intended to be gone so long."

Baby sat up and signed urgently, his face molded into a pout.

Tears tingled behind Martyr's eyes as he watched Baby's story and took in the horrible bruises on his friend's face and neck. Iron Man and Fido had done plenty of damage while he'd been away.

"What's he saying?" Abby asked.

"He's telling me he spent two days in the infirmary." Martyr laughed. "He says he can eat all the food he wants in the infirmary and no one bothers him."

Baby's expression sobered. He glanced warily at Abby, signing and grunting with fury.

"He says you are very kind and you smell nice, but he is worried for you because … No. We will keep her safe, you and I. I think it's part of our purpose." He tapped his chest, then reached out and tapped Baby's chest. "Purpose."

Baby grunted and banged his chest.

"Shh." Martyr reached out to calm Baby, but the doors swung open. Martyr jumped up, staring into the dark void beyond the storage room door, heart pounding. No one made a sound. Had Martyr not pulled the door closed all the way? Maybe it had simply fallen open?

"Look who came back, Fido."

Fear doused Martyr like a cold shower. He backed in front of Abby while Baby scrambled behind them both. A white-clad figure stepped out of the darkness and stopped just inside the door.

Iron Man.

[CHAPTER TWENTY-TWO]

J.3.3

ABBY PEEKED AROUND MARTY'S LEG. A massive
JD Kane stood in the open doorway, looking like some kind of
wrestling superstar. This had to be the guy Marty said hung out
with a clone named Fido and terrorized all the Brokens. He was no
taller than Marty or JD, but his white T-shirt clung to his he-man
chest and arms. It was almost gross.

Something growled in the darkness behind him. Slowly,
another clone, also dressed in white, prowled into the storage
room. It was beyond weird how they all had the same face. This
one stood hunched, bug-eyed, licking his lips, and sniffing. Fido,
no doubt. Not only was he emitting a perpetually low growl, saliva

dribbled out the corner of his mouth and glinted under the light. Was it cloning gone wrong or psychological abuse that had him behaving this way? If the guards had told him he was a dog all his life, he might believe it.

No wonder the boys who lived on the Farm needed a protector. These guys were messed up.

Iron Man gazed down at Abby with lupine eyes, but his words were for Marty. "Who is this?"

Maybe it was best not to show fear. Abby stood and shook out her hair, mustering up as much confidence as possible. She stepped around Marty and held out her hand to shake. Marty moved with her. She could feel him hovering behind her like some kind of static cling.

"I'm Abby Goyer. Marty has told me so much about you. Never thought I'd actually meet you two, but what do you know? Dr. Kane made an exception to his *no visitors allowed* policy. It's my lucky day, I guess." She laughed, and it came out in a nervous whinny.

Iron Man looked down at her hand, clearly uncertain what he was meant to do with it.

Think, Abby. The Farm doesn't teach social skills.

Fido sprang forward, snatched her hand with both of his, and brought it to his face. He sniffed it—each breath a raspy growl— then licked it with one long swipe of the tongue.

Abby cringed, holding back the gasp of disgust that wanted to leap from her throat. She forced herself to remain still. Show no fear. Maybe they all just wanted to play, like overgrown children. She spotted a ball on the floor. Maybe Fido knew fetch.

Iron Man clapped twice. Fido dropped Abby's hand and shrank back as Iron Man stepped toward her, devouring every inch of her with those hungry JD eyes.

Uh oh.

"Where did you find him?" Iron Man's eyes didn't leave Abby's. She kept her gaze fixed on his, determined that looking him in the eye proved she wasn't scared.

"Outside," Marty said softly.

"Lies." Iron Man stepped past Abby, nearly knocking her over with his sandbag arm. He instead used the momentum on Marty. Marty cried out as his head slammed up into one of the shelves, bumping the metal plank off its pegs and over Marty's left shoulder. Five-pound weights clanged to the floor one at a time. Two landed on Iron Man's bare foot, but he didn't seem concerned, focused instead on the massive hand that gripped Marty's neck.

"He's not lying." Abby pulled at Iron Man's fingers. "My father is Dr. Goyer. He works here."

Iron Man dropped Marty and swung toward Abby. He looped his arm around Abby's waist and hefted her against his side like carrying a stack of books. Fido followed obediently. Abby looked back at Marty, who was scrambling to his feet, gasping.

Baby lay in a little ball on the floor.

Iron Man towed her across the dark track. Fido ran alongside, occasionally circling them like an excited animal. They walked down the long hallway to the stairs and paused as Iron Man flung open one of the double doors. Abby turned to see Marty sprinting after them. Baby loped behind like a wounded gazelle. This was starting to look like something from *National Geographic*. Abby hoped she wasn't the carnivore's prey.

She felt off balance, like her top half could swing over at any moment. She clutched Iron Man's forearm with her right hand and let her left arm hang limp. Her left shoulder was a throbbing numbness she was sadly growing used to. "I can walk, you know."

If he heard, he didn't show it. Her leg snagged on the railing as Iron Man whipped around the landing, climbing the stairs to level two. She winced and shook off the sting. At least her weight appeared to be slowing the behemoth clone down; by the time he pushed the doors open on level two, Marty had caught up.

"Please." Marty's voice was an urgent whisper. "We must keep her from the guards. Dr. Kane is—"

Iron Man spun around in the dark hallway, swinging Abby's head out like a pendulum. Her left arm slapped the wall, sending a violent tremor through her shoulder.

"No one is on guard," Iron Man said. "They all left."

Because the guards had been out chasing her. So why hadn't the guards come down after them yet? A quick scan of the hallway ceiling brought a small, gray camera into view. It pointed toward a door a few steps away. Perhaps the guards were watching, waiting to see what their massive clone and his wannabe dog were going to do? Her chest constricted as her breath grew ragged. This was her life, not reality TV. She had to get away.

Marty met her eyes, his face a mask of concentration.

Abby sucked in as deep a breath as possible. Iron Man's grip was cutting off the circulation to her legs, making it impossible to run even if she could overpower the guy.

Fido padded ahead and burst through the third door on the left, holding it open. Abby's boots scraped the doorframe as Iron Man carried her inside. Marty followed.

Someone turned on the lights. Abby found herself in a large room filled with bunk beds, four on each side wall. An open, tiled area with showerheads, urinals, and toilets filled the back. No dressers, no TV, no personal items of any kind, no bathroom stalls.

Over a dozen half-dressed Jasons squirmed to life on the beds. Some sat up, some rolled over, and all of them squinted in the halogen lights.

Abby looked from face to face, taking in glimpses of JD Kane from junior high on up.

Unreal.

Iron Man finally put her down. She massaged her waist, certain he'd left a welt.

A skinny boy wearing nothing but a pair of gray sweatpants staggered out of his bed. "What's wrong?"

Abby jumped as a hairy bare leg swung past her ear.

"Who is he?"

"*What* is he?"

"*She*," said Marty. "Women are she."

"Martyr is back."

"Martyr!"

The skinny boy in the sweatpants sidled up to Marty and clapped him on the back. "Where did you find the she?"

Abby wrinkled her nose as a chubby Jason, wearing nothing but a pair of tighty whities, stalked toward her. She averted her eyes from the horror and shrank back against Marty as the Jasons closed in.

Her *National Geographic* episode had turned sci-fi. Instead of *Gorillas in the Mist*, she was now living out some kind of *Planet of the Apes*. Make that Planet of the JD Kanes. The clones were intelligent, but—because of her—they were acting like primates: staring and grunting at each other.

"Ow!" She scowled at a shorter Jason, who'd plucked out a few strands of her hair.

Another boy stroked her cashmere sweater. A purple sweater. She winced, remembering Marty's fascination with bright colors. Another Jason mauled the side of her face with his clammy hand.

Pawing at her like animals.

No. They weren't animals. They were people. Children. Who had been psychologically abused.

And not loved.

Regardless, Abby thought back to the gorilla show she'd seen on the Discovery channel a few weeks back. Don't show fear. That had been the main thing. Marty took her right hand in his and pulled her close, and his touch filled her with warmth. A Jason grabbed her other hand and rubbed it, frowning at her painted fingernails and purity ring.

"I don't see what's so special about him," the bare-legged Jason said. He was still sitting atop his bunk bed.

Tighty-whitie boy fisted her hair. "His hair's soft."

"And long and twisting," said the boy holding her hand.

"Like the dog." Iron Man clutched her left arm at the bicep.

She sucked in a small gasp at the pain his grasp caused. *Dog?*

"His pants are like Rolo's eyes."

"What color is his shirt?"

"Purple," Marty said.

"He's small, like a Broken or a J:10."

"No, like a J:8. Like Mikey."

Someone honked a dorky JD laugh. "Mikey! That's funny."

"Can he speak?"

"Is he like Baby? Martyr, does he speak signs too?"

Marty crushed her hand, almost at Iron Man's strength. He didn't look so hot at the moment. His eyes were bloodshot, and his face was pale—smooth since his recent shave. He wore an expression a father might give a guy taking his daughter out on a date.

The boy holding her left hand had nearly rubbed it raw, like it was some sort of stress ball. Up, down, up, down. Tighty-whitie boy raked his fingers through her hair again. Iron Man still gripped her arm. And Marty still held her right hand. Far too many people were touching her.

She fought to think rationally. The only way out was the elevator or the tunnel, right? She concentrated to remember Marty's map of the facility.

The dumbwaiter she'd seen while snooping. It came out somewhere down here. Marty hadn't mentioned it, but if they could get away, she could look for it. The kitchen perhaps?

"It's my turn," someone called from the back.

"Me too."

Close to twenty Jasons crowded around. Abby surveyed the room and spotted four cameras, one in each corner. Was her dad watching, worrying? Did he know what had happened to Dr. Markley? Abby gulped. Would the same thing happen to her?

"Dr. Kane lied to us," Marty said suddenly.

She turned to find him scanning the faces around them.

"The air outside is not toxic. There is no disease to cure. Abby and Dr. Goyer live in a large house. I saw the sky and a moose eating a tree. Abby has her own cell with lots of colorful clothes. A tiny white dog lives with them. She made me bleeding eggs to eat."

Say what?

"I saw birds and dolphins and huge dogs on a *TV*, which is a monitor with moving and talking pictures. I saw many cars. Some are called trucks and some are called vans. I saw people with different faces and different hair. I saw many women and colors I never dreamed existed. I ate red and green pizza and wore socks."

"Like Rolo's socks?" the tighty-whitie Jason asked.

"Yes," Martyr said, "but they were red and warm and had green triangles on them."

They *were* pretty rockin' Christmas socks. Abby had got them 50 percent off.

The Jasons all started to talk at once about socks and creatures that ate trees. Marty pulled Abby toward the door, but Iron Man's grip on her sore arm remained tight.

Marty yelled, "Quiet!"

The Jasons settled down.

Marty released Abby's hand, reached down, and pulled something out of his waistband. He held it above his head and the Jasons gasped.

"A keycard."

"Where did you get it?"

"Can I look at it?"

"Martyr, let me see."

"It's how I was able to go outside. Listen." The murmuring stopped. "What Dr. Kane has told us is a lie. We don't expire because we turn eighteen years old. Dr. Kane kills us."

The mumbling started up again. A great ache seized her arm as Iron Man released it and blood started to flow. He stepped up to Marty and snatched the keycard, examining it up close. "It's what the doctors carry."

"It will take you outside," Marty said.

Which wasn't exactly true. Two cards were needed to work the elevator. Plus the guards were upstairs. The Jasons wouldn't know that, though. Abby doubted anyone was going anywhere.

Iron Man strode out of the room. A herd of Jasons trailed after him.

Abby pulled Marty close and whispered, "Wait."

They were the last two to leave the room. Baby stood in the hallway outside the door. Abby hadn't seen him in the room. Had he been out there the entire time?

"Can we get to the kitchen? If we can, I think I know a way out."

Marty stared at her, nodded, then led them after the Jasons

down the hallway, keeping a few yards back. The hallway ended, just like the one did on level three below, only instead of ending by the track, this one led into the cafeteria and playground. The small play structure sat off to the left of the open space, and long cafeteria tables stretched across the right.

Marty pulled Abby up to a door and held out his hand. "Give me your keycard."

Abby glanced at the mob charging toward the double doors. She quickly handed the keycard over. Marty inserted it in a smaller reader above the knob and opened the door.

They entered a kitchen lit only by two dim, long halogen bulbs that flickered from the ceiling. Marty waved Baby in and closed the door behind him. "What must we do in here?"

Abby's lips parted, hope swelling inside like a breath of hot air. A steel door of similar size to the one she'd seen on her barn-sleuthing day was set into one of the walls. She walked toward it, trembling slightly. Could it be this easy? A switch hung on the outside of the door, identical to the one in the barn above. Her heart thumped wildly as she pulled the metal door open.

She laughed out loud. "Here!" But it wasn't big enough for everyone. Maybe two, barely. *Maximum Capacity 300 lbs* was etched just above a small latch on the back of the steel door. Abby did the math. Not so good.

Marty walked to Abby's side. "What?"

"This is a dumbwaiter—a mini elevator that goes outside. It's how they get food down to you. I think we can ride it to the outside."

Marty crouched and gathered her into his arms like she was a damsel in distress.

Abby squeaked. "What are you doing?"

Marty carried her toward the dumbwaiter. She put her right hand against the edge of the opening to keep him from putting her inside. "Wait! Marty, please!"

His brown eyes locked onto hers. "Is something wrong?"

Without thinking, she grabbed the back of his neck with her right hand and pulled his beautiful lips to hers. They were soft and slightly parted, spilling warm breath onto her face. He didn't kiss back at first. But when he did it was like something primal clicked and he suddenly knew what to do.

Her heart fluttered. She could feel his strong arms trembling around her. She wanted to stay here forever in the safety of those arms.

Something shifted beside them. Abby pulled back, saw Baby staring from Marty to her and back to Marty, whose eyes slowly opened. Breathless, he hefted her in his arms, stepped forward, and settled her into the cramped dumbwaiter. With extreme care he began tucking her boots inside and smoothing her hair, which clung to the wall with static.

"Will Baby fit also?" he asked.

Wha … ? Not a word about the kiss? No cute thank you or asking for a second? "I … um … I think so." She squished into the corner, tucking her body into itself.

Marty helped Baby inside. Now that they were so close, she noted the little guy smelled like a hospital. He sat on Abby's toes, wedging his feet next to her left hip. *Cozy* was not quite the right word. Sardines said it better.

"Baby, you must stay with Abby," Marty said. "She will keep you safe." His eyes met hers, all business. "Send the *dumwater* back down so I know you got out." Marty gripped the door to swing it shut.

"Marty." Abby grabbed his arm. She had never felt like this about any guy. She couldn't just leave him behind. What if he couldn't escape? What if he wouldn't? "You're coming up next, right?"

Marty's eyes flickered away. Under the low lights, his long eyelashes cast geometric shadows down his cheeks. His words came in a strained whisper: "I must help your father destroy Dr. Kane's research."

Tears welled in Abby's eyes. It made sense that he and her dad should try and stop Dr. Kane, but she didn't want to leave them behind. "Marty, you can't do this alone. Come up with us. We'll go get the cops. Helpful ones this time."

The corner of his mouth twitched. "We want the same things,

Abby Goyer. But I cannot yell at policemen or push buttons on a cell phone to convince anyone I speak truth. That's your way. My way is to use my hands, my head, and see my goal accomplished with my own eyes. That's what works best for me."

Abby swallowed. "But you'll come up as soon as you destroy the files, right?"

He closed his eyes. "Good-bye, Abby Goyer. Pray that the Creator of Everything will help me." Marty swung the metal door closed with a snap and everything went black.

Baby whimpered and shifted with a force that shook the metal box.

Abby's throat felt ready to close up. She blinked back her tears and groped around in the dark until she found Baby's hand. She squeezed it. "It'll be okay, Baby."

But she couldn't convince herself.

A sudden hum jerked the dumbwaiter up. A flood of heat tingled over Abby. Yes, she would soon be above ground. Free, unless the guards were waiting. She hadn't thought to look for a camera in the kitchen.

The dumbwaiter continued to rise. Abby hoped the door would open from the inside. She didn't want to be stuck in this tiny, dark space any longer than necessary. The kitchen was on level two, but there was no guessing how far underground level one began.

Claustrophobia and the darkness brought more maniacal *CSI*-like musings as she rode topside. The episode where one of the characters had been buried alive had always creeped her out. She chewed on her thumbnail and continued to squeeze Baby's hand while considering the myriad of ways this could play out.

A faint sucking bled into the hum of the machine lifting them. Baby had pacified himself with his thumb. Must be nice. Abby's nail chewing never brought actual relief.

Not like being with Marty had.

The dumbwaiter jerked to a stop. Abby scrambled for the latch, pulled, and exhaled when the door clicked open. A burst of cold air filled the tiny space, sending a shiver over Abby's sweaty body.
Praise God.

"Baby, you've got to get out first." She wiggled her toes to urge him along.

As Baby eased his feet out the hole, the door swung wide with a jerk. Abby screamed.

"I've got people here, in the dumbwaiter." A young police officer peered inside at Abby. "Are you Abigail Goyer?"

"Yes."

The officer turned and told someone behind him, "One of them is the girl."

The girl?

Baby kicked and moaned as the officer helped him out the door.

"It's okay, Baby." Abby pivoted and pushed her legs out the hole. A maddening tickle inched through her feet, legs, and rear end. She gasped and shook her lower limbs, desperate for blood flow.

The officer reached in, grabbed her waist, and lifted her out. He was a state trooper, young with black hair and cheeks pink from the cold. His name badge read *WESLEY*.

"Miss Goyer?" Officer Runstrom appeared at her side. "Could you come with me, please?"

Abby scowled at Runstrom and folded her arms. If he would have listened to her in the first place …

"Please?" Runstrom added in a small voice.

Abby shut the dumbwaiter and sent it back down, earning a puzzled look from both officers. She took Baby's hand and followed Runstrom down the row of aluminum storage cabinets and through the metal vault door, which had been opened somehow. It was slightly warmer inside the small, steel-walled chamber. A wide elevator covered the wall opposite the entry door; she hoped Marty or her father would come through it. The officers seemed to be turning the area into a makeshift command central. Runstrom walked behind a small, black desk to her right. Three more chairs lined the fourth wall.

Wesley ran into the room behind her, holding a black bundle. He draped a scratchy wool blanket over Abby's shoulders. She passed it to Baby, and Wesley handed her a second blanket.

She pointed to Baby's bare feet. "He needs shoes or socks or something."

"I'll see what I can find." Wesley left again.

Abby tucked the blanket around Baby and helped him sit down in one of the empty chairs against the wall. She sat in the seat beside him and the cold leather crackled under her weight.

Runstrom was intensely studying a monitor.

Abby's shoulder throbbed, but she didn't want to be taken to the hospital before she knew Marty and her dad were safe. "Officer, what made you change your mind?"

"A couple things happened all at once." Runstrom folded his hands and leaned forward on the desk. "First, your car was found, wrecked and abandoned. Then your friend, Kylee Wallace, brought this sketch to us along with some interesting paperwork. She also brought her brother, Scott Wallace, who corroborated your story. But what really did it was another fellow, named Jim Markley. Markley had a photograph of his wife standing next to a young JD Kane. Only he seemed to think it wasn't JD at all, but your boyfriend, Marty."

When this is all over, I'm getting Kylee the most amazing thank-you gift she could ever imagine. Abby gestured to the vault door. "How'd you get this door open?"

"Markley found a keycard in his wife's things. Just one, unfortunately. But it worked to open the outside door. We discovered we'll need two to work the elevator."

"Were there guards in here?"

"Just one, named Stan Chestnut. Shredded his keycard when he saw us coming. We've already taken him in for questioning. We've got this place locked down, above ground, anyway. We were securing our search warrant for this location when a call came in from a Dr. Kane. Claims a Dr. Edward Elliot is holding him and your father hostage. We're waiting for his demands now. Anyway … I understand your boyfriend drew this floor plan?" He nodded toward Baby, his forehead wrinkled. "Is that him?"

"No. Marty's still inside. With my dad. But that phone call

must have been some kind of scam. Dr. Kane is in charge here. Dr. Elliot works for *him*."

"Employees sometimes turn on their boss. Problem is, we can't get this elevator opened, and the elevator expert is still on his way. In the meantime, I'd like to send a man down the dumbwaiter, but it's not on this sketch." He smoothed his hands over Marty's floor plan of Jason Farms. "Could you show me where it comes out inside the ... farm?"

Abby studied the drawing and pointed at the kitchen. "It's here. But there's a better way in." She turned the map to face her and showed him the end of the hallway on level two. "A tunnel enters the facility, right here. I just don't know where the entrance is."

"A tunnel?"

"After those jerks ran me off the road, they took me into the woods and through a storm cellar-type door, which led to a tunnel about two hundred yards out from the Farm. There were two doors that required two keycards each, but they weren't vault doors. I bet you guys can break them down."

Runstrom picked up a CB radio and spoke into it. "Allam. Get in here. We've got another entrance." He glanced at the monitor on the desk and frowned, leaning closer to the small screen.

Abby circled the desk and looked over his shoulder, staring at the black and white image. She gasped. Her dad was strapped to a table in one of the labs. And Dr. Elliot stood over him.

[CHAPTER TWENTY-THREE]

THE DUMBWAITER RETURNED EMPTY. *Creator of Everything, please keep Abby and Baby safe.* Martyr listened at the door of the kitchen until he was certain he heard no voices. The Jasons were either at the elevator or had gone back toward the stairs.

He eased open the door. The cafeteria was deserted and there was no sign of anyone near the entrance to the elevator. Martyr edged along the wall and peeked down the hallway to the stairs.

He stood there a moment, unsure what to do. He needed to finish Dr. Goyer's plans and destroy the computers on level one. He touched the top of the single keycard, tucked safely into his waistband. The stairwell was his only option.

Martyr eased gently down the hallway. He had almost reached the doors when they flew open, releasing Iron Man, Fido, and the others into the corridor. Martyr turned around and sprinted for the children's play structure.

Iron Man yelled, "Go get 'em, boy!"

Martyr bounded over the spongy playground floor and darted under the slide just as Fido swiped sharp, ungroomed fingernails across Martyr's cheek. Martyr scrambled back and put up both hands as a barrier. Past Fido, he could see the crowd huddled on the edge of the playground, watching with wide-eyed stares. Iron Man stood in the center of the boys, arms folded across his muscular chest.

Martyr tried to reason as Fido inched nearer. "We can defeat the doctors if we work as a team. We're stronger together."

Iron Man scowled. "You lie more than the guards, Martyr. Did you learn that from your woman?"

Fido made another swipe, forcing Martyr to dash from under the slide and scramble up its slippery surface. He stopped on the top of the playground structure.

"That's right, run away," Iron Man yelled. "You always do."

"Fight him, Martyr!" Teddy, a J:4, yelled.

"Yeah!"

"Go, Martyr!"

Martyr did not want to hurt Fido, but it seemed he had no choice as long as Fido stood in the way of destroying Dr. Kane's computers. What would the Creator say to that? Would God forgive him if he hurt Fido on purpose? Martyr scanned the Jasons who stood watching, calling his name. They wanted him to fight. They wanted Fido to lose.

Fido tried to climb the slide on his hands and knees, but his pants caused him to slip backward. *Forgive me.* Martyr grabbed the bar that ran across the top of the slide and vaulted down the plastic chute. He crashed into Fido, and they landed in a tangled heap on the floor.

Fido growled and scratched, and finally sank his teeth into Martyr's hand. Years of anger went into Martyr's free fist as he punched Fido's cheek with all his strength, then he punched him again in the temple. Fido slumped to the floor and lay motionless.

Martyr rose to sit on his heels and wiped his bloody knuckles off on his shirt. Both hands shook beyond his control and throbbed— one from the bite, the other from the force of his punches. He glanced at Iron Man. Their eyes met in a silent challenge.

Martyr stood and stepped around Fido. "Fighting with each other solves nothing. We need both keycards to get outside." He drew the keycard out from his waistband and held it up. "We must work together."

"But what about the stingers?" Brain asked. "As soon as we try anything, they'll activate them."

"Dr. Goyer turned them off." At least Martyr hoped Dr. Goyer had accomplished that part of the plan.

"You're sure?" Iron Man asked.

"No. But Dr. Goyer promised to leave a tool in the computer room in case he failed. If we can get there, we can cut the stingers off." Martyr lifted his pant leg to show that his stinger ring was gone. Dr. Elliot had been about to put on another one when Abby had arrived.

Iron Man stared for a long moment, nodded once, and turned toward the stairs. "Let's go then."

Martyr walked down the hall with Iron Man, watching for any sudden movements from the muscular Jason. The boys followed, mumbling to each other.

"Where is your *woman*?" Iron Man asked.

Martyr paused, searching to find the best way to explain her disappearance. "She's hiding with Baby. I'll come back for them once we defeat the doctors."

"Did you really see outside?" Brain asked. "Was there sky? Did you see clouds?"

"When I first went out, it was night," Martyr said. "The sky is black at night, and it is filled with tiny lights called stars. They don't look like the stars Dr. Max uses on our charts, though. They're dots of light."

"The sun is a star," Brain said. "Did you see the sun?"

"Yes," Martyr said. "In the morning the room was bright, but no lights were turned on."

Brain's eyes widened. "The light came from the sun?"

"It shone through the windows."

Brain frowned. "I don't understand."

"The windows in Abby's house look outside on the trees and snow and sky. The sun was a pale yellow ball in the sky. It hurt my eyes to look at it. Abby says at night the sun goes down and the moon comes up."

"Did you see the moon?" someone behind him asked. They stopped at the entrance to the stairwell, where the Jasons crowded around Martyr.

"Abby says the moon can only be seen sometimes. I did not see it."

Iron Man opened the door to the stairwell. "Come on."

They took the stairs to level one. Iron Man stopped at the door and handed Martyr his keycard. "What should we do?"

The Jasons all fixed their eyes on Martyr. He swallowed. "We must destroy the computer server."

"What's that?" Teddy asked.

How had Dr. Goyer described it? "It's several boxes that hold information about how we were created. If we leave without destroying it, Dr. Kane can make more of us."

Iron Man snorted. "I don't care if he makes more. I want to leave, now."

Several Jasons voiced their agreement.

Martyr raised his voice. "*First* we destroy the computers. Then we restrain Dr. Kane, Dr. Elliot, and the guards. After that we find Dr. Goyer. He'll help us gather the rest of the boys. No one will be left behind."

Iron Man did not look happy but said, "Fine. Where is this *computer*?"

"According to Dr. Goyer, the computer room is the monitor room, just across the hall from here." Martyr ran his keycard through the slot and opened the door. He crossed the hall, peeked into the rectangular window on the door, and snapped back. "Rolo, Johnson, and Erik are in there."

Iron Man cracked his knuckles. "I'll gladly take care of Rolo."

Martyr looked around the group and turned to Brain. "You take Erik, I'll take Johnson. The rest of you help however you can. Ready?"

The boys all nodded, and Iron Man burst through the door.

Johnson rose from his chair as Martyr entered. "Look out!"

Rolo turned and fumbled for his stick. "How'd they get past the—"

Iron Man knocked Rolo to the floor with one punch. Martyr tried the same with Johnson, but the burly man ducked to the side and whacked Martyr's arm with his stick. Martyr shrank back, reminded why he rarely fought. Still reeling, he turned to his right, where a mob of boys had ganged up on Erik.

A shadow appeared on Martyr's left: Hummer, grabbing Johnson's neck from behind. In response, the guard spun around and whacked the boy with his stick. Hummer went down into a ball.

Iron Man stepped beside Martyr. "Allow me."

Before Martyr could answer, a crash turned every head. Brain had slammed into a table that held dozens of small monitors and stretched along the back wall. He lay on the floor, limbs shaking, a silent cry on his lips.

Then Teddy screamed and fell to the floor, his body convulsing. A shiver raced over Martyr.

The stingers still worked.

Martyr ran to the end of the table and reached behind the monitors, searching wildly for the tool Dr. Goyer had left. He spun back to Johnson in time to see Iron Man punch the guard several times, attempting to force Johnson off his feet. Then Iron Man went rigid, grunted, as if fighting the sting. Bean Bag, a scrawny J:6, picked up a monitor and smashed it over Johnson's head. The guard staggered a moment, dropped his stick, and slid to his knees.

Andre—J:5:1—stood over Erik, watching with a proud grin as two J:5s kicked the unconscious guard over and over. Bean

Bag pounded Johnson's limp body with a stick. The others stood watching, cheering as blood matted Johnson's scalp.

Bean Bag dropped the stick and fell to the floor screaming.

Iron Man went to one knee, still grunting against the electricity shooting into his body. Martyr scanned the room. Who to free first? Half the boys were down, though a few still fought without difficulty. Charlie, the round-headed J:5 who wore only underwear, kicked Erik again. Hyde, the other J:5 kicking Erik, wore only his sweatpants. Neither had shirts.

"Stop!" Martyr yelled.

The Jasons froze.

"Take off your shirts. If they can't see our numbers, it's harder for them to activate the stingers."

White shirts flew around the room as the remaining boys tossed them to the floor. Martyr counted eight bare-chested boys left. But the Jason he needed most lay on the floor whimpering. Iron Man would be no more help until his stinger was disabled.

Martyr dug the keycards from his waistband. "Andre?"

The brawny J:5 stepped forward.

"Take Hyde and Newton and Schroder to the security room." Martyr crouched at Andre's side and clipped off the stinger the way Dr. Goyer had done for him. "Go to the left, and it's the first door at the end of the hall. There should only be one man in there." Martyr stepped over to Hyde and clipped his stinger ring. "He's the one who turns on the stingers. Once you take him down, put him in an isolation room." Martyr clipped off Newton's ring, then handed the keycards to Andre. "Go. Quickly. And make sure you take his keycards."

The Jasons ran into the hallway.

Martyr handed the tool to Charlie. "Clip off the rest of the stingers." Martyr bent over Rolo and pulled the key ring off his belt. Martyr found a similar one on Johnson and Erik, all containing two keycards. He removed Erik's belt and strapped it on underneath his T-shirt, then hung all the keycard rings on it.

Once Charlie had cut Iron Man's stinger off, Iron Man pushed to his feet. "What can I do?"

"When the rest of you are strong enough, take Johnson, Erik, and Rolo to the isolation rooms."

Brain stood up. "I'm strong enough now."

"Me … too," said Teddy, who was still sitting on the floor, panting.

While the boys started dragging the guards toward the door, Martyr turned to the monitors. They showed pictures of everything on the Farm. He saw Andre and Hyde dragging a man out of a door on one monitor.

He saw the small boys asleep in their beds on another.

Another one showed Dr. Kane's spacious office. Dr. Kane sat behind his desk, talking on the phone.

On another monitor, Dr. Goyer struggled against the straps that held him to the table in a lab room. Martyr's fists clenched. How had Dr. Kane realized that Dr. Goyer had been helping Martyr? He would have to be freed next.

Several monitors showed deserted rooms throughout the Farm, including the cafeteria.

Martyr looked to the next monitor and saw Abby and a man at a desk. His heart leapt, and he put his fingers to her image on the glass. She sat beside Runstrom, the police officer who had turned Martyr over to Dr. Kane. He didn't look angry with Abby; could he have learned the truth about Jason Farms? Yes, Martyr was sure of it. He was going to help. They would soon be safe.

Though they weren't rescued yet. Martyr remembered what he came to do and sought out the computer server. Dr. Goyer had said it was several computers hooked together with wires under the table. He crouched down and spotted the computers against the far wall.

He crawled to them and sat cross-legged in front. The computer boxes hummed. Martyr pulled the cords out from the wall. The humming noises died. He tugged the first one out from under the table and pulled it into the center of the room, then went back for the next. By the time the Jasons had returned, Martyr had all the boxes in the center of the room.

"Done," Andre said. "What now?"

Martyr returned to the monitors to check each area in case anything had changed. His eyes stopped at an image of the stairwell: A Jason was coming up. He looked to be at least a J:3 or J:4, but it wasn't Fido, and a quick glance confirmed all the others were here or shown on different monitors. *Who is he?*

The mystery Jason turned the corner to climb the next flight, and Martyr caught the number on his sleeve before he stepped out of view.

J:3:3.

Martyr felt a wave of dizziness run through his head. When he was able to focus again, he found the Jason using a keycard at the top if the stairwell, trying to get onto level one.

Martyr tensed. "Lock the door and turn off the light. Now!"

In the darkness, Martyr watched as the stranger opened the door. But instead of walking confidently through the hall, the fake J:3:3 stepped into the hall and paused, looking like he'd never been to level one before. How could that be? Every Jason made it upstairs at least once a week.

The Jason finally chose a direction and walked down the hall. Whoever it was, he seemed harmless, but Martyr was afraid to lead the boys to the front and try the elevators with Dr. Kane, Dr. Elliot, and the mystery Jason up there.

"Turn the lights back on, Andre," Martyr said.

When the switch flipped, Martyr saw every Jason was looking at him expectantly.

"Iron Man?" Martyr removed two sets of keycards off his belt and handed them to Iron Man. "Take everyone downstairs to level two. Enter the double doors that lead to the elevator, then turn right and walk to the end of the hallway. There's a door there—try the keycards to see if it will open. You and Andre will have to swipe a keycard at the same time. If the door opens, get all the Jasons out and wait for me in the tunnel. Hummer and Bean Bag, stay with me. The rest of you, go with Iron Man."

"You heard him," Iron Man said, sounding like Rolo. The boys obeyed just as quickly as they once would have for the guard and scurried out the door.

"We need to burn these boxes," Martyr said to Bean Bag, remembering Dr. Goyer's instructions. He went back to where Dr. Goyer had hidden the clipper tool, and found the items to help him set the fire. A wide roll of gray tape, a yellow can that said "lighter fluid," and some *matches*. He pointed to a box of paper under the desk. "Crumple up that paper and pile it on the computers."

Hummer and Bean Bag dragged the box of paper into the center of the room and began to wad it into balls. Martyr took a roll of gray tape, stood on a chair underneath one of the *sprinklers*, and wrapped tape around it. Dr. Goyer hadn't been certain this would work, but he'd hoped it would give the fire time to destroy the evidence. Once Martyr had taped all the sprinkler heads, he poured the lighter fluid onto the computer boxes. It smelled terrible, seeming to burn the inside of his nose. He hoped Dr. Goyer's instructions on how to *strike a match* would work, and that Dr. Goyer had succeeded in disabling the fire alarms.

"Can't you make it go back?" Abby asked Runstrom. The image of a huge fight between Jasons and guards in a room with computers had flashed away and not returned. Instead, the monitor flickered to other locations: an empty hallway, a dark room with sleeping toddlers, then another empty hallway. Abby was thankful, but somewhat horrified, to see Fido's body lying at the bottom of the slide and no sign of Marty. Did that mean Marty was up with the others, fighting the guards?

"It's not me," Runstrom said. "The monitor flips from camera to camera on a timer. I have no way to control it from— Did you see that?"

Abby had. The image of Dr. Elliot injecting her father with something had left the screen, but the sliver of fright it left on Abby remained. "How long until it repeats?"

"Almost a minute. There must be over thirty cameras on this loop."

Abby stared at the screen, hoping whatever Dr. Elliot had given her dad was only a sedative. "Any word from Allam?"

"Not yet."

Abby watched the black and white images flashing on the monitor for any sign of her dad or Marty.

The empty cafeteria. The track. A classroom. An image of a single Jason walking down one of the hallways on level one, a phone pressed to his ear. "That's him! That's Marty!" The image flashed away.

"How do you know?"

"I saw the number on his sleeve: J:3:3."

"Who would he be calling?" Runstrom asked.

Abby checked her jeans pocket; her phone was still there. "I don't know. He doesn't have a cell."

"He must have gotten one from someone." Runstrom tapped his fingernails on the desk. The image on the monitor flashed from one to another until finally landing on the image of Abby's father.

She whispered, "Daddy," but he was gone in a moment. She furrowed her brows. What was Marty up to? Why hadn't he tried to find her dad yet?

An image of Dr. Kane sitting in his office, speaking on the phone, flashed by.

"Maybe the kid is talking to Kane," Runstrom said.

Abby scoffed. "How would Marty know the phone number of a secret lab?"

"Maybe Kane called him."

Abby couldn't shake the feeling she was missing something obvious. To ease her concerns, she went to check on Baby. Shortly after Wesley had brought him a pair of socks and boots, Baby had fallen asleep on the floor in the corner, curled into a ball.

Runstrom's agitated voice broke the silence. "The feed's gone! It's nothing but fuzz." He slapped the side of the monitor.

Abby ran around the desk and stood beside Runstrom. It was true—the screen had gone to salt and pepper. She looked down at her thumbnail and realized there was little left. She glanced at her watch instead.

The lock expert had been at it a while. The elevator expert was still on his way from Anchorage, and would be at least another fifteen minutes. Her dad was down there, Marty was down there, and they were out of time. She had to do something.

The CB radio crackled, jolting her heart. "Runstrom? You copy?"

"I copy you, Allam. You find anything?"

"Affirmative. We've got a storm cellar of some kind. Pitch black down here. We're getting some lights brought in. We've also got a vault door, not quite the fortress of that one in the barn, though. Can you spare the locksmith? Over."

Runstrom ran his hand over his mouth. "How you coming on that thing, Joe?"

The locksmith kept working as he answered, "I still got a good ten, fifteen minutes. But I'm not confident it will work. I feel like I'm trying to rob a bank."

Runstrom sighed and brought the CB to his mouth. "Allam, I'm sending Joe over to take a look at that door. You send him right back when you're inside, copy?"

"I copy. Over."

Runstrom led Joe out of the room. Abby quickly set her cell phone on the desk where Runstrom's phone lay, slipping the officer's cell into her jeans pocket. She hoped he wouldn't notice her red phone right away. She felt almost felonious, but this would be the easiest way to call him if she needed to.

The barn was empty and still dark as she padded through the interior. Abby's eyes stung from lack of sleep, and she hoped her feet stayed steady. She peered out the open barn door. A handful of cops stood out in the parking lot, corralled around Officer Runstrom as he shouted instructions on how to meet up with Officer Allam.

Abby hurried to the dumbwaiter and opened the door. She flipped the switch to call it back, but didn't know what to do next with no one to flip the switch once she was inside.

Behind her, boots crunched over dried hay. Abby spun around, shocked to see Baby standing before her. "Baby, Marty is still inside. And my dad. I need to go down. Can you help me do that?"

Baby nodded, grunted, and banged his chest.

"I'll get in, and you close the door and flip the switch down, see?" Abby pantomimed each action.

Again he nodded and banged his chest.

The dumbwaiter stopped, and Abby tried to climb in. It was much more difficult than it looked, and she was glad Marty had gotten all chivalrous last time. Baby tried to lift her, but he wasn't strong enough. After many awkward attempts, their pathetic teamwork finally managed to get her inside.

Abby smiled at Baby before pulling the door closed. The humming started almost immediately.

[CHAPTER TWENTY-FOUR]

THE FIRE WAS BLAZING NOW. Water sprayed from every spout in the ceiling, except the center four Martyr had disconnected before lighting the computers. A rotten smell came from the melting plastic, accompanied by a thick, greenish smoke that billowed from the pile. Martyr risked a deep breath and choked on the rancid air. He had sent Hummer and Bean Bag after the others when the water first began to fall. It was time for him to go too.

The fire hissed and popped behind him, warming his back as he walked to the exit. He wrenched the door open and slipped out into the cool hallway, sucking in clean air. A cloud of dense smoke poured out of the room, forcing him to creep to the corner of the hall in order to fully catch his breath.

Once his lungs and eyes cleared, Martyr peeked around the edge. Empty. He ran all the way to Dr. Goyer's lab, but his heart sank—there was no sign of Abby's father. He locked the door and sat at Dr. Goyer's desk, trying to think. If Dr. Goyer was in Dr. Elliot's office, Martyr needed a plan. *I should have kept some of the Jasons with me.*

He glanced around the room and his eyes fell on a vial sitting on the counter.

He went immediately to the cupboards above the counter. Dr. Goyer wasn't like the other doctors—he hadn't used injections. But the day Martyr had been injected with the EEZ, Dr. Kane had told Dr. Goyer he would have to do testing too. Perhaps he had the same vials.

Martyr dug through the cupboards searching for the letters *EEZ*. When he couldn't find them, he slipped next door to look in Dr. Max's office. He found the vial in the back of the top cupboard and filled two syringes up to the twenty mark with the yellow liquid. Martyr didn't want anyone to expire, but he needed to be ready for the doctors who were after his kidneys. Better to be prepared.

The phone rang.

Abby paused on the landing between levels three and two, fumbled to free Runstrom's phone from her pocket, and managed to flip it open. "Yeah?"

"Where are you?" As expected, Runstrom didn't sound happy.

"I'm going to help my dad."

"We're almost in, Miss Goyer. It's not safe for you to be down there."

"Why didn't you send a man down the dumbwaiter?"

"Because Allam's working on the tunnel. I'd rather send several men in so they can cover each other. I certainly wouldn't send a sixteen-year-old girl."

"I'm seventeen."

"Oh. Well that's different, then."

Abby scowled. "No one's down here, not even the toddlers. I checked their rooms. They must all be upstairs or something."

"A good reason for you to come back up." Runstrom's voice faded a moment as he barked, "Wesley! Get over here." His voice was loud when he spoke again. "Wait in the kitchen. I'm sending Wesley down now."

Abby chewed her thumbnail. She could wait a moment longer. A lot could happen in a moment, though. "I can't. My dad's in trouble, and I'm going to get to him before it's too late." Marty had been right when he said there were times arguing didn't get anything done. Abby had to act before the opportunity passed her by.

"No offense, Miss Goyer. But what exactly are you going to do?"

Abby pushed his comment aside and ran up the remaining flight of stairs. Someone had propped open the door to level one with a rolled up white T-shirt, and a haze now filled the stairwell.

"Miss Goyer? Miss Goyer, are you there?"

"There's smoke."

She heard a muffling on the other end. "Wait for Wesley. He's coming down now."

"No time." Abby clicked the phone shut and switched it to vibrate as she crept up the last few steps. She pulled her shirt up over her nose, held her breath, and darted through the door, only to be met with greenish smoke that seeped out the cracks in the doorframe opposite the stairs. She ran back into the stairwell and dialed her cell phone.

"Miss Goyer?" Runstrom's voice sounded strained.

"Someone started a fire. Call some fire trucks and ambulances, maybe even Hazmat."

"What kind of fire?"

"I don't know. It's in the room across from the stairs on level one, but it smells almost chemical." She snapped the phone shut, tucked it back into her pocket, and held her breath. Setting her mouth in a grim line, she ran out of the stairwell, past the smoking door, and around the corner. The acrid smoke gave way to sweet air. She crept down the hall, listening for voices and clues to what lay ahead.

Abby paused outside the reception area and tried to remember which lab was Dr. Elliot's office. *Think, Abby ...* The first one.

She hurried to the door and slipped inside. Her father still lay strapped to the exam table, unconscious, gray duct tape covering his mouth. She ran to his side and ripped the first binding free, then removed the adhesive from his mouth slowly, not wanting to hurt him.

Before she could get the tape off, pain exploded at the back of her head, and she slumped to the floor.

Abby woke to the sound of clinking glass. She blinked a few times and discovered she was sitting in a wheelchair, her wrists and ankles bound with plastic cinch ties. Dr. Elliot stood at the counter on the other side of the exam table, where her dad still lay.

Abby rose in her seat, nearly losing her balance. "What did you give my dad?"

Dr. Elliot spun around, his bulging eyes fixed on hers. "Oh, Miss Goyer. Only a sedative. I've seen enough spy films to know that if the hero is left awake, he can rescue the damsel." He picked up a syringe and started toward her.

Abby flinched, but he capped the hypodermic needle and tucked it into the chest pocket of his lab coat. Just as calmly, he pushed Abby back into the wheelchair.

"Where are you taking me? What about my dad?"

"You and I are going to evacuate, Miss Goyer. Your curiosity has exposed this lab, and, like you, the world is not yet ready for our miracles. Once our valuable subjects are safe, we will set fire to this building, eliminating your father and what he knows about this lab."

"I think someone already beat you to the fire."

Dr. Elliot opened his office door. A fog of thin smoke now filled the hallway. "What?" He grabbed the wheelchair and pushed it out.

Abby leaned forward, throwing herself onto the cool tile. She cried out as her shoulder slammed into the hard floor.

Dr. Elliot kicked the wheelchair aside, grabbed her under the arms, and dragged her backward. She feared her arm might rip off the way he swung her around the corner. Her boots slid over the tile of the reception area, then dragged onto a fine oriental rug. Dr. Elliot dropped her at the front end of a conference table, before an antique desk.

"Miss Goyer. How good of you to return to us," Dr. Kane said from behind the desk. "One less person I have to track down."

"How can you sit here so calmly?" Dr. Elliot screamed. "The building's on fire."

Dr. Kane stood up. "What kind of fire? Why didn't the alarm go off?"

"How should I know? I saw the smoke coming from down the hall."

Dr. Kane turned and opened a file cabinet on the wall behind his desk. "If the alarm didn't go off, it can't be terribly serious. Anyway, the van will be here soon. Any sign of our boy?"

Dr. Elliot sank into a chair at the conference table on Abby's left. "No."

A row of Jasons sat along the wall to her right, arms bound behind their backs. Eight of them. The oldest might have been seven or eight, the youngest mere toddlers. A few had deformed limbs.

"Hi, Abby."

She pushed herself upright and turned back toward the entrance to see Marty sitting in a chair at the other end of the conference table. The sight of him tore a sob from her lungs. "Marty!"

He chuckled, a sarcastic grin splitting his face. "Fooled you. You really thought I was him? What do you see in that lab rat anyway?"

"Oh," breathed out her lips as she registered JD's arrogant tone. But the resemblance was even more uncanny. His head and face were clean shaven, and he was dressed in white Farm clothes. Even the number J:3:3 appeared on his sleeve. "You were the one on the cell phone. What are you doing down here?"

"Took your advice and followed Dad to work yesterday. You were right—well, obviously." JD gave her an apologetic grin. "What was really odd though, Dad doesn't use the top entrance.

He comes in through an underground tunnel. So when the cops came to the house with a warrant to search Dad's office and told Mom about some mad-scientist hostage situation, I took your clone dude's clothes—the ones the cops gave Dad thinking they were mine—and snuck into this place. I wanted to show you I could be a hero too. Turns out the hostage call was a hoax." He glared at Dr. Kane, then sobered as his gaze traveled to the little boys. His Adam's apple bobbed. "I don't know what is going on here. In case you didn't notice, all these kids have my face."

"No. You all have *his* face." Abby raised her bound hands and pointed at Dr. Kane. "Your *dad* is the mad scientist, JD. He cloned himself. A lot."

"That's crazy." JD rubbed the back of his neck and looked to Dr. Kane, who was pulling file folders out of the file cabinet and piling them on his desk. "Dad?"

"Ignore her, son." Dr. Kane opened his briefcase and loaded the stack of files into it.

"Why is Abby tied up, Dad? You can't just tie up girls."

"She'll be a surrogate, of course," Dr. Elliot said. "Why else would—"

"No." Dr. Kane glared at Dr. Elliot, then turned to JD, his expression earnest. "It's only until we're safely gone."

"Whatever," Abby said. "JD, are you aware they strapped my dad to an exam table in Dr. Elliot's office? They're going to leave him to burn with the lab."

JD looked back to Dr. Kane. "Is that true?"

Dr. Kane added one last file to his briefcase and shut it. "We'll discuss this later."

JD ran a hand over his bald head and glanced at the boys again. "Am I …?" He cleared his throat. "Real?"

Dr. Kane punched up a number on his cell and held it to his ear. "Of course you're real."

"A real *clone*," Abby said.

JD's eyes narrowed. "Take that back. It's not true."

"Of course it's true," Abby said. "JD, look around you."

"Dad? Am I just the pick of the litter or what? Do I have a-a ... number?"

"Johnson," Dr. Kane barked into his phone. "Call me back. Now." Dr. Kane ended the call.

"Answer me, Dad!"

Dr. Kane rubbed his right eye. "You're J:3:1, the first in the J:3 batch. Your mother desperately wanted a child and couldn't conceive. The first two subject groups seemed to be coming along, so it appeared you'd live a normal life. In addition, you had the highest protein counts, which meant you'd likely be a poor transplant candidate."

JD squirmed in his seat. "Wh-What does that mean? Transplant what?"

"I have lupus."

"I already know that."

"Which means you'll have lupus. I wasn't officially diagnosed until I was thirty-six."

This set Abby on meltdown again. "You cloned yourself knowing you were sick, knowing that your clones would be sick too?"

"I only wanted to clone my kidneys at first, but the technology that presented itself was too tempting to bypass. Over the years we've tried manipulating the chromosomes, hoping to slow down the disease in the candidates. The pharmaceutical experiments alone have more than funded this lab over the years. I've had four transplants in my life, and the one from this lab has lasted the longest. My body is a perfect match for my body. No complications."

"Except the organs have lupus, too," Abby said, "so in the end they die."

"Raising my kidneys from birth is the best way, and J:3:3 is the healthiest subject we've had yet."

Abby paled. "But Marty's a person. You can't just kill him."

"See? This is why I dislike having women in the lab."

"Because we have a conscience?" Abby asked.

"Because women are weak. Dr. Markley thought the boys were *so cute*. She disliked injecting them, hated the electroshock treatments and the tasers. Look where her love of the little beasts got her."

A voice from behind Abby said, "You're wrong."

She turned to see JD standing just inside the doorway, while at the end of the table, JD still glared at his father. She gasped. "Marty?"

"Excellent," Dr. Kane said. "J:3:3. The time has come for you to serve your purpose."

Marty glanced at Abby, then to Dr. Kane. "Dr. Markley always made me feel like I mattered, like my purpose was worthy. Since I met Abby, I never felt more alive. I love my brothers. They're my family, and I try to take care of them, but Abby makes me want to be better, the same way Dr. Markley did."

"No matter." Dr. Kane waved to Dr. Elliot, who stood and walked to the center of the room. "One last injection, J:3:3, and it'll all be over. You've lived a good life. You even got to see the sky. You've taken care of everyone, now, let Dr. Elliot take care of you for a change."

Dr. Elliot lifted the syringe out of his pocket and uncapped it.

Abby tried to crawl after Dr. Elliot, inching her way like a worm. "Marty, don't listen to him."

Marty walked into the room and stopped when he met Dr. Elliot.

In response, the doctor lifted the syringe. "Give me your right arm."

Abby inched closer and rose to her knees, her voice cracking over her tears. "Marty, please, come away from him. You don't have to listen."

"Fire!" One of the Jason boys pointed at the wall behind Dr. Kane, where a large black blob had blackened the white wall. Flames brushed across the white surface, painting a trail of charcoal ash in their wake.

All eyes turned to the flames. From her position, however, Abby watched as Marty hauled back a fist and punched Dr. Elliot. The doctor cried out and stumbled, dropping the syringe. Marty kicked it away and lunged.

"Help him, son!" Dr. Kane crouched down, and Abby could hear desk drawers sliding in and out, banging shut.

JD stood and stepped tentatively toward Marty and Dr. Elliot.

His eyes were wild and sort of glazed over, darting between the fight and the fire.

"No, JD. Leave him be." Abby walked on her knees, reaching for Dr. Elliot's pant leg.

As her fingers inched closer, Dr. Elliot suddenly screamed. Marty staggered away as the doctor slumped to the floor, face beet red, limbs trembling a moment before his body seized in a convulsion.

Abby forced herself to keep moving. She reached Dr. Elliot's side and looked up at Marty. "What did you do?" It came out light as a breath.

"Only an experiment, Abby Goyer."

Marty's voice had a harsh tone unlike any she had ever heard before. She simply stared, not knowing what to do, as Dr. Elliot's body continued to twitch and his face took on a bluish tinge. "What experiment?"

Marty shrugged. "Something that hurts."

"I'll give you something that hurts," JD said.

Marty turned just as JD swung. Abby shrieked as the punch struck Marty's ear. He tripped over Abby, nearly falling.

Abby waddled on her knees, trying to stay between them. The sprinklers came on then, spraying cold water over her and partially masking the two boys. "JD, don't!"

But JD lunged past Abby and struck Marty again, only to have Marty hit back. The boys came together like wrestlers and fell to the floor, punching and choking and writhing until Abby could no longer tell who was who. One of the little Jasons began to cry.

A gunshot rang out, jolting Abby around. Dr. Kane stood in front of his desk, briefcase in one hand, gun in the other. The water from the sprinklers had plastered his graying hair to his head. The wall behind him was black now, with several gaping holes that provided a view into a room engulfed in orange flames. Swirls of charcoal gray smoke coiled along the ceiling. It was the most hellish image she'd ever seen. Another sprinkler came on over Abby's head, spraying her with dirty water. Two of the toddler boys were wailing now. Abby wished she could go and pick them up.

Dr. Kane redirected the weapon from the ceiling to JD and Marty. "Stand up!"

The boys clambered to their feet, water soaking their clothes. One had a puffy bottom lip and his left eye was starting to swell. The other had scratches down both cheeks and on his neck. His mouth was bleeding terribly.

But which was which?

Abby studied their body language and posture, but at the moment, exhausted from the fight, they looked identical. She sought out Marty's scratches from his run through the forest that afternoon, but fingernails used in grappling and defense had obscured any such evidence. She couldn't be sure without hearing them speak.

A chunk of debris fell from the burning wall and landed behind Dr. Kane's desk.

Dr. Kane flinched and yelled, "J:3:3! Step forward. Now."

The Jasons looked at each other. The one with the scratches on his neck stepped away and crouched to pick up the syringe Dr. Elliot had dropped.

The other Jason mumbled, but Abby couldn't understand him. He grunted and wiped his mouth with the back of his hand, then patted his pants and spun around, looking for something.

The Jason with the syringe turned to Abby. "Good-bye, Abby Goyer." Then he furrowed his brows and plunged the syringe into his arm.

Abby felt as if her heart was being expelled along with her scream.

A small gasp left his lips. With apparent effort, he pushed down the top of the syringe, forcing the contents into his veins. At first nothing happened.

"Marty?" Abby started to go to him, but as soon as she inched closer, Dr. Kane pointed the gun at her.

"Stay right there, Miss Goyer."

Abby paused, trembling, shivering because of the cold water. She stared at Marty as he sank to his knees, then to the floor, a faint whimper on his lips.

[CHAPTER TWENTY-FIVE]

MARTYR BLINKED, UNABLE TO UNDERSTAND what had just taken place. He knelt beside JD, whose limbs were trembling, and asked in a soft voice, "Why?"

JD whispered, "My whole life … lies." His eyelids drooped. Water pooled on either side of his nose. "Besides, you're not the only one … who can"—he closed his eyes—"play … hero."

Martyr looked to Abby, hoping she could explain JD's words, but she wouldn't take her eyes away from JD's face.

JD continued to gasp, but from what effects? Martyr searched again for the second dose of EEZ he'd lost in the scuffle, not sure which needle the other boy had used. Was JD suffering the effects of a deep sleep or a syringe full of EEZ? He had not turned blue.

"Let's go, JD!" Dr. Kane waved the weapon as he jogged toward the door. "Pick him up. I'll get the girl."

The smoke still streaming from the computer lab was now thick in the room, causing everyone to cough. Martyr glanced at Abby and found her still staring at JD's limp body, tears streaming down her cheeks. She turned her gaze to his and her expression changed. Her eyebrows sank low over her eyes, her bluish lips pressed together, and her eyes … Martyr looked away.

He spotted his second syringe—filled exactly to the twenty mark with the bright yellow liquid—just under one of the chairs surrounding the long table. He closed his eyes and thanked the Creator. JD was only sleeping.

"JD! Now!" Dr. Kane coughed and waved the gun. "The van is waiting."

What would Dr. Kane do if he knew Martyr wasn't JD? He needed to keep silent if at all possible. After a deep breath, he dragged JD toward the chair, pretending to straighten him and using his body for a shield. After discreetly tucking the syringe into his waistband, he heaved JD's wet body over one shoulder and stood, buckling slightly under the weight as he walked toward the door.

Dr. Kane set down his briefcase, removed a pair of scissors from his back pocket, and snipped the bindings on Abby's ankles, pointing the gun at her all the while. When he finished, he threw the scissors over the huge table, backed up, and retrieved his briefcase. "Stand up, Miss Goyer. Collect the boys, if you don't mind."

Abby stood and spoke to the Jasons sitting along the wall. "Come on, guys," she said in a raspy voice. "Quickly. Let's get out of here."

As the boys ran, Martyr wondered why they were there. Three Brokens, two boys from Section Three, and three boys from Section Two, including Spot, a boy with a large red birthmark on his forehead. Spot's tear-streaked face met Martyr's.

Martyr winked, unable to help himself.

Spot smiled, then faced forward.

Abby shooed the boys toward the door and paused in front of

Martyr. She slapped his cheek, sending fire through his face. He cowered at the stinging and almost dropped JD.

"This is all your fault," Abby said in a strangled voice. "If you would have helped—" She choked on her words, then coughed. "If you would have just listened … Now Marty is …" She sobbed, long and sorrowful, clapping her hand over her mouth.

He cringed at the mournful sound. He wanted to hug her and stroke her hair. "Abby …"

"To the elevator, Miss Goyer."

She looked up at Martyr with narrowed, puffy eyes. Another chunk of wall fell behind Dr. Kane's desk.

"Move it!" Dr. Kane waved the weapon Abby's direction again.

She shooed the boys through the door and into the cloud of smoke.

Martyr's throbbing cheek sent pulsing despair through his heart. Abby, someone he'd never imagined capable of striking anyone, had struck him because she thought he was JD. Martyr adjusted his grip on JD and followed Dr. Kane to the elevator. Mercifully, the smoke was not as thick there.

Dr. Kane patted his shoulder and chucked. "That was a close one, son. Smart move attacking him. Weakened his resolve, I think. Rolo feels the same way about physical punishment—have to remind subjects like J:3:3 who is in charge."

Surely Dr. Kane would recognize Martyr's tone of voice when he heard it, so Martyr nodded. He glanced at the door to Dr. Elliot's office, not wanting to leave Dr. Goyer behind. He'd tried to rescue him earlier, after he'd seen Dr. Elliot take Abby into Dr. Kane's office, but Dr. Goyer would not wake up. He prayed the Creator would make a way to rescue Dr. Goyer before fire consumed the Farm.

The elevator dinged and the doors slid open. Dr. Kane held the door and waved everyone inside. Martyr watched as Abby crouched down beside the boys in the corner, pulling them close. Spot whispered in her ear and her eyes shot back and forth between Martyr and Dr. Kane, who had inserted a red card into the slot that seemed to activate the elevator on its own. Unaware of the looks behind him, Dr. Kane pushed the L3 button and the elevator jerked down.

Level three was not the level Abby had claimed had a tunnel. Could she have been mistaken? Had Martyr sent the Jasons to the wrong place?

"Shame what he did to Dr. Elliot," Dr. Kane mumbled to himself. "I had planned to sacrifice Dr. Elliot for my escape, anyway. His deviant obsessions were getting far too reckless. But I never intended to kill the man." Dr. Kane sighed, as if Dr. Elliot's death was a problem he'd rather not deal with. "I'll need to call Dr. Parlor as soon as we're in the van. I'll have her meet us at Gunnolf. Dr. Parlor, now that's one woman who's never given me any trouble." He glanced up at Martyr. "I'll need your help, son. Understandably, most of my employees can't be trusted at this point. I warned them yesterday we might be in crisis mode. Just wish I knew where my guards were."

The elevator slid open. Dr. Kane stepped out and held the door, jerking the gun at Abby. "To the right, Miss Goyer, and make it quick."

Abby and the boys trailed out of the elevator, and Martyr lumbered closely behind as Dr. Kane let the doors close. The temperature was cool down here. No fire. No smoke.

"It's a relief you finally know the truth," Dr. Kane said to Martyr as he walked after Abby, pointing the weapon against her back. "I've wanted to tell you for so long, but your mother—"

"Freeze!"

Martyr whipped around and felt JD slide off his shoulder. He went to his knees trying to keep JD from falling onto the tile floor.

While he crouched, a police officer stepped out from the double doors leading to the track and pointed his weapon at Dr. Kane. "Put the gun down, Dr. Kane."

Abby screamed.

"Stay back!" Dr. Kane yelled, holding Abby's hair in one fist and pressing the *gun* against the back of her head with his other hand. He lowered his voice to a whisper. "Get up, son. We need to get out of here."

Martyr reached under his shirt and unclipped the last set of keycards from the belt. If he could somehow get them to Abby …

"Come on, now, Dr. Kane," the police officer said. "We found your secret tunnel upstairs. There's no way out. Put the gun down, and let's all go up and talk things over."

"I'll kill her, I swear!"

Martyr hooked the keycard ring in his thumb and, tucking that hand around JD's leg, grunted to his feet. Dr. Kane waved him back, sidestepping with him. Martyr chose each step carefully, inching back toward Abby, closely enough that Dr. Kane would not see him hand off the keycard ring.

"Easy." The officer took slow, cautious steps forward, holding his weapon out in front.

Dr. Kane stopped at a large metal door at the end of the hallway. He fumbled to keep the gun pointed at Abby and pull the red keycard from his pocket; a flash of red flipped from his fingers and slapped onto the white tile. Dr. Kane swore. "JS:15:13!"—he waved the gun at Spot—"pick that up for me."

Martyr nudged Abby and slipped the keycard ring into her hand. She tensed, then grabbed the ring and slowly moved her hand behind her back.

"Get it for me, boy, or I'll shoot your head off!"

"It's okay," Abby said to Spot.

Spot picked up the keycard and handed it to Dr. Kane, who swiped it in the reader. The light turned green, and he pulled open the door. "JD, you first. Miss Goyer, you tell the boys to go next."

Martyr stepped toward the dark opening, searching for a way to help Abby and the boys escape. He stumbled into Dr. Kane and cried out, faking surprise as best he could.

Abby had been ready. She jerked free from Dr. Kane. "Run!"

Over a dozen feet pattered across the tile. Martyr closed his eyes and pleaded with the Creator of Everything to keep Abby and the boys safe.

"You clumsy idiot!" Dr. Kane shoved Martyr out of the way and fired the gun.

Abby held out her arms, pressing the boys into a corner just past the elevator. She sent up a prayer of thanks that Dr. Kane's shot appeared to have missed; even Wesley looked unharmed.

"Get up!" Dr. Kane's voice drifted from the end of the hall.

She glanced around the corner, still in shock over which clone lay unconscious on the floor. *All this time it was JD ...* Why would he have done such a thing? Had the truth made him suicidal? Or had he deliberately helped them, sacrificing himself? Both were so unlike him.

She winced as the last few minutes replayed in her mind, including her slap across Marty's shocked face. Now he was stuck with Dr. Kane.

Please, God, let this end safely.

"Just put the gun down," Wesley said again.

"He won't really shoot him," Abby whispered.

"You sure?" Wesley asked.

"Positive. One is his son and he needs the other for a transplant."

"It's over, Dr. Kane," Wesley said.

Bang!

Abby screamed at the gunshot. A door slammed shut.

Wesley holstered his gun and sighed. "They're gone through that door, Miss Goyer. Must be another tunnel. You go on up. They'll be thrilled to see you, and to see that elevator opened. Send me down those keycards and some backup, you hear?"

Abby tensed. She didn't want to leave Marty, but her dad was still upstairs, strapped to the exam table in Dr. Elliot's office. "Did s-s-someone get shot?"

Wesley shook his head as he walked toward the elevator and pressed the button. When the doors opened, he ushered her and the boys inside and spoke into his CB. "This is Officer Wesley. I'm sending up Miss Goyer and eight boys. Do you copy?"

"I got you, Wesley. Nice work," Runstrom crackled in response.

"I've also got what looks like a second tunnel on the right side of the—"

The doors slid shut, cutting off Wesley's words. Abby swiped the red keycard, pressed G, and the elevator started to climb. The little boy with the birthmarked face slid his hand into Abby's. She chewed her thumbnail as the elevator passed up through a smoky haze. Marty had just better be careful.

Martyr walked down a dim tunnel, his bare feet numb on the frozen dirt. Every so often a single lightbulb mounted in the ceiling cast a dull glow around them.

"It's because you had a little crush on her, isn't it?" Dr. Kane asked, still rubbing his jaw. "I don't think you understand. She's the only eyewitness who can testify against me, besides her father. The fire should take care of him, but something will have to be done about Miss Goyer."

Martyr looked away. The only sound was the padding of their footsteps.

Dr. Kane no longer pointed the gun at Martyr, but walked alongside as if he thought they'd found freedom. He ran a hand through his graying hair. "Her meddling not only made me a criminal in the eyes of the authorities, it cost me my biggest breakthrough yet."

Dr. Kane had made himself a criminal, but Martyr kept that thought to himself.

"In fact," Dr. Kane said, "if I don't get those boys back, I'm a dead man." He glanced at Martyr. "Those boys were special. Three-million-dollars-a-piece special."

Martyr knew very little of money, other than people who lived outside used it to purchase things, but *three-million-dollars-a-piece* sounded like a lot.

They came to a staircase.

"Wait here." Dr. Kane climbed the narrow, wooden steps, stopping halfway up to open a door in the ceiling.

Martyr shivered. Once he saw the sky it would be time to get away. He felt certain they were almost there.

Something clattered above.

"Okay, JD. Come on up."

Martyr climbed the stairs on shaky legs; he would not be able to carry JD much longer. Thankfully Dr. Kane was waiting with a stretcher, the same kind the guards took Hummer away on whenever he had one of his fits.

"Put him here," Dr. Kane said.

Martyr crouched down and laid JD onto the stretcher. He wiped the water from the sprinklers off his arms and onto his pants, but it didn't seem to help. They were in a small cell of some kind that was freezing cold and dark. Nothing like Abby's house.

Dr. Kane ran across the cell and opened the front door. A pale beam of greenish light seeped inside. He crossed back to the hole in the floor and kicked the door shut, then squatted at the foot end of the stretcher. "Help me carry this out. Grab that end."

Martyr hesitated. If he carried JD out, how would he get away?

Dr. Kane gripped the stretcher. "Come on."

Martyr picked up the front and backed toward the open door. An icy gust of wind whipped around him, but it was nothing compared to stepping on the snow-covered porch. Martyr distracted himself by looking up. The sky was black, dotted with stars. Green slashed back and forth across the black, then a bit of hot pink, then more green, then blue. Martyr stared. It was like someone was painting on the sky, like Speedy painted on paper. The Creator perhaps?

"Look, son," Dr. Kane said. "I know this has been a rough day. I promise we'll talk when I've recovered from my operation, and I'll take you to the other lab, then show you the program at Camp Ragnar. Because I'm not doing this only for my life. You'll also need the work I've done, because no matter how many kidneys I grow, that girl was right. Age is something I can't conquer … yet. You *will* contract lupus, and you *will* need my clones for kidneys and blood. Until I find a cure or a better body, you *will* become me someday."

Dr. Kane's words tore Martyr's gaze from the night sky. He could do it now—he could inject Dr. Kane with the syringe and end it all. What frightened him was he wanted to. He stared down at JD's pale face. He had forgotten about Gunnolf and Camp Ragnar. Were more Jasons kept there? More computer servers holding the secrets of creating clones? He needed to find out.

Martyr slipped and almost fell. His numb feet no longer wanted to walk.

Dr. Kane frowned. "You all right? The van's just up there. See the taillights?"

Martyr glanced over his shoulder and slipped again, only this time he fell, barely managing to keep JD on the stretcher.

"We can rest a second, son, if you need to. I guess that was a long ways to carry a— Where are your shoes?"

Martyr could hardly believe Dr. Kane had just noticed he didn't have shoes on, but he was starting to realize Dr. Kane only noticed what he wanted to. He forced himself to stand, ignoring the numb ache in his feet.

"JD. I asked where your shoes are."

Martyr tackled Dr. Kane, straddling him in the snow. He clamped one hand around the doctor's neck, reached under his shirt, and pulled the second syringe from his waistband. He yanked off the cap with his teeth, spit it into the snow, and poised the tip over Dr. Kane's shoulder. "You will tell me where Gunnolf and Camp Ragnar are or I will give you what I gave Dr. Elliot."

Dr. Kane's lips parted. His eyes flashed to JD, then back. "M-Martyr?"

The elevator dinged open. A gust of cold air swirled around Abby.

"Get a RIC team in there and bring those kids out!" a man yelled from the darkness, his voice a deep growl. "And someone hold that door!"

A fireman rushed forward, stuck his boot against the elevator door, and waved her out.

Runstrom's voice rose over the mob. "Don't let it shut."

Four more firemen followed. They all wore black hard hats and tan gear trimmed with apple-green reflective bands. The first three each picked up a Jason, took another by the hand, and led them from the room.

The fourth fireman picked up both toddlers and carried them out. "Come with me, miss."

Abby followed him into the barn. "My dad's down there. You have to help him."

"Don't you worry about your dad," the fireman said, boosting one of the toddlers higher. "We're gonna get down there, but first we need to get you all out of this barn."

The firemen led Abby outside. The cold air gripped her, worse because of her damp clothing. She realized for the first time that she wasn't wearing her coat. What had Dr. Elliot done with it? The parking lot glittered with flashing red, blue, and white emergency vehicle lights. Firemen milled around. The policemen had moved to the back of the parking lot.

Abby followed the fireman toward an ambulance, but a different fireman stepped into her path with Officer Runstrom at his side.

Runstrom nodded a greeting. "Miss Goyer, this here's Chief Shawn Bremner from the Fishhook Fire Department. He's taken over the scene until the fire is dealt with."

Excellent. The man in charge. "My dad's still down there. Can you go get him?"

"We'll take good care of your dad," Chief Bremner said, "but I need you to tell me a bit about the fire. Can you do that for me?" He held up Marty's map of the Farm, now sheathed in a plastic sheet protector.

Abby took the map and set it on the hood of the fire chief's Chevy Suburban. She rotated Marty's sketch and tapped the monitor room. "The fire was contained to this room, but it started to burn through the wall into Dr. Kane's office here. That was a good ten minutes ago. My dad is in here." She pointed to Dr. Elliot's office on the map. "Please send someone down for him. I don't know if anyone else is left."

"Apparently some unhappy guards," Chief Bremner said. "Rescue One found forty or so boys at the end of your first tunnel. They claimed to have locked the guards in some isolation rooms. Any ideas where those might be?"

"Here on this end, near the staircase, I think." She pointed to three narrow rooms in a row." She dropped the keycard ring on the hood next to Mary's map. "Dr. Kane took Marty and JD out another tunnel. It ran off level three going"—she paused to get her bearings and pointed—"east. It probably goes out at least as far, maybe farther since its ten feet deeper."

"Wesley told me about that," Runstrom said. "I've got men out looking for it."

A young fireman draped a blanket over Abby's shoulders. "That ought to help."

"Thanks." She offered a quick smile then turned back to Chief Bremner. "Can't you just go down the elevator and get my dad?"

"I need to know what we're dealing with first. I don't like how that elevator is smoking. The shaft is a natural chimney—it'll pull the fire like a magnet. But the sprinklers likely kept the fire from spreading. I'd like to go in that tunnel, but it's pretty long for an attack line. You think this other tunnel is going to be even longer?"

"I don't know," Abby said. "Probably."

Chief Bremner raised his voice. "I need two more teams. Get on the radios so we can do this together. Team one is already at the tunnel. Team two, grab the chainsaw and work on a hole through the floor on the east end of the barn, see if you can get to that stairwell and find a standpipe. Team three goes down the elevator. Take plenty of RIC bags with you."

Chief Bremner's radio hissed static, then a voice said, "Rescue One to Battalion Chief."

The chief lifted the radio to his mouth. "Go, Rescue One."

"Yeah, Chief. What are we gonna do with all these kids? I've got forty-six over here. Babies to teens. They're half-dressed, no shoes or socks. Got any ideas what ..."

Runstrom led Abby away from the fire chief toward a group of police officers standing around a cruiser. "Jackson?"

The female officer who'd interviewed Abby at her house stepped out of the crowd. "Sir?"

Runstrom put a hand on Abby's head. "Get her out to an ambulance and make sure she's checked over."

"I'm fine." Abby could handle the pain in her shoulder a bit longer. "I want to be here when you get everyone out."

"You'll see them when you see them. Now, give me my phone and scat." He held out her red cell. It looked funny in his long fingers. She swapped phones and followed Jackson, folding her good arm in front of her body and drawing into herself. The parking lot glittered with flashing red, blue, and white emergency vehicle lights, and the harsh wind made the frigid night seem colder. Her boots crunched over the snow as she walked toward an ambulance.

She said nothing to Jackson, and Jackson said nothing to her.

Jackson addressed a paramedic. "Need you to check this one over."

The young man opened the back door on the ambulance. "Sit down here and let me take a look. Anything hurt?"

"I think my shoulder is dislocated." Abby sat down and chewed her lip. Her gaze caught dozens of flashlight beams flickering in the distant woods. She prayed the men would find Marty and JD.

The paramedic grimaced as he ran his fingers over her shoulder. "When did it happen?"

"I don't know. Hours ago."

"We'd better take you in. I could try to manipulate the shoulder back into position, but it would be best to have an X-ray first, and I'm sure you'd like some anesthesia."

Abby straightened. "I'll go. But not until I know my dad's safe." And Marty.

Martyr kept the syringe poised over Dr. Kane's shoulder. "You lied to us. This world is not toxic."

Dr. Kane looked back to JD's body. "My boy?"

"He pretended to be me. To help Abby."

"No!" Dr. Kane lurched and punched Martyr in the eye, knocking him into the snow.

Martyr rolled over and scrambled back, watching in confusion. He had not expected Dr. Kane to care deeply for any of his clones, even the one he called son.

Dr. Kane crawled to the stretcher and lifted JD's head into his lap. "JD." He glared at Martyr. "You killed my son!"

Martyr was almost positive JD was only sedated. "He chose to do what he did."

"Twenty years I've been in this location. Twenty years, and no one has tried to escape. Why now? You're *my* clone, designed by me to serve *my* purposes."

"I only wanted to see the sky."

Dr. Kane looked up. "What's so great about the sky?"

The colors were still streaking above. "The Creator is painting."

Dr. Kane snorted. "She told you about God?"

"Yes."

"I suppose she told you God created you?"

"Yes. She told me many things about the Creator of Everything."

"You liked that, didn't you?"

Martyr continued staring at the sky. "Yes."

Dr. Kane got to his feet and lifted his side of the stretcher. He pulled it, making a deep stripe in the snow as he went. "Will you help me? I want to take him home. You can stay, if you like, but I want to take him to his mother."

Mother. Yes. Martyr would help JD be with his mother. He pushed to his feet and crouched to lift the stretcher. A branch snapped to Martyr's left. Somewhere in the dark.

Dr. Kane picked up his end of the bed. "Quick. Quick!"

But Martyr straightened. "It is time to stop hiding, Dr. Kane. We will see what the world will do with us now that we have been found."

"No." Dr. Kane dragged the stretcher again, gaining only a few feet at a time. "Help me!"

A light shifted in the distance, further away than where the noise had come from. Martyr sank onto the ground, no longer able to stand on his numb feet. He pulled one foot up and set it across his knee, rubbing the icy flesh.

A voice broke the silence, sounding like it had come from a TV with the volume turned very loud. "This is the Fishhook Police

Department. Lie down and put your hands on the back of your head."

Dr. Kane ran back to Martyr and held the gun to his temple. "I'm taking my son and going home!"

"Put down the gun, and we'll talk this through," the loud voice said. "Far as I can see, you haven't done anything wrong. We only want to ask you some questions, that's all. Just some questions."

"Ask your questions now."

"They're not my questions, sir. I just need to bring you in. Let's not make things difficult."

Dr. Kane pressed the gun harder against Martyr's head.

"Easy," the loud voice said, drawing the word out. "Why don't you lay down the weapon and let us take you someplace warm?"

Martyr liked the sound of someplace warm. He wanted to be away from Dr. Kane, with Abby, wearing the Christmas socks. He didn't like the way Dr. Kane's gun felt against his head. Martyr feared it could somehow inject him with death, like a syringe.

Dr. Kane's arm relaxed slightly, and Martyr grabbed the gun and yanked it down. The doctor grunted and fought to get it back, forcing Martyr to pull with both hands and raise the gun above their heads. Suddenly, Dr. Kane struck Martyr's stomach with his free hand. Martyr gasped and bent over, gripping the weapon with all his strength. Dr. Kane fell on top of him. They rolled in the cold snow in a tangle of limbs until the gun exploded.

[CHAPTER TWENTY-SIX]

ABBY JUMPED OFF THE BACK of the ambulance. "Did you hear that?"

"Sounded like a gunshot," the paramedic said.

Abby sprinted toward the police cars, her injured arm slack and slightly twisted at her side. She found Runstrom talking on his CB. "Did you hear the shot? What happened?"

Runstrom held up a hand and turned his back to Abby. "Park it out on Lakeview. We need to keep this lot clear for emergency vehicles." Runstrom lowered the radio and faced Abby. "You got any idea who else works here?"

"*What?* A gun went off." Abby pointed to the forest.

"We caught Dr. Kane trying to sneak away. They're bringing him over now."

"What about Marty and JD?"

"We'll know soon, okay? In the meantime, I could use your help."

Abby fought the urge to scream. *God, give me patience...* "What do you need?"

He motioned to where Baby sat inside a patrol car with three of the little Jasons she'd brought up the elevator. "They're bringing a bunch more boys over. I've got a bus on the way, but I'm going to need help with some of the little ones. I guess they're crying pretty bad. Allam's a bachelor—he doesn't exactly know what to do with a bunch of screaming kids. And if anyone asks, keep quiet about the cloning for now. I'm not sure how the FBI, or whoever, is going to handle that." Runstrom looked across the parking lot and shouted, "Reeves! Get OCS over here, pronto."

A full-sized school bus pulled up where the driveway to Jason Farms met Lakeview Road. Abby and Officer Allam led the boys to it, four at a time, where a woman from the Office of Child Services wrote each boy's number or name on a list as they boarded.

Abby felt sorry for the boys. They looked around, shivering and confused. No shoes or socks. A few asked for Martyr. Abby glanced at the dark forest, desperate to see him come out.

"I wonder who this Martyr is," the OCS woman said.

"He's one of the older boys." Abby looked again to the forest. "He hasn't come out yet."

"You know how many there are?"

"Marty said fifty-five."

"I've never seen anything like this." The woman tapped her pen against the clipboard in her hands, then glanced at Baby, who stood beside Abby, wearing a pair of boots that looked twice his size. "You got any ideas what they went through down there? Where they came from? Why they all look like they're related?"

Abby took Baby's hand. "Not really." Abby was glad Runstrom had told her to keep quiet about the cloning. If the press got hold of the information … Abby had no desire for Marty and the other Jasons to become celebrities. They had enough trouble as it was.

"Abby, honey?"

Abby whirled around. Her dad stood behind her, a wool blanket draped over his shoulders. "Daddy!"

He folded her into a gentle hug. She rested her cheek on his shoulder and began to cry as Dad rocked her slowly and kissed the top of her head. "Forgive me?"

"For what?"

"For everything."

She sniffled and looked into his eyes. "Yeah, Dad. I forgive you." She swallowed and glanced at the trees. The Northern Lights danced in the dark sky above. She hoped Marty could see it. "Marty's still out there, Dad. JD too."

"It'll be okay. Know why?"

Abby shook her head.

Dad smirked. "Because I prayed."

Even though Dad had only been at Jason Farms a week, the boys responded to his familiar and friendly face. The OCS woman gladly let Dad on the bus. Abby halted on the step just below him and peered over the top of the first seat at all the little, bald heads. Baby stood just outside the bus, holding on to the hem of the blanket draped around her shoulders.

"You need to trust me," Dad said to the boys. "The world is not toxic. Dr. Kane lied to you about that. But he's no longer in charge, and you all deserve to know the truth. You aren't going to live at the Farm anymore. We're taking you to a place for a few days until we can figure out where you'll go next."

"Where's Martyr?"

"Did Martyr expire?"

Dad gave the boys a weary smile as he and Abby stepped back outside. "I promise I'll answer all your questions as soon as I can."

Dad joined the social services woman beside the bus, and tried to explain the boys' situation. "It's imperative you keep them together. Email me a copy of the full roster, and I can check it against mine. I have a detailed list at home. Once we can match each boy to his information, it will help us go from there. For instance, a few are on special medications. We should be able to get most of what we need from a local pharmacy."

Abby stepped away from her dad as a stretcher being carried out from the forest caught her gaze. She jogged toward it, Baby at her heels.

The stretcher held a delirious Dr. Kane, his left leg matted with blood. Abby stopped to watch as the paramedics pushed him into an empty ambulance and went right to work. A man pressed a cloth to his leg and Dr. Kane howled. Abby turned back to the forest to see two more paramedics struggling in the deep snow with a second stretcher. A bald head rested on the white mattress. *Marty.*

She dashed to the stretcher, grabbing on and running alongside. The scratches on his cheeks were not as red as before. His eyelids fluttered, he groaned, but he did not wake.

Abby sighed, her heart torn within her. "Is he going to be okay?"

"He's got a strong pulse. He should be fine."

Abby stopped and let the paramedics carry the stretcher away. Baby stepped up beside her, and she put her good arm around his shoulders. "It wasn't him, Baby."

Inside, she scanned the crowd of Fishhook PD, state troopers, paramedics, firefighters, and Jasons. Fido sat in the back of a squad car, arms handcuffed behind him. Abby wondered how many cops he had attacked to earn such special treatment.

Baby grunted and pulled Abby's arm. She followed his gaze to Runstrom's back.

The officer's voice carried over to where they stood. "Look, I'm just the messenger, kid. He's asking for you. You don't want to go,

I got no problems with that. He's out in the fire-squad ambulance if you care. If not, go ahead and get on the bus."

Behind Runstrom, Marty stood, arms folded, his left eye puffy and dark, though the swelling on his lip had gone down. He had a wool blanket draped over him and wore a pair of black boots. Baby grunted a scream and ran to his friend. Marty hugged Baby close and, over his shoulder, met Abby's gaze. He whispered in Baby's ear, released him, and walked toward Abby. She ran to meet him.

Marty caught her, wrapping his strong arms around her so tightly she could feel his heart beating against her cheek. Abby ignored her throbbing shoulder. Her voice came high-pitched and whiny over her tears. "I heard the gunshot. I thought you'd—"

He released her and put his finger over her lips. "Dr. Kane's gun injected his own leg."

She giggled at his funny phrasing and kissed him. She pulled back when she recalled Runstrom's words. "He's asking for you?"

Marty's voice softened. "Dr. Kane is dying."

Marty and her dad needed to stay for questioning, so Abby reluctantly let the ambulance take her in to have her shoulder looked at. The hospital took X-rays, found no fractures, and popped it back in. She now had it in a sling and would go back in a week to have it looked at. While the doctor hadn't thought it would need surgery, he wanted to be safe and keep an eye on it.

Sometime the next morning, after Officer Jackson got a full statement from Abby, her dad drove her to the high school gym where they were keeping the older boys. According to Dad, the babies had gone out to temporary foster care.

Local OCS workers had filled the gym with enough cots for each Jason. While Abby and her dad visited with the Jasons, a cop with a Walmart sack passed out pairs of socks and sweatshirts, and a social worker passed out disaster kits. The boys played with their kits, wearing the Band-Aids on their faces like stickers. Extra officers milled around to keep order. The boys, smitten with Abby, obeyed every word she said. She did her best to explain what was happening.

But the bigger question was what would happen now? These boys were not runaways or orphans or even kidnapped children. These were cloned humans, without parents to claim them or social security cards to prove they existed. Greedy people would be eager to exploit them. If only Abby could do something.

Worse, in the aftermath it was confirmed that Marty had killed Dr. Elliot. It had been self-defense in a way ... premeditated self-defense. Abby twisted her lips in frustration. Marty would likely go free because no one could prove he'd done anything. Still, what would they set him free to?

Last she'd heard, he was in the hospital, along with JD and Dr. Kane. Abby wondered if the cops didn't simply want Marty under unofficial surveillance.

Lunchtime came and two social workers passed out fast food burritos. The Jasons were enamored with the colorful wrappers. Wesley and another state trooper set up a movie screen and projector at one end of the gym to show *Pinocchio*. Abby found that an ironic choice.

The Jasons crowded around, staring, while Wesley guarded the screen and answered questions about colors and animals and cuckoo clocks and Cleo the fish. A few Jasons tossed wadded-up elastic bandages from their disaster kits at the screen. Every so often one would try talking to the cartoons. Mostly the younger boys. Two of the older boys tried to dance like Geppetto. This cheered Abby up for a bit, but she missed Marty.

As Jiminy ran down the road after Pinocchio and Honest John, Dad received a call from Runstrom. JD had woken and seemed to have recovered fully, but Dr. Kane needed an immediate kidney transplant or he would die. The stress of the gunshot wound had weakened him to the point where his body couldn't wait any longer.

Abby wasn't surprised. "Dad, there's no way he'll be able to get a kidney that soon. I bet he didn't even bother to get on a transplant list this time."

Her dad's lips pursed, and he glanced at the floor.

She knew that look. "Dad? What's wrong?"

"Martyr is giving him a kidney."

Every molecule of air rushed from Abby's body. Tears instantly flooded her eyes.

"Just one," Dad said.

Abby sat on the end of a cot. "Dad, how? Do they think he's JD? Are they forcing him to—?"

"No one forced him. Dr. Kane asked and Martyr agreed. They're doing it as we speak."

Abby stared at the movie screen. Jiminy Cricket tried to free Pinocchio from the cage where Stromboli held him captive. Why would Marty do this? Why would he help that evil, horrible man? Dr. Kane had taken everything from the Jasons. He'd abused them, lied to them, killed them. Why would Marty help him?

"Runstrom said he'd call us when Marty's out of surgery. I'm going to go home for a while. Take a nap. Want to come?"

"No. I'll stay here. Text me when you know anything."

Dad gave her a hug and left. Abby tried to focus on the film, too shocked to think straight.

Minutes after the movie ended, Abby's cell phone trilled. She had a text message.

MRTY OUT OF SRGRY. IM OUT FRNT.

Pro number one.

Abby crossed the gym at a run and found her dad's Silverado idling at the curb.

Marty was awake—alive. Pro number two. He had his own hospital room with a security guard posted outside his door. The room was small and didn't even have a window. She'd have to bring him some flowers. He had an IV and a transport monitor hooked up to him. He looked pale and tired. She wheeled the IV pole back a little, sat on the edge of his hospital bed, and threaded her fingers between his. "Sorry I slapped you."

Marty squished his head into the pillow and grinned. "I forgive you, Abby Goyer." His fingers brushed her arm sling. "Are you hurt?"

"Why'd you do it, Marty?"

His dark eyes seemed to sparkle. "It was the right thing. It was my purpose … for this day."

"How do you know?"

"Because Jesus would have done it."

Abby huffed. "Jesus didn't have the option of giving anyone a kidney, Marty, especially a criminal like Dr. Kane."

Marty licked his lips and spoke softly, like his throat was dry. "In Luke's book, Jesus said to 'love your enemies, do good to those who hate you, bless those who curse you, pray for those who mistreat you.' I have done so for Dr. Kane. That was my purpose for him."

Abby couldn't believe Marty had already memorized a Bible verse and lived it out. Tears flooded her vision. All her life she'd known what to do and say. But JD had been right, she was a self-righteous snob. She might know all the right answers—fortune cookie answers, Dad had always called them—but she had never known how to live them out. She'd always played life safe, regulated by rules and laws, never bothering to take a chance on someone who had broken those rules or didn't deserve compassion. Yet along came Marty, sacrificially loving a villain like Dr. Kane as if it were the most natural thing in the world.

In Marty's eyes, everyone deserved compassion.

Ever since she'd met Marty, Abby had been trying to save him, but she was the one who'd truly needed saving. *Forgive me, Lord. I didn't understand how to love like you.*

"Do not cry, Abby Goyer," Marty said.

She sniffed back her tears, not wanting to worry Marty when he should be healing. "Well, you have blessed Dr. Kane in an amazing way, what is your purpose now?"

"To take care of my brothers. Will they let me? The police?"

"I think so." On the ride to the hospital, Dad had told her that the FBI was preparing a place nearby, and that he had told them that Martyr would be the perfect person to help the boys adjust. As she had since this morning, she prayed the situation with Martyr and Dr. Elliot would be resolved.

Dad had also made a deal with the FBI last night. He gave them a pile of evidence he'd been collecting for the past few weeks, and they let him off for his involvement on the Farm. He'd even found footage of Dr. Markley working there—enough to prosecute Dr. Kane for conspiracy in her murder. Abby was still amazed, and proud, that her dad had been collecting evidence almost from the time he'd started at the Farm.

Not only did the FBI let Dad off, they asked him to be in charge of the new Jason home. The government needed someone who understood the boys, as Dr. Max and the others had disappeared.

And I'd just about gotten used to Fishhook High School. Now she'd be homeschooling herself for the rest of the semester so she could help Dad. It would be strange for her to live in a facility for clones. Not that she minded much.

Despite all the talk and action around the Jasons, no one seemed to be asking too many questions about the most unique clone of them all, JD Kane. He had a mother and a social security card, after all. Still, Abby wondered what would happen. For possibly the first time ever, she wanted to see him.

"There are two other labs," Marty said, interrupting her thoughts. "But Dr. Kane didn't tell me where they are."

Two more labs! The idea made Abby queasy. She watched the fluid in Marty's IV bag drip down the tube, wondering if there might be other Jasons trapped somewhere. "Let the police handle it, okay?"

Marty reached over to the hand that held Abby's, and fingered the steel cuff on his wrist. "What's this?"

She shrugged, not wanting him to freak out about the tracking device.

"I heard the women talking. They said it's because I'm a criminal, so the police can know where I am if I escape. Abby, is it a taser or another tracker? Like the one in my ear?"

"You're *not* a criminal. You're special. The government just doesn't want you to get lost."

Marty's eyes narrowed. "How can I get lost in this little cell? I can't even get out of bed."

"They gave the bracelets to all the Jasons. It's because of the move. There are so many of you, they are worried one of you might wander off and they'll never know. This way, everyone will make the trip safe and sound."

"How's my tough guy?" A nurse dressed in purple scrubs walked into the room, met Abby's gaze, and stopped, her sneakers squeaking on the white tile. "Oh, you've got a visitor! I need to check your lungs, but I'll come back."

"Thank you!" Marty called after her. He tugged Abby's hand until she looked back at him. "What trip?"

"To a new home. They're preparing a place for you to live. All of you. A safe place. They've asked my dad to be in charge, and they want you to help them."

"Me? Why?"

"Because you're the leader."

"Iron Man is the—"

Abby squeezed his hand. "No, Marty. Iron Man told them you're the leader. The boys asked for you. They need you."

"You're coming too?"

Abby smiled. "Yeah. I can't believe I'm saying this, but I'm actually looking forward to homeschooling."

"Abby Goyer?"

"Yes?"

Marty's eyes ensnared hers; his pupils seemed huge. "Now that we will have time, can we slow down a bit and eat?"

Abby frowned, confused by the intensity of his expression and the simplicity of his request. "You're hungry? I don't think you can eat anything for a while."

Marty tilted his head a bit, rustling the pillowcase. "You said that a girl and boy ate for a while before getting married. I would like to eat with you."

Abby burst into laughter. "Not *ate*, Marty, *date*. It's when two people spend time together doing fun things, going places."

Marty's cheeks lifted in a smile. "Can we date?"

"When we all get settled in the new place, yes, we can date, if Dad says it's okay."

"And you'll tell me how the baby got into Aliza's stomach?"

Abby's cheeks burned. "Nooo. I know I said I would, but … Marty, I think that's a question my dad could answer better for you."

She only wished she could see the look on Dad's face when Marty asked.

THE END

THE END

DISCUSSION GUIDE FOR REPLICATION

1. Martyr believes his purpose is to die in order to help save those living outside from toxic air. Why would the scientists tell the Jasons such a lie? And when Martyr learns the truth, why does he care so much about a new purpose for his life? Have you ever wondered about your own purpose?

2. When Abby comes home to find her apartment empty, she weighs the pros and cons. Why do you think Abby does this?

3. Describe Dr. Max's relationship with Martyr. Why is he willing to offer the clones some forbidden things like pictures of the sky and ice cream but refuses to take Martyr to see the sky? Is this type of kindness dangerous for the clones? How does knowledge of the outside world affect Martyr?

4. When Abby and JD are debating issues of pharmaceutical testing on humans, JD calls Abby a "religious type" and Abby surmises that JD is a "liberal extremist." How are such conclusions harmful to a healthy debate?

5. How does the way the Jasons were forced to live and the simple questions they ask about the sky, color, marriage, God, etc. make you think about the freedoms you have each day and how you view the world?

6. What do you think about the lies that Abby and her father tell the police in order to throw the scientists off Martyr's trail? Could they have handled the situation another way? How? Can you name some of the consequences that came from their lies?

7. In a facility with fifty-five boys with the same DNA, where scientists force obedience and conformity, the boys have very different personalities. Why do you think that is? Have you ever been stereotyped based on your age or how you look? How do you seek out individuality and purpose in your life?

8. Abby and her father react differently to Abby's mother's death. For instance, Abby tries to find beauty in ashes. Have you ever tried looking at devastation in a positive light? How might such a practice be helpful? Is there a way it might be harmful?

9. Abby claims to have standards as to who she dates and that JD doesn't measure up. Then later, Abby is the one who kisses Martyr, breaking her own rules. Have you set any standards in regards to dating? If so, have you ever broken your own rules? Why might having standards be a good thing?

10. The police take Martyr and Abby to the station, and Martyr is put into handcuffs. How might such bonds be considered a metaphor for his life?

11. Abby tells the police that Dr. Kane is the real criminal. How has Dr. Kane stolen the lives of all those living on the Farm? As different as he and Martyr are, how might environment influence actions more than DNA?

12. Dr. Corrine Markley gave the Jasons something no other scientist did, and Martyr remembered her for it. What was so powerful about Dr. Markley's presence on the Farm? Was it simply the fact that she was female? Or was there something more?

13. Why do you think JD injected himself with the syringe after having seen what an injection did to Dr. Elliot? Do you think JD wanted to die?

14. Abby and Martyr both have a tendency to try and be heroes. How are they alike and/or different in their motivation and methods? In the end, Martyr donates one of his kidneys to Dr. Kane. How is Abby's interpretation of this act different from Martyr's? How does Martyr's explanation of his choice change the way Abby views herself?

15. Do you feel that the possibility of human cloning is an ethical option for scientists to investigate further, or do you feel that the cost of such experimentation is too high? What are the pros and cons of human cloning? (For more information on both sides of this controversial issue visit *www.cloninginformation.org* and *www.humancloning.org*.)

ACKNOWLEDGMENTS

I have so many to be grateful for.

To God, who continues to amaze me and teach me new things each day, for loving me and allowing me to write books.

To my husband, Brad, for putting up with this time-consuming writing thing of mine, and for liking *Replication* best of all my stories.

To my sister, Beth Britton, for taking me to pick apples that day in upstate New York. There would be no *Replication* without that little adventure.

To the members of the CYAW critique group, who helped me make this story stronger, specifically Mary Hake, Stephanie Gallentine, Gretchen Hoffman, Amy Meyer, Shelley Pagach, Diana Sharples, and Claire Talbott.

To Shawn Grady and Greg Bremner, my firemen, for teaching me about fires and procedures to make those scenes as realistic as possible.

To Jeff Gerke, for publishing *By Darkness Hid* and distracting me from my plans of publishing *Replication* with a different house. Because I got so busy with edits for Jeff, *Replication* eventually went into a drawer until I pulled it out again in the summer of 2010.

To the Oregon Christian Writers organization for putting on

such great summer conferences where conferees like me can find publishers and an agent.

To Kathleen Kerr for liking my ideas and wanting me to be a Zondervan author.

To Amanda Luedeke for liking what I write and wanting to work together.

To Jacque Alberta for championing my book and for being a brilliant editor, who helped make this story the best it could be.

To the fantastic team at Zondervan. Thanks so very much for taking a chance on me.

And to my readers, for sticking with me on this science fiction adventure. I promise I'll write more fantasy soon. ☺

continue the adventure
ONL1NE

[ADVENTURES IN READING]

Over 300 book reviews of clean teen fiction
Search for books by age, genre, or gender

[ADVENTURES IN WRITING]

Ask Jill your writing questions
Download FREE writing help charts

[ADVENTURES IN LIFE]

Share your life story
Find out what Jill is up to next

[JOIN THE ADVENTURE]

jw www.jillwilliamson.com
f www.facebook.com/jwilliamsonwrites
t www.twitter.com/jillwilliamson
YouTube www.youtube.com/jwilliamsonwrites
www.jillwilliamson.com/podcast

HALFLINGS

A Halflings Novel by Heather Burch

After being inexplicably targeted by an evil intent on harming her at any cost, seventeen-year-old Nikki finds herself under the watchful guardianship of three mysterious young men who call themselves Halflings. Sworn to defend her, misfits Mace, Raven, and Vine battle to keep Nikki safe while hiding their deepest secret—and the wings that come with.

A growing attraction between Nikki and two of her protectors presents a whole other danger. While she risks a broken heart, Mace and Raven could lose everything, including their souls. As the mysteries behind the boys' powers, as well as her role in the mission they undertake, unfold, Nikki is faced with choices that will affect the future of an entire race of heavenly beings, as well as the precarious equilibrium of the earthly world.

Available in stores and online!

Eternity's Edge

Book Two

With the secrets behind the mirrors unlocked, Nathan and Kelly set out to save three colliding Earths from certain destruction. But they are not the only ones on a mission: an intergalactic stalker is fighting for control, forcing Nathan and his friends to journey through mystifying realities.

Nightmare's Edge

Book Three

The destruction of the three Earths is imminent, and only Nathan's father knows the secret to saving billions of people. Nathan is tasked with freeing his very-much-alive parents from a dream world, while Kelly sacrifices herself to rescue Nathan. Time is running out, with the universe and Kelly's life hanging in the balance.

Also available in ebook and audio versions.

Available in stores and online!

Dragons of Starlight

Another Exciting Trilogy from Bestselling Author Bryan Davis!

For years, tales of dragons from another world kidnapping and enslaving humans have been circulating in Jason Masters' world, while for a slave girl named Koren, the stories of a human world seem pure myth. Together, these two teens will need to bridge two planets to overthrow the draconian threat and bring the lost slaves home.

Starlighter

Jason Masters always believes the stories of a dragon-ruled planet were pure myth, but when his brothers go missing, and clues point to a mysterious portal, he is determined to uncover the truth. At the same time, a slave girl named Koren discovers gifts that could either save her people from their dragon masters or doom them forever. But a prophecy on the dragon planet is about to be fulfilled, which could make both Jason's and Koren's missions futile.

Warrior

When the black egg hatches, unleashing a new dragon prince, Koren and Jason work to find the one person who can help them free the human slaves. Little do they realize the secrets of Starlight go deeper than anyone imagined, and they may soon snare Koren in a deadly deceit.

Diviner

Koren begins to doubt the path she has chosen, and seeks for a way to use her gifts for a nobler purpose. Meanwhile, Jason and his friend Elyssa attempt to rescue loved ones from the dragons' jaws, and Elyssa uncovers gifts of her own that could be a powerful weapon in the coming war.

Also available in ebook and audio versions.

Available in stores and online!

Talk It Up!

Want free books?
First looks at the best new fiction?
Awesome exclusive merchandise?

We want to hear from you!

Give us your opinions on titles, covers, and stories.
Join the Z Street Team.

Email us at zstreetteam@zondervan.com
to sign up today!

Also—Friend us on Facebook!

www.facebook.com/goodteenreads

- Video Trailers

- Connect with your favorite authors

- Sneak peeks at new releases

- Giveaways

- Fun discussions

- And much more!